SLOWKILL

MICHAEL McGARRITY

SLOWKILL

A KEVIN KERNEY NOVEL

DUTTON

DUTTON
Published by Penguin Group (USA) Inc.,
375 Hudson Street, New York, New York 10014, U.S.A.
Penguin Group (Canada), 10 Alcorn Avenue, Toronto, Ontario, Canada M4V 3B2
(a division of Pearson Penguin Canada Inc.); Penguin Books Ltd, 80 Strand, London
WC2R 0RL, England; Penguin Ireland, 25 St Stephen's Green, Dublin 2, Ireland (a division
of Penguin Books Ltd); Penguin Group (Australia), 250 Camberwell Road, Camberwell,
Victoria 3124, Australia (a division of Pearson Australia Group Pty Ltd);
Penguin Books India Pvt Ltd, 11 Community Centre, Panchsheel Park, New Delhi - 110 017,
India; Penguin Group (NZ), Cnr Airborne and Rosedale Roads, Albany, Auckland,
New Zealand (a division of Pearson New Zealand Ltd);
Penguin Books (South Africa) (Pty) Ltd, 24 Sturdee Avenue,
Rosebank, Johannesburg 2196, South Africa

Penguin Books Ltd, Registered Offices: 80 Strand, London WC2R 0RL, England

Published by Dutton, a member of Penguin Group (USA) Inc.

First printing, August 2004
1   3   5   7   9   10   8   6   4   2

 REGISTERED TRADEMARK—MARCA REGISTRADA

Library of Congress Cataloging-in-Publication Data

McGarrity, Michael.
   Slow kill / by Michael McGarrity.
      p. cm.
   ISBN 0-525-94799-X (hardcover : alk. paper)
   1. Kerney, Kevin (Fictitious character)—Fiction. 2. Police—New Mexico—Santa Fe—Fiction.
3. Horse breeders—Crimes against—Fiction. 4. Ranchers—Crimes against—Fiction. 5. Horses—
Breeding—Fiction. 6. Police chiefs—Fiction. 7. California—Fiction. I. Title.
   PS3563.C36359S58 2004
   813'.54—dc22
                                                                    2004012675

Printed in the United States of America
Set in Sabon
Designed by Leonard Telesca

For Margaret Ann Lupfer Jameson Casady,
aka Ann Casady

ACKNOWLEDGMENTS

In California, Ed and Charmay Allred graciously allowed me to stay at their beautiful Rolling A Ranch, where foreman Dave Martin gave me the run of the place and educated me about racing quarter horses and breeding stock. Captain Gary L. Hoving of the San Luis Obispo County Sheriff's Office brought me up to speed on the workings of his department, as did Captain Robert J. Lowry, Captain Edward P. Szeyller, and Mr. Errol L. Murphy of the Santa Barbara Police Department. Nothing in this fictional work should be viewed as a negative reflection on the professionalism and dedication of the serving officers in either organization.

At Quantico, FBI Supervisory Special Agent John R. Cantalupo, Stephen R. Band, PhD, and DEA Special Agent Karen I. Flowers loaded me down with information, toured me around the facilities, and made my days there very productive.

In Santa Fe, pharmacists David Nunez and Cathy Morlock provided me with technical information about their profession and prescription medications; Tom Claffey dug up information on record retention rules for financial institutions; and Ken Mayers, without even knowing it, gave me an excellent idea I immediately put to use in the book.

Finally, a very special thanks to Major Linda Wrasman of the New Mexico State Police, a good friend who opened many doors for me at the FBI Academy and gave freely of her valuable time and expertise at Quantico and in Santa Fe.

ChapterOne

Ten minutes after Santa Fe Police Chief Kevin Kerney picked up his rental car at the Bakersfield Airport, he was stuck in heavy stop-and-go traffic, questioning his decision to take the less-traveled back roads on his trip to the central California coast.

Congestion didn't ease until he was well outside the city limits on a westbound state highway that cut through desert flatlands. Ahead, a dust devil jumped across a straight, uninviting stretch of pavement and churned slowly through an irrigated alfalfa field, creating a green wave rolling over the forage.

Kerney glanced at his watch. Had he made a mistake in trying to map out a scenic route to take to the coast? By now, he'd expected to be approaching a mountain range, but there was nothing on the hazy horizon to suggest it.

It really didn't matter if he'd misjudged his driving time. He had all day to get to the Double J horse ranch outside of Paso Robles, where he would spend the weekend looking over some quarter horses that were up for sale. He hit the cruise control and let his mind wander.

Kerney had partnered up with his neighbor, Jack Burke, to breed, raise, and train competition cutting horses. Kerney would buy some stock to get the enterprise started, Jack would contribute brood mares, pastureland, and stables to the partnership, and Jack's youngest son, Riley Burke, would do the training.

The sky cleared enough to show the outline of mountains topped by a few bleached, mare's-tail clouds. Soon Kerney was driving through a pass on a twisting road flanked by forked and tilted gray-needle pine trees, into a huge grassland plain that swept up against a higher, more heavily timbered mountain range to the west.

Finally his road trip had turned interesting. He stopped to stretch his legs, and a convertible sports car with the top down zipped by, the woman driver tooting her horn and waving gaily as she sped away.

Kerney waved back, thinking it would have been nice to have his family with him. He'd arranged the trip with the expectation that he'd enjoy his time by himself and away from the job. But in truth, he was alone far more than he liked. Sara, his career Army officer wife, had a demanding Pentagon duty assignment that limited her free time, and Patrick, their toddler son who lived with her, was far too young to travel alone.

Kerney had hoped that the new house they'd built on two sections of ranchland outside of Santa Fe would change Sara's mind about staying in the Army, but it hadn't. Although she loved the ranch and looked forward to living in Santa Fe full-time, she wasn't about to take early retirement. That meant six more years of a part-time, long-distance marriage, held together by frequent cross-country trips back and forth as time allowed, and one family vacation together each year. For Kerney, it wasn't a happy prospect.

He looked over the plains. The green landscape was pleasing to the eye, deeper in color than the bunch grasses of New Mexico, but under a less vivid sky. He could see a small herd of grazing livestock moving toward a windmill, the outline of a remote ranch house beyond, and the thin line of the state road that plowed straight across the plains and curved sharply up the distant mountains.

He settled behind the wheel and gave the car some juice, thinking it would be a hell of a lot more fun to drive on to Paso Robles in a little two-seater with the top down and the wind in his face.

Kerney arrived in Paso Robles and promptly got lost trying to find the ranch. A convenience store clerk pointed him in the right direction, and a few minutes later he was traveling a narrow paved road through rolling hills of vineyards, cattle ranches, and horse farms sheltered by stands of large oak trees amid lush carpets of green grass. He drove with the window down, finding the moist sea air that rolled over the coastal mountains a welcome change from the dry deserts of New Mexico.

He'd been offered free lodging at the ranch along with a tour when he arrived, and he was eager to see how the outfit operated. The condition of the horses would tell him most of what he needed to know before deciding whether to buy. But the people who cared for the animals and their surroundings would also indicate whether his money would be well spent.

Kerney turned a corner onto a wide-open vista, eased the car off the pavement, and got out to take in the scenery. On a hilltop behind and above him stood a large mission-style villa with a portal consisting of a series of arches supported by Georgian columns and topped off with a red tile roof and overhanging eaves. Paired bell towers with identical arches rose above either end of the second story. Two vineyards cascaded down the gentle slope on both sides of the villa. Taken as a whole, the place reeked of wealth.

To the west, densely treed coastal mountains rose up from a green, rolling valley that wandered down to a creek bed. A sign fronting the ranch road into the valley announced the Double J Ranch. In a series of fenced and gated pastures, brood mares and their foals gathered under shady oak trees.

The ranch headquarters bordered the creek bed and consisted of four white houses around a semicircular driveway within a few steps of a birthing barn and a long row of covered, open-air stalls adjacent to small paddocks. Beyond the stalls was a barn, which Kerney guessed was used to house the stud horses.

Sara had asked for pictures, so Kerney got the camera from his travel bag and took some shots, doing a rough mental count of the mares and foals in plain view. There were more than a hundred, signifying a very large breeding operation.

He drove to the ranch and parked near the birthing barn, which had a small office building off to one side. A man in his early forties stepped onto the porch as Kerney approached.

"Mr. Hilt?" Kerney asked as he approached.

The man nodded. "The name's Devin," he said with a welcoming smile, extending his hand. "You must be Kevin Kerney."

Kerney smiled back and shook Devin's hand. "Thanks for putting me up."

"I'm afraid you'll have to share the guesthouse with another party," Hilt said. "The boss has a buyer coming up from Santa Barbara sometime later today."

"That's not a problem," Kerney said as he took a look around. "This is quite a place."

Hilt laughed. He stood six feet tall in his cowboy boots and had a sturdy frame topped off with curly brown hair cut short. "This isn't the half of it. Around the bend a mile away we've got a training track, stables, and pastures for colts and two-year-olds. That's where the boss, his wife, his mother, and the ranch manager have their houses. This area is just for my family, the trainers, and guests."

"It's pretty posh," Kerney said. "I can't remember ever seeing a more beautiful ranch."

Hilt laughed again. "It does make working for a living a bit more pleasant." He pointed down the driveway to a pitched-roof, single-story clapboard house surrounded by a picket fence. "That's the guest cottage. Want to settle in first or take that tour I promised you?"

"Let's do the tour," Kerney said.

"Perfect," Hilt replied as he moved toward the pickup truck.

Hilt drove Kerney around the spread, passing on bits of information along the way. It was a quarter-horse ranch with about four hundred head and a breeding program that foaled more than a hundred newborns yearly. Four stallions at stud were syndicated at more than a million each. Most of the horses were owned by the ranch.

The owner, Jeffery Jardin, lived most of the time in southern California, where he owned a high-tech manufacturing business with major defense and military contracts. But his passion was racehorses, and the ranch showed that he pursued it seriously. Kerney guessed the size of the spread at about five hundred acres. He wondered what the value of the land was on the pricey California market.

Hilt told Kerney that in the morning he'd meet Ken Wheeler, a former jockey who oversaw the operation and culled the horses that weren't suitable for racing. Kerney hoped he'd find what he was looking for: two riding horses for personal use, one stud to service Jack Burke's mares, and some two- or three-year-old geldings Riley Burke could train as cutting horses.

Tucked into a separate part of the valley, away from the road, stood the training track and a set of fenced pastures that held good-looking colts and two-year-olds. Open-air covered stalls and a barn stood adjacent to the track. At one end of the stalls a circular pen contained a hot walker. Driven by an electrical motor, the device had four arms that looked like oversized propeller blades mounted on a triangular-shaped base. After training runs, the horses were hitched to the arms and mechanically walked to cool them down.

On a hill overlooking the track were three houses, one a two-story Victorian with a low-pitched hipped roof and spindlework porch railings. It was flanked by two modest, single-story houses built with wood cladding and brick. All were nicely landscaped and sheltered by oak trees.

As Hilt pulled to a stop in front of the barn, he pointed at a smaller Victorian house on the far side of the track. "That's where Ken lives," he said. "He'll meet you at the office tomorrow at seven. Want to look at some pretty horses?"

"You bet," Kerney said as he climbed out of the truck.

Hilt spent the better part of an hour walking Kerney through the barn, stalls, and into several nearby pastures. The horses were slick and well cared for, and the grounds, barns, and stalls were clean and tidy. Kerney learned that the ranch employed a full-time veterinarian, two tech assistants, two trainers, and a variety of stable hands, groomers, exercise riders, and laborers—many of them Mexican. Low-cost housing was provided for a dozen key employees.

The two men entered a pasture, and several colts came trotting over to greet them. Hilt recited their bloodlines while Kerney gave them the once-over. He found himself enjoying Hilt's company and the talk of horses. He stroked a chestnut colt's neck and ran a hand over its withers, thinking it was decidedly refreshing to get away by himself and forget about being a cop.

Back at the guest cottage, Kerney found an overnight bag and briefcase on the floor of the largest bedroom, but no sign of the man who was sharing the accommodations with him. He dumped his stuff in another bedroom and looked around the cottage. Whoever decorated the place had a penchant for green and an obsession with frogs. The carpet, wallpaper, tile work, and even the kitchen ceiling were all various shades of green. Ceramic, glass, and pottery figurines of frogs sat on every table, dresser, and countertop, and framed prints of jumping frogs, singing frogs, and comical-looking standing frogs hung on the walls of each room. It seemed like a big silly joke that had gotten slightly out of hand. Still, it made him smile.

The kitchen was fully equipped and stocked. But Kerney decided to take himself out to dinner and do a little sightseeing before it got dark. Hilt had told him of a good restaurant in a nearby village and given him directions.

Kerney changed into a fresh shirt, fired up the rental car, and drove away, pleased with how the day had gone.

*   *   *

Always an early riser, Kerney was up at five. He showered, dressed, and sat on the porch of the guest cottage in the cool predawn air drinking a glass of juice and enjoying the sounds of whinnying mares in a nearby pasture. Last night, after an early dinner, he'd driven to the ocean in time to watch a spectacular, romantic sunset, which only made him miss Sara's company.

When he'd returned to the ranch, an imported luxury sedan was parked in front of the cottage, and the door to his bunkmate's bedroom was closed. To avoid disturbing the man, Kerney had read quietly in his room for a few hours before turning in.

From the porch he could see a night watchman moving down a line of corrals where brood mares about to foal were kept under observation. Kerney strolled over to join him. In front of the office was a five-gallon bucket filled with horse biscuits. He stuffed some in his jacket pocket and caught up with the watchman. Even in the dim light he could tell the mares were pampered ladies. He fed biscuits to those who came up to the corral fences to greet him.

He wandered up and down the stalls that held the mares with their newborn foals. Workers, including a veterinarian checking on the expectant mothers, soon began arriving. Barn boys started cleaning stalls and filling feed bins. One young man raked a herringbone pattern in fresh sawdust that he'd spread down the center aisle.

After watching for a while, Kerney went back to the cottage. There was no sound of movement behind the other guest's closed bedroom door. Hilt had told Kerney that the man had an early morning appointment with the owner, who personally handled the sale of all racing stock. Kerney knocked on the door to give the guy a wake-up call. He got no response, so he knocked again and called out. Still nothing.

He opened the door and turned on the light. Lying faceup on the duvet covering the bed was a man, probably in his late sixties. One look told Kerney the man was dead.

He stepped over to the body, checked for a pulse at the carotid artery to make sure, and backed out of the room, touching nothing else.

The last thing Kerney had expected to see was a dead body. He went to find Devin Hilt, knowing full well his morning would be shot as soon as the local cops showed up.

*   *   *

According to the California driver's license found on the body, the dead man was Clifford Spalding, age seventy-one, from Santa Barbara, a two-hour drive down the coast.

Sergeant Elena Lowrey of the San Luis Obispo Sheriff's Department thought it quite likely the deceased had died of natural causes. There were no visible wounds to the body, no defensive marks, no signs of a struggle. But until the coroner agreed with her observations and the autopsy findings confirmed it, she would handle the call as a death due to unknown causes.

If everything looked copacetic, there might be no need to call out the detectives and the crime scene techs.

She stood at the foot of the bed for a minute and watched the coroner begin his examination before stripping off her gloves and exiting the cottage. Outside on the front lawn three men waited: Kevin Kerney, who'd discovered the body; Devin Hilt, who'd called 911; and Jeffery Jardin, the ranch owner.

Behind them, near the barn and stables, two employees, who looked to be Mexican nationals, worked at cleaning out a cool-down corral while keeping a wary eye on the proceedings.

Lowrey, who had an Anglo father and Mexican American mother, bet that neither man held a green card. She had no desire to pursue it. Her grandfather, a migrant worker, had been deported years ago because of a disorderly conduct conviction stemming from a clash with police at a farmworkers rally. He could never legally return to the States, although he did sneak in for occasional visits, especially when Ellie's kid sister, the baby-producing sibling of the family, added another grandchild to the clan.

She stepped off the porch and spoke to Jardin. "Can I use the ranch office to take statements?"

Jardin, a man in his sixties who sported a great tan, a full head of hair, and a worried expression, nodded.

"Thanks," Lowrey said, switching her attention to Kerney, whom she guessed to be around fifty, and good-looking for a man his age. He stood six-one, had a nice build and deep-set, pretty blue eyes.

"I'll start with you," Lowrey said to Kerney. "It shouldn't take too long."

Kerney nodded and followed the sergeant to the office, noting that even with the body armor she wore under her uniform shirt she cut a trim, well-shaped figure. A shade over five-five, she wore her thick dark hair rather short.

Kerney had come to the ranch as a potential buyer, not a police chief, so he doubted anyone knew he was a cop. Nonetheless, he'd told Hilt it would be best to keep everyone away from the cottage, a suggestion Devin readily accepted. Like most civilians, Hilt had no desire to stare death in the face.

Kerney sat with Lowrey in the ranch office and answered her questions directly. He'd never met the man and didn't know him or his name. He only knew that he would be sharing the cottage with another visitor who was looking to buy horses. He'd returned from dinner last night to find a car outside and one of the bedroom doors closed. He'd simply assumed that Spalding was sleeping or desired some privacy. He'd read for a time before retiring and had heard no sounds from the man's room. Nothing out of the ordinary had occurred during the night to arouse any suspicions about Spalding's welfare. He'd discovered the body after attempting to wake Spalding with a knock on the bedroom door. He'd touched only the light switch in the bedroom and Spalding's carotid artery to confirm he was dead.

Lowrey asked for the name of the restaurant where he'd dined, which Kerney provided, and asked how long he'd be staying at the ranch.

"I leave tomorrow," Kerney said.

Lowrey nodded. "We might have to ask you to stay over, Mr. Kerney, until we clear things up."

"If it's possible, I'd rather not do that, Sergeant," Kerney said as he took his police commission card from his wallet and gave it to Lowrey.

The sergeant glanced at it and gave Kerney a reproachful look. "You could have told me who you were up front."

Kerney shrugged and took his ID back. "I knew we'd get around to it," he said. "Besides, until you say differently, I'm a person of interest to your investigation. But I would like you to extend the courtesy of allowing me to go home tomorrow."

He replaced the ID in his wallet and gave her a business card. "You can confirm who I am. Call the dispatch number and ask to speak to Deputy Chief Larry Otero. They'll patch you through to him."

Lowrey nodded. "I'll do that. Until we know more, this looks like an unattended natural death."

"So it seems," Kerney said as he got to his feet. "But it's always best to do it by the book."

"Why didn't you just tell me you were a police chief?" Lowrey asked.

"Because I came here as a civilian," Kerney said, "which occasionally is a very nice thing to be."

Lowrey smiled, and a dimple showed on her right cheek. "Point well made, Chief. Will you ask Mr. Hilt to join me, and stand by in case I have any more questions for you?"

Kerney nodded and left the office.

*   *   *

If Clifford Spalding had expired in his own bed, the coroner, Deputy Sheriff William Price, would probably have done a quick death assessment and let it go at that, trusting the autopsy to pinpoint the cause. Instead, he decided to be a bit more thorough. First he checked the eyes for any signs of changes in the vitreous humor, which usually turns cloudy within eight to ten hours after death. The fluid was clear and there was no evidence of the minute blood clots caused by strangulation that show up as tiny red dots.

He inspected the mouth for any sign of blockage or corrosive burns, the neck for bruising or ligature marks, hands and arms for defensive wounds or needle marks, and fingernails for any traces of skin. He ran a gloved hand over the skull and found it to be intact with no telltale indication of blunt trauma. He stripped off a glove and felt the armpits with the back of his hand. They were cool to the touch.

There were early signs of rigor mortis, which usually occurs within two to four hours after death. That, along with the absence of any changes to the vitreous humor and the coolness of the armpits, indicated that the man had been dead for six to eight hours.

The body was clad in an undershirt, slacks, and socks. Using scissors, Price cut the undershirt and pants away, then turned the body facedown on the double bed and used a rectal thermometer to take the body's temperature. Then he checked the room temperature. The difference between the two readings brought his estimate of the time of death down to no more than six hours ago.

Blood pools and settles after death, appearing as a purple discoloration of the skin, and the lower back showed signs of it. Price pressed a finger against the spot and the color didn't blanch white, which was another good indicator that Spalding had been dead for about six hours, and, more important, hadn't been moved.

He looked over the body one more time. There were no surgical scars. The gluteus maximus and leg muscles were firm, indicating the man had been physically active.

Price guessed that either a heart attack or a stroke had killed the man. He took off his gloves and went to give Ellie Lowrey the news.

*   *   *

After admitting that he had almost no experience with cops or dead people, a nervous Devin Hilt confirmed what he could of Chief Kerney's story. Ellie Lowrey probed with a few more questions to reassure herself that all seemed as it should before letting Hilt go and calling Kerney's deputy chief to verify his identity.

Bill Price came in just as she was about to begin her interview with Jeffery Jardin, the ranch owner.

"The body shows no signs of death by unnatural causes," he said.

"You couldn't seriously think that Clifton Spalding was murdered here," Jardin said in a bit of a huff.

Price smiled benignly. Civilians were always uneasy about the thought of homicide. He'd faced the same reaction from people time and again over the years. "We always try to rule that out first," he said.

He turned his attention to Lowrey. "I'd say he died in his sleep, either from a heart attack or a stroke, about six hours ago. The autopsy will tell us more."

Lowrey nodded. "Thanks. Ask the EMTs to keep everyone away from the cottage until I finish my interviews. I'd like to take another look around before we wrap it up."

"You got it," Price said, stepping out the door.

"Are you people always so suspicious?" Jardin asked.

"Careful would be a better way to put it," Lowrey replied. "How well did you know Mr. Spalding?"

"Well enough, on a business and social basis. Over the past ten years, he's bought about six horses from me, some that he ran in qualifying and small purse races. He didn't seem to care if they won or lost. It was a hobby for him, or rather for his wife, who I think basically liked the social scene at the track. He stabled his horses here and used my trainers. My ranch manager arranged for jockeys and the horses' transportation to and from the track. We basically did everything except race the horses under my colors. His wife keeps two of the horses he bought for pleasure riding, although they're good enough to race. I usually dealt with her."

"That's a pretty expensive hobby his wife has."

"Clifford could afford it. He owns, rather did own, a number of resort hotels up and down the coast."

"You said you knew him well," Lowrey remarked.

"For about the last ten years," Jardin replied, "after he married his second wife. I met them when they were first looking to buy racing stock. After that, I'd see them at the track, and we'd get together occasionally for dinner and drinks. Claudia, his wife, is a good twenty years younger. She divides her time between Santa Barbara and Santa Fe. Clifford built a house for her out there where she could keep some horses. I think she's in Santa Fe now."

"If you usually dealt with Spalding's wife, why did he come here this time?" Lowrey asked.

"Claudia had her eye on a horse she liked, and Clifford said he wanted to buy it for her as a surprise anniversary present."

"Do you have Mrs. Spalding's Santa Fe address?"

"My ranch manager should. He made the arrangements to have the horses she keeps in Santa Fe transported there."

Jardin glanced at his wristwatch, an expensive, wafer-thin gold timepiece that probably cost more than Lowrey's personal vehicle.

"Just a few more questions," she said, "and then we'll be done."

*   *   *

Kerney waited on the porch outside the office with the ranch manager, Ken Wheeler, and watched the coroner come and go. No longer a jockey, Wheeler had still managed to keep weight off his wiry frame. He sported a wide mouth that seemed ready-made to break into easy smiles, and had tiny ears that lay flat against his head. At six-one, Kerney towered over the man.

Wheeler told Kerney that he had two twelve-year-old halterbroken mares, four three-year-old geldings that didn't seem to have the heart to race, and a young stud named Comeuppance available for sale.

Wheeler thought the mares, once saddle broken, would serve well for pleasure riding, the geldings were sure-footed and quick enough to be good cutting horses, and the stallion would do just fine at stud, if the new owner didn't expect fast runners from his lineage.

Kerney knew, if he decided to buy it, the stud horse would be his most expensive purchase. "Is that his only flaw?" he asked.

"I believe so," Wheeler replied, his deep baritone voice quite a contrast to his diminutive size. "But you'll get to see for yourself.

He's got good bloodlines, but none of his yearlings or two-year-olds look promising for the track. The boss says we sure aren't going to make any money keeping him, and I agree."

Before Kerney could reply, Sergeant Lowrey stepped onto the porch.

"Mr. Wheeler," she said, "could you get me Mrs. Spalding's Santa Fe address?"

"Sure thing," Wheeler said as he slipped past Lowrey into the office.

Kerney raised an eyebrow. "Santa Fe, New Mexico?"

"She has a house there," Lowrey said, "and according to Mr. Jardin that's where she is. Do you know her?"

Kerney shook his head. "Do you want my department to make contact with her?"

"That would be helpful, Chief." Lowrey handed him a business card. "Ask your officer to call me first."

"Will do." Kerney reached for his cell phone. "What did the coroner have to say?"

"So far, Spalding's death appears to be from natural causes." Lowrey paused and gave him a once-over. "Quite a coincidence, isn't it, Spalding's wife having a place in Santa Fe?"

"In this particular instance, I would say that it is," Kerney replied.

"Are you sure you've never met her while you've been out riding the range?"

"That's very funny, Sergeant," Kerney said, slightly piqued at Lowrey's sarcasm. "Actually there are times when we still ride the range. But now that the streets of Santa Fe are paved, my officers mostly drive squad cars."

"Maybe you met her at a horse show or a rodeo," Lowrey countered.

"Not that I recall," Kerney said. He turned away from Lowrey and dialed Larry Otero's home number.

After talking to Larry, he waited for Lowrey to reappear. Instead, Wheeler came out of the office and told him Lowrey had a few more questions to ask and would be with him shortly. He agreed to meet

Wheeler at the track when he was finished, and cooled his heels waiting on the porch.

It didn't surprise him that Lowrey wanted another go-round. The "coincidence" that both Kerney and the dead man's wife lived in the same city would spark any competent officer's interest.

Finally, Lowrey called him back into the office. Kerney sat in a straight-back chair, while Lowrey perched against the office desk and studied the coral and turquoise wedding band on his left hand.

"You're married," she finally said.

"Yes," Kerney replied.

Lowrey's eyes searched his face. "And your wife didn't come here with you."

"She's a career military officer serving at the Pentagon. Her schedule didn't allow it."

"You must not be able to spend a great deal of time together," Lowrey said.

"We manage to see each other frequently," Kerney said, watching Lowrey, who was busy scanning him for any behavioral signals that might signal deception.

"Have you been married long?"

"A couple of years."

"Children?"

"One son, ten months old."

Lowrey smiled. "Your first?"

"Yes," Kerney said. "Now, why don't you get to the part where you stick your face in mine and ask me if I might be lying about not knowing Spalding's wife?"

Lowrey laughed. "As I understand it, Mrs. Spalding is about your age, and spends a great deal of time alone in Santa Fe, away from her husband. You seem to be in the same situation with your marriage."

"I am happily married, Sergeant. Don't turn a perfectly reasonable coincidence into a soap opera about two lonely, unhappy people."

"Obviously, you and Mrs. Spalding share an interest in horses."

"Along with about five million other horse lovers."

"Mr. Spalding was rich and considerably older than his wife."

"So I understand, from what you've said."

"And neither you nor Spalding have ever stayed here before," Lowrey noted.

"Apparently not," Kerney replied. "Do you find a chance occurrence tantalizing, Sergeant? That would be quite a stretch."

"Perhaps you're right. Do my questions upset you?"

"Not at all." His cell phone rang. Kerney flipped it open and answered.

"What kind of fix have you gotten yourself into out there?" Andy Baca, Kerney's old friend and chief of the New Mexico State Police, asked.

"What's up?" Kerney asked, raising a finger to signal Lowrey that he'd only be a minute.

"I just got a call from my district commander that some deputy sheriff, a Sergeant Lowrey out of San Luis Obispo County, wants an officer sent to inform a Mrs. Claudia Spalding of her husband's death and to determine your relationship to the woman, if any."

"Interesting," Kerney said.

"I've got two grandchildren in my lap, one on each knee," Andy said, "ready to head off to the Albuquerque zoo to see the polar bears. What's going on with you?"

"I'll call you when I know more."

"That's it?" Andy asked, sounding a bit exasperated.

Kerney laughed. "I'll talk to you later."

"I'll be home by dinnertime," Andy said. "Unless you get locked up, call me then."

"I'll do that. Have fun." Kerney disconnected and smiled at Lowrey. "Are we done here, Sergeant?"

Lowrey smiled back. "We'll talk again after I've heard back from your department."

"I'll be around," Kerney said, thinking Lowrey was doing her job and doing it well. Still, he didn't have to like it.

*   *   *

Ellie Lowrey made another visual sweep of the cottage before the EMTs took Spalding's body away. After they rolled him out, she gathered up the dead man's luggage, put it in the trunk of her cruiser, and drove a back road to the sheriff's substation in Templeton.

The station was housed in a fairly new single-story faux western frontier–style office building with a false front and a slanted covered porch. It had been designed to fit in with the old buildings on the main street left over from the town's early days as a booming farming and ranching community. Now, the charm of the village and its convenience to Highway 101, which ran the length of the West Coast, drew droves of newcomers looking to escape the sprawl of the central coast cities, creating, of course, more sprawl.

As second-in-command of the substation, Ellie Lowrey served under a lieutenant who was on vacation with his family in the Rocky Mountains. She parked in front of the closed office, carried Spalding's luggage inside, and placed it on her desk.

She'd secured the dead man's effects to ensure their safekeeping, which required her to do an inventory. She got out the forms she needed and glanced at the wall clock, wondering how long it would take to hear back from the New Mexico authorities.

Ellie had decided not to rely on Kerney's department for information until she knew for sure whether there was or wasn't a personal relationship between the chief and Mrs. Spalding. Of course, if there was something going on between the two, both of them could lie about it. It was best to get corroborating information from an independent source such as the New Mexico State Police, in case they did have something to hide.

Spalding's overnight bag yielded nothing but toiletries and a change of clothes. The attaché case was a bit more interesting. A manila envelope contained a photograph of the horse Spalding was planning to buy, along with a record of its race results and bloodlines.

The cover letter from Jardin listed the price at a few thousand dollars more than Ellie's gross annual salary.

Other paperwork in the case pertained to Spalding's hotel holdings. Lowrey recognized a few of them by name: very swanky places in upscale California resort communities. A sleeve held a small number of business cards. Lowrey thumbed through them. One was from a Santa Barbara police captain who headed up the Major Crimes Unit. What was that all about?

Lowrey wrote the information in her notebook. Tomorrow was Sunday. She doubted the autopsy would be done quickly, given the likely absence of foul play. If the results came back as death due to natural causes, she'd drop the matter completely. Until then, she would keep the case open and call the Santa Barbara P.D. captain on Monday to satisfy her curiosity.

Ellie got up and poured a cup of coffee. She felt good about how the morning had gone. She'd spent five years as an investigator before earning her stripes and taking a patrol assignment. It was fun to work an investigation on her own again. In truth, she missed her old job, but accepting a promotion to the patrol division had been the only way to move up in the ranks.

She returned to her desk and started in on the paperwork, hoping it wouldn't take all day for the New Mexico cops to find Spalding's widow and report back.

ChapterTwo

After his retirement as an Army nurse, William Price had returned home to California and started a new career as a deputy sheriff. He'd put in three years as a patrol officer and then transferred into the detective unit as an investigator/coroner. During his ten years on the job, Price had seen just about every possible kind of dead body, from gruesome murder victims and gory traffic fatalities to little old ladies who died peacefully in their sleep.

Until her promotion and transfer out of investigations to patrol, Ellie Lowrey had worked with Price on a number of homicide cases. He admired her meticulous attention to detail. Although Price saw no evidence of foul play in the death of Clifford Spalding, Ellie was right to assume a worst-case scenario until it was proved otherwise.

The department contracted for autopsy space with a mortuary in the town of Los Osos, close to the coast. In an office outside the embalming room, Price went through the clothing he'd removed from Spalding's body. The scent of flowers from the viewing rooms at the front of the mortuary made his nose itch.

In a pocket of the expensive Italian slacks he found a small gold pill case with Spalding's initials engraved on the hinged lid. It contained a single, small, pale yellow pill shaped in the form of two blunt arrow points with the name of the manufacturer stamped on it.

Price reached for the *Physicians' Desk Reference* he carried in his briefcase, known by all who used it as the *PDR*, and looked up the drug. It was a hormone replacement medication used in the treatment of Graves' disease, a form of hyperthyroidism. He read through the entry and called Ellie Lowrey to give her the news.

"Would having a thyroid condition kill him?" Lowrey asked after listening to Price's report.

"I'm no expert on immune system diseases," Price replied. "But not taking the medication would be dangerous, perhaps even life threatening, especially if Spalding had other health problems."

"Wait a minute," Lowrey said. "There was a physician's business card in Spalding's briefcase. Here it is, Dr. Daniel Gilbert. His office is in Santa Barbara."

Price reached for a pen. "You want me to call him?"

"Right away," Lowrey replied. "Get all the information you can and call me back." She read off Gilbert's phone number. "And pull the pathologist in to do the autopsy right now."

"Aren't you rushing things a bit?" Price asked, knowing that Ellie might catch some flack from the brass for authorizing a priority autopsy for what appeared to be nothing more than a routine unattended death.

"I've got a feeling about this," Lowrey replied, "and a possible suspect I'd rather not lose sight of before I get some answers."

"Who's your suspect?"

"The man who found Spalding's body. His name is Kevin Kerney. He's the chief of police in Santa Fe, New Mexico, which coincidentally, is where Spalding's wife has a house."

"This could come back to bite you," Price said.

"Just because he's a cop doesn't mean he gets a free pass," Lowrey said.

Price hung up, contacted the pathologist, and then tracked down

Dr. Gilbert by phone, who fortunately was handling weekend calls and emergencies for his group practice.

Gilbert responded to the news with surprise. "Clifford was in three months ago," he said. "His health was good and his blood work results were fine."

"What about the original course of treatment for the Graves' disease?" Price asked.

"Radioactive iodine was used to destroy the thyroid gland and stop production of the hormone. It was completely successful."

"When was that?" Price asked.

"Ten or eleven years ago," Gilbert replied. "Clifford had all the classic symptoms, but he'd let them go untreated thinking it was just stress related. He'd recently divorced his first wife and was about to remarry. He came in for a prenuptial physical exam and that's when I made the diagnosis."

"Were there any complications?" Price asked.

"It caused some weakening of his heart muscles," Gilbert answered. "But I put him on a diet and exercise program that he religiously maintained. I saw no further deterioration."

"Would not taking his pill cause heart failure?"

"Certainly not by forgetting to take his medication for a day. But in the long term, too little or too much of the drug can put the patient at risk for a variety of medical problems. The key is to maintain the patient on a stabilized thyroid hormone replacement regime. That's why periodic blood work to determine medication levels is vital."

Price described the pill he'd found, and the dosage for it listed in the *PDR*.

"That's what I prescribed," Gilbert said. "I haven't changed the dosage in two years."

Price thanked the doctor, hung up, and reported back to Lowrey.

"Bag and tag everything you have," she said, "and turn it in to evidence."

"Will do," Price said, nodding to the board-certified forensic pathologist, who stood in the office doorway looking not at all pleased and rather impatient.

He dropped the headset in the cradle and stood.

"Am I here because of one of Ellie Lowrey's legendary hunches?" the pathologist asked.

"You could say that," Price said. "Mind if I assist?"

"You damn well better," the pathologist said. "I have a dinner party to go to tonight."

*   *   *

Using a borrowed western saddle lent to him by one of the trainers, Kerney rode each of the four geldings around the track, first in a slow trot using the reins to see how they responded to the bit, then moving them quickly from a canter to a gallop, letting them run for a while to test their endurance. Of the four, he favored a red roan and a gray, because of their smooth gaits, calm dispositions, and swift, tight turns.

He watched Sergeant Lowrey drive up to the stalls just as he finished saddling Comeuppance, the stud horse. Other than the sheer fun of having a racing stallion under him, he had no compelling reason to check out Comeuppance on the track. He'd already decided to buy him, ship him home, and get him started servicing the mares. But he wanted the experience of running him full-tilt along the rail of the racetrack.

Lowrey was still a good thirty feet away as Kerney swung into the saddle and nodded at the stable hand, who opened the gate to the track. He adjusted the strap to the helmet Wheeler had asked him to wear, touched his heels against Comeuppance's flanks, and the horse surged through the gate at a full gallop.

Why the horse couldn't sire fast runners was anybody's guess. He had good speed and power. Bent low over Comeuppance's neck, Kerney gave him his head for a full quarter-mile, enjoying every second of the ride. But he sensed that the horse was running under protest, with little enthusiasm. He slowed the stallion gently to a walk and circled the track, deliberately letting Lowrey cool her heels.

From phone calls he'd received, Kerney already knew that contact had not yet been made with Spalding's wife. Both the state police and Detective Sergeant Ramona Pino, one of Kerney's officers, had reported that the woman was away on a weekend trail-riding trip with friends somewhere in the Pecos Wilderness outside of Santa Fe.

At the stalls, he turned Comeuppance over to the stable hand, returned the borrowed helmet, and walked to the track railing where Lowrey waited.

She gave him a smile. "You ride well."

Kerney nodded at the compliment.

"So what are you, a cowboy or a cop?"

"A little of one, more of the other," Kerney replied.

Lowrey laughed. "In that order?"

Kerney nodded again.

"I don't think I've ever met a cop who kept racehorses as a hobby."

"I don't plan to race them, and it's not a hobby."

"Still, it must be expensive," Lowrey said, the smile fixed on her face.

"Ask your question, Sergeant."

"The last time I checked, police work wasn't in the top ten high-income professions," Lowrey countered.

Kerney stayed silent.

"How many horses do you own?"

"Right now, none. By the end of the day, probably four."

"That's interesting," Lowrey said, her smile fading.

Kerney knew he had to give Lowrey more information or face her continued probes, starting with why a man who owned no horses would come to this ranch, at this particular time, to buy some animals.

"I own a small place outside Santa Fe," he said, "and I'm partnering with my neighbors to breed cutting horses. Except for ones I'm looking to buy, they'll supply the brood mares. I'm also fronting the costs for the stud horse and two geldings. We plan to start training the geldings as soon as possible."

"On a ranch outside of Santa Fe," Lowrey said.

"Yes."

"I've never been there," Lowrey said in a casual tone, "but I've heard it's where the rich people like to go and play."

"It's one of those places," Kerney said. "Let me answer some of the other questions you haven't asked me yet. How can I afford a ranch outside of Santa Fe? I came into a sizable inheritance several years back. Do I live anywhere near Mrs. Spalding? I know all my neighbors and she's not one of them. Why did I come to this ranch to buy horses? My partner suggested it. Some of the finest cutting horses in the country have been bred here."

Lowrey laughed and turned to face the track, where a trainer was running a frisky two-year-old. "You don't like being the subject of an inquiry."

"Would you?"

"Probably not. Are you going home tomorrow?"

"That's the plan," Kerney replied.

"Maybe I'll have to come see you in Santa Fe," Lowrey said as she returned her gaze to Kerney.

"That would be a waste of your time."

"You haven't asked me if Mrs. Spalding has been advised of her husband's death."

"I figured you'd tell me if she had been."

"Of course I would." She handed Kerney a business card. "Call me if you'd like to get anything off your chest."

Lowrey stepped away in the direction of her police cruiser. Kerney stuffed her card in his shirt pocket. Clearly, the sergeant was just doing her job, and doing it very well. But that didn't ease the irritation he felt at being treated like a suspect.

He laughed at himself. No matter what Lowrey thought, he had nothing to worry about. He went to take a closer look at one of the four geldings. It seemed a bit shallow in the flank and somewhat razor-backed, which wouldn't do at all.

*   *   *

In her unit, Ellie Lowrey checked with Price by radio on the status of the autopsy and learned it was still under way. She decided to drive to Los Osos and get a firsthand report from the pathologist. She had deliberately given Chief Kerney the impression that he'd be free to go back to Santa Fe tomorrow. But that depended on what the doctor had to say.

Ellie knew she was operating solely on her intuition. But coincidence was always questionable in a criminal investigation. Happenstance, fate, and chance were often used by subjects to camouflage the truth.

She pondered a scenario. Kerney lived in the same town as Spalding's wife. Both of them were apart from their spouses a good deal of the time. Kerney, who owned no horses, came to California to buy stock at the same time Clifford Spalding was at the ranch. They shared accommodations, which allowed Kerney to conveniently find Spalding dead in his bedroom in the morning.

According to Jeffery Jardin, Spalding had never stayed at the ranch before, and had arrived surreptitiously to buy a horse as a surprise anniversary present for his wife. Did Claudia Spalding know Clifford's whereabouts? Wives often have a way of keeping track of husbands.

And what about Kerney? Who better to orchestrate a crime than an experienced cop? Who better to stage a death that looked natural, leave no evidence behind, and have plausible explanations at hand?

Motive, opportunity, and means made up the three major components of any criminal investigation. So far, all she had for sure was opportunity, and a lurking suspicion that perhaps Kerney and Claudia Spalding were lovers who'd plotted and carried out a murder. But why?

She'd watched Kerney carefully, and he hadn't shown any nonverbal signs of lying. But cops, the good ones anyway, were masters at lying. A lot of dirtbags were in the slam because of well-formulated, totally believable lies told to them by police officers.

Ellie tapped her fingers on the steering wheel. Was she completely off base? She hoped the autopsy would answer the question one way or the other.

She reached the mortuary in Los Osos, and the thought struck her that calling such places funeral homes was totally incongruous. If you were there to get buried, you were about as far away from home as you were ever going to get.

Inside, she found Price moving the body from the autopsy table to a gurney. "Where's Doc?" Ellie asked.

"He left," Price answered.

"And?"

Price shook his head as he covered the body. "It looks like straightforward heart failure. But Doc said he'd have the lab run exhaustive blood and chem tests, just as you asked. He's particularly interested in learning what the levels were for the hormone replacement medication."

"Did he say why?" Ellie asked.

Price laughed as he pushed the gurney into an open locker and closed it up. "For two reasons: to keep you happy, and to see if the drug may have contributed to the death. Spalding's heart blew a valve and the muscles showed signs of fairly rapid and recent deterioration."

"Getting the lab results could take several days."

Price hosed down the autopsy table, stripped off the bloody gown and gloves, and dumped them in a hamper. "Not much we can do about it," he said.

In his late fifties, Price had a fatherly air about him that always calmed Ellie down. Maybe she'd pushed the investigation as far as she could for the time being.

She gave Price a resigned smile and nodded. "Do you think I'm wrong about this one?"

Price responded with a shrug of a shoulder and a grin. "I've learned never to bet against you, Sarge."

Ellie's smile turned mischievous.

"What are you thinking?" Price asked.

"Did you do a plain-view search of the cottage?" she asked.

"No, just the bedroom."

"I took a quick tour around the other rooms," Ellie said, "and didn't see anything out of the ordinary. Maybe we should go back there and look again, this time more carefully. Perhaps Chief Kerney will let us search his personal property."

"He could challenge you on that," Price said.

"I hope he does." Ellie dialed Jardin's number on her cell phone, and when he answered she asked for permission to search the cottage to look for any evidence that might help determine the cause of Clifford Spalding's death.

"Is this absolutely necessary?" Jardin replied.

"It would be a great help to the investigation," Ellie said.

"Do your search, Sergeant," Jardin said.

"Thank you, sir." Ellie disconnected and winked at Price. "Let's go see what we can stir up."

"Don't you mean stir Chief Kerney up?"

"Exactly."

*　　*　　*

Kerney found doing business with Ken Wheeler enjoyable. The man had given him lots of space and made no attempt to influence his choices. In the ranch office, Kerney signed the paperwork for the animals he'd selected, and arranged to have Wheeler contract on his behalf to transport the horses to Santa Fe. He was one mare short, but he could probably talk Jack Burke into selling him an eight-year-old bay he had his eye on.

"You picked the best of the lot," Wheeler said as Kerney wrote out the check.

"They'll do nicely," Kerney replied. "Have you ever been to Santa Fe?"

Wheeler shook his head as he took the offered check. "Why do you ask?"

"I thought maybe you could tell me about Mrs. Spalding."

Wheeler laughed. "I can't help you there. As far as she's concerned, I'm just hired help, and I'm sure not the type that would turn her head."

"Meaning?" Kerney asked.

Wheeler scratched his chin. "She seems to have an eye for men. But they're all a hell of a lot taller, younger, and better-looking than me. I've never heard that it went any further than that. But playing around isn't all that unusual among the horse-racing set."

"She got along okay with her husband?"

"Yeah, as far as I could tell. Why wouldn't she? The guy was fronting some big bucks to keep her happy."

"Did Spalding ever say anything about his marriage?" Kerney asked.

Wheeler wrinkled his nose. "Not directly to me. I did overhear him once bellyaching to a friend before a race that he had a hard time getting her to travel out to the coast. There was always something that would come up and keep her in Santa Fe. Why are you asking me these questions?"

"I have the feeling the sheriff's deputy thinks I may be personally involved with Mrs. Spalding," Kerney said, "and that her husband's death may not be as uncomplicated as it appears."

Wheeler's genial attitude vanished as he looked Kerney up and down. "You're saying the cops think Spalding might have been murdered?"

"They haven't discounted it."

"Well, you sure fit the type she'd be drawn to." Wheeler shifted uneasily in his chair. "Not that I'm saying you're involved in anything."

"I'm sure it will all get sorted out," Kerney said.

He picked up the paperwork from the desk and thanked Wheeler for making the transaction pleasurable. Outside, two sheriff's units were parked in front of the guest cottage.

Kerney walked across the circular driveway thinking that what Wheeler had told him lent credence to Sergeant Lowrey's gut instincts about the case. The idea of going home as a suspect in a homicide held no appeal. He decided to delay his return to Santa Fe and poke around a bit to see what more he could learn about Clifford and Claudia Spalding.

*   *   *

Ellie Lowrey didn't see any hint of surprise or uneasiness in Kerney when he entered the cabin.

"Have you found anything interesting, Sergeant?" he asked. In the kitchen, the coroner was bagging the juice glass Kerney had rinsed out and left on the counter.

"Not yet," Ellie replied.

He turned to leave. "I'll wait on the porch until you're finished."

"Mr. Kerney," Lowrey said.

Lowrey had deliberately avoided addressing him by rank. It was a neat psychological trick to establish dominance. Kerney countered by reducing Lowrey in rank. "Yes, Deputy?"

Color rose on Lowrey's cheeks. "I'd like permission to search your luggage."

"Go ahead," Kerney said. "I'll be on the porch."

"Don't you want to be present?"

"It's not necessary."

She held out a clipboard. "Please sign the permission slip," she said tersely.

He scrawled his name, went outside, and sat on the stoop. Woodpeckers were busy in the trees and mares grazed lazily in the adjacent pasture. The afternoon sun, hazy in the sky, cast a soft, golden light that looked like melted butter. A mare rubbed her rump against the thick, curling lower branch of a live oak tree as her foal lay asleep close by, legs folded. Leaves shimmered in a whispering breeze, and a crow swished overhead, wings spread wide, croaking as it passed to drop down and perch on a creek-bed rock.

It had been an unusual day. Some of it had been as pleasant as the warm afternoon sun now on Kerney's face, and some of it as chilly as the early morning air, the darkened bedroom, and death. He wondered what other events might be in store for him before it ended.

An hour passed before the coroner hurried out carrying a small cardboard box. He loaded it in the trunk of his unit and drove away. Lowrey soon followed, stopping to thank Kerney for his cooperation.

"No problem," Kerney said.

"I still haven't heard back if Spalding's wife has been notified," Lowrey said.

"I take it she's not the first Mrs. Spalding."

"No, ex-wife number one lives in Santa Barbara."

He decided to tell Lowrey his plans. "I'm staying over until this gets resolved. How long do you think it will take?"

Lowrey blinked. "Through tomorrow night should do it."

Kerney stood, brushed off the seat of his jeans, fished Lowrey's business card from his shirt pocket, and waved it at her. "Good. I'll find a motel and let you know where I'm staying."

"Don't you want to know what I found in your luggage?"

"Nothing of any consequence, I'm sure," Kerney replied.

Lowrey nodded and walked away.

Kerney went inside, found his return airline ticket and car rental agreement, and changed his travel itinerary by phone. Then he called long distance information and got a phone listing for an A. Spalding in Santa Barbara.

A woman answered on the first ring. Kerney identified himself as a police officer and asked if she was Clifford Spalding's former wife.

"I am not," the woman replied. "That would be my employer, Alice Spalding."

"May I speak to her?" Kerney asked.

"What is it in reference to?"

"Her ex-husband."

"Talk to Mrs. Spalding's lawyer. I can give you her office number to call in the morning."

"Clifford Spalding died early today." Silence greeted Kerney's announcement.

"Where are you calling from?" the woman finally asked.

"Paso Robles," Kerney said. "It's important that I speak to Mrs. Spalding."

"Why? What happened?"

"I can't discuss it with you until all family members have been notified," Kerney replied. "It's policy. May I speak to Mrs. Spalding?"

"It's best that you do it in person," the woman said. "Alice has Alzheimer's disease, and she doesn't use the telephone much anymore. It confuses and upsets her."

"How advanced is her condition?" Kerney asked.

"Deteriorating. It's quite likely she won't understand all of what you tell her, but I can never be sure. Sometimes she's lucid, at other times she's incoherent. Her mind wanders, her memory is impaired, and she goes off-topic frequently."

"I can be there in two or three hours."

"Don't make it any later than that," the woman said. "Alice fades in the evening."

Kerney asked for directions and scratched them down on his road map, starting with which Highway 101 off-ramp to take once he reached Santa Barbara.

He left the ranch and headed south. Given Alice Spalding's medical condition, Kerney wasn't sure what he might gain from meeting her. But it felt good to be doing something.

*   *   *

The route to Alice Spalding's house took Kerney through a tidy Santa Barbara neighborhood of charming Spanish Mission and Romanesque houses. He passed the Presidio, a low-slung adobe building joined to a large mission church with twin bell towers that framed the coastal mountains rising behind it. Tour bus visitors busily took pictures as they strolled the grounds.

Beyond the Presidio, the winding road climbed into hills where the houses were much larger, and more difficult to see through an increasing profusion of plants, shrubs, and trees. None of the flowering vegetation, a riot of rich blues, deep reds, vivid purples, and vibrant yellows, was familiar to Kerney. About all he recognized were the towering palm trees.

He found the right street and house number, and turned into a driveway barred by an electronic gate. He announced himself over the intercom, and the gate swung open.

He parked next to a high-end Japanese sedan and looked around. Pink and red flowers bordered a step-down cobblestone walkway to the house. Tall, thin evergreen trees that reached to the second-story tile roof line bracketed the entry.

Before he could knock on the thick, antique plank door it swung open to reveal a woman with blue eyes, long dirty blond hair, and a fair complexion. She was somewhere in her mid- to late forties.

"Officer Kerney," the woman said, looking him up and down, taking in the jeans, boots, and western shirt. She hadn't expected a cowboy cop to come to the door. But then, Paso Robles wasn't as stylish as Santa Barbara.

Kerney nodded and flashed his shield, which he'd carried to California in his overnight bag.

The woman gave it only a quick glance as she extended her hand. "I'm Penelope Parker," she said with the slightest hint of a Southern accent. "Come in."

Kerney followed Parker into a large room with a line of windows looking out to a covered loggia supported by four columns and surrounded by a semicircular wall. Beyond was a view of mountains, the city below, and finally the bay, where masts of pleasure boats bobbed like tiny toothpicks in the water.

"Alice is napping right now," Parker said, "and I don't want to wake her. It shouldn't be too long before she rings for me."

"I don't mind waiting," Kerney said.

Parker gestured to the patio, opened the door, and led Kerney outside. "How did Mr. Spalding die?" she asked.

"For now, it appears to be by natural causes," Kerney said as he joined her at the patio wall. Below him an abandoned three-story stucco house sat with a patched tar-paper roof and plywood-covered windows and doors. A paved drive ran behind the building to a dead-end parking area where a few benches had been positioned to take in the view of the bay.

"Alice won't be happy to hear this," Parker said. "She'll probably reject what you have to say."

"Why is that?" Kerney asked, wondering why a derelict house on an overgrown lot with a parking area stood in the middle of such an expensive neighborhood.

"Because of her condition, and because of Mr. Spalding's legally binding agreement to make continued good faith efforts to locate their only child, a son named George. Alice had her lawyer make that language part of the divorce settlement, and she refers to it obsessively."

"They have a son who's gone missing?" Kerney asked. The grounds around the abandoned house overflowed with huge palm trees, and more lush shrubbery, vines, and flowers he didn't recognize. But these plants were growing wild, not carefully tended like those in the gardens of the houses all around.

"If only it were as simple as that," Parker replied. "George was killed in the Vietnam War. However, Alice refuses to accept that reality."

"Because of the Alzheimer's?"

"Oh, no," Parker said. "The onset of the Alzheimer's occurred two years ago. The hunt for George has been going on much longer, almost thirty years. Alice's obsession about it was one of the things that drove a stake in her marriage."

"You knew them back then?"

"No," Parker said with a shake of her head. "I've been Alice's personal assistant since the divorce. In fact, in a way, I'm also part of the divorce settlement. Mr. Spalding pays my salary and benefits. Before they split up, I worked for both of them for about two years."

"Has the son's death in Vietnam been fully documented?" Kerney asked.

"Completely," Parker said. "Still, Alice persists in her belief that he's alive. You'll see what I mean after she's up. There's a room in the house devoted completely to George. But no one's allowed in it unaccompanied. Not even me. If you ask, she'll show it to you."

"Do you know the current Mrs. Spalding?" he asked.

"I've never met her," Parker replied. "Clifford bought her a Tuscan-style mansion in Montecito. But as I understand it, she rarely stays there."

"Do you know where it is?"

Parker nodded. "I can give you directions before you leave."

"That would be great," Kerney said. He pointed at the abandoned house. "What is that place?"

Parker leaned against the patio wall. "It's a park owned by the city but rarely used. Originally, it was a residence and a plant nursery started by an Italian named Francesco Franceschi, who came here in the 1890s. He was responsible for importing almost a thousand foreign species and varieties of horticultural plants to the area. They still grace many of the older homes and mansions. He almost single-handedly beautified the city. These were treeless, brush-covered hills back then."

"Why is it so run-down?"

Parker laughed. "The city would love to restore the house and grounds as a venue for concerts and community events. But the neighbors won't hear of it. They don't want the peace and quiet of the area disturbed."

A bell sounded from inside the house. "That's Alice," Parker said. "I'll go prepare her for your visit."

Kerney stood on the patio and looked up. A covered second-story balcony dominated the back of the house, and, he guessed, gave onto the master bedroom. He wondered if an adjacent room served as George Spalding's shrine. Although Mrs. Spalding's obsession with her son probably had nothing to do with her ex-husband's death, it was intriguing.

A ground-floor breezeway connected to what Kerney assumed were Parker's living quarters. Parked in front was a sporty silver SUV that had probably never been off the pavement.

Penelope Parker stepped out on the patio and beckoned to him. He followed her through a spacious living room filled with ornate Spanish Colonial period furniture and tapestry rugs, and up a staircase to the master bedroom, where he was introduced to Alice Spalding.

A tiny woman dressed in powder-blue slacks and a creamy white blouse, Spalding smiled up at him from a beige leather easy chair near the windows. Her feet barely touched the floor.

She smiled vaguely at him. "What do you have for me today, Captain Chase?"

Parker touched Spalding on the shoulder. "This is Officer Kerney from Paso Robles, Alice, not Captain Chase."

"Oh," Spalding said, looking worriedly from Parker to Kerney. "What happened to Captain Chase?"

"Nothing," Parker replied. "The officer has something to tell you."

Spalding's expression brightened with anticipation. "Yes?"

"I'm sorry to tell you that Clifford Spalding is dead," Kerney said.

Confusion and anger washed over Alice's face. "George isn't dead."

"I'm talking about your ex-husband, Clifford," Kerney said.

"Well, he isn't dead either," Alice said emphatically. "Have you found George?"

"Not yet," Kerney said, thinking he'd wasted his time coming to see her.

"I didn't think so," Alice said huffily as she rose. "Come with me, I have something to show you."

She took him into an adjacent room. It was indeed a shrine, filled with framed photographs of George Spalding as a child, boy, teenager, and finally a young man in his Army uniform. On a heavy oak table were stacks of out-of-state newspaper clippings, some of them slightly yellow with age, others worn from constant handling.

She removed two recent news stories posted on a bulletin board behind a desk and handed them to Kerney. One, from an El Paso newspaper, had a picture of a middle-aged man accepting a civic award. The other article, with a photograph of a different man pushing a shopping cart filled with aluminum cans, was a story about homelessness.

"That's George," Alice Spalding said. "Now, all you have to do is go get him and bring him home to me. I never should have let him go. I need to tell him how sorry I am."

Kerney stifled the impulse to ask *which* man was George, since neither one at all resembled the young soldier in Mrs. Spalding's photograph. He glanced at Parker, who shook her head sadly.

"I'll get right on it," he said.

Among the photographs on the wall was a picture of Alice, Clifford, and a very young George Spalding in front of a pueblo revival—style motel that had been popular in the Southwest before the advent of the Interstate highway system. Kerney asked about it.

"It was our first motel in Albuquerque," Alice said. "On Central Avenue. We owned it for years."

"You lived in Albuquerque?" Kerney asked.

"I think so," Alice replied as she glanced questioningly at Parker.

"Yes, you did," Parker said.

Alice smiled in relief.

On the desk was a framed photograph of George in his Class A Army uniform, probably taken after his graduation from basic training. Next to it was a picture of a pleasant-looking teenage girl.

"Who's the young woman?" he asked.

Alice Spalding glared at him. "You know very well that's Debbie Calderwood."

"Yes, of course it is," Kerney said.

"Find her and you'll find George," Alice said.

"She's also missing?"

"You know she is," Alice replied hotly.

"Debbie left Albuquerque soon after George died," Parker explained. "Alice believes she was pregnant with George's baby at the time."

"I want to see my grandbaby," Alice said. She made a cuddling motion with her arms.

Kerney had heard and seen enough. He excused himself and let Parker escort him downstairs.

"See what I mean?" Parker said as she led him toward the front door.

"Who is Captain Chase?" Kerney asked.

"He's the commander of the Santa Barbara Police Department Criminal Investigation Unit. Alice usually has me call him once a week to report another lead about George. He's handled the case—if you want to call it that—for years."

"Can he tell me anything about Mr. Spalding?"

"I'm sure he can," Parker answered. "As well as probably more than you'll ever want to know about Alice's search for George."

"How did Spalding handle Alice's obsession?"

"Indulgently, for years, until it got the best of him."

"What about Debbie? Is she really missing?"

Parker had her hand on the front doorknob. "She probably just moved away. The police aren't looking for her. They never have. Years ago, before my time, Alice talked Clifford into hiring a private detective to look for Debbie, but it didn't get anywhere."

"Does the private detective live here in Santa Barbara?"

"Yes, but he's retired now, and I don't know his name. Alice will eventually ask me about Clifford. What can I tell her?"

"What I said earlier, that he probably died from natural causes in his sleep."

"What a peaceful way to go."

"You'll be able to get a report from the San Luis Obispo Sheriff's Department within a few days."

"Could you bring it to me?" Parker asked, smiling winningly.

"I'll see what I can do."

Parker gave him directions to the second Mrs. Spalding's Montecito estate, and Kerney decided to find a room for the night. After his visit with Alice Spalding, he wondered if staying over in California to chase down information would turn out to be nothing but a waste of time.

He pulled into a motel parking lot on State Street, a few blocks beyond an area of hotels, high-end department stores, movie houses, restaurants, and retail shops that formed the tourist center of the city. His cell phone rang as he killed the engine.

"Hey there, Kerney," Andy Baca said.

"How were the polar bears at the zoo?" he asked.

"Playful," Andy said. "The grandkids loved them. We're on our way home to Santa Fe, and they're asleep in the back of the car."

"Wasn't I supposed to call you later tonight?" Kerney asked.

"Yeah, but I've got news," Andy said. "I told my district commander to do whatever it took to find Mrs. Spalding pronto. So he contacted the state game and fish officer for the Pecos District and asked him to go looking for her and her trail-riding buddies up in the mountains.

"The game and fish officer found her all right, along with only one, I repeat, one, trail-riding pal: a white, forty-year-old male named Kim Dean. It was just the two of them. Mrs. Spalding gave the officer a line of bull about the rest of the group having gone on ahead to Elk Mountain. But from what the officer saw, he didn't buy it."

"What did he see that led him to that conclusion?"

"A cozy tent for two and no sign of any other riders entering the trailhead during the last three days."

"Interesting," Kerney said. "Where's Mrs. Spalding now?"

"Still in the mountains," Andy replied. "The officer just called in his report. He said she had a good three-hour ride before she would get back to where their horse trailer is parked."

"Did he say how Spalding reacted to the news of her husband's death?" Kerney asked.

"Yeah, tears, shock, and surprise."

"Uh-huh."

"Larry Otero has Ramona Pino checking out this Dean guy."

"Good. Has the San Luis Obispo Sheriff's Department been informed?"

"They will be as soon as we hang up and I give my people the go-ahead to make the call."

"I'm staying over an extra day," Kerney said.

"Why? If something is fishy, the focus of attention should be on this guy Dean, not you."

"You're probably right," Kerney said. "But just to satisfy my curiosity, I'll give it another day. I don't want this situation biting at my heels back in Santa Fe."

"Okay. Try to stay out of any more trouble while you're there," Andy added with a chuckle.

"Thanks for the vote of confidence," Kerney said.

"See you when you get home."

Kerney disconnected, walked into the motel office, and paid for a room. As he left with the key, he had half a thought to call Sara and tell her what was going on, and decided against it. Better to wait until things got sorted out.

He dumped his overnight bag on the double bed, and looked around the plain room. Cheap salmon-colored drapes adorned with seashells and sea urchins covered the window, and a faded print of a sailboat in a plastic frame was screwed into the wall over the bed. On a small desk was a pile of brochures for the major local tourist attractions.

He hadn't eaten all day, which was more than enough of an excuse to leave the dreary room, get a meal, and come back only when it was time to sleep.

ChapterThree

Kerney ate a light meal on the patio of a State Street restaurant where a blues band entertainied appreciative patrons, and then went looking for the Spalding estate in Montecito. All the houses in the neighborhood hid deep within their grounds behind privacy walls, mature trees, and hedges. Only here and there could Kerney glimpse the partial outline of a roof or facade through the treetops or a gateway.

He found the estate on the road to a private college in the hills, protected by a ten-foot-high stone wall with three gated entrances, one for the owners and their guests, one for staff, and another for service and deliveries.

He stood in front of the ornate wrought iron gate at the delivery entrance and pushed the intercom button. Beyond the gate, all he could see was a tree-lined driveway that wound through a forestlike setting. After waiting a few minutes with no reply, he pushed the button again. Finally a young man in a golf cart drove down to meet him. He wore damp swimming trunks and a cotton T-shirt that showed off his muscular arms. Wet black hair drooped over his forehead.

Kerney showed the man his shield and asked if he might speak to someone about Mr. Spalding's recent travel itinerary.

"Why do you want to know about it?" the man asked.

"Has Mr. Spalding been in Santa Fe during the last few days visiting his wife?" Kerney asked.

The man shook his head. "I can't answer that. Everyone who works here has to abide by a confidentiality agreement not to discuss anything about Mr. and Mrs. Spalding."

The man stepped closer to the closed gate and eyed Kerney's rental car. "That's not a cop car. Let me see that badge you showed me again."

Kerney held his badge case up so the man could look closely at his official ID.

"You're from New Mexico," the man said, studying the ID carefully, "and a police chief to boot. What are you doing here asking these questions?"

"Do you know a man named Kim Dean?" Kerney asked. "Perhaps he's a friend of the family from Santa Fe who has visited here."

"Never heard of him. What's this about?"

"Mr. Spalding is dead," Kerney said.

The man blinked and looked shocked. "What happened?"

"We're not sure what caused his death," Kerney said. "Has he been to Santa Fe recently?"

"No, not in the last two months."

"You know that for certain?"

"Yeah, he left his prescription medication behind, or lost it, or something. Sheila, his personal assistant, had to get a pharmacy in Santa Fe to fill it."

"He had a medical problem?" Kerney asked.

"Graves' disease," the man said. "It's a thyroid condition."

"Other than that, was his health generally good?" Kerney asked.

"Well, he's been complaining about blurred vision and not sleeping well recently. Does Mrs. Spalding know about this?"

"She does," Kerney said. "I expect she'll get here as soon as she can."

The man suddenly shut down. "Where did he die?" he asked suspiciously.

"In Paso Robles, at a quarter-horse ranch."

His expression cleared. "That's where he was going this weekend. What have you got to do with it?"

"I was at the ranch when it happened," Kerney said, thinking it might be best to stretch the truth a bit. "Since Mrs. Spalding lives in my jurisdiction, I'm assisting with the inquiries. Is Sheila here? I'd like to talk to her."

The man shook his head. "She's off for the weekend, down in L.A."

"An officer may want to speak with her," Kerney said.

"I'll call her on her cell and let her know what's happened."

"Was Mr. Spalding in residence before he left for Paso Robles?"

"No, he hasn't been at home for two weeks. What's that got to do with anything?"

"Since we're not sure of the cause of death, it's important to know where he's been," Kerney replied, making it up as he went along. "He may have been exposed to a virus, or had food poisoning, or become infected on his travels, especially if he was out of the country. But the proper tests can't be conducted unless we know his itinerary."

The man nodded as though Kerney's answer made good sense. "He was visiting several of his hotel properties. One in Mexico, and several in British Columbia. Sheila would have his exact itinerary."

"Good," Kerney said. "But the name Kim Dean doesn't ring a bell?"

"No. The only person from Santa Fe who has been here as a guest is a neighbor of Mrs. Spalding's, a woman named Nina Deacon. She's visited five or six times."

"Thank you for your time," Kerney said.

"That's it?" the man asked.

"For now," Kerney answered. "If there are more questions, you'll probably be hearing from a Sergeant Lowrey."

*   *   *

On the short drive back to Santa Barbara, Kerney called Santa Fe and left a message for Detective Sergeant Ramona Pino to contact him as soon as possible. On State Street, near the pier, he stopped at a bicycle rental store and asked a clerk how to get to police headquarters.

Following the clerk's directions, he continued along State Street, turned on Figueroa, and found the police headquarters building sandwiched between the old county courthouse and two small, somewhat run-down 1920s cottages, apparently rental units, in need of fresh coats of paint. They were the first houses he'd seen in Santa Barbara that didn't look picture-perfect. In an odd way, Kerney was pleased to see them after driving through so much opulence. Maybe some real, ordinary working people lived in the city after all.

He drove by the two-story headquarters building. A series of steps with landings leading up to the front entrance were bordered by carefully tended, terraced planting beds. On the second landing a large tree towered above a flagpole where an American flag fluttered in a slight breeze. The building was white with a slightly slanted red tile roof, and two rows of rectangular windows ran across the front, their symmetry broken only by an arched, recessed entry.

Kerney figured the public access door would be locked on the weekends, so he parked and walked to the back of the building where he found the staff entrance. He pressed the bell and held his shield up in front of the video camera mounted above the door.

A uniformed officer wearing sergeant stripes on his sleeves opened up and inspected his credentials. "You're a long way from home, Chief," the sergeant said. "What can I do for you?"

"I'd like to speak to Captain Chase," Kerney said.

"He doesn't work on weekends unless he's called out."

"Can he be contacted?" Kerney asked.

"Is this important?" the sergeant asked.

"I wouldn't be here if it wasn't," Kerney replied.

"Let me see if he's home." The sergeant stepped aside to let Kerney enter and led him down a corridor past a line of closed doors, around a corner, and into an empty bullpen office filled with standard issue gray desks, file cabinets, and privacy partitions that defined work cubicles for investigators.

The sergeant got on the horn to Chase, explained that he had a police chief from Santa Fe who needed to see him, and turned the phone over to Kerney.

Kerney gave Chase a rundown of the events that had brought him down to Santa Barbara.

"Jesus H. Christ," Chase growled. "Okay, I'll be there in a few. Wait for me in my office."

Chase's office was also standard issue: a desk, several chairs, a file cabinet, a desktop computer, and the usual personal and cop memorabilia displayed on the bookshelf and the walls. Kerney spent his time waiting by reading a back issue of the *FBI Law Enforcement Bulletin* that featured a cover article on criminal confessions. Through the window he could see the sky darkening into dusk. He was almost through the article when a burly man with a day-old beard and a broad face stepped into the open doorway.

"So Clifford Spalding is dead," the man said with a rueful smile. "God help me. Now I'll never get his ex-wife off my back." He offered his hand. "Dick Chase."

Kerney set the bulletin aside, stood, grasped Chase's hand, and introduced himself.

"So, is this a homicide?" Chase asked as he settled into the chair behind his desk.

"Possibly," Kerney said, "possibly not."

Chase grunted. "That clarifies things. What brings you into it?"

Kerney decided to level with Chase. "For now, it appears that I'm a person of interest to the investigation."

"You're a suspect?" Chase asked as he gave Kerney a hard, sideways look.

"Not yet," Kerney replied. "I'm trying to extricate myself from that possibility."

Chase leaned back in his chair, his tight smile showing no teeth. "You'd better lay it all out for me."

Kerney told Chase about his reasons for coming to California and his early morning discovery of Spalding's body at the ranch. He emphasized that Claudia Spalding had been in the company of a man on a remote, high country trail-riding trip when notified of her husband's death, and finished up by summarizing the conversations he'd had with Alice Spalding and Penelope Parker. He deliberately skipped over his visit to the Spalding estate.

He put Sergeant Lowrey's business card on the desk. "That's the San Luis Obispo sheriff's deputy who's handling the inquiry," he said. "Give her a call, Captain, and get her side of the story."

Chase nodded. "Wait out in the bullpen, and give me a few minutes."

Chase closed the door behind Kerney and spent a good ten minutes on the phone with Lowrey. When he reappeared he didn't look too happy. He motioned for Kerney to enter.

Kerney's cell phone rang as he sat.

"It's Sergeant Pino, Chief," Ramona said when he answered.

"What have you learned about Kim Dean?" he asked.

"He's a divorced father of two. The ex-wife and kids reside in Colorado. He's a pharmacist and the owner of one of those franchise pharmacies. He's got a house in Canada de los Alamos and keeps a couple of horses. The neighbors say Claudia Spalding's vehicle is frequently parked at his house overnight."

"Find and talk to a friend of Claudia Spalding's named Nina Deacon," Kerney said. "She lives in Spalding's area. Learn what you can from her about Dean's relationship to Spalding."

"Will do. Anything else, Chief?"

"Who's working with you?"

"Russell Thorpe."

Thorpe was a young, capable state police officer Kerney knew personally through his involvement in several major felony cases.

"Good. Check your facts carefully," he said, hoping Ramona and Thorpe would get the hint and sit on what they'd learned for a little while.

"Will waiting thirty minutes before we pass on the information do?" Ramona asked.

"Perfect," Kerney said, then disconnected and looked at Chase. "Well?" he asked. "What did Sergeant Lowrey have to say?"

"You've pissed her off, big-time," Chase said flatly, "and frankly, I'm feeling that you've put me in an awkward situation. I don't know whether to hold you for questioning or let you walk."

"I'm not going anywhere for a while," Kerney said. He gave Chase the name of the motel where he'd rented a room. "What did Lowrey tell you?"

Chase ran his hand over the stubble on his chin. "You know the drill: no details or information gets released to potential suspects or targets of investigation."

"Fair enough," Kerney replied. "Can you talk about Alice Spalding and her search for her missing son?"

"That I can do," Chase said with a small, derisive laugh. "There is no missing son. George Spalding was killed in a helicopter accident in Vietnam near the end of the war. He was a military policeman transporting one of the last prisoners from the stockade at Long Binh when the chopper went down. Both Spalding and the prisoner were killed in the crash."

Kerney knew about the Long Binh Jail, located on a U.S. Army base near Bien Hoa, twenty miles north of Saigon. The troops referred to it contemptuously as the LBJ, for Lyndon Baines Johnson, the president who'd escalated the war through deceit, misinformation, and lies.

Kerney had been in-country as a lieutenant at about the same time as George Spalding, serving as a member of the last U.S. Army combat unit in Nam, the Second Battalion, Twenty-first Infantry.

"You've got DOD verification of George Spalding's death?" he asked.

"Up the wazoo," Chase replied.

"So why is Alice Spalding convinced her son is still alive?"

"Long before the Spaldings ever moved to Santa Barbara, she saw a wire service photograph in a newspaper of some people with injuries being treated at a traffic pile-up on the interstate. One of the victims in the photo looked like her son, and I grant you he did. But a check with the California Highway Patrol and the EMT who treated the man confirmed that it wasn't George Spalding. As I understand it, that started the whole thing."

"How did Clifford Spalding handle it?" Kerney asked.

"It was his cross to bear," Chase said. "He asked me to contact him every time Alice called to report another sighting. She sees George everywhere, on television, in the newspapers, walking down the street, at shopping malls in Timbuktu. Most of the time the subject doesn't even resemble George. I've been dealing with her obsession about her son for the past fifteen years."

Kerney nodded sympathetically. "Why is she so obsessed?"

Chase shrugged. "I don't know."

"How do you handle her?" Kerney asked.

"In the past, she used to call me herself. But now it's mostly her personal assistant who phones in to report a new sighting. I take down the information, tell her we'll look into it, and then let Mr. Spalding know about it. He'd take it from there. He had a way of calming her down, at least for a while. Usually it would be a month, maybe two, before I heard from her or her assistant again."

"Didn't Spalding at one time hire a private investigator at Alice's urging?" Kerney asked.

"Yeah, Lou Ferry," Chase said. "He retired from the department about twenty years ago. I heard he got sick and had to shut down his business. Spalding used Ferry once or twice right after he moved here to placate Alice when she felt like we weren't doing enough."

"What about Debbie Calderwood?"

Chase held out his hands in a gesture of supplication. "Oh yeah, the girlfriend from Albuquerque. Wouldn't it be great if she just dropped out of the sky into our laps? According to an Albuquerque PD report from back in the early seventies, she quit college and left town soon after George died. Nobody knows where she went or where she is. She's just another person out there somewhere in the great unknown who doesn't want to be found."

"Not missing?"

"Who knows?" Chase replied. "She was never entered into the national missing persons data bank. For the life of me, I don't see how any of this has any bearing on Spalding's death or your situation."

"When you don't have a suspect, you focus on the victim," Kerney said.

"That would be a smart thing to do," Chase said, "especially if you did kill Spalding. It makes everybody think you're just trying to clear yourself, protect your good name, and keep your job as Santa Fe police chief."

"You have a cunning mind, Captain."

Chase stretched, put his hands behind his head, and gave Kerney a friendly smile. "Tell me about this Dean guy you were talking about on the phone."

"I already have," Kerney said.

"Yeah, but it sounded like you got some fresh information."

"It hasn't been confirmed yet."

"Is Dean someone you know?" Chase asked. "A friend perhaps?"

"I don't know him at all," Kerney said.

"Am I right to assume the phone call you got came from someone in your department who is keeping you advised?"

"My department is cooperating with Sergeant Lowrey's investigation."

"And keeping you advised," Chase said.

Kerney decided it was time to end the game. "Of course. But I'm sure you know from your little talk with Sergeant Lowrey that she has asked the New Mexico State Police to verify any information my department passes on. It would seem she doesn't trust my people."

"Given the circumstances, wouldn't you be cautious and skeptical?"

Kerney stayed silent.

"Tell me about this Santa Fe neighbor of Mrs. Spalding's."

"For now, there's nothing to tell."

"Holding out on Lowrey isn't going to help your cause," Chase said.

"I'm holding out on you, not Lowrey," Kerney said, getting to his feet. "I see no reason to use you as an intermediary in this matter. It's not your case or your jurisdiction. You know where I'm staying for the night. I'm sure Sergeant Lowrey will want to know how to contact me. Are we done here?"

Chase's lips got tight and thin again. "Yeah, we're done."

"Good night, Captain."

"See you around, Chief," Chase replied.

In the rental car, Kerney drove in the opposite direction from the motel until he found a gas station, where he looked up Louis Ferry in a phone book and got an address.

He figured that Lowrey, by now fully briefed by Captain Chase, was on the road to Santa Barbara, prepared to read him out once she arrived for meddling in her case. He decided it would be best not to meet with her until Ramona Pino and Russell Thorpe finished up with Nina Deacon and hopefully had enough information to put the spotlight on Kim Dean as a possible murder suspect or accomplice— if indeed a homicide had been committed.

He'd never completely discounted the possibility of murder, or disagreed when Lowrey took the investigation to the next level to see if it proved out. That wasn't the issue. Kerney simply didn't like the idea of Lowrey polishing her shield by tarnishing his reputation.

With the station attendant's directions to Ferry's address in mind, Kerney started off, aware that he might be on a wild-goose chase. Still, the story of Alice Spalding's search for a son who'd been dead for thirty years continued to intrigue him. He wanted to learn more about it.

*   *   *

Lou Ferry lived in a trailer park on Punta Gorda Street, a dead-end lane cut off by the freeway. The rumble of traffic rose and fell as the cars and trucks rolled by.

Ferry's residence was the first space in two long rows of small and medium-size camper-trailers that stretched down a paved drive filled with parked jalopies and older-model cars. The only modular home along the lane, it was enclosed by a five-foot-high wooden fence and gate.

Kerney knocked at the front door and a sour-looking, middle-aged Mexican woman greeted him.

"I'm looking for Lou Ferry," he said.

"He don't know you," the woman replied.

"I'm a police officer," Kerney said, displaying his shield.

"Just a minute," the woman replied, closing the door.

Soon she was back, gesturing for Kerney to enter. "He's in the bedroom," she said, pointing to a passageway before walking away.

The sound of clattering dishes from the kitchen followed Kerney down the short hallway. In the back room, he found Ferry sitting up in bed watching television.

"Mr. Ferry?"

"Yeah," Ferry said in a wheezy voice as he turned off the TV, "and don't make any wisecracks about my name. I've heard them all."

The nightstand held an array of prescription bottles and an empty drinking glass.

"My wife, who wants me to hurry up and die so she can sell the trailer park and move back to Mexico, says you're a cop."

"That's right."

Ferry made a gimme motion with his hand. "Let's see your shield."

Kerney handed him the badge case and watched Ferry reach for his reading glasses. He was a short man who'd lost weight and had the frail look that comes with an end-stage illness.

"Santa Fe Police Chief," Ferry said, handing back the badge case with a slight smirk. "Impressive. What you want from me?"

"I hear you retired from the job," Kerney said.

"After thirty-six years. I started when I was twenty-one. I've been on a pension for over twenty. You do the math."

"You were a PI for a time."

"Eighteen years, until I got sick." Ferry dropped his reading glasses on his lap and coughed into his fist. "Get on with what you came here for. I could die before you finish asking your questions."

"You did some private work for Clifford Spalding. I'd like to know about it."

Ferry shook his head to ward off the inquiry. "That's it. End of questions. Get out."

"He's dead," Kerney said.

Ferry absorbed the information and relaxed slightly. "How did it happen?"

"We're still looking into it."

Ferry smiled sardonically. "Crazy Alice Spalding didn't kill him, did she?"

"Why do you say that?" Kerney asked.

"For giving her the runaround all these years," Ferry said as he adjusted the pillow behind his head.

"Explain that to me."

Ferry propped himself up against the headboard. "Since he's dead, I guess I finally can tell somebody. Spalding came to see me soon after he moved to Santa Barbara. Walked in the door of my office one day with a legal document he'd had drawn up. Said he would hire me to do some work for him if I agreed to do exactly what he wanted and sign a binding nondisclosure agreement. I looked it over. It basically said I couldn't reveal any information I gathered about George Spalding or Debbie Calderwood to anyone but him, and that I'd forfeit any sums paid to me if I did."

"And?"

Ferry took a deep breath that rattled in his chest. "I told him I needed a hell of a lot more information before I'd even consider taking on the case like that. That's when he showed me the official Army documents of his son's death in Vietnam and explained the situation with his wife. He said he'd tried everything to help her accept the fact that George was gone, and since that hadn't worked he'd been forced to live with an obsessive wife who was driving him crazy and hounding cops all over the West to find her lost son. He gave me copies of missing person reports Alice had submitted to a half dozen police departments in three or four different states."

Kerney scooted a straight-back chair to the foot of the bed and sat. "So you took the case."

"After he put ten one-hundred-dollar bills in my hand as an advance and told me what he wanted me to do."

"Which was?"

Ferry chuckled. "Nothing. Make stuff up. The deal was that he'd call and ask me to follow up on one of Alice's crazy leads. Then I'd write up a report about my phony investigation into it, wait a week or two, and mail it to him. He paid me five hundred dollars a pop."

"Easy money," Kerney said. "How many reports did you concoct for him?"

"About twenty, twenty-five, over the next couple of years."

"What made the cash cow dry up?"

Ferry laughed. "I blew it. When I started running out of creative ways to lie, I decided to do some actual investigating to freshen up my reports."

"Tell me about that."

"Alice had tracked down an old college friend of Debbie Calderwood living in Portland, who said she'd gotten a card from her about a year after Calderwood disappeared. So, I called the friend, who told me Calderwood had written to her from Taos, New Mexico, where she was living on a commune at the time. Remember, that was back in the early seventies when all that flower power and antiwar stuff hadn't completely faded away yet."

"What else did the note say?" Kerney asked.

"That she was moving with an unnamed boyfriend to a small town in southern Colorado. But she'd didn't say exactly where. So, I got out the atlas and phone book and called a bunch of places trying to locate her. When that didn't work, I phoned some town marshals, sheriffs, and police departments, and still came up empty."

"Did you tell Spalding that you'd actually done some real work on the case?" Kerney asked.

"Nope. But I put everything I'd learned in my report. That's when he fired me. End of story." Ferry coughed hard into his hand again. "It got me to thinking that maybe Spalding was up to maybe something more than trying to appease his unbalanced wife."

"Like what?"

"Don't know," Ferry said breathlessly, waving the question away as if it was an angry hornet buzzing around his head.

"Did you check out Spalding before you spent the retainer he gave you?" Kerney asked, switching gears.

"Smart question." Ferry smiled slyly and held up a trembling index finger. "Rule number one for a PI, always know who you're working for. I made some calls, but I can't remember most of what I learned."

"What stands out?"

"He'd made a lot of money in the hotel business in a relatively short period of time. He went from owning a mom-and-pop motel in Albuquerque to building a resort hotel outside of Tucson in something under five years. That's what got him started playing with the big money boys."

Ferry's head sank against the pillow and his eyes closed. The fatigue in his face ran deep into the wrinkles of his cheeks and cut into the furrows of his forehead. A vein throbbed in his skinny neck.

"Did you keep copies of your reports?" Kerney asked.

"No copies," Ferry said in a weak voice. "That was part of the deal."

"You need to sleep," Kerney said as he stood.

Ferry's eyes fluttered open and he winced in pain. "Yeah, maybe I'll get lucky this time and won't wake up."

Kerney left the bedroom quietly. In a dining area off the front room, Ferry's wife sat at the table talking softly in Spanish on the telephone. She looked at him with cool disinterest when he waved good-bye and left.

Outside under the street lights, some kids were kicking a soccer ball around, and two teenagers sat in an old primer-gray Chevy smoking cigarettes and playing loud rap music on the car stereo.

It wasn't the Santa Barbara in the travel posters or real estate ads. Not that there was anything mean or menacing about the area. It was just another one of those tucked-away places you could find in any city that the underclass lived in and everyone else avoided.

Kerney drove away thinking about Lou Ferry. He'd spent a lifetime on the job as a cop and a PI. All he had to show for it was ownership of a run-down trailer park and a woman who couldn't wait for him to die. It wasn't the happiest of endings.

What Kerney had learned about Clifford Spalding's efforts to defeat his ex-wife's search to find her son gnawed at him, as did the New Mexico connection that kept popping up. He decided, if time allowed, to speak to Penelope Parker again and get a little more background on the man.

He glanced at the dashboard clock. But first there was Sergeant Lowrey to deal with. He hoped she was stationed outside his motel room waiting for him to show.

*   *   *

Five blocks from his motel, Kerney's cell phone rang. He pulled to the curb and answered. It was Ramona Pino.

"What have you got for me, Sergeant?"

"Interesting stuff, Chief. We've just finished up with Nina Deacon. It seems like Claudia Spalding and Kim Dean started out as horseback-riding buddies and the relationship segued into a hot love affair about two years ago that's still going strong. Recently, Claudia has been crying on Deacon's shoulder about the prenuptial agreement she signed with her dead husband."

"She wanted out of the marriage?" Kerney asked.

"Affirmative," Ramona replied. "But she didn't want to lose the Santa Fe house or her lifestyle. According to Deacon, any divorce caused by infidelity on Claudia's part cuts her out of Spalding's will. The way Deacon tells it, the Santa Fe property is in his name as the sole owner, with a legal agreement signed by Claudia to back it up. About all she could walk away with would be her horses, other gifts he's given her over the years, a half interest in the furnishings they bought together for the house, and whatever is in her personal checking account."

"What else?" Kerney asked.

"Spalding was out here about two months ago for ten days. He got sick about halfway through the visit. Fatigue, heat intolerance, the sweats. Deacon said Spalding thought he was just having a reaction to the dry climate and the change in altitude."

"Did he see a doctor?" Kerney asked.

"No, Claudia nursed him, cared for him hand and foot until he left."

"The loving wife. Where is she now?"

"At the Albuquerque airport waiting for a flight to Burbank. According to Deacon, she keeps a car in Burbank and drives up to Santa Barbara."

"Did Deacon see her before she left?"

"Yeah. Claudia told Deacon that probably Spalding's heart had given out."

"Will Deacon keep her mouth shut about your visit?" Kerney asked.

"She'd better. Both Thorpe and I made it clear that warning Claudia about our inquiries would make her liable to be charged as an accessory."

"Did that sink in?"

"Big-time, Chief," Ramona said. "She squirmed in her seat and promised to be a good girl."

"Put somebody on Kim Dean to keep an eye on him. I don't want him suddenly disappearing."

"It's already done."

"Have you got Sergeant Lowrey's cell phone number?"

"I do."

"Call her now and brief her."

"You don't want me to do time-delayed information sharing on this go-round?" Ramona asked with a hint of a smile in her voice.

Kerney laughed. "No, let's get this over with so I can come home without a black cloud floating over my head."

"Ten-four to that, Chief. Thorpe is on the horn to Chief Baca with the news right now. Get ready to have him rib you about all of this when you get home."

"He's already started," Kerney said. "Good job, Sergeant. Pass on my appreciation to Officer Thorpe."

"Thanks, Chief. Will do."

He disconnected, sat back against the car seat, sighed with relief, and looked at the dashboard clock. He'd give it five minutes before driving to the motel in the hopes that a sheepish Sergeant Lowrey would be waiting for him with an apology in hand.

*   *   *

Ellie Lowrey watched Chief Kerney enter the motel parking lot and ease to a stop next to her unit. Although she'd been rehearsing what to say to him, her mind suddenly went blank and her mouth got dry. She motioned at him to join her.

He slid into the passenger seat, closed the door, and nodded a silent greeting.

Ellie waited a few beats, hoping Kerney would say something to break the ice and let her off the hook. When the silence between them became unbearable, she said, "I guess I had my eye on the wrong target, Chief Kerney."

"Your instincts were good," Kerney said, keeping his voice flat.

"It wasn't personal," Ellie said, hoping Kerney would make eye contact with her.

Kerney stared straight ahead. "I know that."

"I'm sorry for the hassle."

Kerney glanced her way and smiled. "It's okay, Sergeant. You were doing your job, and doing it well."

"You've talked to Santa Fe?" Lowrey asked, trying to keep the relief she felt out of her voice.

"I have. Now it's your turn to fill me in."

Ellie told Kerney about the preliminary findings from the post mortem, the discovery of the hormone replacement medication in a pill case in Clifford Spalding's clothing, and Price's telephone conversation with Spalding's doctor.

"You only found one pill?" Kerney asked.

"Yeah. Is that important?"

"I talked to a caretaker at Spalding's estate who told me Spalding had been on a business trip for the past two weeks before he went to the ranch. I doubt he'd be foolish enough not to keep a supply of medication on hand."

"We didn't find a prescription bottle," Ellie said.

"Did you search his car?" Kerney asked.

Ellie shook her head.

"It might be a smart thing to do. The caretaker also told me that Clifford Spalding forgot to take his medication with him while visiting his wife in Santa Fe two months ago, and had to get his prescription refilled locally. Don't you find that interesting, given who Claudia Spalding has been sleeping with?"

"I do," Ellie replied.

"Who better to tamper with or alter medication than a pharmacist? And if it was Dean who filled the prescription, did he dispense a one-month, two-month, or three-month supply?"

Ellie mulled it over. "Claudia Spalding told Nina Deacon her husband probably died of heart failure, which comes pretty close to the autopsy findings. Now, how would she know that, given the fact that Spalding was in good health at the time of his last checkup?"

"Exactly," Kerney said.

"So how would Dean have done it?" Ellie asked.

"I don't know," Kerney replied, as he opened the passenger door. "But the caretaker mentioned that since his return from Santa Fe, Spalding had been complaining about sleeping poorly and blurred vision."

"Which means his condition may have been deteriorating," Ellie asked, reaching for her cell phone.

Kerney got out of the unit.

"Where are you going?"

"To find an address for an all-night pharmacy while you call in for a search of Spalding's car."

*   *   *

The on-duty pharmacist at the discount drugstore, a woman with a button chin and a long, narrow nose, stood behind the counter at the back of the store and listened carefully as the female police officer described a well-known brand of thyroid medication.

"Yes, it's used as a hormone replacement."

"If, as a pharmacist, you wanted to alter or tamper with it, how would you do it?"

"The easiest way would be to coat it with a clear substance. That way the pill would look perfectly okay."

"Barring that, what could you do?" Ellie asked.

"I'm not sure I understand the question."

"What if you wanted to change the actual composition of the pill?" Ellie asked.

"Well, this is a medication that you can get in a powdered form. Some pharmacists who specialize in mixing their own compounds like to fill prescriptions that way. But it wouldn't look anything like the pharmaceutical version."

The tall, good-looking man with the female officer smiled at her.

"How could you change the dosage or ingredients and yet have it look identical to the real thing?" Kerney asked.

"Same size, shape, color, and brand name?" the pharmacist asked.

"Yes. Could it be done?"

"I suppose, if you made it with a mold. But it would be painstaking work."

"How would you go about it?" Ellie asked.

"Well, I'd start with making an impression of the lettering on the pill so I could duplicate it," the woman said. "Then I'd have to build a mold to form it based on the precise measurements of the pill and its lettering."

"What kind of a mold?" Kerney asked.

The woman tapped her finger against her chin. "Ceramic perhaps, but certainly something that wouldn't break under pressure when you formed the pill, especially if you wanted to imprint a brand name."

"What about the coloring?" Ellie asked.

The pharmacist smiled. "That would be the easy part. I'd use a natural dye."

"Could you duplicate the shape of the pill by hand?" Kerney asked.

"Sure, but it would take some time to make a good supply, and the brand name would still need to be stamped on the pills to make them look authentic."

"What's the usual refill supply that's given to patients?" Kerney asked.

"Three months is the norm, if the patient is stabilized on the dosage."

"You've been a big help," Ellie said.

The woman looked from the female cop to the man. "Now, please tell me what this is all about."

"Crime, of course," Kerney said, stepping away from the counter.

Ellie waited until they were in the parking lot before asking Kerney what he thought should be done next. He suggested having the pill found in Spalding's pocket analyzed and getting started on the paperwork for a search warrant of Dean's pharmacy and residence in Santa Fe.

"I don't have enough evidence to get a search warrant approved yet," Ellie said as she unlocked the passenger door to her unit.

"I bet you will have after the lab results come back tomorrow," Kerney said as he ducked into the cruiser. "But you may not need to have the search warrant served right away. If you play your cards right, Claudia Spalding might just crack under questioning. Then you can go for an arrest warrant on Dean and serve both simultaneously."

Ellie got behind the wheel and fired up the engine. "Want to be there for the Q&A with Claudia Spalding?"

Kerney shook his head and laughed. "Not a chance. Because of you, I'm spending an extra day in California, so I might as well enjoy it."

"Sorry about that, Chief," Ellie said as they arrived at Kerney's motel. "I'll call you when things shake out."

"Leave me a message," Kerney said as he climbed out of the unit.

Ellie watched Kerney unlock his motel door and step inside. He'd never once flared up under the pressure she'd put on him. Beyond that, he'd gathered important information to advance the investigation and had graciously accepted her apology without laying into her.

She'd come to Santa Barbara ready to ream Kerney out for meddling in her investigation. As she drove away, Ellie thought that Chief Kerney would be a hell of a good boss to work for.

ChapterFour

Kerney slept hard, got up early, showered, dressed, and studied a tourist map that promised to guide him to Santa Barbara's finest dining, shopping, and entertainment experiences, including an adult video store and a gentlemen's club featuring fully nude live dancers.

He located a restaurant that looked interesting at a place called Hendry's Beach outside of town. On the drive there, he enjoyed the quiet of the morning, the absence of traffic, and a view of the bay with gentle waves of surf rolling in.

The restaurant, located next to the beach, wasn't open for business when he arrived, although several servers were busy setting the tables on an outdoor patio. He took his boots and socks off, rolled up the cuffs of his jeans, and walked in the shade of the cliffs that lined the shore. Only a few people were out, including some joggers, a couple walking two dogs, and several tourists snapping pictures near some rocks where a young seal seemed to be calmly posing for a photo shoot. Out beyond the surf, a dolphin briefly surfaced, drawing the attention of a lone seagull circling overhead.

On top of the cliffs, which showed signs of constant erosion, houses surrounded by tall, skinny palm trees looked out at the ocean. Steep stairs, some rickety and dangerous, provided access down the cliff face to the beach. Kerney wondered how long it would take before the sea, the wind, and the rain brought everything crashing down. A hundred years? A thousand? Ten thousand? Eventually, it would happen.

His thoughts turned to Sara and the beaches they'd walked together on their honeymoon in western Ireland. There, cliffs of solid rock towered over them and a heavy surf threw angry plumes of white foam into the air. It had been a happy time on the shore of a turbulent sea under misty gray skies.

Sara had spent hours inspecting and gathering seashells, stuffing the choice ones in the pockets of her windbreaker, enlisting Kerney to fill his pockets as well. The shells now sat in a large, hand-blown glass bowl on Sara's desk at the Pentagon.

He wondered how Sara and their son, Patrick, were doing back on the East Coast. He pictured her getting Patrick out of bed, fed, and ready for the day, Patrick banging his rattle on the high chair and giggling, Sara dressing hurriedly and running a brush quickly through her strawberry blond hair.

The restaurant was open when Kerney returned, and he took breakfast on the patio, careful as always not to eat too much. He'd been gut shot in a gun battle with a drug dealer some years back, and it had damaged his stomach badly.

He finished his meal and decided it wasn't too early to call Penelope Parker. She answered on the first ring and readily agreed to meet with him again. He left the restaurant just as a smiling young couple with a toddler sitting happily on the man's shoulders entered. The sight of the family made him miss Sara and Patrick all the more. But soon he'd be with them for two solid weeks. He would be teaching some classes and taking a top-cop seminar at the FBI Academy in Quantico, Virginia, thirty miles away from the small house Sara and he had bought in Arlington, Virginia.

The thought of seeing his family made the day seem much brighter. He smiled as he headed down the road to visit Penelope Parker.

*   *   *

Ms. Parker seemed pleased to see Kerney when he arrived. There was a nervous energy to her greeting that he couldn't quite decipher. He wondered if it came from spending her days cut off from the world tending to Alice's needs. She escorted him to the patio where coffee, juice, and a platter of warm scones were arranged on a table, and seated him so he could have the best view of the city and the bay.

Parker had dressed up for the occasion. She wore a pair of dainty, open-toe shoes, black slacks that accentuated her slender legs, and a short-sleeved, partially unbuttoned Hawaiian shirt that emphasized the curve of her breasts. Without prompting, she told Kerney that Alice still didn't understand that Clifford was dead.

"I don't know if she's able to process it," Parker said as she leaned over Kerney's shoulder and poured his coffee. "She may never be. Her mental capacity is diminishing rapidly."

The color rose on her cheeks when Kerney looked up and thanked her. He quickly realized Parker was lonely for more than simple companionship.

"Do you have any help to look after her?" he asked.

Parker nodded as she sat and served Kerney a scone. "Trained caregivers are here at night, and I do get an occasional weekend off. But when Alice becomes confused, I'm the only one who can deal with her, so I always try to be fairly close at hand."

"Where is Alice now?" Kerney asked.

Parker smiled as she stirred cream into her coffee. "She's in her room. I asked the caregiver to stay over for a while to be with her so we could talk without any interruption."

"What can you tell me about the origin of Clifford Spalding's wealth?"

"As I understand it, he owned an old motel in Albuquerque adjacent to a very large shopping mall that wanted the land for expansion. The developer had a pending lease agreement with a national chain to build an upscale motor lodge for vacationers and out-of-town weekend shoppers. Clifford negotiated a deal that gave him some working capital and a minority ownership in the franchise. That's how it all started."

"When did this happen?" Kerney asked.

"Long before my time," Parker replied. "The same year George was killed in Vietnam, or soon thereafter."

"How did Clifford parlay his profit into a hotel empire?" Kerney asked.

Parker leaned forward, revealing a bit more cleavage. "Another hotel company wanted to establish a presence in Albuquerque and offered an attractive buyout deal for the property after the new motel was up and running. Mr. Spalding retained his minority interest as part of the deal and used his cash-out from the profit he'd made to buy a ninety-nine-year lease on a run-down motel in downtown Santa Fe. He got some investors to put up money for the renovation, and turned the place into a thriving boutique hotel operation."

"Did he live in Santa Fe?" Kerney asked.

"No, he and Alice had a house in Albuquerque."

Parker stood and filled Kerney's juice glass, this time touching him lightly on the shoulder as she poured.

"Why would Alice want Clifford tied to a divorce decree that made him responsible for the continued search for George?" Kerney asked, after Parker, cheeks slightly flushed, returned to her chair.

"Partially out of spite, and partially to use every possible way to hit Clifford in the checkbook," she said.

Kerney sipped his juice. "Explain that to me."

"She hates the fact that Clifford never believed George was still alive. It got to the point, just before the divorce, where Mr. Spalding was publicly demeaning her about it to their friends. It was her way of striking back at him."

"Yet Spalding cooperated in Alice's hunt for George," Kerney said. "He hired a private investigator, and stayed in touch with the local police."

"I always felt he did that more to placate Alice than to really look for George."

"What about the search for Debbie Calderwood?" Kerney asked.

"George's personal effects included love letters Debbie had written to him while he was in Vietnam. Those letters convinced Alice that Debbie knew something about George's military service the Army wasn't telling her."

"Like what?"

"That George had some secret duty, a special operation or a hush-hush assignment."

"Where are the letters?" Kerney asked, remembering Lou Ferry's story of how Spalding had made him fake a report on Calderwood's possible whereabouts.

"Alice and Clifford had a big fight just before he walked out on her," Parker replied. "She came home to find him burning everything about George and Debbie that she'd accumulated over the years. He destroyed all of it."

"Interesting," Kerney said. "Did this happen while Clifford had the private investigator working on the case?"

Parker nodded. "Right about then, as I recall."

"But you never met him, or knew his name," Kerney said.

"That's right," Parker said. "Nor did Alice. Mr. Spalding was something of a control freak. When Alice challenged him about it, he said the man couldn't possibly remain objective unless he was free to do his job without her interference."

Kerney folded his napkin, placed it on the table, and stood. The morning haze had lifted and the calm ocean glimmered like a deep blue mirror, reflecting the sunlight. "I've taken up enough of your time," he said.

"Will you be in town long?" Parker asked wistfully.

"Just through today," Kerney replied.

Parker covered her disappointment with a cheerful smile. "Please come back if you have any more questions. I'll be here all day."

"Thank you."

Parker walked close beside Kerney to the front door and waved good-bye as he left. On the trip down the hill, with the scent of Parker's perfume still lingering, he decided to pay another visit to Captain Chase. There had to be some documentation about George Spalding on file with the department. He also wanted to probe into what kind of working relationship Clifford Spalding had forged with the good captain.

*   *   *

Ellie Lowrey got to the lab just as it opened and extracted a promise from the supervisor to have Spalding's toxicology work done and the medication found in the pill box analyzed before the end of the day. Last night's search of Spalding's car had turned up nothing. But Bill Price was busy calling every pharmacist in Santa Barbara in an attempt to learn what drugstore in Santa Fe had requested a copy of the prescription.

While Price worked the phones, Ellie drove to Santa Barbara to meet Claudia Spalding, who had called her after arriving in Montecito early in the morning. On the phone, the woman had sounded sincerely grief-stricken. Ellie deliberately played into it, offering Claudia Spalding as much sympathy and understanding as she could muster.

On the freeway, Lowrey pondered possible approaches to take with Mrs. Spalding. Hardball wouldn't work, not without proof that she had had the opportunity and means to arrange for her husband's death. Ellie figured the best she could do was to open a few trapdoors for the woman and see if she fell into any of them.

Ellie arrived at the estate and announced herself on the intercom. When the ornate wrought iron gates swung open, she followed the cobblestone driveway up a hill that curved and dropped into a vale. Her mouth almost dropped open at the imposing three-story stone residence that came into view. At one end, a majestic watchtower rose above a long portico with Romanesque columns. It looked like a stage set for a nineteenth-century costume drama.

A labyrinth of boxwood hedges enclosed acres of lawn, ornamental plantings, and gardens. Towering stands of trees covered knolls and filled vales. Ellie half expected to see corseted women with parasols and men in breeches and top hats strolling leisurely through the gardens.

A woman whom Ellie took to be Claudia Spalding stood under the portico. Tallish, with long curly black hair, she hurried forward as Ellie got out of her cruiser.

"What happened to Clifford?" Claudia Spalding asked as she closed in on Lowrey.

"I'm very sorry for your loss," Ellie said. "We don't know yet exactly why he died."

"Why was he at the ranch?" Spalding asked. "He's never gone there before."

"As I understand it, your husband was arranging to purchase a horse for your anniversary."

Spalding's hand flitted to her chest. "Oh my."

"Had your husband been sick recently?" Ellie asked.

Spalding gestured toward the house. "Please come inside. Except for a cold, not at all. He played tennis regularly and swam every day. He had a thyroid condition, but it was controlled by medication."

"Yes, I know," Ellie replied. "We found the medication in his belongings."

Spalding didn't react one way or the other. Following along behind her, Ellie entered a large room with a vaulted ceiling and an enormous stone fireplace at one end. The floor was antique terra-cotta accented by a big Tibetan rug that would have overwhelmed an ordinary room. A mixture of Italian antique tables, soft leather couches, and upholstered easy chairs done up in subtle Moorish patterns were arranged at either end of the room. Ellie sat with Spalding in front of the fireplace and watched as the woman took a deep breath and composed herself.

"This must be very hard on you," Ellie said.

Spalding nodded. "Clifford was a special man. Brilliant, worldly, caring. I loved him dearly."

Ellie studied Spalding's face. Her large blue-green eyes were attention grabbing. Her thin lips with a hint of small lines at the corners made her appear secretive in a provocative way. Her creamy, flawless skin spoke of expensive spa treatments.

Something about the woman didn't ring true. Ellie decided to abandon her game plan. "Your neighbor, Nina Deacon, has suggested that you might not have loved your husband as much as you claim," she said.

"Excuse me?" Spalding said, with a look of haughty surprise.

"I'd like to hear your side of the story regarding your relationship with Kim Dean," Ellie said.

Spalding's expression turned cold. "Would you, now. For what reason?"

"To set aside any suspicions I might have about you."

"My husband died in his sleep."

"Every unattended death is investigated, Mrs. Spalding, and from what Nina Deacon told a Santa Fe detective, you weren't as happily married as you'd like me to believe."

Spalding got to her feet. "There are certain facts you're not aware of. Wait right here."

She left the room with her back stiff and her head held high. She returned with a folder, handed it to Ellie, and said, "Read this."

In it was a legal amendment to the prenuptial agreement specifying that the removal of Clifford Spalding's prostate had rendered him unable to engage in connubial activity with his wife, and thus she was free to engage in discreet sexual liaisons without suffering any financial loss, as long as such relationships did not occur in Montecito or nearby environs, and that the terms of the amendment remained strictly confidential between the two parties.

It was dated four years ago, signed by both of them, witnessed, and notarized.

In her years as a cop, Ellie had encountered a good many people with unusual private lives. But this definitely was a new wrinkle on matrimonial bliss. "Interesting," she said.

Spalding looked down at Ellie. "It was Clifford who instigated this agreement. In fact, he had to talk me into it."

"I see," Ellie replied, not sure that she did at all.

"What Nina Deacon may have told you about my personal relationship with Kim is true. He is my lover. Nina is a neighbor and close friend, and it would have been impossible for me to hide everything from her. Letting her believe I was trapped in a loveless marriage was preferable to breaking the confidentiality of this agreement with my husband."

"She said the Santa Fe house was in your husband's name only."

"I lied," Spalding said curtly. "It's my house free and clear."

"Did your husband know of your relationship with Dean?"

"No."

Ellie waved the papers at Spalding and stood. "Does Dean know about this agreement?"

"Heavens, no."

"I'll need to keep this document for a time to verify the contents with the lawyer, and I'll also need to speak to the doctor who removed your husband's prostate."

"Of course. Just make sure I get it back. Now, when can I claim my husband's body?"

"Today," Ellie replied, handing Spalding her business card. "Once you've made arrangements with a funeral home, have them call me."

"I did not have anything to do with my husband's death."

"I never said that you did."

"I am not a brainless trophy wife, Sergeant," Claudia Spalding said. "I hold an MBA and a PhD in organizational psychology, and clearly understood the implications of your questions. You'd better be very careful with your investigation, or you may find yourself swimming in deep legal waters."

"I'll be in touch," Ellie said. "One last question: Do you know a man named Kevin Kerney?"

Claudia knitted her brows. "I've heard that name before. Who is he?"

"I thought you could tell me."

She left the mansion convinced that notions of normal behavior— if there was such a thing—simply didn't apply to the very rich.

*   *   *

Captain Chase was out of the office attending an all-day meeting, but a detective who was helping a young Hispanic woman amend a stolen property report from a recent burglary at the front counter took a moment to buzz Kerney through the door to the restricted area. From there a uniformed officer took him to the cold case office, a windowless room with two desks and a big chart on the wall that tracked the status of the cases under review. George Spalding's name wasn't on it.

At one of the desks, a young man sat in front of a computer screen scrolling through a file. A nameplate on the shelf above the desk read DET. JUDE FORESTER.

Forester had an eager, intelligent look about him, which was offset by dark circles under his eyes and a skin condition that turned his forehead bright pink.

Kerney explained he'd like to take a look at the George Spalding case file, and Forester gave him a quizzical look.

"Why bother with that piece of garbage?" he asked, gesturing at an empty chair.

"Professional curiosity," Kerney said as he sat. "There are some New Mexico connections that interest me."

"Well, actually, we don't really work it as an active case."

"So I understand," Kerney said. "How is it handled?"

"You know about the situation?"

"Your captain filled me in," Kerney replied.

"Then he probably told you we do nothing more than take down the information Alice Spalding gives us and forward it to him. He takes it from there."

"Where does he take it?" Kerney asked.

"He talks to Alice and then gives the ex-husband a heads-up on the situation."

"Talks to Alice about what?"

"Just to reassure her that we've looked at whatever she told us and there is nothing to report. Of course, we really don't do squat."

"Do you have the case record?"

"Do I ever," Forester said with a laugh. He opened a desk drawer, removed a thick file folder, and put it in Kerney's hands. "Have at it, Chief," he said, grinning. "You can use the other desk."

Kerney spent an hour paging through the file. Most of what Chase had talked about was documented in the record. A U.S. Army report described the helicopter accident in Vietnam that had caused George Spalding's death. The chopper had gone down for unknown reasons, probably due to mechanical defects. There was nothing in it that spoke about a secret mission or hush-hush duty, as Penelope Parker had mentioned.

Kerney had been in-country during the same time as George Spalding. He wondered if he'd ever met the man.

According to the rescue and inspection team sent to the crash site, only two passengers who'd been thrown free upon impact had survived. Everyone else—four people—had been fried to a crisp when the bird exploded.

He scanned the missing person reports that Alice Spalding had called in to the department over the years. In the material he found an old memorandum from a former police chief assigning Detective Chase to the investigation.

Kerney thought that a bit unusual, but not completely out of the realm of possibility. Perhaps Clifford Spalding had taken his initial request for special handling straight to the top.

It was also curious that Chase had remained involved with the case over the years. Why did he find it necessary to be the primary contact with Alice and Clifford Spalding? Why hadn't Chase passed the job on to somebody else as he rose through the ranks? After all, it was supposedly nothing but a big nuisance.

Kerney looked up from the file and asked Forester about the ex-chief who'd given Chase his initial assignment.

"Ed Ramsey?" Forester replied. "He retired about five years ago, just after I joined the force."

"Where is he now?"

"Teaching at the FBI Academy. Management, or something like that."

Kerney shook his head, smiled at Forester, and patted the folder. "Man, if I'd been Chase, I would have dropped this baby in somebody's lap the first chance I got. Somebody like you."

Forester chuckled. "Then I'm sure glad you're not running the show here, Chief. Cap says he'd rather not have us wasting our time on it. Besides, Clifford Spalding likes to deal directly with him."

Forester's choice of words suggested that he didn't yet know that Spalding was dead. "But Alice doesn't seem to mind whom she talks to in the department," he said.

"Yeah, but then, she's crazy," Forester said. "Crazy Alice, we call her."

Kerney handed the file to Forester and stood. Asking more questions about Chase might raise a red flag. "Thanks for letting me have a look-see," he said.

"Learn anything helpful, Chief?"

"Yeah, it's time to stop spinning my wheels and go home."

Kerney left police headquarters telling himself to put the riddle of George Spalding aside for a time and think about something else, *anything* else. He walked past the rental car in the direction of State Street, turned the corner at the busy boulevard, and joined the tourists wandering along the crowded sidewalk.

A red light held Kerney up at an intersection and soon a throng of people waiting to cross the street surrounded him. The walk sign flashed and Kerney stood his ground as pedestrians surged around him. Chase had mentioned an old newspaper photograph of a traffic accident that had triggered Alice Spalding's search for her son.

Although noted in the case file, the newspaper photograph wasn't in the record. Kerney changed directions and walked down a less busy side street. Chase had told him that one of the victims in the news photo resembled George Spalding, which meant that he must have seen the picture.

Also missing from the record was any documentation of the attempt Chase said had been made to identify the man. Supposedly, a highway patrol officer and an EMT who'd responded to the accident had been queried about the victim. But there was nothing in the file that noted their names, any statements taken from them, the true identity of the man Alice had believed to be her son, or even the date and place of the accident.

Additionally, there was no mention of Debbie Calderwood in the file. Was there another record? Perhaps one that Chase kept in his office?

As Kerney strolled back toward the car, another inconsistency surfaced in his mind. Chase said Alice always called in her sightings. But when Kerney had first met Alice, she mistook him for Chase. Did Chase visit Alice periodically? If so, why?

Kerney stopped in front of the old courthouse, where a group of tourists led by a guide were getting the scoop on the historic building and the fabulous view of the bay from the bell tower. He called Penelope Parker on his cell phone.

"Does Captain Chase stay in close contact with Alice?" he asked when she answered.

"Not so much since she got sick," Parker replied.

Kerney moved out of the way as the tour group hurried inside. "And before that?" he asked.

"Oh, yes," Parker said. "Alice relied on him heavily. He would even visit her to report in person."

"On a regular basis?"

"Monthly, I'd say."

"Did she know Chase was passing on what she told him to Clifford?"

"Alice never would have stood for that," Parker said.

"Did Chase give her verbal or written reports?"

"Only verbal, as far as I know. It's interesting that you should mention Captain Chase. He called here after you left this morning, asking questions about you and what you were up to. I told him what we'd talked about."

"You did the right thing," Kerney said, responding to the anxiety in Parker's voice.

"Oh, good. I was worried that perhaps I had caused you some problems."

"Not at all," Kerney said. "Thanks."

He disconnected before Parker had a chance to get chatty, and the phone rang almost immediately.

"I've been trying to ring you," Ellie Lowrey said.

Kerney chuckled. "Ring me? What a terribly British thing to say."

"Yeah, well, sometimes I also like to say lorry instead of truck, and knickers instead of underpants."

"How revealing. What's up, Sergeant?"

"Can you meet me for coffee?" Ellie asked.

"Tell me where," Kerney answered.

*   *   *

The diner was, of course, the kind favored by penny-pinching cops, who were always on the lookout for a decent meal and a good cup of coffee at a reasonable price. Kerney sat with Lowrey in a booth and read the prenuptial legal amendment that gave Claudia Spalding the right to seek sexual fulfillment outside her marriage without penalty.

"My, my," he said as he returned the document to Lowrey.

"It's valid," Ellie grumped, "and moreover, the attorney I met with said Claudia Spalding is due to get one-third of her husband's estate after probate; Alice Spalding, by the terms of her divorce settlement, gets a third; and the rest goes into a trust foundation that Spalding established to do good works."

Lowrey motioned at the waitress for a coffee refill. "I confirmed Spalding's operation with the doctor who removed his prostate. He told me it is not uncommon after surgery for men, especially the elderly ones, to become unable to perform in bed."

"Are you taking Claudia Spalding off your suspect list based on what you've learned?" Kerney asked.

Lowrey paused for the waitress to fill her cup and move away before giving Kerney a sour look. "Not necessarily, but it weakens the circumstantial evidence, which is further undermined by the fact that Kim Dean did not fill the prescription for Spalding in Santa Fe. It was handled by a different pharmacy."

"That's not what we wanted to hear," Kerney said. "What about the neighbor's assertion that Claudia was unhappy in her marriage?"

"Mrs. Spalding said she lied to Deacon and Dean so as not to violate the confidentiality clause in the agreement. But there is some good news. I asked the lab to test first for the presence and levels of thyroid medication in the blood sample that was drawn during the autopsy. The results came back way below what they should have been, given the daily dosage Spalding was supposed to be taking."

"Would that have killed him?" Kerney asked.

"Over time, quite possibly, according to our pathologist. Too little thyroid hormone would cause a slowing of the heart rate and force the endocrine system to overcompensate. So while the heart struggles to pump blood, the patient could simultaneously have symptoms such as blurry vision, heat intolerance, restlessness, digestive disorders, and the like."

"Some of which Spalding had been complaining about," Kerney said.

Ellie nodded. "Exactly. Given Spalding's already damaged heart muscles, our doc suggests he could have easily gone into cardiac arrhythmia and thrown a clot that blew his pump."

"What about the pill you found?" Kerney asked.

"It's under the microscope," Ellie said, crossing her fingers. "Here's hoping we find something. But even if the lab does confirm it was altered or duplicated to look like the real thing, I doubt I can get a search warrant approved."

"What if Dean was acting on his own and somehow managed to switch Spalding's medication?" Kerney asked.

"Give me the evidence to nail that idea down," Ellie said, "and I'll get a warrant signed today."

Kerney shrugged. "It's speculation, but worth looking into, nonetheless. Let's say Dean bought into Claudia's fairy tale about how unhappy she was with her hubby, and that Dean truly didn't know about the confidential agreement. Maybe he decided, without Claudia's knowledge, to set her free from her burden."

"So he could claim her as his own," Ellie added. "Good thinking, Chief. Now, tell me how we get from your theory to hard facts."

Kerney took the check from the waitress and paid the bill. "I'll have my peelers look into it."

"Your what?" Lowrey asked with a grin.

"Peelers," Kerney said, grinning back, as he slid out of the booth. "It's an Irish slang word for cops."

*   *   *

Ten blocks from the diner, a city police cruiser with headlights flashing came up behind Kerney's car. He pulled off the road and the cop car followed, slowing to a stop when he braked and killed the engine. With his eye on the rearview mirror, Kerney watched as the officer called dispatch by radio, trying to figure out exactly what traffic ordinance he'd violated. He rolled down the window as the officer approached, his driver's license and badge case in hand.

The cop took the license, glanced at it, handed it back, and looked at the open badge case Kerney held out the window.

"Captain Chase would like to see you in his office, Chief Kerney," the officer said politely. "If you'll follow me, please, sir."

"Certainly," Kerney said, wondering what he might have done to draw Chase away from his all-day meeting and require an escort to headquarters.

At his office, Chase greeted Kerney with a big smile and a hearty handshake.

"Sergeant Lowrey tells me you're off the hook as a possible suspect," he said.

"The truth is a persuasive argument for innocence," Kerney replied.

"That's for sure," Chase said, settling into his chair. "Jude Forester said you came by and looked over the Spalding materials."

"I did," Kerney said as he sat across from Chase.

"Well, he didn't show you everything," Chase said, sliding a slim file folder across the desk. "That's my file I keep here in the office. Have a look."

Kerney scanned the contents. It contained Chase's brief handwritten notes of conversations and contacts he'd had with Clifford and Alice Spalding over the years.

"There's not much here," Kerney said.

Chase laughed as he took the folder back. "What did you expect?"

"I was hoping there would be a copy of that newspaper article and photograph about the interstate traffic accident that originally caught Alice Spalding's attention," Kerney said. "It wasn't in Detective Forester's file, nor were the statements of the cop and the EMT on the scene who confirmed that the man in the photograph wasn't George Spalding."

"It's not in Forester's case material?"

"I didn't see it," Kerney replied.

Chase shook his head apologetically, but his expression was wary.

"I haven't looked at that file in years, but it should be in there. Maybe it's just misplaced."

"Probably," Kerney said with an easy smile. "I guess it really doesn't matter, since Spalding, his ex-wife, and their dead son are no longer of any concern to me."

"Lucky you," Chase said with a laugh. "Did you get a chance to talk to Lou Ferry?"

"Yes, last night," Kerney answered. "But he was in too much pain to tell me much, and now it doesn't matter."

"He died early this morning," Chase said.

"Good for him," Kerney said. "That's what he said he wanted to do. Hopefully, he went out easy."

"In his sleep," Chase replied with a nod.

"The best way to go." Kerney slapped his hands on his legs and stood. "Thanks, Captain, for your courtesy and understanding," he said, hoping it didn't sound as disingenuous as it felt.

"My pleasure, Chief." Chase rose, walked around his desk, and put a hand on Kerney's shoulder. "Call me the next time you're in Santa Barbara, and I'll stand you to a drink or two."

"You've got a deal."

With the afternoon sun in his face, Kerney drove out of the police parking lot. At the very least, it had been an interesting two days, nicely topped off by Chase's sly gambit to probe Kerney's intentions and do some subtle grilling about what he'd learned from Lou Ferry.

Kerney decided to drive to the beach later on and catch another sunset. He also decided to start a background check on the Spaldings—all three of them—and Debbie Calderwood when he got home to Santa Fe.

But first, he needed to find an electronics store, buy a tape recorder, and dictate everything he'd learned about the Spaldings, Debbie Calderwood, and Captain Dick Chase while it was still fresh in his mind.

ChapterFive

The next morning, Kerney's flight took him over the oak woodlands and chaparral-covered hillsides east of Santa Barbara, the evergreen coastal mountain forests, and the glittering low California desert. He changed planes in Phoenix and from his window seat looked down on the high mountains and rolling grasslands of the remote Gila Wilderness, which gave way to mesquite-covered desert scrubland cut by wide, sandy arroyos. It felt good to be going home.

After landing, Kerney went straight to his office. Within minutes, Helen Muiz, his administrative assistant, swooped in bearing paperwork. She immediately asked about his California misadventure, currently the hottest back-channel gossip topic in the department.

In her late fifties, Helen had worked for the PD for over thirty-six years, longer than any other employee, civilian or commissioned. Stylish, witty, and a grandmother twice over, among her many duties Helen served as the lightning rod for rumors, hearsay, and prattle that circulated throughout the department, all of which came to her sooner rather than later. She dispensed with it quickly, separating fact from fiction and squelching the falsehoods.

In private, Helen dealt with Kerney as an equal, which he didn't mind at all.

"Well, are you having an affair with a woman currently under suspicion for the murder of her husband?" Helen asked from the comfort of the chair at the side of Kerney's desk.

Kerney tried hard to act put-upon by the accusation. Instead, he broke into a smile and laughed. "Not guilty."

"Does your lovely wife know about this?" Helen asked with a twinkle in her eye.

"Not yet," Kerney said.

"I shouldn't wait too long to tell her, if I were you. Some evil person might delight in putting a nasty spin on what happened in California, and feed Sara some misinformation."

"Who would do something like that?" Kerney asked.

"Not everyone in this department loves you as much as I do, Kevin," Helen said with a devilish wink.

"Name these malcontents," Kerney jokingly demanded.

Helen laughed. "And destroy my network of informants? Never."

She handed him a number of letters on department stationery, each neatly paper clipped with file copies and addressed envelopes. "Please sign these so they can go out today."

"Perhaps I should read them first," Kerney said.

Helen rose to her feet. "Good idea. Do you have anything for me?"

Kerney gave her the cassette tape of his recorded notes on the Spalding affair. "Have it transcribed and ask Sergeant Pino to come see me in ten minutes."

"As you wish," Helen said from the doorway. "Did you buy any horses, or were you too busy professing your innocence to the police?"

"I got four good ones," Kerney said.

*   *   *

Kerney's open office door signaled that all were free to enter without knocking. Sergeant Ramona Pino stepped inside to find Kerney reviewing and signing letters. He smiled at her and raised an index finger to signal he needed a minute to finish up.

She took a seat at the small conference table that butted against Kerney's desk, opened her notepad, and quickly reviewed her activity log on the Spalding case to make sure she was totally up to speed for her briefing report.

Ramona had stumbled badly on a major homicide case late last summer, but that hadn't kept the chief from approving her promotion to sergeant. Since earning the new shield, Ramona had returned Kerney's vote of confidence by doing her best possible work.

Kerney signed the letter, tossed it in the out basket, and sat back in his swivel chair. "So, where are we?"

"According to the pharmacist here in town who filled Clifford Spalding's prescription, his wife called to say that the pharmacy in Santa Barbara was faxing the refill information to him, and she would pick it up when it was ready, which she did. She paid by credit card. Just as a matter of interest, I queried the credit card company and got a copy of her charges for that monthly billing cycle. On that same day, twenty minutes later, she charged a bottle of expensive perfume at Kim Dean's pharmacy."

Kerney's eyes glinted with pleasure at the news. He interlocked his fingers, and tapped his thumbs together. "Go on."

"A clerk who works at the pharmacy and knows Mrs. Spalding as a customer said Dean waited on her personally. The clerk found that odd, because Dean never bothers with customers who come in to buy sundries. She thinks, but isn't sure, that Dean left Spalding at the perfume counter for a few minutes to do something in the back before he rang up the sale."

"Did Sergeant Lowrey inform you about the pill found in Spalding's possessions?" Kerney asked.

"She did," Ramona said. "Not only is it a fake, but the analysis of the active ingredient in it perfectly matches the medication level in the blood sample that was drawn during the autopsy."

"Which suggests Dean and Claudia Spalding switched the pills," Kerney said.

"Yes, it does," Ramona said. "If Spalding had lived one more day the evidence would have been gone, Chief. According to the Santa Barbara pharmacist Sergeant Lowrey spoke with, Spalding was down to his last pill when he died."

"Was Dean present when you spoke to the clerk?" Kerney asked.

"No," Ramona said. "I didn't talk to her at the pharmacy. I hung around until she went next door to a deli for lunch and spoke to her there."

"Will she keep her lip buttoned about your inquiry?"

Ramona nodded. "Dean's a pushy, demanding boss who contradicts himself and then lays the blame on the clerk. She puts up with it because she's older, divorced, timid, and needs the job. She promised not to say a word."

"What else have you got?"

Ramona flipped back to a page in her notebook. "I checked with both Dean's and Spalding's cellular telephone providers. There has been a flurry of calls between the two, starting almost immediately after Sergeant Lowrey talked with Claudia Spalding in Montecito."

"How many?" Kerney asked.

"Five yesterday and two this morning. Mrs. Spalding made first contact."

"Do you have anything that can connect Dean to the fabrication of the pill?" Kerney asked.

"We know the inert ingredients are different, the weight is slightly off, and the shape isn't uniform based on the manufacturer's specs," Ramona replied. "So, I took a cue from your research into how he might have done it, and called a pharmacist here in town who said that duplicating the exact size and shape of the original pill wouldn't be easy, but it could be done. He suggested we look for all the compounds Dean used."

"Did the pharmacist have any idea about how Dean might have shaped and sized the pills?" Kerney asked.

"He said that except for the grooves on either size of the pill, it's oval in shape, which is very common. Pharmacists use that kind of pill all the time, in many different sizes. He said if he were to do it, he'd make each pill as close in size to the original oval as possible, match the color, and then hand-cut the grooves to make them look right. The tedious part would be the final shaping."

"How does all of this help us?" Kerney asked

"The analyzed pill shows small striations in the grooves. We've got tool marks, Chief."

Kerney grinned. "Coordinate with Sergeant Lowrey and get an affidavit done for a search warrant at Dean's home and business," he said. "We want to look for the tools he might have used and the raw ingredients identified by the lab findings."

"Will do," Ramona said.

"Then take everything we have that supports motive, opportunity, and means directly to the district attorney and ask if he'll approve arrest warrants for Dean and Spalding based on circumstantial evidence. If he agrees that we have probable cause, synchronize the busts with Sergeant Lowrey so both of them are picked up simultaneously."

"Shouldn't we take a statement from Dean first?" Ramona asked.

"Normally, I'd say yes," Kerney said. "But according to Dean's clerk at the pharmacy, he's a bully. If we stuff the facts we have down his throat, maybe he'll crack."

"I'll make the collar at his store," Ramona said, "and tell him Claudia is talking. That should shake him up."

"Give the newspaper a heads-up and ask them to have a reporter and photographer standing by outside. Take two uniforms with you and have them take their time putting him into a unit."

"Make it a perp walk," Ramona said.

"You've got it," Kerney said. "Good work, Sergeant."

"Thank you, sir," Ramona said as she closed her notebook and rose. She hurried out of the office before the pleasure she felt at the chief's compliment turned into a noticeable blush.

*   *   *

District Attorney Sid Larranaga personally scrutinized carefully any arrest and search warrant affidavits prepared and submitted to his office by Sergeant Pino. He held her partially responsible for mistakes in a homicide case last year that resulted in the death of two innocent, mentally ill individuals, one in a totally uncalled-for SWAT gun battle, the other by suicide.

Ignoring Pino, who sat quietly in front of his oak desk, Larranaga read through the affidavits a second time, jotting notes as he went. Because of the complexity of the facts, the suppositions, and jurisdictional issues, he wanted to be absolutely clear that probable cause existed.

He punctuated his last entry on the legal pad with a flourish and looked at Pino. "As far as the arrest affidavits go, you and this Sergeant Lowrey have given me only the possibility of a motive for murder. The rest of it is just an interesting theory regarding opportunity." He tapped the paperwork with his pen.

Ramona waited a beat before responding. She and Ellie Lowrey had each put in at least three hours of intensive work preparing a strong circumstantial case. "The forensic evidence proves the victim was murdered," she said, "and both Dean and Claudia Spalding had the opportunity to do it."

"Yes, but which one?" Larranaga countered, crossing his hands over his belly. "Dean? Possibly. Claudia Spalding? You can't seriously expect a judge to approve an arrest warrant for Mrs. Spalding based on the fact that she bought perfume at Dean's pharmacy after picking up her husband's prescription somewhere else."

"It establishes a chain of events," Pino said. "Quite likely Spalding met with Dean to switch the medication."

"Or Dean could have switched the medication without Mrs. Spalding's knowledge"—Larranaga shifted his weight in the chair— "at some other time or location. Dean could have been acting on his own. The fact that Dean left Mrs. Spalding alone for a few minutes in the front of the store to do something in the back room doesn't establish collusion or conspiracy between the two parties. I'm sure if the clerk had seen the actual exchange you would have included it in your affidavit."

Larranaga brushed a hand over his new-look, swept-back haircut. "Also, you don't have a strong motive for Mrs. Spalding to plot and carry out the murder of her husband. In fact, I don't see that you have one at all. She was literally having her cake and eating it too, and she was bound by the amended prenuptial agreement to keep Dean in the dark about it."

"What about the arrest and search warrants for Dean?" Pino asked.

"Again, a motive for Dean isn't clearly articulated," Larranaga said. "Other than noting he was Mrs. Spalding's lover, you've presented nothing that points to an inducement or reason to kill on his part. Was it jealousy? Money? Did he want Spalding dead so he could marry Claudia? Or was he perfectly happy with the affair as it stood? Why hasn't he been interviewed?"

"Given how the victim was killed and what went into accomplishing the crime," Ramona said, "I think probable cause has been established that Dean committed murder, and that the evidence to that effect can be found at his house or business."

"Even with the lack of a clear motive, I agree that it is probable that Dean, with his expertise as a pharmacist, could have done it. That's why I'm approving the search and arrest affidavits for Dean only. If he confesses and implicates Mrs. Spalding, then your problem is solved, and the California authorities can pick her up without a warrant."

Larranaga signed the affidavits and Ramona went to find a judge. During a ten-minute wait outside chambers, she called both Sergeant Lowrey and Chief Kerney to give them the news about the rejected Spalding arrest affidavit. Lowrey promised to take another crack at Claudia after Dean was in custody. Kerney told her to stick with the plan to rattle Dean and break him down if possible.

The judge issued the warrants without any probing questions. Five blocks away from Dean's place of business, Ramona met up with two uniformed officers and went over how she wanted the bust staged. At the pharmacy, a photojournalist from the newspaper waited in the parking lot. The three officers hustled inside to find only the store clerk, Tilly Gilmore, and a female customer standing at the counter.

Ramona gestured for Tilly to approach her at the front of the store. "Where's Dean?" Ramona asked when she arrived.

The woman averted her eyes. "He left in a hurry."

"When?"

"About an hour ago," Tilly said tentatively, her eyes fixed on the floor. Immobile and hunched, she looked like a tense, frightened animal trying hard to be invisible.

Ramona let out a disgusted sigh. "What happened?"

"He saw you follow me into the deli," Tilly replied.

"And?"

Tilly looked at Ramona through glasses that magnified her anxious eyes. "I had to tell him," she said apologetically, like a child hoping to avoid punishment.

Ramona turned to the two officers. "Send the reporter away and put out an all points bulletin on Dean pronto."

At the drug counter, the middle-aged woman clutched a prescription bottle in her hand and stared at Ramona, unsure of what to do.

"You can leave if you like, ma'am," Ramona said to her. The woman scurried down an aisle and out the door, her shoes clacking noisily on the tile floor.

Ramona studied Tilly's drained, beaten-down expression. Had Dean simply bullied the woman into becoming a wet rag over the years, or had she always been easy prey? Ramona guessed the latter, but it didn't matter. She now had to deal with the consequences of Tilly's inability to keep her mouth shut.

"Okay," Ramona said soothingly, as she guided Tilly away from the front of the store. "Let's talk about what happened."

*   *   *

At a restaurant on Cerrillos Road close to police headquarters, Andy Baca stirred sugar into his refilled glass of iced tea and listened as Kerney spoke to Ramona Pino on his cell phone.

"Problems?" he asked when Kerney disconnected.

"Our murder suspect seems to have disappeared," Kerney replied, looking a bit vexed as he hooked the phone on his belt. "Pino has issued an APB and is on her way to search Dean's house."

"Do you need to go?" Andy asked.

Kerney shook his head and waved off the waitress as she approached to refill his glass of lemonade.

"Well, then, finish your story," Andy said.

Kerney continued, recounting the events in Santa Barbara that had prompted his request to have Andy meet him.

When Kerney stopped talking and sipped his lemonade, Andy jumped in with a question to back him up a bit. "What made this Sergeant Lowrey think you'd be stupid enough to kill Spalding and then stick around to report it as an unattended death?"

"She didn't know I was a cop," Kerney replied, "until she questioned me. Once she picked up on Claudia Spalding's connection with Santa Fe, she decided to probe it. I probably would have done the same thing."

"Still, it was no fun," Andy said.

Kerney pushed the glass aside. "Not really. But that's not what I wanted to talk to you about. Alice Spalding's thirty-year search for her dead son, George, has some unusual wrinkles to it. I think Clifford Spalding may have sabotaged his ex-wife's quest for the truth."

Andy shot Kerney a quizzical look. "From what you said, it sounds more like the woman has been in total denial of the facts for decades."

"Has she? If so, why would Clifford Spalding continue to maintain a long-term arrangement with a local cop to stay informed of

Alice's activities? Why would he hire a PI to feed false reports to Alice and then fire the gumshoe after he'd done some real work that might have lead to finding the son's old girlfriend?"

"If the ex-wife was unstable, maybe Spalding was just indulging her and trying to stay on top of her obsession at the same time," Andy suggested.

"So he burns all the information she'd gathered over the years just before their divorce," Kerney replied with a shake of his head, "and openly denigrates her to their mutual friends. I don't buy it."

"People do ugly things when they get divorced," Andy said.

"I also have trouble with the scarcity of information contained in the police file I reviewed. There was no documentation that Alice Spalding's assertion that a newspaper photograph showed her son to still be alive had ever been proven false. The photograph was missing, as were the statements of people who identified the subject as someone other than George Spalding."

"So track them down and talk to them," Andy said. "That should satisfy your curiosity about whether or not Clifford Spalding was hiding something from the ex."

"Can't," Kerney said. "Neither were identified by name, just referenced in passing by the police captain I spoke with, who seemed a little uncomfortable with my questions."

"Do you think this captain was helping Spalding keep the truth from his ex?" Andy asked.

"I don't know," Kerney said. "But another point troubles me. Look at the sequence of events. Thirty some years ago, George Spalding allegedly dies in Nam."

"Verified by military authorities," Andy said.

"Soon after the helicopter crash, George Spalding's girlfriend goes missing, never to be found, and his father, owner of a mom-and-pop Albuquerque motel, starts building a hotel empire."

"Which means what, if anything?" Andy asked, throwing his hands up in the air. "Maybe Spalding cashed in his son's G.I. life insurance policy and parlayed it into his first big step up the corporate food chain."

"Maybe, but again, I don't know," Kerney answered.

"You're not going to let this drop, are you?"

"Not yet. I've started background checks on all the players, but I could use some help from your department."

"To do what?"

"To chase down information on Clifford Spalding's early business dealings in New Mexico," Kerney said. "Can you free up some of Joe Valdez's time to take a look?"

Agent Joseph Valdez, a certified public accountant with a master's in business administration, handled most of the financial crime cases for the state police, which meant he was usually overworked.

"Not easily," Andy said.

"It doesn't have to be given priority," Kerney said.

"Here's what I'll do," Andy said after a pause. "You talk to Joe. Tell him what you know and what you *want* to know. If he's interested and willing to peck away at it, then it's okay with me. But don't expect too much. He's a busy man."

Kerney smiled. "That went a lot smoother than I expected. Thanks."

Andy paid the check and stood. "I know how you are, stubborn and bullheaded. Why should I waste my time letting you wear me down until I finally give you what you want?"

Kerney laughed and added some money to the tip. "Come on, admit it. This is worth taking a look at."

"Either that, or you have an overactive imagination," Andy replied with a grin.

*   *   *

Ramona Pino brought in a squad of four detectives to assist in the hunt for Dean and the search of his pharmacy and residence. She assigned two of them to work the pharmacy. The others followed her to

Dean's house in Canada de los Alamos, a small settlement in the foothills of the Sangre de Cristo Mountains a few miles southeast of Santa Fe.

Once part of a land grant, Canada de los Alamos had remained a sleepy, forgotten place well into the 1960s. Situated next to the national forest in a protected valley, it held a mixture of mobile homes, small adobe houses, and a growing number of more upscale residences that had been built by newcomers over the past forty years. Anchored by a pretty church along a dirt road that cut through the center of the valley, the settlement had no businesses or stores.

Old fences, corrals, sheds, and outbuildings that bordered an arroyo still gave the area a rural feel. But the landscape was changing, and it wasn't only because of a recent increase in population. Drought had so dried out the piñon and ponderosa forest that the trees could no longer stave off their long-standing enemy, the bark beetle. In wetter times, the trees suffocated the beetles by releasing sap. Now, the beetles had the upper hand and were killing whole stands of trees, sometimes turning their needles brown in a matter of days.

The die-off of the forest throughout the mountains and foothills of northern New Mexico was creating a major wildfire hazard. According to the forestry experts, not much could be done about it.

Kim Dean's house, a solar adobe on five acres, overlooked the old settlement. Two huge dead piñon trees at the front of the property drooped burly barren branches over the driveway. On the off chance that Dean was home, Ramona blocked the driveway with her unit and, accompanied by the two detectives, went in on foot. A quick perimeter check of the house and horse barn turned up nothing other than Dean's two geldings.

Dean's flight to avoid arrest and the search warrant for his premises were all the justification needed to enter the house. They knocked first, waited a minute, then kicked in the front door with weapons at the ready, and cleared the house room by room.

In a workshop attached to the two-car garage, Ramona found a number of small knives and cutting tools on a table made of sawhorses and plywood, several of them coated with a thin layer of pale yellow dust. She bagged and tagged them right away.

Six-foot-high steel shelves filled with paint cans, bottles, coffee cans, and plastic storage bins lined one wall. Waist-high, built-in cabinets made from plywood and rough lumber ran along the opposite wall. Boxes of junk were strewn around the floor. From the looks of it, Dean was a total pack rat, which was an encouraging sign.

Ramona put the two detectives to work going through the shelves, the toolboxes, and cabinets. She cleared a space on the floor, covered it with clear plastic, and started emptying the trash basket next to the table piece by piece. She found a crumpled paper bag containing traces of yellow dust and a number of loose, oval-shaped, empty capsules.

Her cell phone rang, and the senior detective at the pharmacy search reported in. In Dean's desk he'd found a full, unopened packet of the active thyroid ingredient and a copy of the wholesaler's invoice showing that two packets, not one, had been delivered to Dean a month before Clifford Spalding's last visit to Santa Fe.

"Describe the packet to me," Ramona said.

"A small white box, two by three inches, sealed at both ends, with the name of the drug on a manufacturer's label."

"Good deal," Ramona said. "Make sure it's dusted for prints."

"Already done," the detective replied.

Ramona disconnected, whistled at the two detectives, and told them what to start looking for. Then she called Sergeant Lowrey in California and gave her a status update.

"I hope you find that packet," Lowrey said.

"If not, we still may come away with enough evidence to tie Dean to the crime."

"You think Dean may be on his way out here?" Ellie asked.

"Possibly," Ramona said. "Have you talked to Claudia?"

"Not yet. I'm on my way to her house right now," Ellie said. "I'll get back to you."

Ramona put the cell phone away and went through the trash again until she was satisfied nothing had been overlooked. The two detectives were digging through the cabinets and pulling the plastic containers off the shelves. It would take time to go through everything, but they just might get lucky.

*   *   *

Ellie Lowrey found the Spalding estate no less mind-boggling on her second visit. In the past, she'd read newspaper articles about celebrities and their multimillion-dollar Montecito properties. But it had been impossible for her to imagine what that kind of money could buy until she'd seen it firsthand. In some ways, it still didn't compute.

The solemn-looking secretary who met Ellie at the driveway took her through the vast living room, down a wide, long, arched corridor with tiny recessed ceiling lights that softly illuminated the paintings on the wall, and into a sunroom filled with exotic plants and wicker furniture that opened onto a patio at the rear of the house.

In the center of the patio were a large swimming pool and a separate hot tub surrounded by marble tile. Scattered around the pool was enough lawn furniture to accommodate forty or more people. Off to one side of the house stood an outdoor kitchen with stainless steel appliances, a built-in gas barbecue grill, and a work island protected by a freestanding pergola.

Beyond the swimming pool four cabanas sat near two tennis courts. A large swath of carefully groomed lawn in front of a low garden wall served as a putting green. At the bottom of a gently sloping hill, a gardener pruned shrubbery lining a pathway to a guesthouse three times the size of Ellie's modest home.

Claudia Spalding stepped out of the guesthouse and paused along the pathway to speak to the gardener. She wore black slacks and a sleeveless black scooped top. At her neck a large solitary diamond glimmered in the sunlight.

"This is not a good time," Spalding said stiffly when Ellie drew near. Her thin mouth was pinched, but her makeup, right down to the long lashes, eye shadow, and creamy red lip rouge, had been perfectly applied.

"I'm sorry to disturb you," Ellie said.

"What do you want, Sergeant?"

"Have you spoken to Kim Dean recently?"

"Yes, I called him yesterday to tell him about Clifford's death, as I have many other people. We've spoken several times since then."

"Did he say anything to you about leaving Santa Fe?"

Spalding pushed a wisp of hair away from her cheek. "No."

"An arrest warrant charging him with murder has been issued in Santa Fe," Ellie said.

Spalding's aloof expression vanished. She drew her head back sharply. "Impossible."

"Why is that?"

"Kim is perfectly happy with our relationship as it is. He has no reason to harm my husband."

"Can you think of any reason for him to leave work suddenly?"

"Perhaps he had an emergency of some sort at home," Spalding said.

"He's not at his house," Ellie replied.

"Have you checked with his ex-wife in Colorado?" Claudia asked. "She constantly calls Kim to come and deal with his son when the boy acts out. The child has serious behavior problems."

"That's good to know," Ellie said. "Where else might he have gone?"

"I have no idea," Spalding said.

Ellie looked meaningfully at the guesthouse. "Would he be coming here?"

"No," Claudia said emphatically.

Ellie stared hard at Spalding. "If you know where he is and refuse to tell me, you can be charged as an accessory to murder."

Spalding waved her hand in annoyance. "You must be joking."

"I'm not."

"Then tell me what in the world makes you think Kim killed Clifford."

"I can't go into that, Mrs. Spalding."

"Well, whatever your reasons, it's all absurd."

"Why do you say that?"

"Because Kim isn't a violent person by nature. He's very low-key. Calm and easygoing."

"Why did you go to Dean's pharmacy immediately after you picked up your husband's thyroid prescription?" Ellie asked.

Claudia's eyes turned angry. "I'll answer your silly question and then you must leave. It's the only store in Santa Fe that carries the perfume I use. Kim stocks it especially for me. Now, I have a funeral to arrange and a husband to bury. If you have any more questions, speak to my lawyer. Please wait here; Sheila will show you out."

Ellie watched Spalding move across the patio and into the house. Was Dean a bully who, according to Ramona Pino, browbeat his employees? Or a low-key, pussycat kind of guy, as Claudia Spalding characterized him? The steel inside Claudia Spalding made Ellie doubt the woman would be attracted to a subservient man. But anything was possible. Maybe Spalding was a closet dominatrix.

Ellie tried to visualize Claudia Spalding cracking a whip while wearing spike heel boots and leather. The idea of it almost made her laugh out loud.

Sheila, the woman who'd escorted Ellie to the patio, arrived and guided her back through the house. Along the way, Ellie learned that Clifford Spalding's corporation was headquartered in Los Angeles, at Century City, and that Spalding had been in his office briefly the same day he'd driven to the horse ranch in Paso Robles.

Tomorrow, Ellie started her days off. She decided a trip to LA was in order.

*   *   *

The afternoon sunlight drenched the mountains with a golden hue. Cramped from sitting on the floor digging through boxes of junk, Ramona stood, bent over, touched her toes, and stretched. Behind her, Detective Matt Chacon was on his hands and knees with a flashlight trying to fish something out from behind the back of one of the built-in cabinets. Paul Austin, the other detective, was labeling Baggies filled with samples spooned from the various containers for analysis.

"Let's wrap it up," Pino said. "We'll take everything we've got to the lab and see what they can make of it."

"What some folks won't do to commit murder," Chacon said with a grin as he got to his feet, holding a dusty, white pharmaceutical packet in his hand. He shook it gently. "It's got stuff in it."

"Bag it, tag it, load everything up, and let's get the hell out of here," Ramona said, grinning back at Chacon.

*   *   *

Kim Dean was still on the run and, according to Ellie Lowrey, apparently not in hiding at the estate in Montecito. Even with that bit of bad news, Kerney finished up his day at the office feeling good about the progress of the investigation. Thanks to the evidence found at Dean's house, they now had a much stronger case. Not perfect enough to go unchallenged by a good defense attorney, but compelling nonetheless.

Claudia Spalding's possible involvement still bothered Kerney. He hoped that once Dean was in custody he'd provide some answers.

Earlier, Kerney had hand-delivered a copy of his transcribed Spalding notes to Agent Joe Valdez and explained his suspicions. Joe agreed to delve into Clifford Spalding's business and financial dealings in New Mexico as his time allowed, and report back.

A check of public records on the Spaldings and Debbie Calderwood was proceeding. Kerney didn't expect too much to come from it, but sometimes routine sources yielded valuable information.

The second-floor administrative suite was empty when Kerney left headquarters. He spent a minute chatting with a gang unit detective in the parking lot before heading out to Arroyo Hondo where Claudia Spalding lived. As far as Kerney knew, only one neighbor, Nina Deacon, had been interviewed, and he wanted to see who else might know something about Claudia Spalding and Kim Dean.

Tucked out of view from the highway, Arroyo Hondo contained the ruins of an old pueblo owned by the Archeological Conservancy, and a nearby parcel preserved as open space. The land away from the arroyo was a semirural residential area of ten- and twenty-acre tracts populated by a well-to-do horsey set. Houses, paddocks, corrals, and barns speckled the fenced pastures and piñon-juniper woodlands that flowed down from the foothills.

Kerney found the driveway to Spalding's house on Laughing Pony Road and paid visits to the closest neighbors on either side. Nina Deacon wasn't at home, and the people he talked with only knew Claudia Spalding casually and weren't acquainted with Kim Dean at all. No one told him anything of value.

He drove away from the last house ready to pack in his impromptu canvass, go home, and call Sara. Up the road he saw a pickup truck turn into Spalding's driveway. He followed and found an older Hispanic man unloading hay bales from the bed of his truck parked next to the horse barn.

"Mrs. Spalding isn't here," the man said as Kerney got close.

"I know," Kerney said, displaying his shield. "Who are you?"

"Sixto Giron. Is there trouble?" Giron dropped a hay bale on the ground and brushed off his dusty shirt. He had a heavily wrinkled face and a guileless manner.

"No trouble," Kerney said. "Do you work for Mrs. Spalding?"

"Yes, part-time. A few hours now and then every week, and I look after the horses when she is gone."

"What about Nina Deacon?"

Giron nodded. "Same thing. She's also out of town, judging a horse show in Canada."

"Do you know about Mr. Spalding's death?"

"Yes, Mrs. Spalding called and told me. That's why I'm here."

"Tell me about Kim Dean."

"I work for him also, when he needs me. Mostly I haul away manure, or bring fresh straw for the stalls. He does most of the other work himself."

"What can you tell me about his relationship with Mrs. Spalding?"

Giron shrugged. "Not much. They trail ride together, usually on weekends. Sometimes I see him visiting here, sometimes Claudia is at his house. They're good friends."

"Do they have a favorite place to trail ride?" Kerney asked.

Giron pushed his cap back and scratched above his ear. "They like to take the horses on some property Dean owns up on the Canadian River. He bought canyon land that doesn't have a right-of-way road access to it, so he got it for real cheap."

"Where is it, exactly?" Kerney asked.

"I don't know. But Tito Perea, my *primo*, does. Kim hired him to pack in some building supplies so he could fix up an old cabin. Tito made four or five trips with his mules two summers ago."

"How can I reach Tito?"

"He lives in Pecos, but he isn't home. He's outfitting for a group of *turistas* who are riding in the mountains for a week."

"I bet Tito has a cell phone," Kerney said.

Giron laughed at himself. "I forgot. He gave me the number, but I never use it." He pulled out his wallet, and read off Tito's cell phone number.

Kerney helped Giron unload the hay before he left. It was too late in the day to have anyone go looking for Dean on the Canadian. Northeast of Santa Fe, the canyon lands were a place with few roads, bad trails, quicksand, twisting gorges, and dangerous rimrock passages.

If he could contact Tito Perea tonight and get directions, he'd call the Harding County sheriff in the morning and ask him to check out Dean's cabin.

ChapterSix

Agent Joe Valdez of the state police had grown up on the east side of Santa Fe in an adobe house a few blocks away from Canyon Road. When he was in high school, his parents had sold the house at what was then a tidy profit and moved the family into a new home in a south-side subdivision. Many neighbors followed suit, and the exodus of Hispanic families quickly transformed the area into an enclave for rich Anglos.

Now, whenever a house in the old neighborhood came on the market, it was invariably advertised as "a charming, upgraded adobe within easy walking distance of the Plaza and Canyon Road," with asking prices in the high six-figure range and beyond.

Only a few of Joe's old neighbors had stayed put. One family, the Sandovals, still owned two houses on East Alameda, plus a property that had once been an old motor lodge built in the 1930s.

When motels replaced motor lodges, the family converted the units into a number of small retail stores. A later transformation turned the property into a boutique hotel, the very one that, according to Kerney's notes, Clifford Spalding had leased from the Sandoval family for ninety-nine years.

Trinidad Sandoval, the *patrón* of the family, had rolled the dice when Spalding made his offer to lease. He mortgaged everything he owned, borrowed more money, then completely gutted the building and made major additions to it, including two-story suites with balconies, fireplaces, and hot tubs.

The risk paid off and the family became wealthy. Trinidad, now in his eighties, still lived up the street from the hotel in the unassuming house where he'd been born.

Early in the morning, Joe Valdez parked his unmarked unit under a cottonwood tree and knocked on Trinidad's front door. He'd called the night before, asking for a few minutes of Trinidad's time. Sandoval greeted him quickly with a smile and a pat on the shoulder.

Still arrow-straight, but an inch or two shorter than when he was in his prime, Sandoval had lost weight since Joe had last seen him. He wore a starched white shirt and pressed blue jeans pulled up high above his waist cinched tight by a belt, and freshly polished shoes.

"What do you need to see this old man for?" Trinidad asked.

Joe smiled. "For a cup of coffee, perhaps?"

Trinidad nodded. "Come in, and tell me about your family."

A widower for many years but doggedly self-sufficient, Sandoval had a daughter who lived next door and kept an eye on him. In the kitchen, a tidy room that reflected Trinidad's fastidious nature, he served Joe coffee and asked about his wife and sons.

"So, everyone is healthy and well," Trinidad said, when Joe finished bragging about his family. "That is what is most important, to be happy and well. But you didn't come here for an old man's philosophy of life. What brings you to see me, Mr. Policeman?"

Joe laughed. "I'd like to talk to you about Clifford Spalding."

"For what reason?"

"Spalding has died under suspicious circumstances, and I'm looking into questions about his finances."

Sandoval shook his head. "When you get to be my age, it seems like everyone you know dies. What are these suspicious circumstances you speak of?"

"He may have been murdered," Joe replied.

Trinidad quickly crossed himself. "I will say a prayer for him at Mass."

"How did Spalding come to do business with you?"

"First, he tried to buy the property through a Realtor. But I wouldn't sell. Because of the zoning, I knew it was valuable. It was only one of a few commercial parcels close to the Plaza that could be developed into a hotel without difficulty. When he offered to lease it, I accepted, because it kept everything in the family."

"Who were his partners?" Joe asked.

Trinidad blinked. "His partners? He didn't have any."

"Perhaps they were silent partners," Joe replied. Chief Kerney's notes had specifically mentioned that the property lease had been secured by a partnership that included Spalding.

"I don't think he had any partners," Trinidad said.

"Could I see the original paperwork?" Joe asked. "I'll keep the information confidential."

Trinidad thought a long minute before nodding in agreement. He left the kitchen and soon returned with a thick packet, which he placed on the table in front of Valdez.

Joe spent an hour reading the material, taking notes, and asking Trinidad some clarifying questions. Spalding had paid the first two-year lease up front. The agreement had a rate renegotiation clause that kicked in every twenty-four months. It was tied to current costs per square foot of similar properties, which had risen dramatically over the last three decades.

Along with the money he'd borrowed, Trinidad had used Spalding's first payment to renovate and enlarge the building. When the initial lease came up for renewal, the monthly rate jumped significantly to take into account the expansion and improvements Sandoval had made to the property.

From day one, Trinidad had wisely retained complete control over the property, which he now owned free and clear. The hotel generated a sizable chunk of money every month, enough to support every member of the Sandoval family comfortably for the foreseeable future.

Joe left with the name of the Albuquerque law firm Spalding had used to draw up the lease agreement in his notebook. When time allowed, he'd call and see what he could learn about the source of the six-figure payment Spalding had made to secure the lease.

Other than the question of Spalding's financing, nothing looked out of the ordinary.

*　　*　　*

Mid-morning found Kerney at his desk reviewing the information that had come in on the Spalding family and Debbie Calderwood. Interestingly, Clifford Spalding had filed a bankruptcy petition three months before the death of his son in Vietnam. Before the court could act on the matter, Spalding had withdrawn the filing and paid his creditors in full.

A real estate transaction record dated six months later showed that Clifford and Alice Spalding, doing business as Sundown Properties, had paid a mall developer for a land parcel to build a motel in Albuquerque. That seemed to jibe somewhat with what Penelope Parker had told him.

He went back through his notes. Parker had said the developer had wanted to buy Spalding's old motel, tear it down, and put up a franchise hotel next to the mall.

He thumbed through the bankruptcy paperwork. The motel Spalding had listed as an asset was several miles away from the shopping mall. Kerney wondered about the disparity. Maybe Parker's version of how Spalding had started his hotel empire was flawed. Kerney didn't doubt her honesty, just her knowledge of events prior to her involvement with the family.

Putting that issue aside, Kerney still wondered how Spalding had been able to bail out of his financial difficulties so quickly and come up with enough cash to pay for land next to a major shopping mall. Did he have help from a national hotel chain, as Parker reported? If so, why would any large corporation partner with a small-time operator who was about to go broke? It made no sense.

He had Helen Muiz fax copies to Joe Valdez, and took a call from the Harding County sheriff, Luciano "Lucky" Suazo, who reported that his horseback trek along the Canadian to look for Dean at his cabin had been fruitless.

"Nobody's there," Lucky said, "and I saw no sign of anybody coming or going."

"What about his vehicle?" Kerney asked.

"Didn't see it. His closest access would be at the Mills campground. He'd have to leave his vehicle there and cross the river on horseback or on foot to get to his land. From the campground, it's two hours by horse, three on foot, to get to his cabin."

"Are there any other jumping-off points?"

"Yeah, on private land. I'm calling all the ranchers up and down the river now," Lucky replied. "So far, nobody has seen Dean or his vehicle, and believe me, they're out there looking."

"What about the cabin?" Kerney asked.

"Locked up tight, with shutters over the windows. No fresh footprints. Looks like it's been a couple of months since anyone has been around."

"Thanks, Sheriff," Kerney said.

"No need for that, Chief," Lucky replied. "Just doing my job. I'll get back to you if anything turns up."

Kerney hung up and went looking for Ramona Pino, who was in her cubbyhole of an office, fingers clacking away at a computer keyboard.

"I just got off the phone with the Harding County sheriff," he said, as he sat in a straight-back chair. "Dean wasn't at his cabin. Do you have any news?"

"Nothing yet, Chief," Ramona replied. "We've got the Denver PD staking out Dean's ex-wife's house, and I just finished calling all the airlines. He hasn't flown out of either the Santa Fe or Albuquerque airports."

"Did you talk to the ex-wife?" Kerney asked.

"Yeah, and she's not a big fan of her ex-hubby. She's about to file against him for failure to pay child support. He's in arrears for almost fifty thousand dollars."

"What's up with the evidence?" Kerney asked.

"The knives are on the way to California," Ramona said. "Hopefully the lab out there will be able to match one of them to the tool marks on the pill. The stuff I pulled out of the trash bin at Dean's house had traces of thyroid medication on it, and we lifted Dean's prints off both packets the drug wholesaler shipped to him. The packet we found in the workshop contained a mixture of all the ingredients Dean used to make the pills. I guess Dean decided to keep his concoction for another attempt on Spalding's life in case the first batch of pills didn't kill him."

"So, where the hell is he?" Kerney asked.

Ramona shook her head. "I wish I knew. Ellie Lowrey has the Montecito estate under observation in case he shows."

"Okay," Kerney said.

"I'd like to rework the arrest affidavit on Claudia Spalding and have it ready to resubmit, Chief."

"What can you add to it?" Kerney asked.

"The only way Dean could possibly have known the specifics about Spalding's medication and heart condition is through knowledge he gained from Claudia Spalding. Where else could he have gotten it?"

"I agree that it's a good supposition," Kerney said. "But a defense lawyer would argue that the information was innocently passed on to Dean by Claudia Spalding. We need something that irrefutably ties the two of them together as coconspirators."

"We've also got the last phone call Claudia Spalding made to Dean at the pharmacy just before he took off."

"Again, unless we can prove that Claudia actually warned Dean of the arrest warrant, it's circumstantial. What's Sergeant Lowrey up to?"

"She's on her way to Clifford Spalding's corporate offices in LA.

He stopped there before driving to Paso Robles. She's hoping to find the prescription bottle from the Santa Fe pharmacy. She thinks Spalding may have transferred the contents into his pill case, knowing he'd have a refill waiting for him when he got home."

"As a pharmacist, Dean had to be fingerprinted, right?"

"And photographed," Ramona said. "I've sent both his prints and picture to Lowrey by computer."

"Hold up for now on reworking the Spalding arrest affidavit until you hear back from Lowrey. Go for another search warrant on Dean's business instead. Focus on his finances. It's possible that we may have multiple motives for murder. Not only does Claudia Spalding inherit a considerable estate, she frees herself to have an open relationship with Dean and bail him out of his financial woes. Use the statement you took from Nina Deacon about Claudia wanting out of the marriage to back it up."

"But what about the amendment to the prenuptial agreement that validated her right to extramarital affairs?" Ramona asked.

"Her lies to Nina Deacon went way beyond what was necessary to adhere to that agreement," Kerney said. "She told Deacon that she wasn't happy in the marriage but didn't want to get off her husband's gravy train."

"Should I go after Claudia Spalding's financial records also?" Ramona asked.

Kerney stood up. "Not yet. Let's see what kind of backdoor information we can get from Dean's records. Has he increased his borrowing lately? Does he have large or overdue accounts payable? Are there frequent cash transactions? Has he been bouncing checks? If Dean is hurting for money, he has a ready supply of drugs he can peddle illegally. Make sure the warrant covers his pharmacy inventory and prescription records."

"Anything else?" Ramona asked.

Kerney smiled. "Find Dean."

"He's either still traveling or has already gone to ground."

Kerney nodded. "Probably some place that's familiar enough

where he can stay low and feel safe. Get people started talking to everyone who knows him. Contact the ex-wife again and get a list of the names and addresses of family members and old friends. Where does he like to vacation? Where does he go on business trips? Is there someone—a sibling, a parent, a college chum—he visits regularly?"

"Dean and Spalding may have scouted out a hiding place for him on their trips together, in case things went sour," Ramona said. "I'll check his credit card charges. That may give us a lead."

"Keep me informed," Kerney said as he stepped into the hallway.

*   *   *

Century City, an incorporated municipality of 176 acres, had once been the backlot of a major motion picture studio. Now its office towers, high-rise condos, and luxury hotels filled the West Los Angeles skyline. It boasted a major outdoor shopping center with trendy, high-end stores and retail businesses that drew people from all over Southern California and beyond.

In the stop-and-go traffic of the freeway, Ellie Lowrey had a view of Century City through her windshield for a good twenty minutes before she could ease onto an exit ramp and park in an underground garage. Until today, she'd been here only once, a long time ago, on a weekend shopping spree with her kid sister. She'd left suffering from sticker shock and sensory overload, wondering why all the beautiful clothing, expensive jewelry, fine art, and custom home furnishings had left her feeling so dejected. Did people really need all that stuff to be happy?

She took an elevator to street level and made her way to one of the twin office towers that rose behind a large water fountain. Inside, a security guard directed her to the floor where Spalding's offices were located.

On the top floor, Ellie explained to a receptionist the reason for her visit and was asked to wait. While the woman whispered into a telephone, Ellie gazed out the plate glass windows at the barely visible Santa Monica Mountains, veiled by brown smog. Far below, she could see traffic flowing on the streets. Except for a package delivery man rolling a dolly into a store there was nobody else on the sidewalks.

She turned back to the receptionist, who gave Ellie a nervous smile as she quickly dialed another extension. On the wall behind the woman's desk were three rows of framed, enlarged color photographs, eighteen in all, displaying Spalding's hotel properties. One of them showed the high-rise hotel Ellie had just been looking at out the window.

After a few minutes, a man in a suit came down a hallway, introduced himself as the corporate counsel, and took Ellie to his office, where he questioned her closely about the investigation.

She told him what she was looking for and why. Satisfied that her visit was tied to a murder investigation and had nothing to do with corporate matters, he accompanied her to Spalding's corner office, and watched while she searched.

Light flooded the big room through two window walls. It was sparsely furnished with two angular leather couches separated by a low coffee table, and a large, highly polished writing table with steel legs and a matching desk chair.

Ellie looked through the drawers of a built-in cabinet behind the desk and glanced at the framed photographs on the shelves above. There were several of Claudia Spalding, but most were of Clifford Spalding posing with movie stars and politicians.

There were no drawers in the desk and the wastebasket was empty. In Spalding's private bathroom, Ellie found some personal toiletries in a travel kit and another empty wastebasket, but no prescription bottle.

"Was anyone here when Mr. Spalding returned to his office from his business trip?" she asked the lawyer.

"I doubt it," the lawyer said. "We were closed for the weekend."

"Where does he park his car?"

"In the underground garage," the lawyer said. "But when he travels on business, he leaves his car at our hotel here and takes the VIP limo to the airport."

Ellie thanked the lawyer for his cooperation, went back to the garage, found Spalding's reserved parking space, and searched the area. There was the usual accumulation of trash under and around the nearby cars, but no prescription bottle.

She drove to the hotel and spoke to a bell captain, who called inside for the limo driver. An older, skinny man wearing a black suit, white shirt, and black tie hurried out the lobby doors.

"Did you pick up Mr. Spalding at the airport last weekend?" Ellie asked.

The man nodded. "Yes."

"Did he leave anything behind in the limo?"

"Yes, he left an empty prescription bottle on the backseat. It had refill information on the label, so I kept it in case he needed it."

Ellie broke into a big smile. "Where's the bottle?"

*   *   *

Ramona Pino wanted her next case to be a cakewalk. Maybe a gang member who popped a round into somebody's ear in front of ten witnesses, or a body dump case with enough physical evidence at the crime scene to lead her right to the perp, drinking a beer and watching the tube at home, just waiting to be arrested. Even a good old-fashioned domestic disturbance that had escalated into a murder of passion would be a welcome change of pace.

Santa Fe averaged only two homicides annually, but last year had been a real bitch, in terms of numbers and complexity. A lone, smart killer with a bad attitude had chalked up seven victims. One of them, the perp's mother, had been killed years ago and buried under some backyard shrubbery. The rest were all fresh kills done within a matter of days. The perp had been stopped just short of adding Chief Kerney, his wife, and their newborn son to his tally.

Since Spalding had died in California, Ramona wondered if the case even technically qualified as a local homicide. Maybe an argument could be made that murder was committed the instant Spalding's medication had been switched. That made it a slow kill, Ramona thought.

With a new search warrant in hand and three detectives to assist her, Ramona walked into Dean's pharmacy to find Tilly Gilmore, the clerk, and a pharmacist talking in low voices behind the counter. The pharmacist wore a name tag on his white smock that read GRADY BALDRIDGE.

She showed them the warrant and explained what the detectives were about to do.

"Where is Kim?" Baldridge asked. "He should be here for this."

"I wish he was here," Ramona said as she motioned to the officers to get started. Matt Chacon steered Tilly to a back office, while the other two men began looking through the filing cabinet and desk behind the pharmacy counter.

"Do you work for him full-time?" she asked Baldridge.

He shook his head and the folds below his chin jiggled. Ramona put him in his late sixties. The smock he wore bulged at his hefty waistline. His pasty skin almost perfectly matched his gray hair.

"No," Baldridge said. "I'm basically retired. Kim uses me as his relief pharmacist. This is the last day I can be here for three weeks. The wife and I are leaving tomorrow on vacation."

"Were you supposed to work yesterday?" Ramona asked.

"No, Kim called me at home early in the morning and asked me to come in."

"Did he say why?"

"Just that he needed coverage," Baldridge replied.

"Was that unusual?"

"I'd say so," Baldridge said. "In fact, Tilly and I were just talking about it. He's only called me to come in on short notice before when he's been sick. We don't know what to do if he doesn't come back tomorrow, except refer his customers to other pharmacies. I only came in today because people were waiting to have their prescriptions filled."

"What a nice thing to do before your vacation," Ramona said. Baldridge smiled at the compliment.

"Do you know Dean's customers well?" she asked.

"Most of them. I've filled in here for the past five years."

"How about Claudia Spalding?" Ramona asked.

"Oh yes, she has several current prescriptions on file."

"For what?"

"Unless your warrant specifically permits you to gather prescription information about our customers, I can't tell you that."

"It does," Ramona said, showing Baldridge the appropriate paragraph in the search warrant.

"I'd have to look it up," Baldridge said.

"Please do," Ramona replied.

Baldridge spent a few minutes at a computer, then returned and rattled off Claudia Spalding's current prescription information. Ramona had him translate it into language she could understand. Baldridge told her one script was for a mild muscle relaxant and the other was for a narcotic painkiller. She asked Baldridge to pull the hard copies, and while he went off to do so, she called the doctor who'd prescribed the medications and asked him to verify the information.

"The muscle relaxant, yes," the doctor said. "But I never gave her any painkillers."

"What did she need the muscle relaxant for?" Ramona asked.

"You know I can't tell you that, Sergeant."

"If you talk around the subject a little bit, Doctor," Ramona said, "I might not have to pay you a visit."

"Do you ride horses, Sergeant?"

"Not since I was a little kid," Ramona replied.

"Let's say you did, and you took a bad fall from a horse and strained the muscles in your back. Not severely, but enough to cause discomfort. The muscle relaxant, in a very low dosage, provides relief."

"That helps," Ramona said. "What about the narcotic painkiller?"

"It had to be forged," the doctor said. "Mrs. Spalding has no medical condition I'm aware of that requires it."

"Your records confirm that?"

"Absolutely," the doctor said before hanging up.

Baldridge hovered next to her with the hard copy scripts in hand. Both looked real, but who better to forge a doctor's prescription than a pharmacist?

"Tell me about this painkiller," Ramona asked.

"It's hydrocodone acetaminophen, a Class III controlled substance," Baldridge said, "which means it doesn't have to be as strictly inventoried and accounted for as Class II drugs under federal regulations."

"How is it accounted for?" Ramona asked.

"We do an annual report and give an estimate of how much was dispensed and what's on hand. It doesn't have to be absolutely accurate."

"Would the painkiller give the user a high? Make them nod out?"

"It's a downer, so I'd imagine so," Baldridge said. "In normal dosages, other than relieving pain, it tends to cause drowsiness, dull the senses, and flatten the affect."

"Can you find out how many other people have had this medicine dispensed to them at this pharmacy?"

"Easily," Baldridge said, returning to the computer. He came back with the names of twelve individuals, all with scripts written by Claudia Spalding's doctor.

"Did you fill any of these?" Ramona asked.

Baldridge shook his head and pointed to a line on one of the scripts. "Each prescription must be numbered and initialed by the pharmacist who filled it. All of these were filled by Kim."

"What about phone-in prescriptions?"

"That's in a different computer file," he said, stepping back to the monitor. He printed out another ten names of persons receiving the medication, all supposedly phoned in from the same doctor who'd treated Claudia Spalding.

Ramona called the doctor again and asked about the names on both lists Baldridge had provided.

"I've never treated any of those people," the doctor said.

"You're certain of that?"

"I don't like your implication, Sergeant," the doctor snapped. "I do not supply narcotics to drug users. You can come here any time you want and look at the master chart log and my patient appointment calender."

"Thank you, Doctor," Ramona replied. "We may have to do that." She disconnected and turned to speak to Baldridge, who was pulling hard copy files and printing information from the computer. He brought everything to her, and she scanned them quickly one by one. On the hard copies, she noticed that although the doctor's signature and prescription information looked real, the patients' names seemed to have been written with a slightly different slant. The printouts from the phone-in scripts showed Kim Dean's initials as the dispensing pharmacist.

"Do you have a sample of Dean's handwriting?" she asked Baldridge.

He nodded, stepped into the back office, and brought out a large, leather-bound address book.

Ramona paged through it and noted the same slight backward slant. She wrote out a list of all the scripts, added Dean's address book to it, gave a copy of the list to Baldridge, and told him that he needed to keep it as part of the inventory of seized evidence.

"Show me the narcotic medication," she said.

Baldridge took her to rows of freestanding medication shelves and handed her a large, almost empty white plastic bottle.

She looked at the pills, snapped the lid back on, and shook the bottle. "How frequently does Dean reorder this?"

It took Baldridge a while to dig out the invoices. He finished with a distraught look on his face, and asked Ramona to give him back the hard copy prescriptions and printouts.

One by one, Baldridge tallied up the total number of narcotic pills Dean had dispensed, including refills. He shook his head sharply, mouth tight with disapproval. "Kim's been ordering three times the amount he needs," he said.

"Anything else?" Ramona asked.

"There should be two unopened bottles of five hundred pills each in inventory," Baldridge replied as he peeled off his pharmacist's smock and stuffed it under his arm. "They're not on the shelf."

"Where are you going?"

"Home. I can't work here anymore."

Ramona gave Baldridge a sympathetic smile and touched him on the arm. "You'll need to stay for a while longer, Mr. Baldridge. Lock the front door, arrange for another pharmacy to handle any prescriptions that still need to be filled, and work with me. It might mean the difference between leaving tomorrow on that vacation with your wife or being delayed."

Baldridge sighed and looked glum. "Very well, if you insist."

*   *   *

Three hours into the record search at the pharmacy, the detectives had uncovered enough evidence with Baldridge's help to prove that Kim Dean had been moving large quantities of drugs containing narcotic painkillers, barbiturates, morphine, and amphetamines onto the streets of Santa Fe. Forged and phony call-in prescriptions from a number of local physicians had been used to falsify the records. To hide inventory shortfalls, Dean had altered invoices from suppliers and lied on required reports to the state pharmacy board.

Although they were only halfway through the prescription and inventory records, Ramona decided to call a halt and bring in the Drug Enforcement Administration, which by law had jurisdiction. She told her team to switch their attention to Dean's financial records, and gave Grady Baldridge the news that he would have to delay his vacation trip with his wife. Clearly disgusted by what had been unearthed, Baldridge made no complaint.

Sitting in her unit outside the pharmacy, Ramona reported in to Chief Kerney. "When we stopped tallying, the street value of the drugs was at least a hundred thousand dollars," she said. "Who knows how high it will go once the final count is in. I need DEA here, Chief."

"I'll get them on it," Kerney said. "Do you know if Dean was selling the drugs directly or supplying a dealer?"

"We haven't gotten that far yet," Ramona replied.

"What about the forged prescriptions? Are the patients' names real?"

"Except for Claudia Spalding, we don't know."

"I doubt that they are," Kerney said. "But I know a man who might be able to tell us quickly if any of those people on the list are part of Spalding's or Dean's social circle. He knows just about everyone with money in Santa Fe. He's been helpful to me in the past."

Kerney read off a name and address. The man worked as a stockbroker in a professional office building on St. Michael's Drive.

"Got it," Ramona said, wondering if the chief was sending her to meet with a confidential informant or an undercover cop.

"I'll let him know you're coming," Kerney said.

"Ten-four."

*   *   *

For the past year, DEA Special Agent Evan Winslow had masqueraded as an estate, retirement, and wealth management consultant in the Santa Fe office of a national brokerage house. Only the branch manager, a naval academy graduate and former JAG lawyer, and the local police chief, who'd arranged his cover, knew Winslow was a DEA cop.

Winslow wasn't interested in the low-end market that catered to the street junkies. Instead, he was in place to go after a supplier with Bogotá cartel connections who was using a new drug pipeline that stretched from California to New York. Based in Los Angeles, the man flew in a private jet to deliver his goodies to high-end customers across the country who wanted to get loaded in the privacy of their million-dollar homes while remaining under the radar of the local cops.

Winslow was one of four agents in different cities tasked with gathering enough evidence to seize the drugs in the pipeline, bust the supplier, and provide intelligence to DEA agents in South America about the traffickers. If everything worked as planned, a major national roundup of celebrity addicts and users would go down, drawing national media attention, and victory in a battle of the war on drugs would be proclaimed.

So far, Winslow had hard evidence to burn the supplier's Santa Fe customers, including a fading film actor, a famous jazz musician, a world-renowned chef, a New York City fashion designer, a minor British royal, and a network television producer. But he still hadn't been able to score directly from the source, which was key to breaking up the cartel.

The call from Chief Kerney had surprised Winslow. But after hearing the chief out and being reassured that his cover wouldn't be blown, he'd agreed to meet with Ramona Pino.

The receptionist showed Pino into his office. No more than five-three, she was a looker, with perfectly round dark eyes, high cheekbones, and a shapely figure.

"I understand you have some names of people you think I might be able to tell you something about," Winslow said before Pino had a chance to speak.

"Yes." Ramona sat in front of the desk and passed Winslow the list of names taken from the forged prescriptions.

"These aren't people I know," Winslow said, lying through his teeth. At least six were part of the upscale drug party scene, and one, Mitch Griffin, when he wasn't building houses, dealt stolen pharmaceutical drugs to his trendy friends. Winslow had always wondered where Griffin got his drugs. Now he knew.

"You're absolutely sure?" Ramona asked.

Winslow scanned the list again.

"Nobody?" Ramona asked.

"I'm sorry, no." Winslow tapped his finger on the desk. "Unless a first name might be helpful."

"Which one is that?" Ramona asked.

"Mitch," Winslow said, waving the paper. "I don't know his last name, but it's down here as Griffin."

"What can you tell me about him?"

"If it's the right Mitch, he's a general contractor."

"Do you know him personally?" Ramona asked.

"Just in passing."

"Describe him to me."

"Six-foot-three, in his forties I'd guess. He's a big guy who likes to work out and party."

Ramona took back the list. "Thanks for your help."

Winslow smiled and stood. "I don't think I've done anything help-ful at all." He ushered Pino to the door. "If you ever decide to invest in the stock market, come back and see me."

He waited for Pino to leave the building before calling Kerney.

"Did Pino make you?" Kerney asked.

"I doubt it. But let's not make a habit of this, Chief Kerney."

"Not a chance. Thanks."

*   *   *

Finding where Mitch Griffin lived took one phone call to the state agency that licensed general contractors. With the chief's blessing, Ramona assembled a team of officers, including two narcotics detec-tives and some uniforms, and drove to Griffin's house in La Cienega, a few miles south of Santa Fe. The house was sited behind a hill on a private dirt lane. In among the surrounding trees were piles of lum-ber, beams, doors, and windows, some of them covered with clear plastic sheeting.

Griffin's extended-cab pickup truck sat in front of a detached garage, and parked next to it was Kim Dean's SUV. Ramona laughed out loud. Maybe the gods had heard her plea for an easy bust after all.

She spread her troops around the building and used a bullhorn to call out Dean and Griffin. After checking the firepower in his front yard through a window, Mitch came out first, totally stoned and shirtless in his six-foot-three, buff glory. Dean followed behind, rumpled and scared, pumping his hands up and down in the air.

She ordered them facedown on the ground with their hands clasped behind their heads and watched as they were cuffed and frisked. Then she had her officers stand them up while she told them the charges and read them their rights.

She looked Dean over carefully. He wasn't anything to write home about. Maybe the fear in his eyes and his trembling chin made him seem insignificant and ordinary.

"We need to have a nice long talk about Claudia," she said as a uniform led him away.

"Claudia Spalding?" Griffin mumbled lethargically, his eyes blinking rapidly in the harsh afternoon light. "Man, I built her house."

"It's such a small world, isn't it?" Ramona replied cheerily.

ChapterSeven

Kim Dean was scared, but he wasn't stupid. He asked for an attorney and immediately dummied up. Ramona took him directly to the county jail, booked him on a murder one charge, and left him with a detention officer. The officer let Dean make his phone call to a lawyer and put him in an isolation cell, the first step on the way to being processed, fingerprinted, and strip-searched.

Ramona used the time to fill out additional booking forms on Dean, charging him with drug trafficking, conspiracy to commit murder, accessory to murder, forgery, distribution of controlled substances, and possession with intent to distribute. Although it only counted as a misdemeanor, she threw in an evading arrest charge for good measure.

She had a detention officer bring Dean to an interrogation room where she read off the additional charges, Mirandized him again, and asked if he'd like to make a voluntary statement.

Dean shook his head and said no.

Ramona knew his refusal barred her from asking questions, but that didn't stop her from talking.

"Just in case you're interested," she said, "each prescription you forged counts as a separate charge. Let's be conservative and say you did fifty. That's a hundred and fifty years, if a judge sentences you to consecutive terms. Throw in all the other counts and I'm guessing you'll get about 250 years in the slam. Of course, you may get time off for good behavior."

"I want to talk to my lawyer," Dean said. Color had come back to his face and his rosy cheeks clashed with the orange jail jumpsuit. He sat with his feet crossed under the table and his hands hidden from view.

Chief Kerney thought that Dean might break easily under interrogation, but it wasn't happening. Maybe he wasn't the kind of bully who pushed people around to hide his own inadequacies. Maybe, instead, Dean was the control freak type who got off on dominating and manipulating people.

About six feet tall, Dean had light brown hair that receded over his temples and exposed his tiny ears. He had a long, slightly turned up nose that gave him a haughty look. But his rapidly blinking brown eyes signaled underlying stress.

"When the lawyer comes," Ramona said, gathering her paperwork, "ask him about the federal sentencing laws for drug trafficking, possession, and distribution."

"Why should I do that?" Dean asked.

Ramona stared past Dean at the dull gray concrete wall of the room. Jail was a grim place nobody ever really got used to. It always gave her the willies.

"The feds have harsher penalties," she replied curtly. "You may want to deal with us instead of them."

She left Dean and went to check in with Matt Chacon, who'd booked Mitch Griffin into custody. Ramona stepped into the interrogation room and found that big, buff Griffin had waived his Miranda rights and was talking.

He had a pretty face with even features. Combined with the day-old stubble on his chin, he vaguely resembled a country music singer who'd been a teenage heartthrob some years back before quickly fading into obscurity.

Ramona wondered if Mitch had ever slept with Claudia Spalding.

She asked him about it, and he shook his head. Matt Chacon told her Mitch was willing to testify against Dean on the drug trafficking charge if he could cut a deal.

"You didn't promise him anything?" Ramona asked, eyeing Griffin.

"*Nada,*" Matt replied.

"Let's hold off on asking the assistant district attorney to make any offers until we search Mitch's house. I'll call for a warrant."

"Why do you want to do that?" Griffin asked, his glance nervously flitting from Chacon to Ramona.

"Do you ever gamble at the Indian casinos, Mitch?" Ramona asked.

"Yeah, sometimes."

"Then you know what a punt is, right?"

"Yeah, you bet against the banker in faro and games like that."

"Consider me the banker in this game," Ramona said, smiling cheerfully at Griffin. "Depending on the amount of product we find, you may be facing the possibility of life without parole. If I seize enough to put you away for life, I'll be holding all the cards. So, there will be no plea bargain until I know exactly what your maximum bet is going to be."

Griffin slumped in his chair. "How much stash do you have to find?"

Ramona waved a finger at Griffin. "No fair asking, Mitch. That's cheating."

Ramona stepped into the hallway to the sounds of an opening door and footsteps down the corridor. Chief Kerney, an ADA, and Dean's lawyer walked in her direction. The ADA peeled off into the room where Mitch Griffin was parked, and Ramona directed the defense attorney to the room where Dean waited.

"Where are we?" Kerney asked.

"Dean's not talking," Ramona said.

"How many charges did you lay on him?" Kerney asked.

"Seven felonies, including multiple counts of forgery," Ramona said, "plus one misdemeanor."

"That should get him talking eventually," Kerney said with an approving nod. "A DEA team is at the pharmacy. I told our people to stay and assist."

The ADA poked his head out the door of the interrogation room. "You've got Griffin's voluntary permission to search his house," he said. "His drug stash is in a cabinet above the refrigerator." He handed Ramona a signed search release form.

"What did you promise him?" Ramona asked.

"Nothing," the ADA replied in a voice loud enough for Griffin to hear. "He wants immunity from prosecution. He isn't going to get it. At least, not yet. Maybe not ever."

The ADA retreated into the room and closed the door.

"I want Griffin to do time," Ramona said. "Lots of it."

"He probably will," Kerney said. "I asked the ADA to play him for a while to see if he knows anything about the Spalding murder. If that doesn't pan out, we can use what he tells us to nail down the drug charges on Dean and round up his customers."

"We're not backing off on the murder charges against Dean, are we, Chief?" Ramona asked.

Ramona's tight voice gave away her apprehension. Kerney smiled reassuringly. "Not at all. I want him to roll over on Claudia Spalding. We can go to trial without Dean testifying against her, but we'll have a much better chance at a conviction if we have him in our pocket."

"What will the DA offer Dean?"

"He'll drop all but the murder one and drug trafficking charges if he cops a plea and gives us Claudia."

"Has Dean's lawyer been advised?" Ramona asked.

"No, and he won't be until after the preliminary hearing and bail has been set. Since Dean's a flight risk, Sid will request that he be held without bond."

Ramona flashed a pleased smile.

"One more thing, Sergeant," Kerney said. "Remember, the DEA can file against Dean in federal court on the drug and forgery charges that we drop, and I fully expect that they will. His lawyer should snap to that immediately, and listen hard to any plea bargain offer."

"That won't happen until a couple of days from now," Ramona said.

"Exactly. Use the time wisely, Sergeant. If Dean doesn't play ball, you'll need as much as you can get on Claudia Spalding to make a strong case."

"Will do, Chief."

As Kerney turned and walked away, Ramona wondered what else she could possibly do to link Claudia Spalding directly to the murder of her husband. She paused in front of the door to the interrogation room where Mitch and the ADA were meeting. After she finished up at the jail and did the search for drugs at Griffin's house, she would give Ellie Lowrey a call.

Maybe between the two of them they could brainstorm something.

*   *   *

Kim Dean had been cutting legal corners for a long time, but up to now he'd never needed the services of a criminal trial lawyer. He'd used his one phone call from the jail to contact the only attorney he knew, a woman who specialized in real-estate law. She was unable to clear her schedule, but promised to send a junior member of the firm to see him as soon as possible.

Stubbs was the lawyer's name, Howard Alan Stubbs, and he was talking to Dean about all the things he needed to do to get a clear picture of the situation.

Stubbs called it a "situation," but Kim knew better; he was in a pile of shit ten feet deep. He also knew he needed a sharper, more experienced lawyer who could dig him out of a hole.

Stubbs looked like his name: short arms and short legs with a Humpty Dumpty body. He wore a brown suit, brown shoes, and a paisley tie that stopped just below his belly button. His pale young face was round as a beach ball.

Dean interrupted Stubbs's ramblings and asked him when he could get out of jail.

"We won't know that," Stubbs replied, "until your arraignment."

Dean nodded. His right foot tapped a staccato beat on the floor. He pushed down hard on his leg with a hand to make it stop.

"But from what you've told me," Stubbs said, "you may not be released. The DA will ask that you be held without bond, and of course I'll argue against it. Perhaps I can get the judge to agree to a large cash bond. If not, you're here until the preliminary hearing. That's when I'll get a first look at the evidence against you."

"Not until then?" Dean asked.

Stubbs shook his head. "And we won't see everything right away."

"I want out of this place," Dean said.

"I can't guarantee that," Stubbs said.

"The cop who arrested me said something about federal drug laws. She said I should talk to you about it."

"As I understand it," Stubbs said, "the federal laws are more severe. You could find yourself facing trial in both state and federal courts."

"As you understand it?" Dean snapped.

Stubbs flushed. "I'll research the statutes."

That sealed it, Dean thought. Stubbs was in way over his head. "I want you to call someone for me."

"Sure," Stubbs answered agreeably.

Dean gave him Claudia's cell phone number. "Tell the woman who answers where I am and that I need help, lots of it, right away," he said.

"Who is this woman?" Stubbs asked.

"Just a friend."

"What's her name?"

"Just call her and tell her about my situation. She'll know what to do."

Stubbs frowned and packed his notebook in his briefcase. "Don't talk to anyone unless I'm present," he said.

"Don't worry, I won't."

Dean didn't move after Stubbs left the room. He sat with the fingers of his hands interlaced, hidden from view under the table. If he eased up and stopped squeezing his hands together his whole body would start shaking.

None of this was supposed to happen. He wanted to push it aside, smash it to bits, stomp it into oblivion. He could feel sweat under his armpits dripping down his rib cage, taste it on his upper lip.

Dean knew he had to stay in control and not do any talking to the cops. And he had to replace Stubbs with somebody sharp. A good prosecutor would push Stubbs around as easily as he had. He needed a crusading defense lawyer with a high profile who knew how to work the media. He had to stay calm and wait for Claudia to come through for him.

A jailer stepped into the room and took him down the hall. Doors slammed closed behind him, glaring light bounced off the polished tile floors, buzzers sounded as electronic locks opened, eyes followed him. The jailer took him back to the isolation cell, locked him in, and peeked at him through the small window.

There was an elevated concrete slab built into one wall to sit or lie on, a steel sink with one cold water tap, three shielded, recessed lights in the ceiling, a steel toilet with a flush valve. Just that, nothing more.

He sat on the concrete slab, stared at the floor, and told himself over and over again to say nothing and wait. It didn't erase the fear he felt, but it helped.

*   *   *

There were enough pharmaceuticals in Mitch Griffin's house to keep dozens of dopers, pillheads, and speed freaks happy for weeks— and that was just from the stash Ramona and the officers found in the kitchen cabinet above the refrigerator. Further searching turned up ten pounds of marijuana Griffin had hidden in a locked contractor's truck box that sat on a shelf in the garage. Additionally, seventeen thousand dollars in cash was found in a trombone case under Mitch's bed.

While detectives continued searching the house, Ramona stood outside and looked down the lane. Although the hill hid the small village of La Cienega from view, she could see the tops of the old willow trees that lined the valley. A few puffy white clouds drifted overhead in a washed-out, pale blue sky.

Unless Dean talked, she had two days at best to gather enough evidence against Claudia Spalding to arrest her. If Dean didn't implicate Spalding, and no physical evidence tied her to the crime, what would it take?

Ramona had worked circumstantial evidence cases before, and knew that sometimes they were successful in court and sometimes not. She flipped open her cell phone and dialed Sergeant Ellie Lowrey's number in California, hoping for some good news.

"Have you got anything?" she asked when Ellie answered.

"Yeah, and it's all bad," Lowrey replied. "We got partials off the medicine bottle. They belong to Clifford Spalding and the limo driver. That's it."

"Dammit," Ramona said.

"Tell me about it. What's up on your end?"

"Dean's in custody. I booked him on a half dozen felony counts, including drug trafficking and murder. He's got a lawyer and he isn't talking."

"Well, at least you've got him," Ellie said. "That's half a victory."

"Not even, if we can't make a case against Claudia," Ramona replied. "Any ideas?"

"Just one," Ellie replied. "Chief Kerney told me that the ranch manager in Paso Robles characterized Claudia as a big flirt."

"Do you think Claudia has other lovers besides Dean?" Ramona asked.

"I think anything is possible with that woman," Ellie replied. "What if she wanted out of the marriage in spite of the sexual freedom she had?"

"Or maybe she violated the terms of her agreement with Clifford and he found out about it," Ramona said.

"Exactly," Ellie said. "If we could prove that, we'd have a solid motive for murder."

"So let's find out if there have been any other lovers in Claudia's life during the past four years," Ramona said.

"It's a deal," Ellie said. "Keep in touch."

"Talk to you later," Ramona said.

She disconnected, turned the house search over to a senior detective, and headed back to the jail. Although Mitch Griffin had denied any sexual involvement with Claudia, Ramona decided it was time to push the subject a bit harder with him to see where it led.

*   *   *

Kerney's house was built on a shallow depression along a gently sloping ridgeline above a red sandstone canyon. From the portal that ran the length of the south-facing house, he could look down on the meadow below. Cut by a wandering, sandy arroyo and bordered by a stand of old cottonwood trees, the meadow was frequently visited by a small herd of antelope that grazed on the native bunch grasses that grew in the poor soil.

Beyond the canyon, the Galisteo Basin stretched out to meet the Ortiz Mountains, which tumbled against the higher peaks of the Sandias, a good fifty miles distant. Behind the house, a swath of pine-studded pastureland rose up a hill, framed in the background by the Sangre de Cristo Mountains outside of Santa Fe.

In Spanish, Sangre de Cristo meant "blood of Christ." Tradition had it that the mountains were so named by the Spanish settlers because of the deep red color that washed over the peaks at sunset. To the native people who had lived at the foot of the mountains for hundreds of years before the Spanish arrived, they were "the place where the sun danced."

To Kerney, both names perfectly described the mountains. At times, he'd seen a deep mahogany-red color tint the peaks, and on certain monsoon days had watched shafts of sunlight flit like nimble waves across the rain-darkened range. One night he'd stood in awe as the full moon rose, backlighting a bank of clouds behind the mountains, creating a creamy white mantle that draped down to the foothills.

With Sara and Patrick on the other side of the country, Kerney filled his free time with home improvement projects that kept his hands busy and his mind occupied. His latest undertaking was a rock wall that, when finished, would enclose a long planting bed on the east side of the house. He'd bought a truckload of flat landscaping rock from a quarry and was teaching himself how to cut, fit, and dry stack the stone to create a three-foot-high wall. So far, he'd trenched the foundation and leveled the grade. Now it was time to start laying in the largest, widest stones as the base course.

He arrived home, changed into jeans and a long-sleeved shirt, and started working up a sweat in the late afternoon sun. He'd planned the wall to curve and join up with the end of the south-facing portal, and he found that cutting the stones to make the bend was no easy matter.

He stood up to get another rock and saw a car enter the ranch road through the meadow and move up the hill. Even from a distance Kerney could see it was an unmarked police unit. The make of the vehicle, the spotlight mounted on the driver-side door, and the two trunk-mounted antennas were dead giveaways. But he didn't have any idea who the driver might be.

At a hose bib, he splashed water on his face, wiped a sleeve over his damp, matted hair, put his cap back on, and walked to the car as it slowed to a stop in the driveway.

Agent Joe Valdez got out and walked to him. "Building a wall?" he asked as he shook Kerney's hand.

"Trying to," Kerney asked. "What brings you out to the boonies?"

"I'm driving down to Carlsbad for an early morning meeting," Joe said as he walked over to the line of rocks Kerney had laid. "Since you're on my way, I thought I'd stop by to tell you what I've learned about Clifford Spalding."

Valdez knelt down and studied the partial line of rock Kerney had placed in the trench. "Are you planning to dry stack or use mortar?"

"I plan to dry stack," Kerney said.

"How high is the wall going to be?" Joe asked as he jiggled a stone to test its stability. It was firmly placed.

"Three feet," Kerney replied.

Joe shook his head and rose. "Your foundation is too narrow. You'll need to double the size of it."

"You know about this stuff?" Kerney asked.

"My grandfather was a stone mason," Joe said, with a nod of his head. "I used to work for him in the summertime. Will it be a free-standing or a retaining wall?"

"Retaining," Kerney said. "I'll backfill it with topsoil and eventually put in a flowerbed and a flagstone path."

"You'll need to slope it for drainage, otherwise it will give way over time," Joe said as he walked along the empty part of the trench. "That's one of the reasons your foundation has to be wider, so you can step it back a bit and still have support at the base."

"Should I start over?" Kerney asked.

"I would," Joe said, glancing at Kerney's rock pile. "And you might want to order more rock. You've only got half of what you'll need."

"Thanks for the advice," Kerney said.

"That's about all the help I can give you," Joe replied with a smile, "because this thing with Clifford Spalding is a washout. There's no way I can track down the source of the money Spalding used to buy the leasehold for the Santa Fe hotel or pay his way out of bankruptcy. Nobody keeps financial records for thirty years, unless there are potential litigation issues, and there weren't any with Spalding."

"How much money are we talking about?" Kerney asked.

"All together, a little over three hundred thousand," Joe said, "and none of it came from the life insurance policy on Spalding's son. That was for ten grand, and the beneficiary was Debbie Calderwood, who cashed it in, according to the insurance company records."

"Where do you think Clifford Spalding got that kind of money?" Kerney asked.

Valdez shrugged. "One source told me Spalding had no partners. Another, the lawyer who handled the lease agreement for the Santa Fe property, said he had an investor. The state has no record of a part-nership contract, so I'm assuming it was an informal, handshake arrangement."

"Did the lawyer give you the name of the investor?" Kerney asked.

"Nope," Joe replied. "He didn't handle that part of it, and Spald-ing made the first payment on the lease through his personal checking account. Even if I could have found the bank account he'd used, the record wouldn't be there. Banks only keep checking account informa-tion for six years."

"What about state and federal tax records?"

"You'd need to make a strong case for tax evasion first, before we could access that information," Joe replied. "Same with bank de-posit reports to the feds when the amount is in excess of ten thou-sand dollars."

"Did the insurance company have a record of where they sent the policy proceeds to Debbie Calderwood?" Kerney asked.

"Yeah," Joe replied, stepping off toward his unit. "I'll get my notes." He came back and opened a file. "It was sent to general deliv-ery in Taos."

"Thanks, Joe," Kerney said.

"Sorry I couldn't have been more helpful," Valdez replied. "Good luck with the wall."

Kerney glanced at his project. He'd put a lot of hours into doing it wrong, and now he'd have to start over again from scratch. "I might as well get it right," he said.

Valdez laughed and nodded in agreement.

Kerney waved as Joe drove away, thinking maybe his research hadn't been a complete waste of time. According to Lou Ferry, the PI Clifford Spalding had hired and then fired for failing to continue falsifying his investigative reports, Debbie Calderwood had spent some time in Taos living on a commune before disappearing into southern Colorado.

While the communes around Taos were long gone, many of the old hippies from the sixties and early seventies remained. They formed an alternative lifestyle community of fringe artists, environmental activists, ski bums, building contractors, and reconstructed small business owners.

Kerney decided to pay the Taos police a call in the morning. Given the small size of the town, surely the local cops had to know someone with connections to the old communes who remembered Debbie Calderwood.

It was worth a shot.

He turned to the rock work, and started lifting out the stones he'd so carefully leveled at the bottom of the trench.

*   *   *

Ramona Pino had left Mitch Griffin's house weighing a question that had troubled her all afternoon. Why had Griffin waived his rights and given carte blanche permission for the search without demanding a deal from the ADA? It made no sense. Surely, Griffin had to know what the cops would find. Was he just plain stupid, or protecting someone or something? If so, who or what?

Pino knew that a successful interrogation never happened unless you had enough information to pursue the facts by asking the right questions. Was Griffin afraid of somebody? His marijuana supplier perhaps? Or was there another, larger issue at stake that had caused Griffin to cave in so readily?

Ramona didn't think Griffin was stupid, which meant she had to try to get a handle on his motivation before questioning him again. She stopped her unit near the on-ramp to the interstate and thought about what he might be hiding. Nothing came to mind. She decided to make some phone calls to other law enforcement agencies in the morning to see if Griffin's name rang any bells.

Commuter traffic on the interstate had eased up. Ramona glanced at the dashboard clock, sighed, put her car in gear, and headed toward the office. Her shift had been over for hours and there was still reams of paperwork that had to be done for submission to the DA in the morning.

Sometimes she wondered why she liked her job so damn much.

ChapterEight

Kerney woke up stiff and sore. He'd worked on the garden wall until dusk, removing stones from the trench and expanding it so he could lay in a wider foundation as Joe Valdez had suggested. After a good hot soak in the shower, he dressed and drank a cup of tea at the breakfast table. Before he'd been gut shot by a drug dealer, Kerney had been a heavy coffee drinker, and sometimes he still missed the aroma and taste of it.

Always an early riser, Kerney watched dawn break through the French doors that opened onto the pergola. A thin layer of clouds on the horizon, washed pink by the first light, faded into pale ribbons as the sun bleached color from the dark blue morning sky, foretelling a still, dry day.

Across the pasture, peppered with dull green rabbitbrush and bunches of bluestem grass withered by drought, he could see the horse barn, sunlight now reflecting off the slant of the metal roof. It had stood empty since a day last summer when he'd found Soldier, a mustang he'd bought and gentled some years back, brutally slaughtered by a man who'd then tried to kill Kerney's family.

Behind the barn at the top of the hill stood an ancient piñon tree.

He'd buried Soldier in its shade and placed a boulder on top of the grave.

The tree was dead now, a victim of drought and bark beetles, the bare branches rising and jutting at odd angles against the skyline. He'd lost a lot of trees on his 1,240 acres and had cut most of them down, especially the dead thickets that dotted the land and posed the greatest fire danger. But the tree on the hilltop he'd let stand in Soldier's memory.

After rinsing out his cup, he walked into the living room and gathered up his keys, handheld radio, and cell phone. He took his sidearm from the locked gun cabinet, put it in a clip-on holster, and attached it to his belt. Today, he wore civvies, jeans, boots, and a white western-cut shirt, for his trip to Taos. But that would come later. First he'd stop by the office to see where things stood with Griffin and Dean, and make a call to the Taos PD to let them know he was coming and what he was looking for.

He glanced around the room. Sara's sense of style was everywhere. The matching soft Italian leather couch and love seat were arranged to give a view through the picture window to the canyon below. Cherrywood end tables held handsome pottery reading lamps, and under the glass coffee table a Tibetan area rug picked up the warm color of the Mexican tile floor. On the walls Sara had hung two western landscapes, the larger one an oil painting of his parents' ranch on the Tularosa Basin done by Erma Fergurson, his mother's lifelong friend and a renowned artist. Upon her death, Erma had bequeathed it to Kerney along with a parcel of northern New Mexico ranchland that had made him a rich man.

Right now, having money was the furthest thing from Kerney's mind. He was lonely for his wife and son and weary of seeing them so infrequently. He counted the days until he left for Arlington. He'd be with Sara and Patrick for two solid weeks, commuting to the FBI Academy at Quantico to attend an executive development seminar and teach several classes.

He would fly east on Friday, and the time couldn't pass quickly enough.

Day shift started at 6:30 in the morning and radio traffic on his handheld picked up as officers began broadcasting their call signs and reporting in. As he left the house he heard Sergeant Pino announce her arrival at headquarters. He'd ask her for a briefing as soon as he'd finished scanning the reports and paperwork.

*　　*　　*

It was mid-morning before Ramona Pino found the time to call other cop shops to ask if Mitch Griffin might be the target of a probe or a person of interest in an ongoing case. She came up empty, which wasn't surprising. Queries about suspects ate up time and often resulted in dead ends. But going through the exercise narrowed the focus and usually enhanced the investigation.

Unwilling to let her suspicions about Griffin's motives drop, Pino put in requests to federal, state, county, and municipal agencies asking for a records search of his name in all appropriate databases. The bureaucrats she spoke to warned that it would probably be several days before she heard anything back.

She pulled into the public parking lot at the county jail just in time to see Barry Foyt, the ADA who'd secured Griffin's voluntary permission to search, get out of his car. She honked the horn to get Foyt's attention, and he waved and waited for her at the front entrance.

"Did you get my evidence report on the Griffin house search?" Ramona asked as she approached Foyt. At five-three, she could almost look Foyt directly in the eye. He stood no more than five-six and was seriously balding, which made him look much older than his thirty-something years.

Foyt nodded. "It was a good haul," he said. "Congratulations. Let's hope we can use it."

"What do you mean?"

"Griffin lawyered up after we talked to him. He hired Patricia Delgado as counsel. Last night she got a court order to take a urine sample from Griffin for drug and alcohol screening by a private laboratory. The results should be in anytime."

"What does that do to us?" Ramona asked.

"If it tests positive, Delgado will likely argue that Griffin's permission to search should be excluded because he was under the influence and therefore not coherent at the time to make a rational decision. The same applies to Griffin's waiver of his Miranda rights."

Ramona shook her head. "He was coherent, dammit. Did you argue against Delgado's request?"

Foyt scowled humorously. "No, I let Delgado walk all over me. Of course I did. But the judge saw no reason not to sign the order. Under Miranda, any waiver must be knowing, intelligent, *and* voluntary. The judge would've been foolish to disallow it."

Foyt shifted his briefcase from one hand to the other. "If Delgado can make a strong case that both the Miranda warning waiver and the voluntary permission to search occurred while Griffin was mentally debilitated due to drugs or alcohol use, we could lose all the evidence you seized."

"The fruit of the poisoned tree," Romana said.

"Exactly. But we're not there yet. Pretrial discovery will require Delgado to show the results of the test and provide an expert opinion about the findings before asking the judge to exclude Griffin's confession and the evidence."

"I think Griffin rolled over on himself because he's hiding something or protecting someone."

"Like who or what?" Foyt asked.

"I don't know."

"Well, get a handle on it, Sergeant," Foyt said, "because this case might need all the ammunition we can muster."

"Are you here to make a deal?"

Foyt shook his head. "No, to listen to one. Want to come along?"

"You bet I do," Ramona replied, pushing open the door. "What's up with Dean?"

Foyt followed her into the public reception area where three female citizens were waiting to speak to their incarcerated loved ones. "He's in a holding cell at the courthouse awaiting arraignment."

"No problem with him, I hope," Ramona asked.

"Not so far."

They signed in and got buzzed through to the corridor that led to the interview rooms. Patricia Delgado stood in the hallway by an open door. At five-nine, she towered over both Pino and Foyt.

A former basketball star at one of the smaller state universities, Delgado kept in shape by running marathons, usually finishing in the top five for her age group. Single, still in her thirties, and attractive, she was romantically linked to a state senator rumored to have his eye on the governorship in the next election.

Ramona thought of Delgado as an ice princess, who hid her self-absorbed personality behind a veneer of charm. Today she wore a tailored tan pantsuit that accentuated her long legs. The smile on her face held all the false enthusiasm of a media spokesperson peddling a beauty aid.

"I'd almost given up on you," Delgado said, nodding at Foyt and giving Ramona a quizzical look. "I didn't realize you were bringing Sergeant Pino along."

"Is that a problem?" Foyt asked.

Delgado shrugged and gestured at the table inside the room where Griffin waited. "Not at all. I just hope you don't have any more little surprises for me."

"If your client has told you everything," Foyt said as he sat down, "there won't be. What's on your mind, counselor?"

Ramona slid into the seat next to Foyt and studied Griffin. He'd shaved and combed his hair back so that it stood up at his forehead like strands of wispy wire. He no longer looked like a faded country music star. The stress and anxiety of yesterday were gone, replaced by a blasé, untroubled expression.

"If you give him a pass on the drug dealing charges in exchange for his testimony against Mr. Dean," Delgado said, "he's agreed to cooperate."

"Mr. Griffin made that same offer to us yesterday," Foyt said huffily. "I didn't take it then. Why should I take it now when I've got more than enough evidence collected at the pharmacy to nail Dean on drug trafficking without the help of your client?"

Delgado leaned forward in her chair and smiled winningly. "Because he might be able to help you with the murder charges you've filed against Dean."

"I'm listening," Foyt said.

"Before we get into that, let me tell you that the lab report on Mr. Griffin's urinalysis came back positive for both alcohol and barbiturates. In fact, he was barely below the legal limit for intoxication hours after his arrest, and the thin layer chromatography and infrared spectrophotometer analysis shows that Mr. Griffin had ingested a significant amount of Seconal prior to being taken into custody.

"You'll get the details at the preliminary hearing when I move to have the evidence suppressed, the confession thrown out and the charges dismissed. I also plan to bring along expert witnesses who will testify that my client was in no condition to intelligently understand his rights or give an informed consent to search his premises."

Clearly irritated, Foyt rolled his tongue around his lips before speaking. "I'm not going to bargain with you based on a report I haven't seen."

Delgado flipped slowly through a leather-bound notecase with her long fingers and perfectly manicured nails. She extracted the report and gave it to Foyt. He read through it quickly and passed it to Ramona.

Delgado hadn't exaggerated. Ramona pushed the report across the table to Delgado. "Exactly what evidence will you ask to have suppressed?" she asked.

"The pharmaceuticals, of course," Delgado replied.

Ramona smiled. "But not the ten pounds of marijuana we found in the locked contractor's truck box on a garage shelf?"

The expression on Griffin's face turned from smug to stunned. "What?"

"All neatly wrapped in plastic bundles."

"That's not mine," Griffin said. "I don't know anything about that shit."

"Regardless of who it belongs to," Delgado said, putting a hand on Griffin's shoulder to shut him up, "it's still part of an illegal search."

"That's yet to be determined," Foyt said, switching his gaze from Delgado to Griffin. "Whose grass is it?"

"Not mine," Griffin repeated hotly.

"Let me do the talking, Mitch," Delgado said.

Griffin shook his head and the swept-back hairs on his forehead flopped and waved. "That's not my toolbox. It was left there by one of my subcontractors last week."

"Does this person have a name?" Ramona asked.

Delgado held up a hand. "Stop right there. This goes no further unless we have a deal."

Ramona watched Foyt think it through. If he went for Delgado's deal, he'd earn bragging rights for nailing three bad guys in one fell swoop and have one less case to prosecute. Faced with the possibility that the judge would rule in favor of Delgado's motions, Ramona didn't think Foyt would turn her down.

"Griffin gives us the marijuana dealer," Foyt said, "tells us what he knows about the Spalding homicide, and pleads out to intent to distribute."

"Unacceptable," Delgado replied. "This is his first offense."

"No, it's just the first time he's been caught," Ramona said.

Delgado sighed as she reached for her notecase. "I'm sorry we couldn't reach an agreement. We'll see you in court."

"But," Foyt said, "if Mr. Griffin would show some good faith and tell us what he knows about the Spalding murder case, I'll consider dropping the current charges."

"Agreed." Delgado nodded at Griffin.

He looked directly at Pino. "Like I told you, I never slept with Claudia Spalding, but I know this guy who said he did. He works as a wrangler at a horse rescue ranch down by Stanley, in the southern part of the county, or at least he used to. I haven't seen him in years."

"Go on," Ramona said.

"Anyway, Claudia was like a big supporter of the program, gave it money and volunteered to tour the schoolkids around who'd come out to the ranch on field trips. This guy tells me that he got pussy action from her, but cut it off when she asked him to help her arrange a little accident for her husband."

"What kind of accident?" Ramona asked.

"She wanted to bring Spalding down to the ranch, have the guy take them both out on a horseback ride, and then fake a bad fall. You know, the horse spooks, throws Spalding, and he dies in front of two witnesses."

"When was this?"

"While I was building her house, before she met Kim."

"Give me a name," Ramona said.

"Coe Evans," Griffin said. "I haven't seen him in two, three years."

Ramona got a physical description of Coe Evans and the location of the ranch before Delgado stopped the questioning, gave Foyt a toothy smile, and asked him to affirm the agreement.

Foyt met her smile with a cool look. "Only if your client is willing to give us the names of everyone he's sold to, every dealer and supplier he knows, precise information about this subcontractor he says stored the marijuana in his garage, *and* agrees to testify against Dean on both the murder and drug charges, if needed."

Griffin nodded. "That's cool with me. When can I get out?"

"As soon as you deliver," Ramona said, getting to her feet. "I'll have detectives here within the hour. How long it takes is completely up to you."

Foyt used his cell phone to clear his calendar for the remainder of the day so he could supervise the interrogation, and joined Ramona at the door.

"I'm hungry," Griffin said, grinning and patting his stomach.

"We'll have your lunch brought in," Ramona said. She walked with Foyt to the lobby and used her cell phone to arrange for a narcotics officer and detective to meet her at the jail pronto.

"You're not disappointed with the plea bargain, are you?" Foyt asked.

"A little bit," Ramona said, slipping the phone on her belt. "But I understand your reasoning."

What she didn't mention was her plan to have Griffin arrested for harboring a fugitive as soon as the interrogation was over and the current charges were dropped. She had the unshakable feeling that Griffin was still hiding something.

*　*　*

Marched into the courtroom by a uniformed officer, Kim Dean looked around for Stubbs, the moon-faced young lawyer, and didn't see him. Except for a judge, bailiff, court stenographer, a guy in a suit talking to the judge, and the cop who'd escorted him, the room was empty.

Dean had spent a miserable, sleepless night and an anxious morning at the jail. He'd almost abandoned any hope that Stubbs had gotten through to Claudia. But maybe he had, and Claudia was in the process of lining things up and getting him a good criminal attorney.

The cop put Dean in a seat and hovered behind him. What if the guy in the suit was his new attorney? Kim watched the man eagerly, waiting for him to turn from the judge and make a sign of recognition in his direction. Instead, he picked up his briefcase and left the courtroom just as Stubbs rushed in.

"Did you call my friend?" Dean whispered.

Stubbs scrunched into the seat next to Dean, and looked at the cop, who moved out of earshot.

"I did."

"And?"

"She thanked me for the call," Stubbs replied.

"That's it?" Dean hissed. "What did you say to her?"

"I told her where you were and what the pending charges are."

Kim took a deep breath. "Have you been contacted by another attorney?"

"Listen," Stubbs said in a terse whisper, the color rising on his cheeks. "You made it clear yesterday that I am not the lawyer you want. That's fine with me. Let's just get you through the arraignment. You'll be formally charged, given copies of the criminal complaints, and informed of your constitutional rights. I'll enter no plea on your behalf and you won't have to say anything. In fact, I don't want you to. The DA will ask for bail to be denied, and I'll argue against it. Don't get your hopes up. The charges are serious."

Feeling sorry for himself, Dean sighed with resignation.

"Have the police tried to talk to you since yesterday?" Stubbs asked.

Kim shook his head.

"Good. Keep it that way. If you want, I'll call around to several good criminal trial attorneys. You're going to need one."

Kim had waited long enough for Claudia to come through for him. "Why don't you do that?" he said brusquely

The judge shuffled papers and called Dean's case.

"Gladly," Stubbs said, getting to his feet.

*   *   *

The drive from Santa Fe to Taos was always a hassle, especially along the section of the two-lane twisting highway that paralleled the Rio Grande, where Kerney got stuck between two slow-moving motor homes.

In town, summer tourist traffic clogged the narrow main street, and it was stop-and-go all the way until Kerney reached the turnoff to the police station a few blocks north of the old plaza.

Inside, he met with Victor Pontsler, the police chief, who'd held the top cop position on three separate occasions over the span of his thirty-five-year career with the department. Twice in the past, Pontsler had been given the boot after a change in city administration, reverting back to his permanent rank of captain. Now he was back in the chief's chair again, this time to clean up the mess left behind by a heavy-handed predecessor who had driven officer morale into the ground and alienated the city fathers.

No more than five or six years older than Kerney, Pontsler kept himself in good shape. He weighed in at about a hundred and sixty pounds on a five-ten frame. He had a full head of hair and a crooked nose with a thin pink surgical scar that ran down to his nostrils. It had been badly broken years ago when Vic had responded to a fight in progress that turned into a bar brawl between cops and drunks.

Pontsler sat behind his cluttered desk and twirled a rubber band around his fingers. "I spent time after you called thinking about who you should talk to," he said. "Michael Winger would be your best bet. Back in the old hippie days he called himself Montana. He grew up in Manhattan and dropped out of college to come west and be part of the love generation. Moved here from San Francisco in the early seventies. He knew just about everybody who lived in the local communes."

"What else can you tell me about him?" Kerney asked.

"He's part of the establishment now, a successful businessman. Chamber of Commerce member, museum foundation patron, and all that. Owns the Blue Mountain Restaurant on the Paseo and the Blue Moon Gallery just off the plaza."

"He likes the color blue, I take it," Kerney said.

"You've got that right. He lives in a primo old hacienda on a ten-acre parcel off Kit Carson Road. He likes to play the cowboy role. Wears his hair pulled back in a ponytail and dresses in jeans and boots. He's divorced and has a Scandinavian girlfriend who teaches writing workshops and makes documentary films about oppressed women."

"Is he into anything shady?" Kerney asked.

"As far as I know, Winger is a solid, upstanding citizen."

"No trouble during his early days in town?"

"I know he smoked pot, but he never was busted."

"How did he get started in business?" Kerney asked.

Pontsler rubbed his thumb and fingers together. "He likes to say he started out buying southwestern art for himself before the market for it took off. But it was really family money that bankrolled him. His father was a big-time New York City architect."

Before leaving, Kerney got a rundown on a few more people Pontsler thought might be helpful. He locked his sidearm in the glove box of his unit, stuck his shield in his back pocket, and walked to Winger's restaurant.

Although it was touted as a mecca of Native American culture and had a long history as a famous art colony, Taos had never appealed much to Kerney. Parts of it were charming and the surrounding landscape was majestic. But the city was also a magnet for modern-day rogues and ruffians, frauds and fugitives, many of whom could be belligerent and nasty. Pontsler's sterling character reference aside, Kerney wondered if Winger fit into any of those categories.

The Blue Mountain Restaurant occupied an old adobe house with a lovely tree-shaded outdoor dining patio and two small separate dining rooms with low ceilings, light blue walls with framed photographs of early Taos scenes, and Mexican tile tables. The hostess, a tall, rather aloof woman with a clipped English accent, told Kerney that Winger was never at the restaurant until late in the afternoon and could most probably be found at his gallery. He half-expected her to say "ta-ta" or "cheerio" when he thanked her and left.

He walked down the Paseo toward the plaza. Slow-moving road traffic with its incessant noise lurched in both directions as groups of shoppers wandered in and out of the retail stores lining the street. Many establishments had sale signs in the windows, others displayed rugs, apparel, and handcrafted furniture in the front yards of old houses that had been converted to shops. Here and there a bored store clerk stood in a doorway watching the foot traffic pass by.

The hot, dry day had brought the tourists out in shorts, pullover short-sleeved shirts, and athletic walking shoes. Some were building up to painful sunburns, while others shaded their faces with newly purchased cheap straw cowboy hats or billed caps that proclaimed their visit to Taos.

The Blue Moon Gallery was an austere, modern space a few steps from the plaza. Overhead track lights and exposed heating and cooling ductwork hung from the ceiling, and the walls were filled with the works of the Taos Society of Artists, established in the early part of the twentieth century by a group of bohemian artists drawn to the area's culture and landscape.

Kerney trailed behind two couples cruising the gallery and immediately recognized the distinctive styles of Joseph Henry Sharp, Eanger Irving Couse, and Ernest Blumenschein, three of the founding members of the society. Only the placards next to the smaller paintings displayed a price. There was nothing on sale below twenty thousand dollars until you got to the lesser-known artists who'd joined the society later on, and even those works were pricy.

In the center space, randomly placed pale blue stands of various heights and widths held sculptures by Frederic Remington and Charles Russell.

Kerney admired everything before moving on to a small display of Maynard Dixon pencil drawings that were hung on a corridor that led to a suite of offices. A comely woman with curly hair and a bright smile approached him holding a gallery brochure and asked if he needed any assistance.

Kerney shook his head, showed the woman his shield, asked for Winger, and when she showed concern, quickly reassured her there was no reason for alarm.

She led him down the corridor and knocked on an open office door. Michael Winger sat at a large cherrywood desk in front of a flat screen LCD computer monitor. Behind him was a floor-to-ceiling shelving unit crammed with art reference books.

Winger looked up from the monitor and studied Kerney with interest as the woman explained the reason for the interruption. Then he stood, shook Kerney's hand, and gestured at an empty chair.

"You're the Santa Fe police chief," Winger said with a smile as Kerney eased into the chair.

"How do you know that?" Kerney asked as the woman left the office. Winger's gray, neatly tied-back hair draped several inches below the back of his neck. He had on an expensive blue designer work shirt that matched the color of his eyes, which held a look of amusement. On his left wrist he wore a vintage watch with a leather strap. His face was narrow, long, and deeply tanned.

"I have some business interests in Santa Fe," Winger replied, "so I spend a lot of time there. What can I do for you, Chief?"

"I'd be interested in what you could tell me about Debbie Calderwood."

Winger laughed. "Boy, I haven't heard that name in years. Debbie Calderwood. I may be the only person around who knew her real name. At the commune, she called herself Caitlin, after Dylan Thomas's wife. She was always quoting his poems to anyone who would listen. She liked to say he was the only true poet of the twentieth century."

"Certainly one of the best," Kerney said. "What was she like?"

"Waiflike in a very sexy way. She was tiny, but perfectly proportioned, with these huge innocent eyes. Every guy who saw her wanted to sleep with her, but she'd have none of it. She was really smart and had a steel-trap mind. You could talk to her about something and weeks later she'd remember the conversation almost verbatim."

"How did you meet her?"

"She just wandered into the commune with a sleeping bag and a backpack one day and stayed. Said she need to crash with us until her old man returned from Guatemala. Things were going downhill at the time. People were bailing to go back to the city, couples were breaking up, cash was tight, and the cops and the locals were hassling us. She had money, which helped a lot."

"How much money?"

"I don't know, but she was pretty free with it. She'd pay for the supplies we needed and put gas in the bus without anyone asking."

"How did you learn her real name?" Kerney asked.

Winger smiled. "We were all a bit paranoid about newcomers who showed up back then, worried about the lowlifes who wandered in, or outsiders nobody knew who might be narcs. This one guy showed up, stayed for a week, and then stole the International Scout we used to till the garden with an old plow. So I searched through her stuff one day after she came back from town, and found some general delivery letters addressed to her."

"Did you read the contents?"

"Yeah, they were innocent, chatty notes from some girlfriends in Albuquerque and Oregon."

"Did you confront her about her name?"

Winger laughed and shook his head. "No. We were all into giving ourselves or each other new names. Jimmy called himself Beaner; Sammy, a surfer guy from Hawaii, was Bear; Judy had an acid ceremony to change her name to Peachy Windsong. We had girls who called themselves Star, Feather, Aurora, Chamisa; guys who went by Owl and Rabbit. Owl held a drum circle to celebrate his new name."

"And you were Montana," Kerney said.

Winger looked sheepish. "You heard about that. I guess I grew up watching too many cowboy movies. In retrospect, it's funny now. But we were all just kids who'd dropped out of the establishment to create a brand-new society, live peacefully, and change the world. Free love, flower power, new identities, and lots of dynamite drugs. We wanted truth, enlightenment, sex, and freedom to get high without any bullshit."

Winger shifted in the chair, with a sunny look on his face as he warmed to the memories. "Looking back, we didn't have a clue what we were doing. We built chicken pens and then let the birds run wild, put up a big dome—sort of an aboveground kiva we used for family meetings—that almost blew down during the first big storm. Hell, the most substantial structure on the whole place was the outhouse. It had six seats and was made of scrap slat lumber."

"Looks like you came through it all right," Kerney said, thinking of his year in Nam, which occurred probably right about the time Winger and his friends had been trying to build their utopia.

Winger smiled. "Yeah, and most of it was fun. The one thing I learned was that you can't live without rules. It's a great idea but it doesn't float."

"Did Debbie do a lot of drugs?"

"She smoked some pot, but that's about it."

"How long did she stay?"

"Three, maybe four months, until her boyfriend showed up. They split two days after he arrived."

"When was that?" Kerney asked.

Winger closed his eyes and thought hard, "Shit, I don't know. Sometime in the summer. I was on a really bad head trip at the time. People were staying wasted, not pulling their share, or just bitching each other off right and left about the crops we couldn't raise, the goats that got into the garden, the pig nobody knew how to slaughter, the tools that had gone missing. There were maybe a dozen of us left and nobody was getting along or doing any work."

It was clear that Winger had told the story of his youthful, hippie escapades many times. Kerney decided Winger wasn't a rogue or ruffian, fraud or fugitive. He was just a guy who wore his counterculture experiences as a mark of his individuality.

"Tell me about the boyfriend," he said.

Winger made a face. "Now, that was strange. He showed up one day driving a new truck with Mexican license plates. It was like he didn't want to talk to anybody but Caitlin. They went off together in his truck. Two days later they came back, picked up her stuff, and left. That was the last time I saw her."

"Describe him to me."

"Average height, real fit looking, with a shaved head that he covered with a bandana. Oh yeah, and a fairly new mustache he was cultivating. Somebody asked him what had happened to his hair, and he said he'd picked up head lice and had to shave it off in Guatemala."

"Did he have a name?"

"Caitlin called him Breeze."

"Can you give me a little more detailed description of him?"

Winger chuckled. "I can go one better than that. Photography was my thing back in those days. I was documenting communal living and keeping a journal. My plan was to write a book about it someday. Never did get around to it. Anyway, I snuck around taking pictures of everyone and everything with a telephoto lens. Before Caitlin and Breeze left, I snapped a couple of frames from a distance for my rogues' gallery. Got a nice tight head shot of both of them."

"I need to see those photographs," Kerney said.

"Hell, I'll give you copies if you'll tell me what this is all about."

"If I'm right, Breeze may be a solider named George Spalding who faked his death in a helicopter crash in Vietnam. Why he did it, I still don't know."

Winger's eyes widened. "A deserter. Isn't that something?" He scribbled on a piece of paper and passed it across the desk. "Meet me at my house in an hour. It shouldn't take longer than that for me to dig through my archives and find the photographs."

"One more question," Kerney said, pocketing the address. "Do you have any idea where they went?"

Winger shook his head. "They could have gone anywhere. South to Silver City. There was a commune down there. Maybe up to Trinidad, Colorado. All I know is that they didn't hang around Taos."

Ninety minutes later, Kerney waited patiently in the library at Winger's house, a spacious room with massive ceiling beams, double adobe walls, and tall casement windows, painted on the outside in turquoise blue. Bookcases along three walls were filled with Native American artifacts, pre-Columbian pots, and rare first editions of early Southwestern archaeology studies. The room held two oversized antique Mexican tables that served as desks, each laden with books, old maps, file folders, photographs of high-end artwork, and related provenance documents.

He sat in front of the stone fireplace, impatiently waiting for Winger's return from what he called his archives room, located somewhere in the back of the rambling adobe. The sound of hurrying footsteps brought Kerney to his feet. Winger appeared, photographs in hand, which he passed to Kerney.

"Sorry to take so much time," Winger said. "I had to make copies and dig out my journal to look up when I took the photos."

"What?" Kerney asked, staring at the head shots of a young Debbie Calderwood and her boyfriend Breeze, also known as U.S. Army Specialist George Spalding, killed in action. His mother had been right on the money all along.

"I looked up the date I took the pictures," Winger repeated, "in my journal."

"When was that?" Kerney asked.

Winger told him.

"You've been a big help," Kerney said.

"So what happens now?" Winger asked.

"I'm going to find out where Spalding's grave is located and see who's buried in it."

ChapterNine

The day's events had forced Ellie Lowrey to focus solely on her duties as a patrol supervisor. She'd been called out to three major incidents: a domestic disturbance at a trailer park, a fatal traffic accident on a busy county road, and the pursuit and apprehension of an armed robber who'd knocked over a convenience store. At the Templeton substation, she hurried through her officers' shift and arrest reports, daily logs, and supplemental field narratives, before starting in on her own paperwork.

She left the office late, wondering what was up with Bill Price. Much earlier, he'd reported the mid-morning arrival of the evidence sent from Santa Fe by overnight air express, and had promised to walk it through the lab and get back to her with the results.

On Highway 101, heading toward San Luis Obispo, Ellie tried with no luck to reach Price by radio and cell phone. She called the detective unit main number, got put through to Lieutenant Macy, her old supervisor, and asked for Price.

"Where are you?" Macy asked.

"Halfway to headquarters," Ellie said, wondering why her question about Price's whereabouts hadn't been answered.

"Good," Macy replied. "See me when you get here."

Located outside of San Luis Obispo on the road to Morro Bay, headquarters consisted of the main sheriff's station, the adjacent county jail, and a separate building that housed the detective unit. Both the jail and the main station were flat-roof, brick-and-mortar structures landscaped with grass, shrubs, palm trees, and evergreens. The detective unit, on the other hand, was in a slant-roof, prefabricated building with aluminum siding. From a distance, it looked like a large industrial warehouse.

She found Macy in his office with Bill Price, who gave her a slightly woebegone glance and sank down in his chair.

"Ellie," Lieutenant Dante Macy said heartily, flashing a big smile. "Take a load off."

Ellie's antenna went up. Cordiality wasn't Macy's strong suit. She sat and studied her old boss. A former college football player with a degree in police science, Macy had fifteen years with the department. Big, black, and bright, he'd cleared more major felony cases than any other detective in the unit, past or present. Except for the rare times when Macy lost his temper, Ellie had enjoyed working with him.

Macy's quiet manner hid a strong-willed, compulsive nature. His passion for order, thoroughness, and adherence to rules showed in the way he dressed and the almost obsessive neatness of his office. Every day he came to work wearing a starched white dress shirt, a conservative tie knotted neatly at the collar, slacks with razor-sharp creases, highly polished shoes, and a sport coat. Ellie had never seen him with the tie loosened or his sleeves rolled up.

Macy's work space was no less formal: family pictures on the desk arranged just so, file folders neatly stacked in labeled bins, and behind the desk, rows of books and binders perfectly aligned.

Ellie fixed her gaze on Macy. "What's up, Lieutenant?"

"We got some results back from the lab on that evidence the Santa Fe PD sent us," Macy said, staring back at her. "The compound recovered from Dean's garage matches perfectly with the altered pill found in Clifford Spalding's possession. And there were traces of it on several of the tools."

"Was it the same potency?" Ellie asked.

"Yeah," Price interjected, mostly to break up the locked-in eye contact between the two officers. He'd seen them clash before and didn't want any part of it. "Way under the amount Spalding's doctor had prescribed."

"That's great," Ellie said, giving Price a glance. "I'll call the Santa Fe PD and give them the news."

"Already done," Macy said softly.

"I drove down here for you to tell me that?" Ellie asked hotly, her eyes riveted on Macy's face.

"Listen to me, Sergeant," Macy said calmly, "you're a patrol supervisor, not a detective anymore. You should have wrapped up the preliminary investigation at the ranch and immediately referred the case to my unit. That's procedure. If any uniformed officer had done differently while you were serving under me, you would have been in my office bitching up a storm about it. Correct?"

Ellie flushed and nodded.

"Instead, you call out the pathologist to do a rush autopsy without getting authorization, put an out-of-town police chief on the spot as a primary suspect, and then go tearing down to Santa Barbara where you manage to piss off the victim's widow, not once but twice."

"Is that your version of what I've been doing?" Ellie asked.

Macy spoke with care, giving equal inflection to every word. "That is what the sheriff would have heard if Detective Price hadn't been covering your ass, with my permission, I might add. Otherwise, I would have been compelled to write you up for failure to follow policy and engaging in activities outside the scope of your present assignment."

"I did most of that work on my own time," Ellie retorted, sending a quick smile of thanks in Price's direction, "and you've been getting all my field interview and follow-up narrative reports."

Macy nodded. "True enough." He looked at Price. "Give us a minute."

Price nodded, slipped out of his chair, and hurriedly left the office, closing the door behind him.

Macy leaned forward in his chair, clasped his hands together, and paused before speaking. "The question is, Sergeant, do you want to remain a patrol supervisor or voluntarily give up your stripes and return to your old job?"

"I worked hard for my promotion," Ellie said, shaking her head.

"But you didn't like the idea that you had to leave the detective unit to get it," Macy said.

"It's a dumb policy," Ellie said, "when officers have to leave their specialty to move ahead."

"If you want to rise through the ranks, you take the opportunities as they come," Macy said. "That's the name of the game."

"So it seems," Ellie replied.

"I am not faulting the work you've done on the case. In fact, I can easily understand why you were drawn to it. The complexity of the situation intrigued you. But you are a supervisor now, in a position that requires you to apply the rules to those who serve under you. Failing to do so weakens the entire command structure."

"Duly noted," Ellie said.

"Be glad this one-time warning comes from me and not your immediate superiors," Macy said, his tone edgy, a stern look fixed on his face. "Are we clear?"

"Yes, sir."

Macy relaxed and leaned back. "Do yourself a favor, Ellie," he said, now much more friendly. "Put in two full years as a patrol sergeant and then ask for a transfer back to my unit. I'll be looking to add another sergeant around that time."

"You'd take me back?" Ellie asked.

"In a flash," Macy said, breaking into a smile, "if you learn to lead by example."

*   *   *

Price walked Ellie out to the parking lot and said nothing until they reached her cruiser. Before retiring as an Army nurse, he'd supervised an intensive care unit, overseeing other nurses, technicians, and support staff, coordinating services with physicians, therapists, and pharmacists, managing the day-to-day operations.

Price wholeheartedly supported Macy's position. Ellie had to stop being a loose cannon for her own good and the department's.

"You don't look too badly chewed on," he said as Ellie unlocked the cruiser door.

"I'm not. Is Macy going to keep you on the case?"

"Yeah. Why do you ask?"

"Because unless Claudia Spalding's lover confirms her complicity in the murder, which he hasn't done yet, we won't be able to charge her. The hard evidence just isn't there."

"What are you saying?" Price asked.

"Right now, the only way to implicate her is by building a circumstantial case. Spalding showed me a legal document that supposedly gave her permission from her husband to engage in extramarital affairs. The lawyer who drew it up said it was valid, but is it truly?"

"Good question. I'll get a warrant for the original and run it through questioned documents."

Ellie began to say more, shook it off, and got into the vehicle.

"What?" Price asked, holding the door open.

"Nothing," Ellie replied. "But if a Sergeant Ramona Pino from the Santa Fe Police Department passes along any anonymous tips, you might want to check them out."

Ellie's intuition, her ability to absorb details, her perseverance, and her superior intelligence put her far beyond the pack as an investigator. But she could be bull-headed, a trait that had caused her trouble in the past.

"Don't risk your stripes, Ellie," he said.

"I wouldn't think of it," she said, pulling the car door closed.

Price watched her drive off, wondering if he should share his gut feeling about her with Macy. He decided to let it ride. Maybe Ellie could keep herself from going over the line.

*　　*　　*

The six-hour interrogation of Mitch Griffin combined with other details and facts developed during the day made Ramona Pino feel overloaded with tasks to accomplish, information to sort through, and assignments to make.

First off, Kim Dean had been denied bail and remained in jail, just where Ramona wanted him. He'd fired his lawyer, hired an experienced criminal trial attorney, and still wasn't talking.

Even if Dean continued to stay dummied up, the lab results from California added heavy weight to the evidence against him. As for the other charges, Griffin's testimony would go a long way toward securing multiple convictions.

But that still left Claudia Spalding in her California mansion as free as a bird. Finding Coe Evans, the man Claudia Spalding had allegedly asked to help murder her husband, was critical if Ramona had any hope of turning that situation around. But Evans, who no longer worked at the horse rescue ranch, had dropped out of sight, whereabouts unknown.

Ramona had detectives on the phones, talking to Evans's former coworkers and old acquaintances, checking with utility and phone companies and the postal service, querying banks and credit card companies. So far, he remained off the radar screen.

Locating Evans was just one of the tasks Ramona was juggling. Griffin had identified his framing subcontractor, Greg Lacy, as the man who'd left the ten pounds of grass in his garage. A detective sent out to Lacy's house had reported no one at home. A neighbor confirmed Griffin's statement that Lacy was camping somewhere down in the Gila National Forest.

Ramona had questioned Griffin closely about why Lacy's toolbox had been stored in his garage, and his response had sounded plausible. Many of the subs he hired used his garage and land to store tools and excess materials. They would often come to pick things up or

drop things off even when he wasn't home. Besides, his current building projects were just a few miles away from his house, which made it
all the more convenient as a storage site.

Still, Ramona hadn't bought it. Was the grass really Lacy's, or was
it all a big lie on Griffin's part? Until they found Lacy and talked to
him, that question remained unanswered.

Through her open office door, Ramona could hear her team at
work. All of them were well into their second shifts, clacking away at
keyboards, talking quietly on phones, stapling reports and shuffling
papers, compiling information. Before she turned out the lights and
called it a day, she would screen every bit of it.

Two narcotics officers, with the assistance of a member of the Tri-
County Drug Enforcement Task Force, were working to verify the
identities of the users, dealers, and suppliers Griffin had named. Detective Matt Chacon was on the horn calling around to learn more
about Greg Lacy's personal life, business dealings, employees, and
friends. Other team members were working up evidence sheets, doing
field reports, writing narratives.

Her phone rang and she picked up.

"Why didn't you tell me you were going to arrest Griffin on harboring a fugitive charges?" Barry Foyt asked, his voice sputtering
with anger.

"Did you really want to let him completely off the hook?" Ramona
replied calmly.

"You blindsided me."

"No, I upheld my sworn duty," Ramona said.

"Don't give me that technical bullshit. You were there when I
struck the deal with Delgado."

"Nothing pertaining to dropping any future charges was agreed
to, as I recall."

"I can recommend to the DA that we decline to prosecute."

"I'm sure Delgado and Griffin would appreciate that," Ramona
said, trying to bite back on the heavy sarcasm without success. "Is
there anything else you wish to say to me?"

"Griffin made bail thirty minutes ago."

"Thanks for the heads-up."

Foyt grunted in reply and disconnected.

The phone in Ramona's hand brought to mind Ellie Lowrey. Earlier, she had left Lowrey a brief voice mail message summarizing the events of the day, particularly the news that Claudia Spalding might have tried to mastermind her husband's murder with another lover long before Kim Dean took up the gauntlet and actually did it. Surely, that should have sparked Ellie's interest enough to return her call.

She shrugged Lowrey off for the moment, put the phone down, and turned her attention back to matters at hand, only to be interrupted by Matt Chacon, who swooped into the office waving a piece of paper.

"This came in from Lacy's credit card company," he said as he settled into the straight-back office chair. "In the last four years, he's taken five international trips, one to Haiti, two to Amsterdam, and two to Bangkok, all sex tourist destinations."

Ramona looked at the faxed report. "Okay, so he likes whores. What else have you learned about him?"

"He's a bachelor with no current girlfriend," Matt replied. "Like Griffin, he lives alone and runs his business out of his house. Hires mostly locals and a few Mexicans, pays them decent wages, and has a good credit rating. He has several close friends, but according to Lacy's foreman, Griffin isn't one of them. Their relationship is strictly business."

"No wants or warrants?"

Chacon shook his head. "He's got a clean sheet, a good reputation with other contractors who use him, and requires all his employees to undergo periodic drug screening. I think Griffin made a bogus accusation."

"What kind of vehicles does Lacy own?" Ramona asked.

"Just one, according to motor vehicles: a late model, midsize, four-wheel-drive pickup truck."

Ramona pushed back her chair and stood. "Let's go."

"Where to?" Matt asked.

"Griffin lied. The toolbox that held the grass fits a full-size truck bed. He just made bail on the harboring charge. We've got to find him before he runs."

*   *   *

To keep himself informed of activities in the field, Kerney often listened to radio traffic while working. He was in his office about to call Alice Spalding and Penelope Parker when a be-on-the-lookout advisory for Mitch Griffin went out, followed by a secure channel broadcast from Ramona Pino alerting dispatch that she and Detective Chacon were on their way to Griffin's house.

Kerney was certain that Pino and Chacon didn't know what he'd put into play with Griffin. Did they have fresh information they'd gathered from some other source? Or were they just looking to find him for another round of questioning?

He had half a notion to call Pino for an update, or order her back to headquarters. He passed on both ideas. He thought about tagging along to get a firsthand look at the action, and decided against it, although it certainly wouldn't be out of character. Instead, he dialed a cell phone number and told the man who answered that Pino and Chacon might be coming his way.

He sat back, wondering what he might have to deal with when Pino and Chacon returned. Because he didn't run his department by flying a desk in an office, Kerney had built a reputation as a hands-on chief. When time allowed, he liked to get out into the field and watch his officers in action. It reduced the bureaucratic filter between himself and his people.

Occasionally he'd work a patrol or detective shift, pull duty on the Plaza during a major community event, oversee a crime scene investigation, or assist at a DWI checkpoint on a holiday weekend.

He thought back to the event that had established his reputation. During his second week on the job, he'd been driving back to headquarters after a meeting with city hall honchos when a lowered, raked, two-tone '57 Chevy traveling at a high rate of speed cut him off in heavy traffic on Cerrillos Road. Driving an unmarked unit and wearing civvies because his uniforms weren't ready, he'd given chase. He forced the driver into a parking lot and put the young Hispanic male facedown on the pavement.

When he approached to do a pat down for weapons, the kid told him he was a city undercover narcotics officer on assignment with the Tri-Country Drug Enforcement Task Force. He carried no credentials, and was dressed like a gangbanger in baggy jeans, an oversized baseball shirt, and expensive athletic shoes.

Kerney questioned the kid, who rattled off the name of his supervisor and said he was on his way to a drug buy at a city park. Unconvinced, Kerney asked dispatch to send a patrol supervisor to his location ASAP, and left the young man spread-eagled with his hands clasped at the back of his head in full view of traffic on Cerrillos Road.

A patrol supervisor rolled up within minutes. The sergeant took one look at the kid on the pavement, killed his emergency lights, and approached Kerney, trying hard not to smile.

"Chief," the sergeant said, "I see you've met Officer Aragon. What was he doing?"

"Speeding, reckless driving, and public endangerment," Kerney said.

"Okay," the sergeant said slowly in a voice loud enough for Aragon to hear. "Then I think I'd better pretend to arrest him, otherwise we might blow his cover. He's an undercover narcotics officer, you know."

Kerney tried to keep a straight face. "So he said." He watched the sergeant cuff Aragon, pull him upright, and put him in the backseat of his unit. After a brief exchange of words, the sergeant closed the door and returned.

"Thanks for your help," Kerney said, trying not to look sheepish.

"Sure thing, Chief," the sergeant said cautiously. "You do know that only uniformed officers in marked units are authorized under state law to enforce the motor vehicle code and write traffic citations."

"I do know that," Kerney said flatly. "What did Officer Aragon have to say for himself?"

"Except for being worried that he started out on the wrong foot with the new chief, Officer Aragon said he doesn't mind that you busted him. He thinks it will give him credibility with the gang-bangers he's infiltrated."

"Tell him I was glad to be of help," Kerney said, "and to slow it down."

"Yes, sir. I'll give him the word." The sergeant eyed Kerney cautiously. "Technically, I should record this incident in my log and dailies."

"Write it up, Sergeant," Kerney replied. "There's no reason for both of us to be rule breakers."

The sergeant smiled with relief.

"Don't embellish the story too much, Sergeant."

The sergeant's smile changed to a grin. "There's no need for that, Chief."

As Kerney expected, news of the incident had spread like wildfire throughout the department, creating a lot of amused head shaking among the troops about their new chief.

Kerney returned his thoughts to Sergeant Pino. It was quite likely she'd come looking for him with blood in her eye if she happened to encounter DEA Special Agent Evan Winslow.

He called Penelope Parker, hedged a bit on the details, and told her he had some indication that George Spalding might not have died in Vietnam.

"Oh, Alice will be so happy to hear that," Parker replied, a pleased lilt to her voice. "Will you be coming out here to do more investigating?"

"I doubt it," Kerney said. "I need to know where George is buried."

"At the Fort Bayard National Cemetery in New Mexico," Parker said. "At least what could be found of him."

"Meaning what?"

"The bodies had basically been incinerated in the crash. Identification was made primarily by dog tags, remnants of uniforms, and dental records."

"Who supplied the dental records? The military or the family?"

"I don't know."

"Were all the victims' identities verified?" Kerney asked.

"You're asking me for information I don't have," Parker replied. "Remember, this happened long before my time. I do know that after the divorce, Alice wanted George's remains disinterred so that a DNA test could be made. She wanted to use the latest technology to prove that he was still alive. But Clifford stopped it by getting a judge to rule that both parents would have to agree to the exhumation."

"Who was the judge?"

"I don't remember his name, but he was located in Silver City, New Mexico, near the cemetery where George was buried. I typed all the original correspondence. Alice's lawyer should have the particulars."

"I'll need those," Kerney said. "Would Alice be willing to resubmit a request to disinter the body and also provide a DNA sample for comparison purposes? A simple cotton swab for saliva inside her mouth should be all that's required."

"I'm sure she'll want to cooperate."

"Give me her lawyer's name and phone number and I'll get the ball rolling."

"How quickly do you plan to act?" Parker asked, after reading off the information.

"I'd like to move fast and get the skeletal remains tested and compared to Alice's DNA as soon as possible," Kerney replied. "We can use a private lab in Albuquerque to do the analysis. How soon can you get Alice in for a mouth swab?"

"Her doctor makes house calls," Parker said, excitement rising in her voice. "I'll see if he can come out right away. Otherwise, I'll make an appointment and take her to his office as soon as possible."

"Tell him exactly what the swab is for and ask him to handle it like evidence. He's to wear gloves and seal the swab in a clear plastic bag. Have him send it to me by overnight air express."

"Should I tell Captain Chase about this?" Parker asked, after Kerney gave her his mailing address. "He called a day ago asking if I've spoken to you again."

"Please don't tell him anything."

"You make it sound like a conspiracy," Parker whispered delightedly.

Kerney sidestepped the remark. "You'll get a call later today from a New Mexico judge who will want to verify Alice's willingness to have the body exhumed. Make sure she's prepared to give consent."

"That shouldn't be a problem."

"If you have a fax machine at the house, give me the number and I'll send you an exhumation request form. Fax it back as soon as Alice signs it."

"What are you planning to do to the body?"

"We'll take a bone sample from the skeleton and have it compared to Alice's DNA. Also, I'll ask for fresh X-rays of the teeth."

"Who will do the examination?" Parker asked.

"A forensic anthropologist," Kerney replied.

"How long will this take to accomplish?"

"Disinterring the body can be done quickly," Kerney said. "Using a private lab for the testing will cut the turnaround time significantly. We should have results and some answers within a matter of a few weeks, if not sooner."

"I'd better go get Alice ready for all of this," Parker said.

"Thank you, Ms. Parker."

"Please, it's Penelope," Parker replied with a girlish, teasing tone. "Although I must say I like a gentleman with good manners."

Kerney laughed politely, got the fax number, disconnected, and called Alice Spalding's lawyer.

*   *   *

Ramona Pino and Matt Chacon rolled up to Griffin's house to find the front door ajar and nobody home. They did a quick visual room check, and found clothes missing from the master bedroom closet and a laptop computer gone from a desk in the home office.

Ramona stood in the middle of the living room and gazed out the open front door. "Okay, he's running," she said. "But why? What for? And where?"

Chacon wandered around the room pulling furniture away from the walls, kicking over scatter rugs, pummeling the pillows on the eight-foot-long couch. "Drugs," he said. "It's gotta be drugs."

Ramona walked to the telephone, punched in the code to connect to the number of the last incoming call, listened to a clerk answer at a local building supplier, and disconnected. "He's dealing pharmaceuticals and weed," she said. "What else?"

"Harder stuff," Chacon suggested, "or maybe a heavy volume of grass."

"Ten pounds isn't exactly lightweight." Ramona listened to the messages on the answering machine. One from a slightly pissed-off homeowner, demanding to know why Griffin hadn't yet fixed the tile caulking on the kitchen backsplash, caught her attention.

"But let's assume," she said, "he has a really big stash warehoused somewhere. Do we know where Griffin is building houses? Supposedly, it's nearby."

Chacon shook his head. "There are new houses going up all around La Cienega."

Ramona played back the message again, wrote down the irate homeowner's number, called, and got a busy tone. "Think upscale houses," she said as she flipped through a phone book. The homeowner wasn't listed.

"Willow Creek Estates," Chacon said, "near the interstate."

Ramona dropped the phone in the cradle. "No listing." She pawed through a file drawer in the desk and pulled out a copy of the construction contract for the homeowner. "The guy who called Griffin lives on La Jara Way."

"Which means scrub willow in Spanish," Chacon said.

Ramona headed for the door. "Let's take a tour of Willow Creek Estates."

The subdivision covered a lot of territory and was so new none of their maps included it. They divided it up into halves, and cruised the paved streets. Once a ranch owned by a former governor, it was slowly being transformed into a gated residential community. There were large faux adobe houses on five- and ten-acre lots. Some were nestled along a tree windbreak that shielded the highway from view, while others were tucked out of sight behind low hills. Occupied homes were scattered here and there between houses in various stages of construction. All of them were typical Santa Fe style, with flat roofs, enclosed courtyards, portals, earth-tone stucco finishes, two or more fireplaces, and attached garages. Although not as expensive as the more exclusive foothills houses favored by the very rich, Ramona figured they had to be selling in the mid-to-high six-figure range.

She topped out on a hill and saw four unmarked vehicles, all with emergency lights flashing, parked in front of an unfinished house covered in a plaster scratch coat. Griffin's pickup truck stood next to a small construction trailer. Men wearing Windbreakers were going in and out of the house and trailer.

By radio, she gave Matt Chacon the word, gave dispatch her twenty, and asked what was up at her location.

"We have no reported activity in your area," dispatch replied.

"Well, get ready for some." Ramona hit her emergency lights and drove toward the house. The man who stopped her at the driveway had a DEA ID attached to a lanyard around his neck.

"This is as far as you go, Sergeant Pino," Special Agent Evan Winslow said.

"What a surprise," Ramona said. "Shouldn't you be at the broker-age office managing wealth for your clients? I need Mitch Griffin."

"You can't have him," Winslow said as he opened the car door and gestured for Ramona to get out.

"Why not?" Ramona asked, refusing to budge. In the rearview mirror she could see Matt Chacon's unit coming down the road.

Winslow gauged the angry look on Pino's face. "Well, I suppose you deserve some explanation."

"Damn right I do," Ramona said, picking up her radio microphone, "and if I don't get one, I'm calling in this little undercover DEA raid so that every citizen with a police scanner can hear what's going on. It will be in tomorrow's paper, along with your name."

Winslow considered the threat and nodded slowly. "Ask your partner to stay back and I'll tell you what I can, if you promise to discuss it only with your chief."

Ramona pulled her car door closed, radioed Chacon to hold his position, and told Winslow to get in.

Winslow settled into the passenger seat and turned to face her. "I need your promise, Sergeant Pino."

"Yeah, you got it," Ramona said, still steamed.

"Griffin may be able to give me a major drug supplier we've been trying to bust and flip for the past year, so we can shut down a Colombian pipeline."

"How does Griffin figure into your plan?" Ramona asked.

"The supplier offers one-stop shopping to wealthy clients in the privacy of their homes—coke, heroin, speed, grass, designer drugs. He imports the hard stuff and buys whatever else he needs from independent wholesalers here in the States. That ten pounds of grass you found in Griffin's garage put us on to him. We knew the supplier was buying weed locally, but we didn't know from whom."

"Who in the hell told you about the ten pounds of grass?" Ramona demanded. "That's confidential information. Nothing has been released about it."

"Think it through, Sergeant," Winslow said.

Ramona leaned back against the headrest and let out a frustrated sigh. It all made sense; the chain went from Chief Kerney to Special Agent Winslow to Griffin. "What's in the construction trailer?"

"About three-quarters of a million dollars of high quality mari-juana freshly imported from Mexico. According to Griffin, it arrived right after you busted him. He was planning to hitch the trailer to his truck and tow it away when we got here."

"So you bailed Griffin out of jail and put a tail on him," Ramona said. "Where is he?"

"Inside the house," Winslow answered.

"I need to speak to him now."

"Not yet," Winslow replied, opening the passenger door. "Maybe never."

"You can't be serious," Ramona snapped. "He's a major witness in a homicide case. I need his testimony."

Winslow got out of the car, bent down to look at Pino, and nodded in the direction of Matt Chacon's unit parked on the road at the top of the hill. "Talk to your chief, Sergeant, and tell your partner noth-ing about me or this conversation."

"What in the hell do I say to him?"

"You're a sergeant. Pull rank, if you have to. Tell him he has no need to know. If that doesn't work, I suggest you tell him to ask for a sit-down with Chief Kerney."

Winslow closed the door and walked away just as dispatch asked Ramona for a status update. She cleared herself from the twenty, and told dispatch she and Chacon were returning to headquarters.

Matt came on the air, asking for information. Ramona had him switch to the secure channel, gave him the ten code for an undercover operation, and told him they'd talk more back at headquarters. Frus-trated by Chief Kerney's actions, she squealed rubber backing out of the driveway.

ChapterTen

Kerney's attempts to hurry along the approval process for the exhumation of the body buried at the Fort Bayard National Cemetery ran into some serious snags. He thought that Alice Spalding's permission and a judge's order would be all he needed, and hadn't considered the additional layers of bureaucracy he had to go through to get final authorization.

Because George Spalding was a soldier buried at a national cemetery, Kerney faced the daunting task of dealing with the federal government. Both the U.S. Attorney's Office in Albuquerque and the Department of Veterans Affairs had to sign off on the petition, and they wanted extensive documentation, plus authorization from the Department of Defense.

While Helen Muiz faxed documents to the agencies, Kerney decided to call Sara at the Pentagon. As a military police corps lieutenant colonel, perhaps she tell him how to push things along with the Army.

"You rarely call me at work," Sara said. "Are you missing me?"

"Badly," Kerney said, "but this is business. What would it take to get expedited permission for me to exhume the body of a soldier buried at a national cemetery?"

"Well, that just wiped a cheery smile off my face," Sara said crossly. "Start at the beginning and tell me why this is such an emergency."

He gave her the full rundown on George Spalding and the very real possibility that there was a misidentified body in a military grave.

"Okay," Sara said, "that's serious and definitely needs to be looked into. But why the urgency?"

The question pulled Kerney up short. "You're right. I'm being impatient."

"You always get frustrated when you have to wait for other people to get things done," Sara said. "I don't know what I can do to help. I'll look into it. Have Helen fax me copies of everything you have and I'll call you back when I know something. You're going to owe me for this one, Kerney."

"What's the price I'll have to pay?"

"We can dicker about it once you're here. I've got to run. Talk to you soon."

Over the radio, he heard Ramona Pino and Matt Chacon announce their arrival at headquarters to dispatch. Within minutes, Pino poked her head inside his open door and moved briskly to the nearest chair, her back straight and shoulders squared. Kerney could tell she was steamed, and why not? Losing the chance at a slam dunk major felony conviction would piss off any good detective.

"You gave Mitch Griffin to Winslow," she said, "and I'd like to know why."

"I'm sure Agent Winslow told you what he could."

"Not nearly enough," Ramona said, "and he won't give me access to Griffin."

"To use an old cliche, Winslow has bigger fish to fry right now. If you're concerned about not getting credit for the good work you've done, don't be. I'm aware of the significant contribution you and your team have made. So is Winslow."

Ramona blushed angrily. "That's not what's on my mind, Chief. Griffin made a deal with us, got major charges dropped because of it, and now he walks, free and clear courtesy of the DEA, with no commitment to testify against Dean on the murder one and trafficking charges. That weakens my case substantially."

"The lab results from California pretty much confirm that Dean substituted Spalding's thyroid medication."

"That doesn't get me any closer to filing charges against Claudia Spalding."

"We've talked about this," Kerney replied. "If Dean doesn't crack, you'll have to take a different route to implicate her."

"That's already under way," Ramona said. "We're checking to see if Claudia made overtures to other men to help murder her husband. Griffin told me a story about a guy who turned down such an invitation before Dean arrived on the scene. It may be a tall tale, but we've got a name and we're trying to find him."

"Establishing prior intent helps," Kerney said. "But we haven't nailed down a clear motive yet."

"We know she stands to inherit a bundle of money," Ramona said.

"It would be reasonable to assume that she was eager to get her hands on Clifford's wealth. But why the hurry? Spalding indulged her. She lacked for nothing, including his permission to get her sexual needs met elsewhere."

"Right now, I'm stymied, Chief," Ramona said, "and losing Griffin as an informant and a witness doesn't help matters." She stopped short of saying more and took a deep breath.

"You're angry because I kept you in the dark about Winslow."

Ramona gave a tight nod of her head.

"Until now, except for me, no one in this department or any other local law enforcement agency knew about Agent Winslow's undercover operation. I have full confidence that you and Detective Chacon will also honor that commitment to silence. Or do I need to be more emphatic?"

"No, sir," Ramona said tersely.

"Good. Don't let this situation shake your focus, Sergeant. Griffin still may do time. But if not, he's permanently out of business and DEA has gained a major informant. You've got Dean for murder one. Make the same thing happen with Claudia Spalding."

Ramona smiled thinly and rose. "Yes, sir."

Kerney smiled. "Put your frustration aside, Sergeant. Most of the time you handle it well."

Ramona got the sugarcoated warning. "I'm sorry if I seemed abrupt, Chief."

"No harm done," Kerney replied.

Ramona left and Kerney thumbed through a plan Larry Otero had prepared for rearranging offices and renovating space in the building now that the department's dispatch and 911 unit had moved to the new regional communication center housed at the county law enforcement center.

It was a good plan, but it didn't capture Kerney's interest. He wanted Sara to call with word that she'd cleared the decks and he could get on with the exhumation.

He occupied himself by working on the details of the George Spalding matter that he could control. He lined up a forensic anthropologist, arranged for a private lab to do the DNA testing, confirmed that Alice Spalding's saliva sample had been sent by overnight express, and got the judge's signed exhumation order faxed to Sara, the VA, and the U.S. Attorney.

When he finished, he thought about calling Sara and dismissed the idea. He'd already asked her for a big favor. The least he could do was wait patiently to hear back. Holding that thought in mind, Kerney forced his attention on a fresh stack of documents Helen Muiz had deposited on his desk.

*   *   *

Dressed in stonewashed blue jeans, lightweight walking shoes, and a peach-colored pullover top, Ellie Lowrey left her house, greeted by a fair evening with calm, blue skies showing the first hint of sunset. The air, still moist from a brief shower that earlier in the day had brushed the coastal mountains, felt cool against her face.

She drove with her car windows down, trying hard to put the Spalding murder investigation behind her. Lieutenant Macy's lecture should have been warning enough. But over a light dinner, a summer salad with orange slices, greens, and a vinaigrette dressing, Ellie couldn't convince herself to leave things well enough alone. She'd promised Ramona Pino she'd take a closer look at Claudia Spalding's extramarital love life, and she felt honor-bound to follow through.

According to her phone message, Ramona had scored a possible lead on one of Claudia's former lovers, a man named Coe Evans. Supposedly, Evans had been approached by Claudia to join in a murder plot that predated Kim Dean. For now, it was nothing more than hearsay. But Ramona had made some progress, which was more than Ellie could claim.

She took a back road out of Templeton past soft, hilly pastureland dotted with cattle resting under oak trees, yearlings and colts trotting along enclosed white fences bordering the lane, and tidy rows of grapevines winding up gentle inclines.

She drove quickly through Atascadero, a city gutted by the El Camino Real and Highway 101, a place with no true heart left, no real sense of community. Outside of town, she stayed on country roads, driving aimlessly, trying without much success to shake thoughts of Claudia Spalding from her mind.

Spalding was an attractive, sophisticated, calculating, and smart woman, with a smugness and a cold edge to her. She'd swatted away Ellie's attempts to crack her defenses. What would it take to break her down?

Ellie sat in her parked car looking down at the training track of the Double J Ranch. Across the way, perched on a small rise, was the house where Ken Wheeler, the ranch manager, lived.

She wondered if Wheeler felt lucky to live on a picture-perfect ranch, working with beautiful, pampered animals, spending every day inside an enchanted bubble sheltered from ugliness, crime, depravity, and violence.

Cops were supposed to be cavalier about the grotesque and monstrous things people do to each other, immune to the hideous and the horrible. At least, that was the way Hollywood and the hard-boiled crime writers portrayed them. Ellie hadn't gotten to that point yet, and doubted she ever would. She didn't even know any cops with that kind of invisible emotional shield.

Sometimes she yearned to be inside an enchanted bubble, away from it all. It was pure fantasy. As an alternative, she'd settle for bursting Claudia Spalding's bubble.

She gazed at Wheeler's house. White clapboard siding beneath a slanted roof with a single chimney, a porch with a neat front lawn enclosed by a low fence, a detached single-car garage with doors on hinges that swung outward. It was far more lovely and appealing to Ellie than the Spalding mansion.

At the house, Ellie knocked on the screen door and was greeted by a pleasant-looking woman, who identified herself as Lori Wheeler and went to fetch her husband.

When Wheeler arrived, he offered Ellie a seat on the porch and a refreshment.

Ellie accepted both and sat sipping raspberry iced tea from a tall glass, enjoying the scenery and the coolness of the evening. On the enclosed dirt track below, a rider exercised a spirited gray along a quarter-mile straightaway, close to the infield railing. On the rise behind the open-air stalls and barn, a small herd of yearlings, bunched tightly together, wandered up the hill. The smell of wet grass from the afternoon shower still clung in the air.

Wheeler remained silent while Ellie watched a noisy killdeer, clearly recognizable by two black breast bands, circle and dip, piercing the silence with its call.

"What can I do for you?" Wheeler finally asked, after the bird had gained altitude to join a scattered flock. An ex-jockey, he was small and thin, but rail-hard. He exuded the quiet confidence of a competent man comfortable inside his skin.

"You mentioned to Chief Kerney that Claudia Spalding is something of a flirt. Could you be more specific?"

Wheeler swirled his glass, two fingers of Scotch poured neat. "I didn't put it that way. I guess you could say she acted coquettish at times, especially with the good-looking younger guys who worked at the tracks. Believe me, she wasn't alone among the other married women in that regard."

"Do you recall any of those younger men she might have seemed particularly interested in?"

Wheeler drank from the glass and put it on the arm of his chair. "I've thought about that some since Chief Kerney asked me about her. It's more like the other way around. There was this trainer out of Albuquerque, name of Coe Evans, who really had the hots for her. He worked a couple of seasons at the tracks out here, then he went back to New Mexico for a time. Now he trains horses on a TV celebrity's spread south of Atascadero."

The mention of Coe Evans made Ellie sit up straight. "Was there any gossip floating around about the two of them?"

"Not that I heard. Evans had a live-in girlfriend who kept a pretty close eye on him, and of course Claudia was married, so if anything was going on they kept it hushed up."

"What can you tell me about him?" she asked.

"He's in his late thirties, I'd guess. Good with horses, but not the best trainer around. He's one of those people who comes and goes. Turns on the charm and personality with the ladies, his bosses, anyone he can curry favor with."

"Anything else?"

Wheeler sipped his Scotch. "My wife can't stand him, thinks he's a real jerk. I can't say she's wrong. He's got a foul mouth when it comes to talking about women. Likes to brag about his conquests."

"Are you sure he's still working in Atascadero?"

Wheeler nodded. "I saw him in Paso Robles a couple of days ago. That's what got me thinking about him."

The killdeers were back, flying in a swirl above the trees, now pale, soaring shapes wrapped in a light fog that had rolled in from the coast with dusk. One of the few birds that flew at night, they trilled and chattered as though welcoming the impending darkness.

Ellie got the name of the TV personality Coe Evans worked for, thanked Wheeler for his time, and drove home. In her living room she sat, picked up the telephone, and hesitated, trying to sort out exactly what she would say to Ramona Pino.

She wanted to share the news about Coe Evans, but she wondered what Pino would think about her ignoring Lieutenant Macy's order to bow out of the investigation. Granted, their few phone conversations had been cordial, but Ellie didn't really know Pino. Was she a by-the-book cop who would feel compelled to rat her out to Macy, or more freewheeling when it came to bending the rules?

It didn't matter. Pino needed to know Coe Evans had been found. She dialed the phone, gave Pino the news, and then explained why she'd no longer be working the case.

"It will make my life easier if you don't let on to Lieutenant Macy or Detective Price that I'm your source of information about Evans."

Ramona laughed. "You've just eased my load, so the least I can do is cover for you. Besides, who's to say a CI can't be another cop? I'll keep your name out of it when I call Detective Price and ask him to get cracking on Evans."

"Thanks," Ellie said.

"Are you really going to stay on the sidelines?"

"I guess I'll have to."

"How about I keep you informed from my end?" Ramona asked.

"That would be great."

The two women talked awhile longer, and Ellie hung up with the feeling that if distance didn't prevent it, Ramona Pino would make a very good friend.

*　　*　　*

Sara called Kerney at home just as he was preparing for bed.

"I want to apologize," he said, wondering why Sara called so late. It was midnight, East Coast time. "I shouldn't be impatient when I'm asking for a favor."

"There's no need for that," Sara said. "But keep that thought in mind and it will stand you in good stead. You've got a green light from DOD to do the exhumation."

"So fast?" Kerney asked.

"We at the Pentagon never sleep."

"Are you still at work?"

"Back at work, actually. Patrick's tucked into bed, fast asleep, under the watchful eye of a sitter, so you needn't fret about him."

"What did it take for you to pull it off?" Kerney asked.

"Once I connected with the right person and showed him the material you faxed me, it went smoothly. We've opened our own investigation into the matter, and I'm your liaison officer. Aren't you lucky? If the remains prove to be those of someone other than George Spalding, the Army will assume control of the case."

"You're a marvel."

"It's about time you noticed. The U.S. Attorney and the VA have been notified. Have fun at the cemetery."

"You sound tired."

"I'm bushed and want to go home," Sara said.

"I won't keep you. Thanks, my love."

"Give yourself a hug from me. Good night."

The phone went dead. Kerney punched in the home number of Jerry Grant, the forensic anthropologist, got him on the line, and told him they were on for tomorrow.

He stood at the window and stared into the night, trying to figure out what feelings were eluding him. He felt distant, empty, and totally preoccupied with George Spalding. But why?

*   *   *

Jerry Grant was a transplanted Easterner who taught at the University of New Mexico in Albuquerque and did contract forensic work for the state police crime lab. Kerney rounded him up at his office early in the morning, and took the fastest possible route south to Fort Bayard.

A big, beefy man, Grant had thick, droopy eyebrows, a full head of hair badly in need of a trim, and a slightly unruly beard. On the drive, Grant, who'd lived in Albuquerque for ten years, talked eagerly about getting to see a part of the state he'd never visited before.

Kerney wasn't surprised by Grant's lack of familiarity with New Mexico. There were many people now residing in the state, especially urban dwellers, who had no inclination to explore their adopted home ground. But they could talk endlessly about exotic, international tourist destinations.

Kerney played historian along the way and filled Grant in on the background of the fort: how it was established on the frontier during the Indian Wars to contain the Apaches; how it had been home to the buffalo soldiers, companies of black enlisted cavalrymen commanded by white officers; how it had been transformed into a military hospital at the end of the nineteenth century and was now a state-run long-term care facility.

When they arrived at Fort Bayard, Grant had to see it, so Kerney took a quick swing through the grounds. He drove by the three-story, ugly block hospital that had been built years after the fort had been decommissioned, and then on to the charming quadrangle where a bronze life-size statue of a buffalo soldier firing a rifle over his shoulder stood on a pedestal.

A row of officers' quarters, stately Victorian houses with two-tiered porches, lined the street, and the restored post headquarters building, low-slung and sturdy with a wide veranda, sat at the far end of the quadrangle. Behind the building, the Pinos Altos Mountains rose up, masking from view the high wilderness of stream-cut canyons, vast upland meadows, and rugged summits that ranged for hundreds of thousands of acres along the Gila River watershed and continental divide.

"This really is an architectural treasure," Grant said.

"I've always thought so," Kerney said, remembering the times he'd visited in the past, first as a child with his parents and later on when he and his best friend, Dale Jennings, had competed in the state high school rodeo championships in nearby Silver City.

At the national cemetery, a Veterans Affairs official up from Fort Bliss met them. Looking none too pleased, he guided the way to the

Spalding grave site, with a backhoe and a private ambulance following behind.

Evergreen trees scattered across the grounds interrupted the stark lines of gray headstones. The brown earth, almost barren except for sparse native grasses, seemed in somber harmony with the scattered trees.

Kerney signed forms and the backhoe operator went to work, carefully trenching and piling excavated dirt into one large mound. The engine's sputtering carburetor and the whining of the hydraulics put Kerney on edge.

He wondered why the noise bothered him so much. Was it because he wanted the dead, many who'd seen so much violence and had been killed in battle, to rest quietly? Or was it also because of his own lingering sense of guilt about the men in his platoon who never made it home from Nam?

The thought hit Kerney in the gut, and feelings he thought he'd resolved long ago resurfaced, pushed away the emptiness, and brought back vivid flashes of combat. He could feel his mouth grimace, his jaw tighten.

Digging stopped when the casket was uncovered. Chains were secured to the casket fore and aft, and slowly it was lifted out of the grave onto a waiting gurney.

The backhoe operator shut the engine down and the silence only somewhat eased Kerney's mood. He watched Grant stop the ambulance driver before he could push the gurney toward his vehicle.

"Might as well take a look before we cart this back to Albuquerque," Grant said matter-of-factly, brushing dirt off the casket lid. "No sense wasting our time."

Frozen in place, Kerney watched Grant unfasten the casket lid and push it open.

"There's no skull," Grant said.

Kerney approached slowly and looked inside at an assortment of bones, wondering if they represented a soldier unaccounted for and still carried as an MIA, one of the 1,800 Americans killed in Vietnam that had yet to be identified, perhaps a man from his regiment or company. Suddenly, putting a name to the remains became as important as confirming that George Spalding was still alive.

"We got a sternum, two sets of tibias and fibulas, one femur, one humerus, assorted ribs, a scapula, two ulnas, iliums—both with an attached pubis, a collarbone, a radius, and a hip joint—that's it."

Grant looked up from the casket. "No skull, finger, or foot bones. Maybe somebody didn't want these remains to be positively identified."

"That could be."

Grant gave Kerney a questioning glance. "Are you okay with this?"

"I'm fine," Kerney replied, his voice cold and distant.

Grant put on gloves and picked up the radius bone. "According to what you told me, Spalding was killed in a chopper crash that exploded on impact, right?"

"That's what I understand," Kerney replied.

"High-octane fuel burns hot and eats flesh away right down to the bone, especially those that lie close to the skin. I don't see any evidence of burns here, but of course I'll run tests for hydrocarbons."

"What else?" Kerney asked. His throat felt scratchy and dry.

Grant pointed into the casket. "Look at the splintered rib and the shattered breastbone. I'd bet this person was fatally shot. Also, the bones look like they've been thoroughly cleaned."

"Is that unusual?" Kerney asked.

"The only people I know who clean bones are anthropologists, not morticians. Whoever did it effectively erased any trace evidence." Grant stripped off his gloves and closed the lid. "Okay, that's it for now. I can't tell you much more until the remains are in the lab in Albuquerque."

Kerney nodded. The ambulance driver loaded the casket and drove away. He could feel Grant's stare and turned away from it. Behind him the backhoe roared to life with a coarse vibration that seemed to penetrate his skin. He watched until the operator finished filling the empty hole.

"You'll keep me informed?" the VA official asked.

"Yes," Kerney said. Without another word, he joined Grant, who was waiting in the car, and headed back to Albuquerque. Preoccupied by his thoughts, he was grateful for Grant's silence.

*   *   *

Tied up with paperwork and phone calls, Detective Bill Price didn't get to leave his office until late morning. The warrant to seize and examine the original document giving Claudia Spalding spousal permission to take lovers was making its way through the system. Additionally, at Ramona Pino's request, Price had asked for a judge's order requiring the release of Clifford Spalding's last will and testament. If all went without a hitch, Price planned to personally serve both before the end of the day.

Sergeant Pino had also passed on some very interesting information about a man named Coe Evans, including his present whereabouts. Based on the details he'd been given, Price had no doubt Ellie had played a hand in tracking Evans down. He'd said nothing about his suspicions when Lieutenant Macy stopped by his office to tell him the surveillance of Claudia Spalding had been dropped.

Tomorrow, Claudia would bury her husband, and Price had already decided to watch from a distance to see what she did after Clifford got planted.

He found the ranch where Evans worked on a lightly traveled two-lane highway that ran from Atascadero to Santa Margarita, a sleepy little farming town. He turned onto the paved driveway, his progress halted by a custom-made gate adorned with the silhouette of a horse, bracketed by two ten-foot squared columns that displayed its famous owner's initials. He announced himself over the intercom, held his shield up to the security camera, and stated his business, and the gate swung slowly open.

The paved drive cut between two low hills where sunlight spilled on pastures and lethargic brood mares stood beneath oak trees, tails whisking, foals nearby. The drive followed the curve of a small streambed, and descended to a hidden valley revealing a compound of buildings stretched out along both sides of the creek.

On the north side of the creek, a sprawling, modern timber-frame house with a wall of vaulted windows was placed to take in the view of the rolling hills coursing southward. On one side of it was a guest-house, and on the other side a detached four-car garage, all tied to-gether by broad cobblestone walkways that wandered through Japanese-style gardens.

On the other side of the creek two barns faced each other across two large fenced pastures. A tree-lined lane ran between the pastures to a cluster of small cottages, outbuildings, storage sheds, and cor-rals, then continued on to a dirt landing field at the foot of a hill where a twin-engine plane sat next to a hangar. Sunlight flashed off the metal roof of the hangar like a beacon.

Price pulled to a stop in front of the house, got out of his unit, and watched a pickup truck coming in his direction rattle over the wooden bridge spanning the creek. The man who jumped out of the truck had an agitated expression on his face.

"What do you need to talk to me about?" he demanded abruptly.

"Coe Evans?" Price asked, looking the man over. He was a pretty-boy, with cropped curly hair, symmetrical features, and a solid six-foot frame.

"Yeah, that's right. What do you want?"

"You sound worried," Price replied pleasantly. "Is something wrong?"

"I don't know," Evans said, glancing up at the big house. "You tell me."

"As far as I know, you're not in any trouble," Price said. "What can you tell me about Claudia Spalding?"

Evans looked surprised, but recovered quickly. "Not much. I barely know the woman."

"How did you come to meet her?"

"At the tracks where I used to work. She likes the ponies—owns a few and races them. I'd see her around and sometimes we would chat. Small talk stuff."

"Just casual conversation about horses and racing," Price rephrased.

"Horses and racing," Evans said. "Exactly."

"That's it?" Price asked. "You had no social interaction with her outside of work?"

Evans smirked and laughed. "Are you kidding, outside of work? She didn't hang out with my crowd."

"So you only saw her at the track."

"I just said that."

Evans was repeating Price's words, averting his eyes, omitting information—all signs of a liar.

Price decided to stop acting so amicable and ask a slightly tougher question. "You never slept with her?"

Evans tilted his head and closed his eyes. "That's bullshit. Who have you been talking to? Who would say something like that?"

Pleased with the response and convinced he was reading Evans correctly, Price backed off. "When was the last time you talked with Mrs. Spalding?"

"I can't recall," Evans replied. "It wasn't like I kept track of her. She was just another rich bitch who hung around during racing season."

"Try to remember," Price encouraged.

Evans gave a slight, cooperative nod of his head. "Probably it was just before she built a house somewhere in the Rocky Mountains. Four, maybe five years ago."

"What would you say if I told you we think Claudia Spalding arranged to have her husband murdered?"

"I heard he died in his sleep."

"What type of woman would do something like that?"

"Man, who knows why women do anything?"

Price glanced at the gold band Evans wore on his left hand. "You're married, I take it. Is it the same woman you were living with back when you knew Claudia Spalding?"

Evans stiffened. "Have you been checking up on me?"

Price smiled. "A little bit. Is she?"

"Yeah, so what?"

"Perhaps I should speak with her. Is she here?"

Evans waved off the notion with a wagging finger. "You have no cause to do that."

"Maybe she'd be interested in learning what your old buddy in Santa Fe, Mitch Griffin, has to say about your relationship with Claudia Spalding, and what you told him about the murder plot she had in mind for her husband."

The cockiness in Evans washed away, replaced by hot-wired apprehension. "Shit. That crazy bitch. I cut it off with her then and there. I swear, I did nothing. My wife would kill me if she ever found out about Claudia."

"I believe you," Price said consolingly as he opened the passenger door to his unit. "Let's take a ride to my office. We'll start all over again, and this time you can tell me the truth."

*   *   *

In a laboratory at the university, Kerney watched Grant assemble the bones into a recognizable partial skeleton, studying each one carefully before he laid it out. After he took measurements, he picked up the breastbone and shattered rib for a closer examination.

"Definitely shot," he said.

"Not shrapnel wounds?" Kerney asked.

Grant shook his head and put the bones back in place. "No way. It's a male. Based on my measurement I make him to be between five-foot-eleven and six feet tall. I'm thinking he was probably in his thirties when he died, but it will take some time to confirm it. Since we're missing the skull, I was hoping I might find an old break that could be compared to medical records, but there are none that I can see. I'll do X-rays."

"What else can you tell me?"

"Not much until I do some tests. The important work will be the mitochondrial DNA comparison of the bones to the blood sample provided by Alice Spalding."

"I only asked for a saliva swab," Kerney said.

"Normally, that would be good enough," Grant said. "But for what I have in mind, I'll need a blood sample."

"Assuming these aren't the remains of George Spalding, is there still a chance a positive ID can be made?" Kerney asked.

Grant smiled. "I've been waiting for you to ask that question. I did postdoctoral work at the U.S. Army Central Identification Laboratory in Hawaii, which has the largest staff of forensic anthropologists in the world. I'd like to query them and ask for a records search of their POW/MIA data bank based on what I can tell them before we get the DNA results back. It might help narrow a search for a likely victim. But don't expect to get a list of names you can easily investigate."

"Why is that?" Kerney asked.

Grant walked to a desk and started rummaging through a drawer for some forms. "Because if this is truly an MIA, the man is probably just a name in their system. Or it could well be that the victim isn't even an American soldier. The laboratory cooperates with over seventeen countries to identify remains of both military personnel and civilians from foreign governments who are unaccounted for in Vietnam. Your task could be daunting."

"How can I narrow the field?" Kerney asked.

Grant labeled a manila file folder with a marker and put the blank forms in it. "Based on what you told me, George Spalding was handled as a KIA, which means after recovery his remains went to one of two well-equipped mortuaries in-country, Da Nang in the north and Tan Son Nhut outside of Saigon. Mortuary affairs are handled by the Army Quartermaster Corps. Finding out which facility handled these remains could be helpful. They keep excellent records."

"What better place to switch remains than a mortuary?" Kerney said.

"You got it," Grant replied. "But we shouldn't stop there. I can short-circuit the process considerably by sending our DNA results to the Armed Forces DNA Identification Laboratory at Walter Reed Hospital. They have thousands of blood samples from POW/MIA family members in their database, and a new high-speed automated robotic processing system in place. Of course, that's assuming the lab has maternal DNA of the victim on hand."

"How long would we have to wait for a report?" Kerney asked.

"Even with the new system, months, I would imagine. Unless, that is, you know some way to get it bumped up on the priority list."

"I don't think that will be a problem," Kerney replied. "The Army is as interested in this case as I am."

ChapterEleven

By choice, Kerney spent very little time in Albuquerque, driving down from Santa Fe only for necessary business or to catch a plane at the airport. But after leaving Jerry Grant he lingered at a diner over a cup of hot tea and called the half-dozen Calderwoods listed in the local phone book. He made contact with four people who professed no knowledge of, or kinship to, the long-lost Debbie, and left messages for the others.

To make sure he hadn't missed anyone, he called the phone company and asked for any unlisted numbers under the Calderwood name. There were none. He closed the dog-eared, grease-stained directory he'd borrowed from a waitress, drank his tea, and looked around the diner. By the front cashier station a row of booths lined one wall. Perpendicular to the booths was a serving station in front of swinging doors that led to the kitchen. Behind a long counter with padded stools a waitress refilled a trucker's coffee cup.

Kerney liked diners, not for the food but because they made great people-watching places. An elderly couple at one of the nearby tables carefully examined their menus and discussed whether they should order the early-bird dinner special. The woman wore loose-fitting slacks and a summer blouse, the man jeans and a short-sleeved shirt topped off by a ball cap adorned with tourist pins from the places he'd visited.

In one of the booths along the wall, a young couple in shorts, T-shirts, and hiking boots sat next to each other studying a map. By the look of their tanned legs, arms, and faces, Kerney figured them to be college students doing some high country backpacking on summer break.

He picked up the phone directory again and turned to the business listings on the off-chance the name Calderwood would appear. There was a Calderwood Farm Equipment Company on North Second Street. He called and got a recording announcing the business was closed for the day. Since it wasn't far, Kerney decided to swing by and take a look at the place.

He avoided rush hour on the interstate and found his way to Second Street, an area of seedy commercial buildings, warehouses, and low-end used car lots that paralleled the train tracks a block away. Calderwood Farm Equipment sat across the street from a city vehicle maintenance yard. Tractors, horse trailers, field cultivators, and large metal water tanks filled the lot behind a chain-link fence. The gate was open and a late model cream-colored Cadillac sat in front of a building that had once been a heavy equipment garage, the tall bay doors now replaced with showroom windows.

The entrance was locked and the man who answered Kerney's knock wore a dress shirt, tie, and slacks that were badly wrinkled around the crotch from too much sitting. Chunky with a fold of loose skin under his chin, the man flashed Kerney a broad smile.

"I don't suppose you're interested in that sweet 480-horsepower tractor out on the lot," he said jovially after inspecting Kerney's credentials.

"I'm looking for Calderwood," Kerney said.

"You're about twenty years too late. I bought him out but kept the company name."

"Can you point me in his direction?" Kerney asked.

"He died two years after I took over the business. I guess retirement didn't suit him."

"Did he have a wife, children?"

The man's expression darkened. "Don't get me started on his wife. When I bought the company I couldn't afford to purchase the property, so Calderwood gave me a two-year option on the building. His wife wouldn't renew it after he died. Said she needed the rental income. I've been paying for her tour ship cruises and European vacations ever since."

"How can I find Mrs. Calderwood?"

"She got remarried ten years ago to a retired university professor. Now she's Mrs. Kessler. She lives on Twelfth Street, not too far from here."

"Does she have any children?" Kerney asked.

"Not that I know of."

"Can you give me her address?"

"Sure, if you tell me what this is all about."

"I'm looking for a missing person named Debbie Calderwood. Does that name ring a bell?"

The man shook his head. "You know, I worked for Calderwood for five years before he sold me the business. Never once did I meet any of his relatives or get invited over to his house. Both he and his wife were the most private people you could ever know. They never talked about anything personal. I can't tell you a darn thing about that family."

Kerney left with an address for Mrs. Kessler and drove to Twelfth Street. Until 1880, Albuquerque had been a small, predominantly Spanish settlement near the Rio Grande River. Within a year after the arrival of the railroad two miles east of the village, a new town sprang up that soon overshadowed the old Plaza as a center of commerce and business.

Over time, the old and new towns began to merge as the city grew. Anglo merchants, bankers, doctors, and lawyers bought up lots near what was to become downtown Albuquerque, and built grand homes for their families. Those houses still stood in a lovely old residential neighborhood that included Twelfth Street.

The Kessler residence was a Victorian classic with a steeply pitched roof running front to back and exposed timbering on the upper story. It had a Palladian window centered in a wall projection that jutted out above a narrow gabled porch supported by heavy square-cut posts.

Kerney climbed the broad porch stairs and turned the crank of the mechanical doorbell attached to the paneled oak front door. The tinny, weak trill of it made him crank the bell again a bit harder.

A few minutes passed before the door opened to reveal a small, lean, elderly woman with sharp features magnified by a peevish expression.

Kerney held out his badge case. "Mrs. Kessler, I'm with the Santa Fe Police Department."

"Yes, I can see that," Mrs. Kessler said, without a hint of humor. "Whatever do you want?"

"I'd like you to tell me what you know about Debbie Calderwood."

Kessler's slate-gray eyes registered no expression, but she wrinkled her nose a bit at the mention of Debbie's name. "Debbie?" she said. "I haven't seen or heard from her in over thirty years."

"Is she related to you?" Kerney asked.

Kessler bared her tiny teeth in a tight, polite smile. "Why are you asking me about her?"

"I'm attempting to locate her," Kerney replied.

"Well, I'm certainly not someone who can help you," Kessler said, her voice tinged with displeasure.

"Learning about Debbie's family could be very helpful. I'd appreciate hearing whatever you can tell me."

Kessler stayed silent for a long moment, so Kerney prodded her a bit. "This is an official police investigation, Mrs. Kessler."

"Debbie was my first husband's niece," Kessler said tonelessly. "Her parents relocated to Arkansas after she finished high school. She stayed behind to go to college and moved into a dormitory on campus. Then she got caught up in all that antiwar, free speech movement that was going on at the time, and started using drugs."

"You didn't approve of her behavior?"

"No, we didn't. Her parents laid the blame for her poor judgment on our doorstep, said we hadn't looked out for her enough. It caused a rift between my husband and his brother that never healed."

Mrs. Kessler obviously wasn't one to forgive and forget. Kerney played into it. "That must have been very unpleasant for you and your husband."

"Indeed, it was. We tried to help Debbie as much as we could. We gave her things to furnish her dorm room, had her over for Sunday dinners, even paid to have her car fixed when it broke down. All it got us was criticism from her parents, especially after Debbie dropped out of college and ran away."

"Did she ever correspond with you after she left Albuquerque?"

"Not a word of thanks or anything else," Kessler said emphatically.

"Young people can be so thoughtless," Kerney said. It earned him a surprised look of approval. "Did she maintain contact with her parents?"

"I don't know," Kessler said as her expression cooled. "After Debbie left, we had nothing more to do with them other than a polite exchange of Christmas cards each year."

"Are they still living in Arkansas?"

"They're both deceased."

"Does Debbie have any siblings?"

"She was an only child."

"What about a boyfriend?" Kerney asked.

"If she had one, we never met him," Kessler answered.

"Does the name George Spalding mean anything to you?"

"No."

"Did she ever talk about boys?"

"Not with us," Kessler said. "She wasn't close to us in that way."

"What about girlfriends, or her college roommate?"

She made a bitter face. "In truth, except for the help we provided,

Debbie wanted very little to do with us. We were much too conventional and uptight, as she so often liked to remind us."

"You never met any of her friends?"

"She often brought someone with her when she came to get a free meal. But the only one we saw more than once was her roommate, Helen. She at least had been brought up well enough to say thank you and offer to help with the dishes."

"What else can you tell me about her?"

"She was from Santa Fe. She was studying art history. My husband liked to tease her about doing something more practical."

"Have you seen Helen since those years?" Kerney asked.

"Once, in Santa Fe, when I was there for the day with a friend. She was working in an art gallery on Canyon Road. Somehow she recognized me and asked for news of Debbie. They'd lost touch with each other. Of course, I could tell her nothing."

"When was that?"

"At least ten years ago."

"Do you remember where you saw her?"

"No, but I do recall we had lunch right next door to the gallery."

Kessler named the restaurant. It was one of the oldest and finest restaurants in the city.

"Thank you," Kerney said.

"Why are you trying to find Debbie?"

"It's a police matter."

Mrs. Kessler nodded as though it was of no importance and closed the front door.

On the drive back to Santa Fe, Kerney couldn't shake the image of the rigid, unforgiving Mrs. Kessler from his mind. Surviving a Sunday meal at the Kessler home must have been pure agony for Debbie.

*   *   *

Although he tried to seem impassive, Kim Dean knew that his fear showed through. Whenever an inmate looked at him, he averted his eyes. His face felt like a frozen death mask, his upper lip was wet with sweat, and he was constantly swallowing, rubbing his nose, or fidgeting with his hands.

A big Hispanic guy with tattoos on his arms and the back of his neck kept eyeing him, as did a black Cuban who grabbed his crotch and smiled wickedly every time Dean glanced in his direction.

He sat by himself at a table in the communal area of the living pod and stared at the wall-mounted television tuned to a Spanish language station no one else was watching. Clusters of inmates were playing cards or talking in tight-knit little groups.

All the metal tables, fabricated with attached benches, were secured to the floor, as were the beds in the cells, the sinks—everything that ordinarily could be disassembled or dislodged was bolted, welded, or fastened down. The stairs to the upper-level cells, the security grates covering a high row of frosted windows, and the bars on the cell and pod doors were gleaming steel.

Four young, tough-looking inmates—kids really—stood in front of the lower tier of a semicircular wall of cells singing rap in low voices, flashing gangbanger signs, and laughing. Two older inmates who were mopping floors and cleaning tabletops moved slowly across the room.

The guy wielding the mop, a small, stoop-shouldered man who looked like a character from a Dickens novel, appeared to be perfectly content with his task. In fact, everyone in the pod seemed completely at ease, like it was no big deal to be locked up. It only served to make Dean more apprehensive.

He kept glancing at the glassed-in guard station and the locked pod door, hoping someone would come to fetch him to meet with his new lawyer, Scott Ingram.

Ingram had called hours ago to say he'd spoken with Howard Stubbs, the inexperienced lawyer Dean had fired, and would be out to see him as soon as he'd received and reviewed the arrest affidavits, warrants, and charges, and talked to the district attorney.

He was about to return to his cell, which Dean figured was the safest place to be if he never fell asleep, when a guard appeared and motioned him to approach the pod door.

"Is my lawyer here?" Dean asked.

The guard nodded as the door slid open. After being patted down and cuffed, he was walked down the main corridor and deposited in an interview room where Scott Ingram waited. Neither man spoke until the cuffs came off and the guard left the room.

"You took your time getting here," Dean snapped.

Ingram smiled indulgently at Dean. "I'm sure you wanted me to be well prepared before we talked."

"Are you a good criminal defense attorney?"

"I'm very good at what I do," Ingram said.

"Has anyone tried to contact you on my behalf?" Dean asked.

Ingram looked down his hawkish nose as he sat at the table. "Do you mean Claudia Spalding?"

Surprised, Dean nodded. "How do you know her name?"

"Because Stubbs told me about the phone call he made at your request, and I've learned that the DA is sitting on a pending murder arrest warrant for her, waiting for the receipt of more information from California."

"Dammit," Dean said.

"Have you talked to anyone about the charges since your arraignment?" Ingram asked.

Dean sat down across from Ingram. "Nobody."

"That's good. But time may be running out on you to enter into a plea agreement."

"I don't want that. I want you to find a way to get me out of here, now." He bit a hangnail off his thumb and spit it out.

"I've already informally approached the judge on your behalf in that matter. Any official request I make to ask him to reconsider setting bail will be rejected. You're to be held without bond."

"Can't you do something? Tell him I'll surrender my passport, sign over the equity in my house and business to a bondsman. Plus my cash. I can put together almost a million dollars."

"I don't think if you had three million in cash and assets the judge would let you out."

"Do something, dammit."

Ingram sighed sympathetically and leaned forward. "Getting you out of jail isn't an option. In fact, as I see it, you don't have many options."

"What are they?" Dean asked.

"As things stand right now, you can cooperate with the prosecution and get the murder charge reduced and most of the other charges dropped. But if the cops develop sufficient probable cause to get an arrest warrant for Claudia Spalding, you may wind up on the short end of the stick."

"How so?"

"She may decide to testify against you. That means the DA will have her, instead of you, in his pocket. He'll go after you full-bore, using Spalding as his star witness. He won't even think about negotiating with you. He'll try you on all the state charges. Once that's done, the DEA can step in and file against you in federal court."

"That's double jeopardy."

Ingram shook his head. "No it isn't, Mr. Dean. The criminal codes in this country are complex, and the federal government has drug laws on the books that aren't duplicated by state statutes."

"Claudia wouldn't do that to me," Dean said.

Ingram raised an eyebrow. "Has she been in touch with you to offer aid?"

Dean shook his head. "I want you to call her."

"I tried that under the pretext of asking her to make a sworn statement on your behalf. I spoke to one of her employees, who told me she refused to take my call. That should tell you something, Mr. Dean."

"Shit!"

"It could get worse," Ingram said. "From what I've learned, Claudia Spalding has the financial wherewithal to hire a team of the best defense lawyers, private investigators, and expert witnesses money can buy. I'm sure if she's arrested, a motion to separate her case from yours will be filed and most likely granted. That will put us in an adversarial relationship with her. Are you prepared to go that route?"

"Can't you do anything to keep that from happening?" Dean asked.

"Certainly I can argue against it, if that's really what you want. But I don't see how it serves any purpose. Actually, I'll use the very same tactic on your behalf, if you're willing to cooperate."

Dean started nibbling at another hangnail. "So where does that leave me?"

"We can go to trial and I'll mount the best defense possible. We can dispute the circumstantial evidence, bring in psychologists to testify that Spalding manipulated and used you, call on medical doctors and pharmacologists to challenge the cause of death findings, file motions to have witness statements excluded, pound away at any evidence collection screwups, and do everything possible to place the preponderance of blame on Mrs. Spalding."

Dean peeled the hangnail free and picked it off his tongue. "Can we win?"

"You never know. But whatever the outcome, you'll most likely still be in jail—maybe even prison—while you're awaiting trial on the other charges. Plus, by then you'll have to ask for a public defender to represent you."

"Why not you? I can pay your fee."

"Now you can," Ingram replied. "But you won't be able to hire a private attorney in the future if the DEA and local cops can trace the money you made on drug trafficking back to your business and personal accounts. If they succeed, your assets will be frozen, confiscated, and disposed of. And believe me, they're doing everything possible to make sure that happens."

Dean sagged in his chair, head lowered, eyelids fluttering. "This wasn't supposed to turn out this way."

"Do we go to trial or do I call the DA?" Ingram asked.

Dean looked up from the table. "Call the DA."

"Are you willing to talk to them right now?"

Dean nodded.

Ingram stood. "Stay put. I'll make the call and be back in a few minutes."

After Ingram left, Dean dropped his head on the table and cried like a baby.

*   *   *

Early in the morning, long before dawn, Ellie Lowrey dressed for work. She set aside the freshly laundered and pressed uniform she'd picked up at the dry cleaner's the day before, and instead put on her best pair of black slacks, a white linen blouse, and a loose-fitting jacket cut long enough to adequately hide the holstered weapon strapped to her belt.

Today, Claudia Spalding would be arrested and charged with murder, and it was Ellie's job to make it happen without a hitch.

It had all begun last night, when it seemed that her telephone would never stop ringing. First, Ramona Pino called to share the news that Kim Dean had given up Claudia Spalding as his accomplice. Bill Price followed with a call soon after to report that Coe Evans had made a sworn statement accusing Spalding of proposing a prior murder plot against her husband.

Then it was Lieutenant Macy on the line, who'd been assigned to coordinate the arrest of Claudia Spalding. Since Ellie was the only officer who had met Spalding face-to-face, Macy wanted her to lead the team assigned to make the collar.

"She may let her guard down with you, and implicate herself," Macy said.

"Maybe," Ellie said doubtfully. "She's not the nervous Nellie type by any means, but it's worth a try."

"Think on it," Macy said. "Be empathetic and give her a reason to show you how smart she is."

Twenty minutes later, Macy called again, this time to pass along instructions from the sheriff and district attorney. In order to avoid adverse publicity and controversy, Spalding was not to be picked up at the cemetery or during the wake. There were to be no leaks to reporters, no lingering guests at the estate when the bust went down, and any employees on-site were to be held for questioning after Spalding was booked into jail. As soon as Spalding was locked up, the sheriff and DA would hold a joint press conference to announce the arrest.

With instructions from the brass out of the way, Macy talked about operational specifics. Surveillance was back on Spalding to make sure she stayed put until Ellie had her team in place. Only plainclothes detectives in unmarked cars would be used, and all exits and entrances to the estate would be watched. Macy would partner-up with Ellie during the operation, and if any adjustments needed to be made to the plan, he would have the final say.

After talking to Macy, Ellie had settled down to a cup of tea and thoughts about how to approach Claudia Spalding. Then the sheriff called. Did Ellie understand she was to make no statements to the press after the arrest? That the case would get national attention? That there could be no procedural screwups?

An hour later, Ellie lay wide-awake in bed, puzzling over how to get Claudia Spalding talking. What was it Ramona Pino had said about Kim Dean? She couldn't remember the exact words, but it boiled down to Dean being easily manipulated by Claudia. Bill Price had noted the same trait in Coe Evans.

Claudia Spalding apparently thrived on domination and control. Prickly and imperious, she was beyond a doubt a formidable woman. Ellie could easily imagine how she used her sexuality, intelligence, and guile on Dean and Evans. Or anybody else she needed to. It was one thing to guess at Claudia's motives for murder, but quite another to understand the forces that had made her act. For a woman who'd been given so much, who had so much, it surely went far beyond simple greed.

A restless night finally over, Ellie was starting the day with no brilliant inspirations or new insights. She checked her appearance in the mirror and left the house, hoping that during the drive to headquarters she would think of some way to get Claudia to take that first small step toward admitting guilty knowledge.

*   *   *

It was a soft summer morning in Santa Fe, unusually cool with moist tropical air coursing up from the Gulf of Mexico, yet without a cloud in the sky or any haze to dampen the sunlight. Kerney found it unusual for other reasons as well. Although the downtown shops were about to open, traffic was light and the tourists had not yet begun to stream out of their hotels to fill the sidewalks.

By the time he reached the turnoff to Canyon Road the brief moment of serenity had passed. People wandered up the middle of the narrow street snapping pictures of the quaint pueblo-style adobe buildings, drivers backed up traffic waiting for parking spaces to become available, and the open-air sightseeing trolley just in front of Kerney's unit was filled with visitors listening to a tour guide's thumbnail sketch of Santa Fe history blaring out from a loudspeaker.

Santa Fe, a city of 65,000 people—not counting the untold numbers of undocumented residents from Mexico and Central America—was the third largest art market in the country. It was awash with art galleries, private art dealers, art consultants, conservators, appraisers, and studio artists. There were foundries, lapidaries, glass-blowing studios, weaving shops, wood-carving shops, and ceramic studios all over town. But the largest concentration of businesses that made Santa Fe an art mecca were to be found around the Plaza and on nearby Canyon Road.

Years ago, old-timers had decried the rapid changes to the street, once a quiet, sheltered neighborhood of adobe homes, a bar or two, and a small grocery store along a dirt lane. Now the transformation was complete: shops, studios, galleries, and restaurants dominated, and the tourist dollar ruled.

Kerney parked illegally in a loading zone and walked over to the art gallery next to the restaurant where Mrs. Kessler had last seen Debbie Calderwood's college roommate. The gallery was gone, replaced by an upscale boutique that sold fringed leather jackets, handmade western shirts, silk scarves, flowing dresses, gaudy, flowered cowboy boots— everything a gal needed to show that she had Santa Fe style.

Kerney wasn't surprised; retail shops along the road came and went with such frequency it was almost impossible to keep track of them.

The store owner told Kerney she'd been in the same location for five years, didn't know who had leased the space before her, and had never met the prior occupants. However, she did provide Kerney with the name of her landlord.

Kerney called the landlord from his unit and learned the building had previously been leased by a woman who now ran a gallery out of her house in the village of Galisteo, southeast of Santa Fe.

"She deals in abstract, modern art," the man added. "A lot of it by well-known European and East Coast artists."

"How long did she lease from you?" Kerney asked.

"About ten years."

"What's her name?"

"Jennifer Stover. Her number is in the business directory under the Stover-Driscoll Gallery. Driscoll is her ex-husband's name. She sees clients only by appointment."

Kerney got the listing from information, dialed the number, listened to a recorded message, and disconnected. He called information back and learned there was no published residential listing for either a Stover or a Driscoll in Galisteo.

When he got to his office, he'd ask the phone company to search for an unlisted number and then try to make contact with Stover again. If that didn't work, Galisteo was ten minutes away from Kerney's ranch. He'd swing by the village before going home in the evening and track Stover down.

*   *   *

From a distance, Ellie Lowrey and Lieutenant Macy watched the hushed, somber crowd assembled at the grave site. Men and women dressed in dark blue, black, and charcoal outfits stood quietly, eyes cast downward. The young children present were anchored close to their mothers' sides to keep them still. Claudia Spalding held a bouquet of flowers and a pure white linen handkerchief in her gloved hands. An ocean breeze ruffled skirt hems, jacket lapels, and ties, and carried away the minister's words.

The wind died away, and for a moment the gathering looked like a staged movie scene. The open grave, the casket of polished wood with brass handles, the abundance of carefully arranged funeral wreaths, the green grass blanket of the cemetery dale with the forested hills rising behind, created a surreal impression.

It was a large crowd of two hundred or more people. Behind the hearse, cars parked on the winding gravel lane stretched almost to the cemetery entrance. Outside the arched, open gate, private security personnel held back photographers with telephoto lenses who were pressed against the ornate wrought iron fence taking pictures.

"We may have a long wait before the last of Spalding's guests clear out after the wake," Ellie said to Lieutenant Macy.

Macy nodded. "I'm more concerned right now about the paparazzi. We need them contained and kept away from the estate."

Ellie had been out of touch with Macy for the past three hours, scoping out the situation in Montecito, making arrangements, and putting her team in place.

"Spalding's rent-a-cops will keep them at the bottom of the hill, and the Santa Barbara PD, at Claudia's request, will be on hand to assist."

"Do they know what's going down?"

"No, I called the estate posing as a newspaper reporter and got the information from an employee. She also told me that invited guests would be screened at the entrance to the estate by private security."

"How do we make sure Spalding doesn't slip away in the backseat of a guest's car?" Macy asked.

"Claudia has hired a valet parking service for the wake. One of our detectives will be an attendant."

"Valet parking for a wake," Macy said in mock disbelief. "How did you manage that?"

"Plus catered food for the guests by a celebrity chef," Ellie said. "I talked to the man who owns the service, flashed my shield, told him I was with dignitary protection for a high-ranking government official, and got him to agree to the substitution. He thinks we're feds and it's all very hush-hush."

"Clever," Macy said.

"Security at the entrance will use the keypad gate opener to let the guests through. We'll use it after they leave to make a quick entry."

"You have the code?"

"I got it from the fire department," Ellie answered. "A local ordinance requires owners of all gated residences to provide emergency access information to the department."

Ellie watched Claudia step away from the crowd, place the bouquet on her husband's coffin, bow her head, and clutch a hand to her throat.

"She's *very* good," Ellie said, still wondering what it would take to break the woman down.

"Let's go," Macy said as people started drifting away toward the waiting cars. The young children, released from their mothers' sides, eagerly skipped ahead of their slow-moving parents and skirted around the tombstones.

*   *   *

After the last guest had left and the caterers and parking attendants were gone, Ellie went up to the estate alone. She found Claudia on the patio seated in a lawn chair next to the pool.

"I don't recall your name on the guest list," Spalding said. "How did you get in here?"

Spalding's modest black designer dress, with a high scooped neckline, half sleeves, and the hem just below the knees, fit her perfectly. She stood, walked to the pergola, poured whiskey into a tumbler, and held it in both hands.

Everything about her was smooth and polished. She glanced at Ellie intently without a hint of uneasiness.

"I know this probably isn't the best time to talk," Ellie said.

"That doesn't answer my question," Claudia replied.

"Would you rather I come back some other time?"

"Don't play games with me, Sergeant. Coming to see me now, at this time, goes beyond rudeness and bad manners. Tell me how you got in or leave."

"A security guard let me in," Ellie said.

A thin smile stretched across Claudia's lips. "I rather doubt that." She put the tumbler down. "Say what you need to and then go."

Ellie waved her off. "Never mind. It can wait."

"Another little trick, Sergeant?" Claudia asked. "Are you trying to make me anxious and curious about what brought you here? If so, you're being much too transparent. Let me show you out."

Ellie followed Spalding through the sunroom, down the hallway with the walls of paintings, into the enormous living room. There would be no breakthrough moment with Spalding. She showed no tiny pang of conscience or fear of punishment that could be used as a lever. There was no gambit of conversation Ellie could use to open her up, lower her defenses.

She was a poised, elegant, armor-plated, stone cold killer.

At the massive front doors, Ellie cuffed Spalding, told her the charges, read her the Miranda warning, and put her in the backseat of the unmarked cruiser.

"I'd like to call my lawyer," Spalding said.

"You can do that from jail," Ellie said, looking in at her through the open car door.

"Were you overweight as a child?" Spalding asked.

"Why do you ask?" Ellie countered, taken aback by the question. In fact, she'd been a little chubby until puberty caught up with her and burned it permanently away.

Spalding smirked. "Never mind."

"Were you?" Ellie asked, hoping at last Claudia wanted to talk.

Spalding turned away. "Please hurry. These handcuffs are very uncomfortable."

ChapterTwelve

With Claudia Spalding in custody and on her way to jail, Lieutenant Dante Macy quickly moved the team of detectives onto the estate. The long lane to the house, shaded by rows of overarching trees, cut the afternoon sun into gleaming flecks of light. On either side, thickets of brambles and tall pines created the illusion of a forest. When the Tuscan-style house and the formal tiered gardens came into view, Macy was stunned by the opulence. Ellie Lowrey's description of the estate hadn't done it justice. He wondered how many tens of millions, or hundreds of millions, it took to own such a place.

Macy put his people into motion. Two men would round up the staff and take their statements. Detective Price and two officers would conduct the search for evidence. Two more detectives would do a visual sweep of the extensive grounds to determine what else might need to be searched under a new warrant.

The five employees consisted of Clifford Spalding's personal assistant, an estate overseer who lived on the grounds, two gardeners, and a resident housekeeper. All of them had attended the funeral services and the wake, staying behind after the last guests departed to tidy up and restore order.

Macy wandered through the house and grounds thinking it would take a platoon of officers a day or more to do a truly comprehensive search. Hopefully, that wouldn't be needed. He watched as the detectives working under Price examined hard drives on the household computers, then stopped by the kitchen where the personal assistant, a nervous woman in her thirties named Sheila, was giving a statement. The rest of the staff were seated silently around the table in the adjacent dining room under the watchful eye of an officer.

Macy found Price exiting the guesthouse by the tennis courts, empty-handed. Price shook his head to signal that he'd found nothing of interest and walked toward the garage and staff quarters. Macy went back to the kitchen and waited for the detective to finish up with Sheila. Then he took her in tow and had her open every locked door on the estate so the officers could do a visual inspection. There was no good reason to waste time trying to do a thorough search of every nook and cranny. At least, not yet.

After the doors had been unlocked, he told Sheila to wait in the dining room, and sat at the far end of the long antique tavern table that filled the center space of the kitchen. The two gardeners, both middle-aged Hispanic men with limited English language skills, were questioned one at a time by a Spanish-speaking officer. They both said they didn't know Kim Dean or what his relationship to Claudia was. The detective probed a bit, but it was clear both men had very little personal knowledge about their employers.

Next up was the housekeeper, a woman with a broad Nordic face and pale blue eyes named Cora Sluka. Under questioning, she was uncooperative and evasive at first, but opened up a bit when the detectives pointed out that Clifford Spalding was dead, his wife was in jail charged with murder, and Sluka might have a hard time getting another job if they had to arrest her.

She talked about a male who'd appeared unannounced within the past year to visit Mrs. Spalding, and recalled serving them drinks on the patio. She couldn't describe the man, but when shown Dean's booking photograph from the Santa Fe County Jail, she identified him as the visitor.

The information pleased Macy. Claudia Spalding had told Sergeant Lowrey that Dean had never been to the Montecito estate. He wondered what else Claudia had lied about.

Macy motioned the detectives to back off and took over the interview. "Were you present at the house the entire time Dean was here?" he asked Sluka.

"No, Mrs. Spalding asked me to take some clothes to the dry cleaners and then gave me the afternoon off."

"Was that an unusual thing for her to do?"

"Yes, it was. She liked to keep us busy."

"Were other employees around at the time?"

"No, just me."

"Did you mention Dean's visit to Mr. Spalding?"

"No."

"Could he have learned about it some other way?"

"Mrs. Spalding might have told him."

"Does Mrs. Spalding treat the staff fairly, without favoritism?"

Sluka lowered her head. "She treats us all pretty much the same, I think."

Macy read the dodge. "She doesn't play favorites?"

"We all try to get along and work together," Sluka hedged.

"No one gets special treatment?" Macy asked.

Sluka's cheeks turned red. "That's not for me to say."

"Okay, Cora, that's all for now. But I may have to speak to you again."

Sluka hurried out, and Glenn Davitt, the estate manager, replaced her at the kitchen table. A man in his thirties, he had jet black hair, dark, deep-set eyes, and a lean, angular face. He looked at Macy with feigned boredom, which raised Macy's curiosity.

"How long is this going to take?" Davitt asked as he slouched in his chair and glanced at the three cops.

Macy countered the question. "Tells us what you know about Mrs. Spalding's lovers."

"I know nothing about any of that," Davitt said, peering over his shoulder as the two detectives moved behind him.

"Please pay attention to me, Mr. Davitt," Macy said softly as he approached. "Would you say Claudia Spalding is a beautiful woman?"

Davitt shrugged. "Sure, for someone her age."

"Hard to resist?" Macy asked.

Davitt crossed his arms. "I don't know what you mean."

Macy chuckled. "Come on, don't give me that. She's a very sexy lady."

"If you say so. To be perfectly honest, I don't think of her that way. She's my employer, that's all."

Macy gave Davitt a friendly pat on the shoulder. "Relax. Talking to me can only help you."

"Help me how? This is a waste of time."

"Let's forget about Mrs. Spalding for a minute. Think about yourself, your future."

Davitt laughed. "Maybe I'll write one of those tell-all books and make a pile of money."

"That's a great idea," Macy said approvingly. "But if you don't tell us the truth, you'll have to write that book in jail."

"In jail for what?"

"Making false statements to the police," Macy said. "Obstructing justice."

Davitt raised a hand. "May lightning strike me if I'm telling a lie."

Macy pulled a chair over and sat close to Davitt. "I don't think you've lied, yet. But if you don't tell us about your relationship with Claudia, you'll be in a world of trouble. We know you've been sleeping with her."

"Who says?"

Macy glanced at the closed door to the dining room where Cora Sluka waited. "Who changes and washes the bedsheets?" he asked.

Davitt bought into Macy's trickery and started talking. He copped to having sex with Spalding, and cast himself in the role of a pursued, put-upon employee who only wanted to keep his job.

When Davitt finished, Macy stood. "Did she ever ask you to help her kill her husband?"

"No way," Davitt said, making good eye contact.

"I believe you," Macy said, "and I can't wait to read your book, if you ever get it published."

*   *   *

Late afternoon turned golden, the clear sky so bright that the peaks of the Sangre de Cristo Mountains were washed in a flood of light. On such days, Ramona Pino could still believe in the enchantment of Santa Fe.

Good news from California earlier in the day had put her in an excellent mood. She hummed a song, off-key as always, on the drive to Claudia Spalding's Santa Fe house, search warrant in hand.

In the two units behind her were Matt Chacon and Chief Kerney, who'd invited himself along without explanation. The chief occasionally went out in the field with the troops, but this was the first time for Ramona. Cheerily, she decided not read anything more into it than that, and turned her thoughts to the work at hand.

The arrest of Claudia Spalding, Dean's confession, and the statements given by Coe Evans and Glenn Davitt were important milestones, but the investigation was far from over. Without an admission of guilt from Spalding, which Ellie Lowrey said was highly unlikely, nailing down motive remained a crucial issue.

Without it, Ramona could visualize Spalding's defense attorney in court, convincing a jury that the grieving widow had no reason to murder her husband, that she was a victim of lies and false accusations by Kim Dean and other men of questionable character.

Ramona pulled into the driveway of Claudia's Santa Fe house. It certainly wasn't the Montecito mansion Ellie had described to her, but it was no adobe shack either. It was a long, rectangular, two-story double adobe under a high, forest-green pitched roof, with deeply recessed doors and windows. A horse stable, corral, and hay shed stood nearby under a stand of trees. Given its Arroyo Hondo location with sweeping views of the distant Sandia Mountains and the tip of Mount Taylor, it had to be a million-dollar property.

She waited at the front door for Matt and the chief to join her, wondering why a woman who had so much would risk so much. Perhaps they'd find the answer inside.

She smiled as the two men approached. "Ready to go hunting for secrets?" she asked.

"Lead on," Kerney said.

She searched for a spare house key and found it under a rock at the base of a large bronze and stone garden sculpture of a life-size raven perched on a boulder. Inside, a great room consisting of living, dining, and kitchen areas ran the length of the first floor. It rose to a high vaulted ceiling bracketed on both ends by two second-story lofts accessed by staircases.

Ramona went over the scope of the search warrant with Kerney and Chacon. All written or electronically stored materials pertaining to or mentioning Clifford Spalding, Kim Dean, Mitch Griffin, Coe Evans, and Glenn Davitt, including financial and legal documents, letters, journals, diaries, business correspondence, handwritten notes, lists, address books, calendars, computers, electronic organizers, and recorded telephone messages were fair game.

She made Matt Chacon the inventory officer, responsible for logging and tagging what was found, where, when, and by whom. Prepared for the role that always fell to junior detectives, Chacon opened his briefcase, took out a clipboard, and started organizing the forms he needed.

"I'd better get started," Ramona said, glancing at Kerney.

"I came along to help, Sergeant," Kerney replied. "Put me where you want me."

"We'll start on this floor," Ramona said, wondering if Kerney was testing her on search protocol, "and clear an area for Detective Chacon to use."

The sun was low on the horizon when they finished searching the ground floor and started on the lofts. One served as the master bedroom, and the other was a combination library and music room with a baby grand piano, writing desk, soft leather reading chairs with matching ottomans, and built-in bookcases.

Kerney had just finished with the contents of the writing desk in the library/music room when Ramona came up the loft stairs.

"Have you found anything interesting, Chief?" Ramona asked.

Kerney fanned the stack of papers in his hand. "Not really. Closing documents on the house, property tax notifications, canceled checks, paid veterinary and feed bills for the horses. The usual stuff. How about you?"

"The same. What about the laptop?"

"It's password protected," Kerney answered as he rose with the laptop in hand to turn over to Chacon.

"What about the books?" Ramona asked, looking at the shelves lining the walls. There had to be at least a thousand volumes, and each one had to be checked.

"That's next on the list," Kerney said from the ground floor.

Ramona glanced at some of the titles on the spines. Carl Jung's complete works; books by Boswell, Swift, Yeats, Samuel Johnson, Oscar Wilde, Gabriel García Márquez, and Jorge Luis Borges; Shakespeare's sonnets; Joseph Campbell's works on mythology; a complete shelf devoted to art and architecture.

She passed in front of a cushioned banco below a large window and inspected the next stand of shelves. A book at eye level, *Premier Nudes*, caught Ramona's attention. Next to it was a tome on the erotic world of wrestling, followed by a book of erotic drawings. In fact, the entire set of shelves was given over to erotica, with many of the titles in French, German, and Italian.

She flipped through several volumes. Some were nothing more than photography books of nude men and women, not at all provocative, while others had more explicit sexual content with heavy sado-masochistic and homosexual themes.

"Well, well," Ramona said quietly to herself.

"Find something?" Kerney asked as he returned to the loft.

She turned and handed him a small softcover German book entirely devoted to photographs of a dominatrix with various men.

Kerney opened it to the first photograph, which showed the finely sculpted buttocks of a woman wearing garter belts, stockings, and spike heels. At her feet kneeled a fat, elderly, nude man with downcast eyes.

"Well, well, indeed," Kerney said.

"There's a whole wall of this stuff, Chief."

"Let's see if Claudia Spalding left any messages inside these tantalizing little volumes," Kerney said, fanning through the pages.

They carefully searched through every book in the library, discovering an errant bookmark or two, a forgotten postcard, an occasional cash receipt for a book purchased but never read. They emptied one shelf at a time, and soon the floor, the desk, the chairs, and the top of the baby grand piano were covered with wobbly stacks of books.

Ramona finished first, thumping down an enormous old copy of *The Oxford Universal Dictionary of Historical Principles* on the last empty bit of floor space. She cleared off the piano bench, sat, and watched Kerney as he pulled a book off the lowest shelf and inspected it in the dim light of dusk that filtered through the window.

Ramona switched on the desk lamp. Her fingers were dirty gray, the creases in her palms etched with grit. During the time they'd been searching Claudia's library, Ramona had learned that the chief shared her love of books. They'd exchanged comments about interesting titles, the discovery of favorite authors, and some of the more valuable signed first editions.

Kerney fanned through the last book to be checked, put it down, and rubbed his hands on his jeans. "That does it. Have we missed anything?"

"I don't think so," Ramona said.

"Have you looked inside the piano bench?"

Ramona opened the bench. Inside there was a stack of sheet music, and under it a diary bound in red leather with gilt edging and a sterling silver clasp lock.

"Is there a key for this in the desk?" she asked, holding up the diary.

Kerney found the key and passed it over. Ramona unlocked the diary and read a random, dated entry, written in neat script.

> *K has a lovely penis, medium in size, but he uses it enthusiastically. He lets me fondle it, but I haven't yet taken him in my mouth. I wonder if he's afraid to give up control.*

She scanned another entry.

> *I'm as twitchy and horny as a brood mare in heat. Masturbated three times this morning.*

Ramona flipped back to a longer entry.

> *Dinner out with K last night. The lovely blonde who arrived soon after us with her escort was enchanting. Tiny waist, long legs, perfect hips, and just a sexy hint of a round tummy. I told him she'd be perfect for us to share, and he made some inane comment that he'd have to sleep with her first before he could suggest a threesome. I'm beginning to wonder if I can take him to the next level. He's sexually possessive and not as open-minded as he'd like to believe. But I'll continue to hold my tongue and stroke his little-boy's ego.*

She read aloud an entry made soon after Claudia's move to Santa Fe.

> *Putting distance between Clifford and myself hasn't worked. It's still bondage of a certain kind, no matter how much freedom I've managed to broker for myself in this*

marriage. It's all an anachronism, lacking only the lordly robes of some duke or earl hanging from Clifford's aged body in testimony of his right to possess me. Even his generosity is a two-edged sword, designed to bind me to him to do his bidding, right down to his need to have me at his side at some absurdly boring event. This cannot continue. I will not be owned.

"I think this clears up a few things," Ramona said as she handed the diary to Kerney.

He scanned a few passages. One detailed how Claudia had used her erotica collection to stimulate Kim Dean's interest in more adventuresome sex. It read like a sex manual. Another spoke directly of Claudia's growing desire to rid herself of Clifford.

Kerney closed the diary. "She may have never put her murder plan on paper, but what's here is damaging."

"What do you make of her?" Ramona asked.

Kerney shook his head. "I don't know, but the psychiatrists on both sides will have a field day in court."

Ramona shook her head. "I never imagined sex could be so devoid of any feelings."

Kerney smiled at the comment. "Perhaps you just didn't expect it from a woman."

Ramona laughed and headed for the loft stairs. "Good point, Chief."

"Make a copy of the diary for me, if you will."

"It will be on your desk in the morning."

* * *

A full moon hung in the clear evening sky, shedding a silvery light over the Galisteo Basin and spilling pale shadows across rangeland, low woodland mesas, and grassy hills.

Kerney's earlier attempt to locate Jennifer Stover, the woman who'd owned the gallery where Debbie Calderwood's college roommate once worked, had failed. He was determined, if possible, to find and talk to Stover before calling it a day.

He knew the village of Galisteo well. For a time, he'd worked on the basin as a caretaker of a small ranch while recovering from gunshot wounds, and now he had his own spread on the north lip of it.

Although some of the land near the village had been carved up into residential parcels, most of the surrounding countryside remained open range owned by ranchers who still ran cow-calf operations and cowboyed every day. There were outfits that encompassed ten and twenty thousand acres, but the largest ranch took up almost ninety thousand acres of grassland, canyons, low-slung mesas, and wide sandy creeks that ran west toward the Rio Grande.

Within the private holdings were the remnants of ancient Indian pueblos, petroglyphs etched on massive rock outcroppings, ruins of early Spanish sheep camps, caves with painted pictographs, and abandoned farmsteads rarely viewed by outsiders. Kerney had been fortunate enough to see many of the sites during the times he'd participated in gathering cows on the neighboring ranches during spring and fall works.

A village of several hundred people, Galisteo still retained the look and feel of a Spanish settlement. Tall cottonwoods spread thick branches over high adobe walls, and dirt lanes wound past flat-roofed haciendas and veered away from the deep channel of the small river, in truth no more than a stream, that defined the eastern boundary of the settlement. A small distance beyond the village stood a narrow old highway bridge with concrete railings, and beyond that were the rodeo grounds, consisting of a fenced arena and corrals, where every summer working cowboys from the basin gathered for a weekend of friendly competition.

An adobe church with stone buttresses and rows of narrow, tall windows defined the center of the village, fronting a two-lane state road that crossed the bridge and wandered up grassland hills to Comanche Gap, an ancient route once used by Plains Indians to raid nearby pueblos. Across the road from the church was a small general store with turquoise-blue wood trim, earthy peach plastered walls, and a hand-painted sign that advertized homemade tacos. To the rear of the church, away from the lush tree cover by the river, was a scattering of more modest houses and a cemetery on a rocky knoll.

There were a few businesses in and around the village, but they were not the usual array of gas stations, diners, and motels found in small towns. There was a bed-and-breakfast inn with an excellent restaurant, a riding and horse-boarding stable, an herbalist's shop, an upscale spa resort, a new age spiritual awareness center, and of course the Stover-Driscoll Gallery which had to be somewhere nearby.

Kerney stopped at a lighted house behind the church to ask where the gallery was, and was directed to the old territorial-style schoolhouse on the county road that cut west toward the Cerrillos Hills.

Two cars were parked in front, and warm light poured out into the silvery night through the tall, open windows. From deep inside came the soft sounds of a piano sonata. Kerney's heavy knock on the original double doors brought a quick response by a woman whose expression of anticipation changed to one of surprise.

She was dark-haired with widely spaced eyes and a softly rounded face that matched the attractive curves of her frame. The plain gold band on the ring finger of her left hand signaled to Kerney that if she was indeed Jennifer Stover, she had remarried.

"Are you Jennifer Stover?" Kerney asked, after introducing himself.

"I am," Stover said. "I'm sorry I reacted the way I did. I thought you were Dennis and Marie."

"There's no cause to apologize," Kerney said. "Have I come at a bad time?"

Stover stepped back and motioned Kerney to enter. "I can spare a few minutes."

"That's all I need."

The inside guts of the schoolhouse lobby had been ripped out, enlarged, and renovated, creating a great room of considerable size that spanned the width of the building. Thick posts and beams had been installed to bear the weight of the roof, a rectangular stone fireplace had been added along one wall, and the old oak floors gleamed with a satiny patina.

A fluffy, overweight cat scurried past Kerney's feet and out the open door. Five seating areas filled the room, each large enough to accommodate six to eight people, strategically arranged for viewing the artwork on the walls, all of it modern, abstract, large canvases.

"I'm looking for an employee," Kerney said, "who once worked in your Canyon Road gallery. Her first name is Helen."

Stover smiled. "Helen Randell is my partner."

"Can you put me in touch with her?" Kerney asked.

"She's my partner in life as well as business," Stover added without hesitation. "Why do you need to speak with her?"

"I'm looking for someone she knew a long time ago, and I hope she might be able to help me."

"She's in the kitchen. Follow me."

Stover led Kerney to a converted classroom off the great room, where Randell stood at a counter in front of a bank of kitchen cabinets. Tall, with curly golden hair, she turned when Stover called her name.

"Who do we have here?" she asked, eyeing Kerney.

"A police officer who is trying to find someone," Stover replied.

"Has someone we know gone missing?"

"Debbie Calderwood," Kerney said.

Randell laughed. "Isn't it odd that you can go for years without ever thinking about or seeing someone and then suddenly they repeatedly reappear in your life, one way or another? Debbie is hardly missing, at least not anymore."

"You've seen her or heard from her?"

Randell nodded. "Less than a month ago, at the opera. I was standing in line at the bar before the performance getting drinks and Debbie was right in front of me. At first I didn't recognize her, but it was Debbie."

"You know that for sure?"

"Of course. We talked."

"What did you talk about?" Kerney asked

"We caught up briefly with each other. She's living in Calgary, Canada, and is married to a man who runs a philanthropic foundation of one sort or another."

"Did she tell you her married name?"

"No, we didn't talk for very long."

"Was she with her husband?"

"She didn't say, and I didn't see anyone with her. She did mention that it was her first trip back to New Mexico since she'd moved to Canada many years ago. From the way she was dressed and the jewelry she wore, she's been living very well up there."

"Does the name George Spalding ring a bell?"

"He was her high school boyfriend. In the Army at the time. She didn't really talk about him much, especially after she got involved in the free speech movement."

"Did you exchange addresses?"

Randell shook her head. "No. It was a rather awkward encounter. Even though we were college roommates for a time, we weren't that close, and Debbie didn't seem interested in chatting."

"Would you be willing to work with a police sketch artist so we can create a likeness of Debbie?"

"If it's important," Randell said.

Kerney handed Randell his business card. "It is. Call my office in the morning and I'll set up an appointment for you."

Randell slipped the card into a pocket of her slacks. "Why are you trying to find Debbie?"

"In order to find someone else," Kerney replied.

A knock at the front door ended the conversation, but Kerney had learned far more than he'd hoped for. He thanked the women for their time, made his way past their arriving guests, and drove home, eager to call Sara and learn what she might have gleaned from George Spalding's military records.

*   *   *

In the living room with the dim light of a single table lamp turned down low, in a house almost always much too empty and quiet, Kerney phoned Sara.

"I was hoping you'd call," she said.

"I wanted to apologize again," Kerney said, "for being so pushy."

"There's no need. What happened yesterday is over and done with, and I've got other things on my mind."

"Like what?

"I've just been handed a major project, an important one, and it's a mess."

"Can you talk about it?"

"If members of Congress can, I guess I can too. A number of female soldiers from the enlisted and officer ranks have come forward with charges of sexual assaults that have gone unpunished or not yet been brought to courts-martial. They're claiming shoddy, flawed investigations, unacceptable leniency for offenders, and inadequate victim services."

"It's that bad?"

"Worse," Sara snapped angrily. "Many of them didn't receive rape kit examinations or treatment for their wounds, evidence wasn't gathered and collected, and their requests for base transfers to get away from their attackers have been routinely turned down by post commanders. Besides that, instead of receiving appropriate sexual trauma counseling, they've been ordered to take polygraph tests, and routinely sent back to work while still suffering from psychological and physical problems."

Kerney sat in the leather easy chair Sara had picked out for him at a local furniture store and put his feet on the ottoman. "How many victims are you talking about?"

"Over ninety that we know about, but probably a hell of a lot more, worldwide. The post commanders are laying the blame on inadequately trained investigators and medical personnel. Pardon my

French, but that's bullshit. Some of these attacks were brutal, Kerney, and the victims frequently weren't believed. You should read the case files, they're gut-wrenching."

Kerney pulled off his boots and dropped them on the floor. "What is it you have to do?"

"Let me quote. I'm to 'Prepare a report on readiness to adequately and fully respond to sexual assault complaints, including an analysis of training needs, recommendations for changes to current investigative protocols and procedures, improvement in the coordination of services with Medical Corps personnel, and an estimate of staffing requirements needed to ensure the sufficiency of trained personnel, system-wide.' "

"That's a military mouthful," Kerney said.

"Don't make me use my French again," Sara said. "Instead of writing a report, we should be mounting a full-scale, widespread Internal Affairs operation into each and every one of these cases."

"You don't sound too happy with the brass."

"I'm not. They tried to promote it as a plum assignment, sure to earn me another commendation. But all they really want to do is assuage the politicians and hope the furor dies down."

"You know that for a fact?" Kerney asked.

"Come on, Kerney, you were an army officer. There are two kinds of orders: the ones that are written down and those that aren't. In a private conversation, the scope of my assignment has been clearly limited." Sara's voice was clipped, filled with frustration.

"Does this mean you've hit the glass ceiling?" he asked hopefully.

"I'm not resigning my commission, Cowboy, if that's what you're asking. I want to pin eagles on my collar at the very least before I retire to civilian life."

"And after that, you'll want your first star."

"Probably. But let's not wind our way down that road again. How are you?"

"Ready to see my family," Kerney said. "Will you have time for me?"

"I've got a hand-picked team assigned to assist me. I'll make the time, don't worry about that. Have our horses arrived from California?"

"Not yet. They'll be here next week while I'm with you and Patrick. Riley Burke will look after them until I'm back."

"I'm ready for a long horseback ride with you under a big sky or a full moon."

"A night ride sounds romantic," Kerney said.

"I get to ride Curmudgeon."

"Why do fast women always seem to like fast horses?"

Sara laughed. "You ponder that, Kerney. I'll see you Friday night."

"See you then."

Kerney hung up, went to the kitchen, and fixed a light meal. Although he'd wanted to, he hadn't asked about the George Spalding investigation. It could wait. Worried about Sara's predicament, knowing he could do nothing about it, he sat and ate his dinner without enthusiasm.

ChapterThirteen

Ramona Pino often chuckled at television cop shows that were riddled with cliches and misconceptions about police work, dreamed up by writers who, for the most part, obviously didn't know jack shit about the job. She especially got a kick out of a show that featured a shrink who hung around a police station giving instant psychological insights into suspects and a bombshell babe prosecutor who ran around tidying up flawed police investigations.

She didn't know any shrinks or prosecutors who did things like that. In the real world, cops did most of the theorizing about suspects and virtually all of the hard grunt work necessary to bring a case to trial.

But this Friday morning, Ramona's job was bringing her an unexpected bonus that had a bit of California glamor to it. She was being sent to work with the San Luis Obispo County Sheriff's Department to wrap up the Spalding homicide case. Her airplane ticket and a per diem check were in her purse. She sat in Chief Kerney's office with all of her case materials crammed into a soft canvas flight bag at her feet.

"When do you leave?" Kerney asked.

"This afternoon," Ramona said. "Sergeant Lowrey has offered to put me up."

"I think the two of you will hit it off."

"We already have, Chief. She's meeting me at the Santa Barbara airport."

Kerney scribbled phone numbers of where he could be reached in Virginia on the back of a business card and gave it to Ramona. "I'll be at Quantico for the next two weeks, and I want you to do something for me while you're in California."

Ramona put the card in her purse. "I'll be glad to keep you informed, Chief."

"It's not just that," Kerney said with a smile. "Although I'd appreciate updates. I want you to take a very close look at Spalding's will and his corporate and personal financial records."

"According to the San Luis Obispo Sheriff's Department, they found nothing in Spalding's will that strengthens our case," Ramona said.

"This is for a completely different matter," Kerney said. "Clifford Spalding had a son by his first wife, a boy named George, who ostensibly died while serving in Vietnam. I believe he faked his death, is still alive, and that his father knew the truth and covered it up for over thirty years."

"Why?" Ramona asked.

"I don't know," Kerney said as he slid a manila folder across the desk to Ramona. "But it could have something to do with money."

Ramona opened the folder, which contained a copy of Kerney's case notes. "I'm not an accountant, Chief. Wouldn't it be better to use auditors for this kind of assignment?"

Kerney nodded. "It would, if I wanted a full-scale financial investigation. All I'd like you to do is find out if Spalding or his company had any financial dealings with four people: Debbie Calderwood, who was George Spalding's teenage girlfriend; Dick Chase, a Santa Barbara police captain; Ed Ramsey, the former police chief; and Jude Forester, a young detective in the department."

"Cops on the pad?" Ramona asked.

"Possibly. I think you'll understand my reasoning after you've read the file."

"So much for sneaking in a day at the beach in sunny California," Ramona said with a smile.

Kerney laughed. "Is your bathing suit packed?"

Ramona grinned, nodded, and got to her feet. "That was wishful thinking on my part, I guess."

"Go swimming, Sergeant," Kerney said. "That's an order."

"Yes, sir." Ramona turned on her heel and left the office.

Kerney lowered his gaze to the desktop, where there were letters to be signed, memos to be read, agendas of meetings to attend, and messages to be returned before he could leave for Virginia.

*   *   *

Kerney put his book aside as the plane taxied for takeoff at the Albuquerque Airport. The afternoon summer sky was an unusually low gray blanket of formless clouds that dissolved at the base of the foothills, allowing sunlight to pour down on the mountains east of the city.

Once the plane was airborne, he tried to return to his book, a biography of Benjamin Franklin, but his thoughts were already in Arlington with Sara and Patrick. He had a vivid memory of the Cape Cod-style house where his wife and son would be waiting, and the events that put them there.

He remembered the long cross-country drive in Sara's SUV with Patrick tucked safely in his infant seat, their arrival in Arlington, and the scramble to find housing within a reasonable distance of the Pentagon.

Sara had thought an apartment would be best, so they toured an area of Arlington known as Crystal City, with high-rise apartments, condominiums, hotels, and malls with trendy stores strung out along a busy thoroughfare.

Many of the apartment and condo rentals had magnificent views that looked across the river and took in the Washington Monument, the long grassy mall, and the Capitol in the distance. Kerney had liked none of them; they were boxy and the rents were totally preposterous.

One evening they left their hotel room with Patrick snug and happy in his carriage and took a walk through a nearby residential neighborhood.

"I don't know why you're so dead-set against an apartment," Sara said as they walked the quiet, hilly streets of older homes with green grass lawns and big trees that towered over them. "Besides, you won't be spending much time there."

"Marble countertops, stainless steel appliances, plush carpeting, cedar closets, and city views aside," Kerney said, "I just wouldn't be happy back in Santa Fe thinking of you and Patrick living in some high-rise box."

"Oh, I see," she said teasingly, "this is all about *you*. Unfortunately, my basic housing allowance won't cover anything but a rental."

"How many real houses have you lived in since you graduated from West Point?" Kerney asked.

"Except for the brief times I'm in Santa Fe, not one," Sara said as she bent down to give Patrick a quick look, who gurgled in response at the sight of her.

They sauntered around a corner and climbed a small rise where the homes and lots were larger, except for one vacant house at the bottom of the far side of the hill. It was a small brick house with a shingled pitched roof containing a row of second-story gabled windows. The front door, accented with pilasters, was reached by three steps. First-floor casement windows were lined up neatly on either side of the entrance. A FOR SALE sign in the front yard advertised "Immediate Possession."

"That looks nice," Kerney said.

Sara gave it a wistful glance. "It's probably way out of the range of what I can afford."

"If it's sound, not overpriced, and meets with your approval, I think we should buy it."

Sara looked at the house with heightened interest and then back at Kerney.

"We can afford it, you know," Kerney said over his shoulder as he went to inspect the backyard. It had a thick carpet of grass, several large shade trees, and one long, raised flowerbed. "It's fenced. Perfect for Patrick."

"I'll only be assigned to the Pentagon for three years at the most," Sara said, not yet willing to get enthusiastic. "What if the house needs repair or renovation? That could be expensive."

"Think of it as an investment," Kerney said when he returned. "We'll put a chunk of money down, pay the mortgage out of my inheritance income, and you can use your military housing allowance to gussie up the place if need be."

Sara's eyes danced. "Are you serious?"

"It would make me happy. Patrick would have a backyard to play in, you'd have a place with some peace and quiet, and I wouldn't feel trapped inside a glass and steel high-rise when I come to visit."

Sara laughed.

"What?"

"So it is really all about you," she said.

Kerney grinned. "Only partially."

The next day, they toured the house with the Realtor, who told them it had just come on the market and would sell quickly. They found it charming, in good condition, and because of its small size reasonably priced for the neighborhood. A similar property in the south capital district of Santa Fe would cost about the same.

Kerney made an offer to the owners through the Realtor, who saw no reason for it to be refused. He gave the man an earnest money check, and together with Sara signed a binder requiring the owners to accept their offer by 5 P.M.

Outside of the house, Sara stood with Patrick on her hip, cradled at her side in a protective arm. She smiled up at Kerney. "Amazing."

Her time in New Mexico had deepened the small line of freckles across her nose, lightened her strawberry blond hair, and given her a bit of a high-desert tan. Her green eyes never looked more lovely.

"What's amazing? Kerney asked.

Sara laughed. "You are. I'm a very lucky woman."

Kerney pulled her close and kissed her. "No, I'm the lucky one," he said seriously.

*   *   *

Nothing pleased Jefferson Warren more than representing clients who were tough-minded, clear-headed, and readily understood that the application of law was institutionalized warfare between citizens and the state, bound by legal rules, court opinions, precedent, and statutes.

Warren liked fighters, and Claudia Spalding was scrappy, focused, and unruffled. He'd had such clients before upon occasion, but never one like Claudia, who seemed to possess an icy inner core coated by a refined but readily apparent sexuality. She aroused him in a strange, exciting way.

As always, Warren's first questions had been the most important ones. Had she made any statements to the police? Confessed to the crime? Talked about her case to inmates, jail staff, prosecutors— anybody?

"Of course not," Spalding answered, as though the questions were absurd. "I've only spoken to the attorney who represented me at the arraignment."

Warren waited for more; in fact, he expected it. Some clients rushed to proclaim their innocence, while others, stung by the reality of jail, feverishly questioned him about what could be done to gain their freedom. Some clients even wanted to confess to him, and were shocked when he stopped them quickly and told them he was a lawyer, not a priest.

Claudia Spalding fit none of those profiles. She sat with her back straight, clear-eyed and poised, her slender elegant hands folded on the table, and looked at him comfortably during the long silence.

"You have no questions for me?" Warren finally asked, amazed at her composure.

"Do you have a plan?" she asked, without a hint of dismay.

"I believe so," Warren said, pushing aside the thought of what she might be like in bed. "Let me tell you what we can do in the short term."

It took only a few minutes for Warren to lay out his strategy and explain the rationale behind it. Claudia asked several questions about the points of law he'd raised, then she stood and offered Warren her hand. Her palm was cool to the touch, her nails perfectly manicured, and her grip sure and firm.

"I'll expect to hear from you directly," she said with a brief, fleeting smile.

"Of course," Warren replied, waiting for an outpouring of relief. None came.

He watched as the guard took her away. Something about the woman was dark, unfathomable, and fascinating, like the ancient maps that marked uncharted waters with the warning HERE BE MONSTERS.

*   *   *

The image of Claudia Spalding, cool and aloof in her jail jumpsuit, stayed with Jefferson Warren as he climbed the courthouse steps in San Luis Obispo on a Friday afternoon and walked through the stylized pediment entrance into the dark hallway.

Outside the judge's chambers, the DA, a pompous man with a wide, horseshoe bald spot that covered most of his freckled skull, intercepted him at the door.

"You're wasting my time if you're planning to ask the judge to reconsider granting bail," he said smugly.

Warren smiled down at the portly DA, smoothed his silk tie

against his cream-colored shirt, buttoned his jacket, and opened the door. "I'm sure you know the judge's mind far better than I ever will."

They found the presiding judge, Truett Frye, in his chambers watching the early evening news on a small portable color television. Frye clicked off the televison and stood, unwinding his lanky six-five frame as the two men approached his desk.

"This better be worth my time, Mr. Warren," he said. "I should have been home an hour ago."

"It's really quite simple, your honor," Warren said. "The alleged murder of Clifford Spalding did not occur within your jurisdiction."

"He died here," the DA interjected.

"Granted," Warren replied. "But the legal definition of homicide requires a willful, deliberate, and premeditated act. According to the arrest affidavit and supporting documents, no such act occurred within San Luis Obispo County in the State of California."

The DA snorted in disbelief. "For a two-month period, Clifford Spalding took medication that was prepared and deliberately given to him by his wife and her lover expressly to cause his death. It doesn't matter where it all started; they were killing him slowly, here, in New Mexico, and wherever else he might have been during that time."

Frye looked at Warren. "Your rebuttal, counselor?"

"There is nothing in the statute that speaks to how long it takes a victim to die, or where he dies, Your Honor. Suppose a man is shot but survives long enough to drive himself to a hospital across the county line, or even into a neighboring state. In what jurisdiction should the killer be held accountable for the act?"

"Where the act took place," Frye said, swinging his attention to the DA.

"Think of the altered medication Clifford Spalding was given as a poison, Judge," the DA said. "He took it every day, as prescribed by his doctor, which means he was poisoned in California."

"Can you prove that?" Warren asked.

"The autopsy blood work confirms it," the DA said.

Warren shook his head. "It only confirms that Spalding ingested the substance, not where he took it. Therefore, arguably, the murder occurred in New Mexico, where my client allegedly acted with specific intent to cause the death of her husband, time and place notwithstanding."

"We have a confession from Spalding's lover," the DA said, "that fully implicates her."

"And proves my point," Warren noted.

Frye gave the DA a cold stare. "Who signed the warrant and affidavit?"

The DA named the judge.

He held out his hand. "Let me see them."

The DA passed the documents to Frye, who put on his glasses, paged through them, and then looked at Warren.

"I see your point, Mr. Warren," he said, "but I don't see what good it will do your client. The DA can drop his charges and continue to hold Mrs. Spalding in custody on the New Mexico warrant."

"There is no New Mexico arrest warrant, Your Honor," Warren said.

"Is that so?" Frye asked the DA.

"I'll get one," the DA answered nervously.

Warren smiled. "Until such time, Your Honor, I respectfully request that Mrs. Spalding be released from jail."

Frye glared at him. "So ordered."

"Thank you. Would you call the jail now?"

Frye slammed his hand down on the telephone. "You'd better make damn sure your client stays put, Mr. Warren."

"She gave me assurances to that effect, Your Honor. She'll be at her home in Montecito. I'll take her there myself."

While Frye made the call, the DA used his cell phone to rally the sheriff's troops.

With a signed release order in hand, Warren left the courthouse, called the jail, and told them he would be picking up Mrs. Spalding in a matter of minutes. Two deputies in unmarked police cars were waiting when he arrived. Warren figured a surveillance team was probably on the way to Montecito to make sure she stayed put while other detectives scrambled to get an arrest warrant from New Mexico.

He went inside and got Claudia, who didn't say a word until they were in his car.

"Well done," she said as she buckled her seat belt.

"I don't think you'll be free for very long," Warren said as he pulled onto the highway, the two unmarked police cars close behind. He explained the situation. "Perhaps no more than a matter of hours."

"I understand," Claudia said softly.

Warren glanced at her out of the corner of his eye. The hem of her black dress rode up an inch above her knees, showing sleek, smooth calves. Her hips were nicely rounded, her neck long and flawless.

She turned her head and smiled warmly at him. "Could you hurry a bit, please?"

Claudia Spalding's allure was subtle yet powerful, and Warren found himself obediently hurrying along.

At the gate to the estate, the two unmarked police cars pulled to the curb as he turned into the driveway and entered the code Claudia provided on the keypad. He drove up the lane not knowing what to expect. But he'd represented many celebrity clients, was familiar with their extravagant lifestyles, and figured the estate had to be top of the line. When the mansion came into view it matched anything he'd seen in Beverly Hills.

He parked and looked at Claudia Spalding. "There's a slight chance the judge will reconsider granting bail if you're here when the police show up with a new warrant. I'll certainly make a strong argument for it."

"That's something to look forward to," Claudia said.

"Would you like me to stay with you until they arrive?"

Claudia shook her head, her hand on the door latch. "No, Mr. Warren, that won't be necessary."

"It would be in your best interest to have me stick around," he said, fully aware his motives were mixed.

Claudia flashed him a knowing smile and stepped out of the car. "Yes, I'm sure it would. Good night, Mr. Warren."

He watched her walk to the house, her posture perfect, body moving in a lithesome rhythm, as though she didn't have a care in the world.

*   *   *

Lieutenant Dante Macy found it no easy matter to have a warrant for Claudia Spalding's arrest issued by a Santa Fe district court judge. Since it was after normal working hours on a Friday, he first had to go through a Santa Fe PD dispatcher, who put him in touch with the highest ranking officer on duty, a patrol captain, who in turn referred him to the lieutenant in charge of special investigations.

Macy called the lieutenant at home, who contacted an off-duty detective named Matt Chacon. Detective Chacon got on the stick in a hurry and talked to the ADA on duty. He reported back promptly to Macy that the original arrest affidavit prepared by Sergeant Pino had been turned down by the DA and would have to be reworked and resubmitted.

Macy knew Pino was on her way to California, bringing with her all the case materials. "Do you have the information you need to do it?"

"We have copies of everything," Chacon replied.

"How long will it take you?"

"I'll use what the sergeant wrote, add in the Dean confession, and that should do it."

"How long?" Macy repeated.

"An hour to do the paperwork," Chacon replied. "I'll hand-carry it to the ADA, who has the judge who signed the warrant for Dean standing by."

"My sheriff, who's not a happy camper, is hovering over my shoulder on this, Detective. When will I get a faxed copy?"

"Give it two or three hours, Lieutenant," Chacon said, "barring any unforeseen delays."

"Like what?" Macy asked.

"The district attorney wants to sign off on it. I think he's talking to your DA as we speak."

"Are there any political issues regarding Claudia Spalding I should know about?" Macy asked.

Chacon chuckled. "I don't think Claudia Spalding has any political clout at all in Santa Fe. From what I know about her, she didn't come here to engage in civic affairs, if you get my meaning."

In spite of himself, Macy laughed. "Okay. Thanks for pushing it along, Detective."

"No problem. I'll have it to you as fast as I can."

Macy called Bill Price, who had a team of officers on stakeout at the Spalding mansion. "Is everything quiet?"

"No problem, LT. She hasn't moved, and no one's been to visit since the lawyer dropped her off."

"We should have a warrant from New Mexico in two or three hours. I'll let you know as soon as it comes through."

"Ten-four," Price said.

*   *   *

Because Ramona's tickets had been booked a day before her departure, she wasn't able to fly directly to San Luis Obispo and had to lay over at the Phoenix Airport and catch the last flight to Santa Barbara.

For a time, she sat in the busy concourse oblivious to the people around her and read through the chief's case notes on George Spalding.

Kerney had put everything in chronological sequence, and his narrative style was crisp, clear, thoroughly detailed, and filled with solid observations. The notes read like a compelling mystery, and by the time Ramona finished she was caught up in the case, eager to know where George Spalding was and why he'd faked his own death.

Ramona wasn't surprised by Kerney's investigative skills. She'd watched him work several major crimes, and knew he'd spent most of his career in the major felony crime unit as he rose through the ranks.

Because of his background in investigations, Kerney paid a bit more attention to the unit than most chiefs normally would. But he didn't shirk his larger responsibilities, and Ramona hadn't heard any complaints of favoritism from members of the other divisions.

She put the case notes away and did some people watching. Businessmen and -women in rumpled suits traveling home for the weekend wandered back and forth pulling their wheeled carry-on bags and talking on cell phones. Weary parents chased after hyperactive children. Electric carts with flashing red warning lights passed by carrying senior citizens, frail and disabled people, and young mothers holding infants. Teenage girls in tight jeans showing bare midriffs clattered along. There were middle-aged men in baggy shorts and T-shirts, and an abundance of overweight people.

Her flight left on time and the small turbojet flew west into the sun, with Phoenix and its suburbs below spreading out for miles across the desert floor. Not yet immune to the fun of flying, Ramona passed the time looking out the window. When the plane banked and turned on its final approach to Santa Barbara the ocean came into view, shimmering like an enormous undulating sheet, each wave tufted in white as it broke against the shore.

The Santa Barbara airport was much like the one in Santa Fe, which also served only commuter jets and private aircraft. Portable stairs were rolled up to the plane to unload the passengers, and the terminal, a quaint, tidy California mission–style building, was just a few steps away. Inside, the passenger area was empty, and a small cluster of people waited behind the security barrier, manned by a bored-looking guard sitting on a stool next to the baggage screening machine.

A pretty woman, perhaps two inches taller than Ramona, with short, dark hair and a dimple in her cheek, stepped forward and waved in her direction.

"Ramona?" the woman asked with an easy smile.

"You must be Ellie." Impulsively, she stepped forward and gave Lowrey a hug.

"Welcome to California," Ellie said. "Let's get your bags and hit the road."

As they waited at the covered baggage stall next to the terminal, Ellie's cell phone rang.

"Is Sergeant Pino with you?" Lieutenant Macy asked.

"Yes, she just arrived," Ellie said.

"Good. I need you both here now," Macy said. "Claudia Spalding is out of jail."

"What happened?"

"The judge threw out the arrest on a technicality and released her. She's home, but I've got people there making sure she stays put."

"Do you want us at Montecito?" Ellie asked.

"No, the sheriff and the DA want you and Pino here to vet the new arrest affidavit before it's served. They want everything in perfect order."

"Does it need vetting?"

"I didn't say that."

"Are they just covering their butts?"

"I didn't say that either," Macy replied.

"We're on our way."

"Problems?" Ramona asked as she picked up her luggage.

Ellie smiled. "We've been called into work. I'll tell you about it on the drive."

"Another Friday evening shot to hell," Ramona said cheerfully as she followed Ellie to her unit.

*   *   *

Much more than three hours passed while Detective Bill Price waited in his unit with all the windows down so that no outside sound would go unnoticed. Every ten minutes he checked in with his team by radio. All the entrances were covered, two detectives were constantly circling the estate perimeter in units looking for any sign of movement, and an officer was on station at the bottom of the hill ready to stop, ID, and question the destination of any drivers entering the street.

Price checked the time as he unwrapped a stick of gum and folded it into his mouth. The night breeze whispered through the trees, soft and soothing, and a full moon flung tangled webs of shadows from the branches across the roadway.

The distant sound of rotors made Price stiffen, listen intently, and look up at the empty sky through the windshield.

He got out and did a three-sixty scan. Tall trees blocked his line of sight in every direction.

The sound grew closer and a helicopter broke into view, traveling fast, descending quickly, veering toward the estate.

Price decided he couldn't wait for Macy's call. He reached into the car and grabbed the microphone. "Go, go, go," he yelled. "Stop that chopper."

Car engines roared to life, entrance gates opened, and police cars barreled onto the grounds from three directions, converging on the house. Price swerved around the lead car and braked hard by the front door just in time to see the chopper rise above the rooftop, displaying only the tail boom and rear fins as it flew away.

His cell phone rang. He took a deep breath to swallow his frustration and answered.

"You're good to go," Macy said.

Price watched the flashing anticollision beacon on the upper fin of the chopper recede in the sky. "It's too late. A helicopter just picked her up."

"Dammit," Macy said. "You're sure of that?"

"It just left, Lieutenant. We're at the house now, but we haven't searched it yet."

"Do it," Macy snapped. "I'll notify all the area airports and local police departments."

Price thought about LAX and Burbank, which weren't that far by air, Santa Barbara just minutes away, and all the other, smaller fields Spalding could land at before any cops could get there in time. It seemed hopeless.

"Ten-four," he said.

"Did you ID the chopper?" Macy asked.

"Negative, I couldn't read the markings."

"Dammit," Macy said, this time with more feeling. "Seal that place off and search every inch of it. I'll take care of the warrant affidavit. I want to know exactly what Spalding took with her."

"Roger that." Price put the cell phone away, gathered his team, and began the search.

The only person they found on the premises was Glenn Davitt, the estate manager, waiting for them in his quarters. He cheerfully admitted that he'd seen Claudia fly away.

"Did she say where she was going?" Price asked.

"No," Davitt replied, "just that her arrest had all been a big mistake."

"Were you with her when she arranged for the helicopter?"

Davitt shook his head. "I didn't even know about it until it landed."

"But you saw her leave."

"Yeah."

"What air charter company did she use?"

"I didn't notice."

"What was she carrying?"

"Two bags and a briefcase."

"Did you see her pack?"

"No."

"Where's the housekeeper?" Price asked.

"She gave herself the night off."

"But you stayed here. Why?"

"Look, I didn't help Claudia, if that's what you mean. And even if I had, like I said, she told me everything was cool and you guys had fucked up."

Price didn't believe one word of it. Pissed beyond belief, Price told Davitt he would be held as a material witness.

"What does that mean?" Davitt asked.

"You're going to jail, and you'll stay there until you're called to appear at Spalding's trial."

"When will that be?"

Price smiled wickedly. "Who knows? Months, maybe. It depends on how long it takes to find her. What air charter company did she use?"

"Valley Air, out of Burbank."

"There, that wasn't so hard," Price said as he dialed Lieutenant Macy's number.

"Do I still have to go to jail?" Davitt asked.

"Maybe not."

*   *   *

The full moon Kerney left behind in Santa Fe was hidden by a bleak night sky and a light wind that carried a mist of rain across the river into Arlington. A warm glow came through the windows of the house, and the exterior light was on in anticipation of his arrival.

He paid the cabbie and carried his bags inside just as Sara stepped out of the kitchen. He could feel the grin on his face spread the moment he saw her. Barefoot, dressed in shorts and a halter top that showed the flat muscles of her stomach, her long, slender legs, and the rise of her breasts, she hurried to him and he held her tight, smelling her scent.

After a long look at Patrick, sound asleep in his crib, they sat in the kitchen, Sara sipping wine and Kerney a glass of iced tea. They talked idly, comfortably, about small matters.

Kerney told her of his faulty attempt to build the rock retaining wall at the ranch, and described in detail the horses he'd bought. Sara told him Patrick was about to start teething, and that she was planning to have the old-fashioned radiators enclosed to protect him from accidental burns.

Later, with the bedsheets tangled at their feet, pillows pushed aside onto the floor, damp legs intertwined, Sara talked more about their son. How he was starting to say words, how he would sit quietly and stare at the pages in his picture books.

"He's already reading and talking," Kerney said. "What a genius. Do the three of us have the weekend together?"

Sara reached for the pillows, brought them up to the bed, and yawned sleepily. "We do."

She ran her foot along Kerney's leg and snuggled close. In the darkness, he listened until her breathing slowed into the quiet rhythm of sleep.

*   *   *

A cooperative Glenn Davitt supplied Price with phone numbers where Cora, the housekeeper, and Sheila, the personal assistant, could be reached. After making contact with them by phone, Price sent detectives to fetch them. Once they arrived, he had them show him the secret places where the Spaldings kept their important papers, cash, and valuables.

Cora took him to the hidden safes in the walk-in closets off the master bedroom. In the library, Sheila opened a sliding wall panel that concealed another safe.

All of them were locked, and since Price and his team didn't know diddly about safecracking, he called in an expert, which meant waiting for the guy to show.

Once they were opened, Price found the closet jewelry safes had been cleaned out. Inside the library wall safe were insurance policies, prior year tax returns, real estate documents, car titles, personal property inventories, and current year quarterly investment statements.

One of the insurance polices carried a three-million-dollar jewelry endorsement. Appended to it was a list of the items with an appraised replacement value for each. A thick envelope contained photographs of the jewelry and watches. He called Lieutenant Macy.

"From what the housekeeper could tell me, Spalding packed casual traveling clothes. I don't know how much money she has with her, or if she took her passport, but she cleaned out three million dollars in jewelry that can be pawned or sold for cash. I've got photographs of the jewelry we can circulate."

"There's a BOLO and fugitive warrant out on her," Macy said. "Customs, the Mexican authorities, and Interpol have been alerted. Valley Air dropped her off at Burbank, where a car was waiting. We don't know yet who picked her up or where they went."

"I'm going to shut it down here, Lieutenant."

"Leave a detective behind until I can get the Santa Barbara PD to put a close watch on the place."

"Affirmative."

Price gave the word to his team, walked outside, and studied the deep marks in the grass left by the helicopter landing skids. A daring escape from justice in a helicopter was something right out of a novel. Who would have thunk it?

Over the years he'd listened to a lot of tales by other cops about their biggest cases, the tough ones, the bizarre ones, the headline grabbers. Price figured he was smack in the middle of a doozie that topped them all.

ChapterFourteen

On his trips to Arlington, Kerney tried to take over as many child-care chores as possible. He got up early Saturday morning while Sara slept, and found Patrick stirring in his crib in need of a diaper change. He cleaned Patrick up, dressed him, and fed him breakfast. Then father and son slipped out of the house for a walk around the neighborhood.

Patrick's affectionate personality, inquisitive nature, and sunny disposition delighted Kerney. Whenever he saw something that stirred his curiosity, Patrick's face lit up in a happy smile.

Kerney let Patrick totter along the sidewalk within easy reach, scooping him up whenever he veered toward the street. While riding safely in his arms, Patrick chewed contentedly on Kerney's shirt collar until it was damp and soggy.

The neighborhood, known as Aurora Heights, fascinated Kerney. Developed prior to World War II, the houses borrowed heavily from Tudor, Colonial, and Craftsman-style architecture, giving the area a settled, prosperous feel. Lush lawns were neatly tended, mature trees canopied homes, and tall shrubs screened front windows.

It was a tame, orderly slice of the world, much different from New Mexico's raw deserts and rugged mountains. Although it was pleasing to the eye, the absence of a distant horizon against an immense, limitless sky made Kerney feel hemmed in.

Back at the house, Sara was soaking in the old cast-iron claw-foot tub, reading a book.

She closed the book and put it on the windowsill above the tub. "You don't know how much I love it when you come to see us."

Patrick stood at the edge of the tub trying unsuccessfully to climb in. Kerney picked Patrick up and let him splash his hands in the bathwater. "I try to be helpful."

Sara smiled wantonly. "Actually, my thoughts were more about last night."

He leaned over the tub and kissed her. "It's my turn to fix breakfast."

"Put Patrick in his high chair while you do," Sara said, "and let him help."

Kerney looked down at his son. "How do I do that?"

"Mash some bananas into two small plastic bowls, and give him his spoon and a teething biscuit. He'll stir it all up, dump it from bowl to bowl, and make a mess."

At the kitchen table, Sara, now bathed and dressed, laid out the weekend plans while Patrick sat in his high chair gleefully stirring gooey banana pulp with his fingers. The plastic bowls and spoon had long ago fallen to the floor at Kerney's feet.

Since moving in, Sara had replaced all the appliances and had a contractor put in a new countertop and sink and restore the original kitchen cabinets. The room had a warm, country feel that Kerney liked a lot.

Sara had arranged for them to stay overnight in Fredericksburg at a bed-and-breakfast inn. They would tour the town's historic district, visit some nearby plantations and Civil War battlefields, and perhaps do some shopping. A history buff, Kerney thought it an excellent plan.

He was washing breakfast dishes at the sink when Ramona Pino called from California and gave him the news about Claudia Spalding's fugitive status. The sheriff's department had tracked her to Los Angeles and lost her there. Detectives were working the phones, talking to everyone in California and New Mexico who knew her, hoping to get a lead on her whereabouts. The story had already hit the newspapers and television networks.

"Keep me informed," Kerney said as Sara stepped into the kitchen with a cleaned-up, freshly dressed Patrick at her heels.

"Problems?" she asked, with a tight, resigned smile on her face.

Kerney put the phone down and smiled reassuringly. "Nothing that will spoil our weekend. Claudia Spalding, our murder suspect, is on the lam, but I'm not about to fly out to California and help find her."

"Then let's get out of here," Sara said, "before the phone rings again."

"Good idea."

*   *   *

Late Sunday afternoon, Kerney and Sara arrived back home with a sleepy, cranky Patrick in tow. In his high chair during dinner, he kicked his feet, waved his arms, and refused to eat. After his bath, Kerney put him in his crib and tried to settle him down. When that didn't work, Kerney rocked him until he fell asleep in his arms.

Leg-weary from tromping through battlefields, plantations, and historic old Fredericksburg, Kerney stretched out on the living room couch and read the Sunday edition of the *Washington Post*. While it hadn't made the front page news, the story of Claudia Spalding's flight from justice got half a column of play inside the front section under the headline "Wealthy Murder Suspect Vanishes."

He passed it over to Sara, who was curled up in an easy chair scanning the house and garden supplement.

She read it quickly and handed it back. "That reminds me, George Spalding wasn't a military policeman. According to his records, he was a graves registration specialist, confirmed by his DOB and Social Security number. The information you got from the Santa Barbara Police Department is false."

"The police captain I spoke with told me George's father provided the military documents to his department, and from what I saw in the file they looked authentic to me."

"They had to be forged," Sara said. "I researched the helicopter crash. No such event occurred in Vietnam on that date. George Spalding was killed in an RPG attack at the Tan Son Nhut Airbase."

Kerney dropped the paper and swung into a sitting position. "Do you have his complete service jacket?"

Sara shook her head. "Not yet. I'll get it tomorrow. When do you expect the forensic results on the skeletal remains?"

"In a week, I hope."

"I'll alert the Armed Forces DNA lab and ask them to give it high priority when the results arrive."

"Jerry Grant, the forensic anthropologist I used, suggested the Joint POW/MIA Accounting Command in Hawaii might also be helpful."

Sara rose and raised the window blinds. Muted evening light bathed the oak floor. "I agree, especially given your theory that the remains in the casket aren't those of George Spalding."

"Why do you say that?"

Sara sat back down. "You raised it in your case notes. George Spalding was five-feet-eight, and nineteen years old at the time of his death. Not five-eleven and in his thirties, as Grant's preliminary findings of the remains suggest."

Kerney nodded in agreement. "There's a cover-up of some kind going on."

"A cover-up of what?" Sara asked.

"I don't know. Clifford Spalding did everything possible to thwart his ex-wife's quest to find her son, and we now know he probably gave forged military documents about George's death to the police. Why? Did George fake his death, desert his post, and somehow make his way back to the States from Vietnam?"

"Possibly," Sara said. "As a graves registration specialist he could have been in a position to send home the remains of another soldier under his name. But that deception should have been caught stateside. The Army goes to extraordinary lengths to confirm the identity of every KIA."

"So how could he get away with it?" Kerney asked.

Sara tapped her fingers together. "He couldn't, without help. In the material you sent me, you noted that Clifford Spalding started building his wealth right around the time his son was reported KIA."

"Up until then, he operated a less than successful mom-and-pop motel in Albuquerque," Kerney said. "But the story of how he got the money, or where it came from, can't be substantiated."

"Maybe George supplied the money," Sara said. "Graves registration is part of the quartermaster corps, which controls the flow of massive amounts of material and equipment. Toward the end of the Vietnam War, there were hundreds of reports of black marketeering in stolen military property, drug trafficking, and currency smuggling, that were run by networks of soldiers in the quartermaster corps. Army CID was swamped with cases. Although a lot of contraband was seized before it was shipped to the States, quite a bit of it got through and was never recovered."

"How do you know so much about this?" Kerney asked.

Sara smiled. "I wrote a paper about it when I was at the Command and General Staff College."

"What would it take to do a CID records search to see if George Spalding was a target of an investigation in Nam?"

"I don't know," Sara said, rising to her feet. "The information may be in Spalding's service jacket. If not, I'll have my first sergeant look into it."

"When is your report on sexual assaults due?" Kerney asked.

"In ninety days. But let's not talk about that now."

"Okay, what should we talk about?"

She reached out, took Kerney by the hand, and pulled him close. "Come into the bedroom and I'll tell you," she whispered playfully.

*   *   *

Early Monday morning, Kerney took Sara and Patrick to the Metro rail station and drove Sara's SUV through the insane Beltway traffic south toward Quantico. Weak light in a gunmetal gray sky dulled the thick woodlands that bordered the road to the FBI Academy. On a 385-acre enclave smack in the middle of a U.S. Marine Corps base, the academy had the feel of an austere college campus isolated from the outside world.

Marine guards in combat fatigues reviewed his credentials at a roadside checkpoint and then passed him through to the main gate where a police officer verified his authorization to enter the secure facility.

In the years since Kerney's last visit, much had changed. A new indoor shooting range had been added, a state-of-the-art forensics center had been built, and the Drug Enforcement Agency had opened a separate academy on the grounds. Kerney was eager to see it all.

A cluster of stark concrete buildings, each ornamented by ground-to-roof pillars and connected by glassed-in breezeways known to the staff, as gerbil tubes defined the main campus. Three high-rise towers served as student dormitories, all within easy walking distance of the classrooms, pool, gym, dining hall, and conference halls in the various buildings laid out in a tight geometrical pattern.

The grassy lawns and stands of trees that surrounded the buildings didn't suppress the Spartan feeling. Woodlands bordering the athletic fields and outdoor shooting ranges were rigorously pruned back and held in check. North, behind the red-and-white striped water tower, the forest spread down to a lake, reserved for the use of military and academy personnel and their families.

In the reception area of the administration building, Kerney's credentials were reviewed again and a temporary visitor's pass was issued. While he waited for his escort, he wondered if J. Edgar, the groundhog who lived in one of the enclosed patio areas, was still in residence.

A secretary from the Leadership and Management Science Unit came through the glass door and greeted him. The woman wore the conservative attire favored by the FBI, a pair of black slacks and a white blouse with a subdued bow around her neck. She led him through a maze of hallways and breezeways to a suite of offices, where he was introduced around to the few staff members who were at their workstations.

Assigned to a small office crammed with three desks, chairs, and file cabinets, he settled in to prepare for his two-week stint as a visiting instructor. First, he looked over his schedule. He would teach two morning-long classes, attend a three-hour seminar on terrorism, participate in a roundtable discussion on leadership development, and speak at an evening conference on community policing for midsize law enforcement agencies. All in all, it was light duty with plenty of free time built in.

Classes were already in session, and his first order of business was to attend a luncheon meeting with full-time and visiting faculty in the executive dining room. He reviewed the list of assigned instructors. Edward Ramsey, of the FBI Law Enforcement Communication Unit, was scheduled to teach an afternoon class next week on public speaking and media relations.

Kerney wondered if he was the same Ed Ramsey who'd once headed up the Santa Barbara PD. The instructor résumés inside the three-ringed binder of student course materials confirmed he was. That meant it should be easy to approach Ramsey and engage him in conversation. He'd be interested to learn if Ramsey knew about his meetings with Captain Chase. He hoped so.

He put the binder aside, took out the lecture notes he'd prepared before leaving Santa Fe, and started adding to them.

*   *   *

After a lengthy morning meeting, Sara returned to her cubicle at the Pentagon to find George Spalding's military service jacket on her desk. Known as a 201 file, it contained, among other things, information on Spalding's military training and occupational specialty, performance ratings and promotions, awards and decorations, medical/

dental records, pay and allowances, permanent duty assignments, and disciplinary actions.

The file confirmed Spalding had been a graves registration specialist and not a military policeman. According to his performance ratings, he'd been a marginal soldier at best; so much so that, had he survived his tour of duty in Vietnam, he would have been denied a Good Conduct Medal. However, he was awarded the National Defense and the Vietnam Service Medals.

While Spalding was in Nam, his promotion from Private First Class to Specialist Fourth Class had been delayed due to a CID investigation into missing personal effects of soldiers killed in action. He'd been cleared of any wrongdoing, but a sergeant in his unit had been tried and convicted for theft under the Uniform Code of Military Justice.

Sara made copies of Spalding's dental charts and the CID report for Kerney, put them in her briefcase, and reviewed her notes from her latest meeting with the brass, which had been a rehash of her original marching orders.

Her immediate boss, a brigadier general, had made it clear that none of the closed sexual assault cases would be reopened. Everything in the report to Congress was to be forward-looking and proactive. He wanted loopholes closed, coordination improved, policies defined, protocols recommended, training proposed, staffing patterns detailed, and nothing more.

Post commanders could be interviewed only to gain feedback about how the system could be improved. No case studies of actual investigations were to be included; only a statistical model of the investigations, with graphs and charts, would be incorporated in the report.

She'd griped to Kerney about the decision by the brass to sanitize the shoddy sexual assault investigations, and her dissatisfaction with the assignment was deepening. The agenda was pure face-saving, buck-passing, Teflon-coated gamesmanship.

Sara had come to her Pentagon post as a realist, knowing full well that not everyone in command operated ethically or honestly. But she was saddled with a petty, childish tyrant of a boss, who was more interested in making rank than doing the right thing.

Two choices faced her: she could play the marionette, get her ticket punched, and move up a rung on the ladder. Or she could exercise initiative and risk short-circuiting her career.

Her gut told her that she really didn't have a choice. No woman willing to serve her country, who'd been viciously assaulted and violated while performing her duty, deserved anything less than justice. The shackles put on her by the higher-ups were unacceptable. She would have to find a way to push the envelope and try to force the brass to confront a reality they dearly wanted to avoid. How to do that without scuttling her career was the question.

She touched the glass jar of seashells she'd collected from the beaches in Ireland. A memento from their honeymoon, it brought back happy memories of early morning walks with Kerney along the wild, misty western coast, whitecaps breaking in ink-black water against the shore.

She turned her attention back to Spalding's 201 file. The CID investigator, Chief Warrant Officer Noah Schmidt, who'd cleared Spalding of any involvement in the decades-old stolen property case, might very well be an important source of information for Kerney.

She put in a request to personnel to see if Schmidt was a lifer still on active duty or retired military now working as a civilian for DOD or a branch of the armed services. Then she called the Defense Finance and Accounting Services in Kentucky, which handled military retirement pay, and the Armed Forces Record Center in St. Louis, and asked for a fast check on the man. Hopefully, she'd know something by the end of the day.

Down the hall, Master Sergeant Wilma Lipinski, who worked for Sara, was at her desk. With twenty-eight years of active duty service, Lipinski had recently rotated into the Pentagon from a first sergeant posting with a military police company. Only exceptional noncoms were authorized to stay in the ranks for thirty years, and Lipinski was one of them.

"Ma'am?" Lipinski asked as Sara stepped into her cubicle.

"Have you read my briefing summary on our new assignment?" Sara asked.

"Yes, ma'am," Lipinski replied cautiously. A sturdily built, middle-aged woman, the daughter of a retired Chicago fireman, she'd won the Bronze Star for valor while serving in Bosnia.

"What do you think about it?" Sara asked.

"On or off the record, Colonel?"

"Off the record, Sergeant."

"It sucks, ma'am."

"Exactly," Sara said, taking a scat. "How many of the sexual assault cases are still carried as active?"

Lipinski consulted a binder. "Thirty-eight at JAG awaiting disposition, and twenty-six are still being investigated by CID."

"The general doesn't want us to touch the closed cases in our report," Sara said. "But he failed to say anything about those that are still active."

Lipinski blinked. "I think it's pretty clear that we're not to do any investigating, Colonel."

"I'm thinking more along the lines of research, Sergeant, that gets to the core issues of what we're charged to address in our report."

"Field research?" Lipinski asked.

"Yes, with information we can append to the report."

"Aren't you splitting hairs, ma'am?"

"Definitely."

Lipinski smiled. "Your orders, ma'am."

Sara's team of six noncoms and officers had been drawn from military police corps personnel assigned to area bases. "We'll field survey one-third of the active cases: nine that are still under investigation, and twelve at JAG. Pick cases that are within a reasonable striking distance and divide the work as equally as you can among the team."

Lipinski scribbled a note. "I could take on some of the cases, ma'am."

"Don't jump into deep water too fast, Sergeant."

Lipinski smiled broadly. "I know how to swim, Colonel."

"Okay, you're on the team. Find an off-site facility were we can meet and go over the details. Did you read Spalding's 201 file?"

"Yes, ma'am."

"Get me what you can on that sergeant Spalding worked for in Vietnam who was busted for theft."

"I've already put in a priority request through channels, Colonel."

"You have a degree in criminal justice and twenty-eight years of service, Sergeant. Care to tell me why you never pursued a commission?"

"A long time ago, I decided it was better to be part of the backbone of the Army rather than part of its head. I've observed that when heads roll, it's frequently the wrong heads."

*　　*　　*

At lunch, Kerney made it a point to sit next to Ed Ramsey, who talked amiably while packing away a meal of meatloaf and soggy mashed potatoes smothered in gravy.

In his fifties, Ramsey looked fit in his brown suit. He had a full head of hair, a ruddy complexion, and blunt, strong-looking hands. Kerney picked at a dry chicken breast and nibbled his salad as Ramsey made small talk.

"I understand you've taught here before as a visiting lecturer," Ramsey said affably.

"Once, some years ago," Kerney replied.

Ramsey nodded. "I've never been to Santa Fe."

"Tourists love it."

Ramsey touched the corners of his lips with his napkin. "Any good golf courses?"

Kerney finished the salad and pushed his plate aside. "Far too many for my taste."

"Why is that?" Ramsey asked, laughing.

"Santa Fe is high desert country. It takes a lot of water to keep fairways green, and we don't have enough to go around. Is golf your game?"

Ramsey grinned. "I hack at the ball every chance I get. If I'm not on the links, I'm sailing. Last month, I taught a police media relations class in Chicago. Stayed over on the weekend and spent two days on Lake Michigan. Pure magic."

"Do you live near the water?" Kerney asked.

Ramsey shook his head. "It's too high-end for me. I have to haul my boat from home, but it isn't that far."

"Where is home?" Kerney asked.

"Do you know the area?"

"Not at all."

"Stafford," Ramsey said with a half smile. "It's a small city south of here. If you have time, you can meet me at the river this weekend, and I'll take you sailing."

"Thanks," Kerney said, "but I'm not much of a water person. Do you miss Santa Barbara?"

Ramsey dropped his napkin on the table. "Not really. As long as I'm near water, I'm happy. Listen, if I can't take you sailing, how about sitting in on my class next week? That civilian task force on community policing and the mentally ill you established last year was really innovative. I plan to use it as an example of how to build good media and community relations. It would be great to have you there to do a Q&A with the students."

"I'd be glad to participate," Kerney said as he got to his feet. The luncheon was winding down. An attractive female agent was gathering the other adjunct instructors around her to take them on a tour. "Guess I'd better join up for the tour."

He shook Ramsey's hand and followed the group out of the building, mulling over his conspiracy theory. Ramsey hadn't said a word about the Spaldings. Maybe Ramsey and Captain Chase hadn't colluded with Clifford Spalding to keep Alice in the dark about her son. Maybe Clifford Spalding had finessed the whole thing.

Kerney decided there were too many maybes. Soon his attention was drawn away by the tour. The new indoor range was a marvel, with high-tech, small-arms combat shooting stations that tested accuracy, judgment, and reaction times in deadly force situations. He got a huge kick out of seeing the Behavioral Science Unit, made famous by a number of movies about serial killers.

Windowless, with mazelike corridors, hidden away in a sub-basement, the unit was unlike the neat, tidy, well-appointed office suites everywhere else in the complex. There were stacks of boxes in hallways, piles of research books spilling off shelves, desks cluttered with reports and paperwork, movie posters tacked to office walls, and dusty, unused typewriters and broken office machines heaped on steel gray work tables.

But the pièce de résistance, the object that truly defined the eccentricity of the staff, was the framed picture of a space alien prominently displayed among the official staff photographs that lined a wall near the elevator.

Outside, within easy walking distance, they strolled the streets of Hogans Alley, a self-contained, completely functional village built to train agents in crime scene scenarios. They finished up the tour with a peek inside the new forensic building and the DEA Training Academy.

During lunch, Ramsey had mentioned that he owned a home in Stafford, a commuter community halfway between Quantico and Fredericksburg. Kerney decided that finding out how Ramsey lived might go a long way to answering some of his questions about the man. With the afternoon still young, Kerney drove south on the congested interstate that ran the length of the eastern seaboard from Maine to Florida.

After a failed attempt to locate Ramsey through the phone book at a gas station in Stafford, Kerney stopped at the county administration building and visited the public utilities office on the first floor, where a very helpful clerk provided Ramsey's mailing address along with driving directions to the house.

Located in a private subdivision surrounding a golf course, the house looked out on a fairway with water hazards, sand traps, stands of big trees, and a paved golf cart lane that wandered up and down the gently rolling terrain. Dense, overgrown woodlands bordered the houses and the golf course. From the lay of the land Kerney could tell the developer had carved the subdivision out of the forest to create a duffer's paradise. A dozen or so golfers were out on the links teeing off and scooting around in their carts.

Ramsey's house was a big, two-story, modern structure with a tall, overwhelming entryway and a red brick facade under a series of pitched roofs. Outside the two-car garage was an expensive sailboat on a trailer and a high-end touring motorcycle. Ramsey obviously liked his toys.

The subdivision was completely built-up and looked fairly new, expensive, and exclusive. Nothing about it felt like an enclave for civil servants. The houses along the streets consisted of a half dozen different floor plans in varying sizes, all with similar exterior treatments and rooflines, probably required by homeowner covenants.

Somewhere Kerney had read, "Americans like sameness." Personally, he found it boring.

A sign at the clubhouse announced that the course was for the use of residents, members, and their guests only. On a putting green near the pro shop, Kerney spoke to an older fellow wearing a golfing cap, and shorts that showed his tanned, spindly legs.

The man chuckled when Kerney said he liked the neighborhood, was looking to buy, and wondered if there were any homes for sale.

"All the houses sell within twenty-four hours after they hit the market," he said. "Your best bet is to get on a Realtor's waiting list."

"If you don't mind my asking," Kerney said, "what's the price range?"

The man pushed his cap back. "The smaller homes are in the $750,000 range. Those are mostly snapped up by empty-nesters or retired couples like me and the wife."

"I've got a growing family," Kerney said, thinking about the size of Ramsey's house.

"Then you're looking at right around seven figures," the man said. "Of course, that gives you equity in the club and unlimited use of the golf course."

Kerney smiled. "That's what I want."

The man nodded knowingly. "What's your handicap?"

Kerney, who'd never golfed in his life, shrugged. "Not very good."

The man laughed again. "I know what that's like. Well, this is the right place to work on your game. We've got a great resident pro."

"That's what I need," Kerney said, looking out at the greens. "Are the natives friendly?"

The man smiled at the comment. "Folks here get along well. There's a good mix of people."

"Civil servants?" Kerney asked.

The man shook his head. "Not too many of those. Some mid-level government appointees live here, but mostly we've got lawyers, doctors, think tank analysts, scientists, and of course old duffers like me."

Kerney left the man to his putting practice, and during the stop-and-go drive to Arlington, with tractor-trailers cutting in and out of lanes and drivers tailgating madly, he did some math in his head. Could a federal employee on a civil service salary and a police retirement pension afford a million-dollar home?

Kerney wasn't sure. Even with a large amount of equity from the sale of a previous house in Santa Barbara, could Ramsey afford a five- or six-thousand-dollar-a-month mortgage payment? What would his annual property taxes be? Was he still paying for his adult toys on top of the mortgage?

Ramsey seemed to be living large, and until he found out more, Kerney decided to keep him in his sights.

He called Sara on his cell, told her he'd pick Patrick up from day care at the Pentagon, and asked if she'd be home for dinner.

"What are you fixing?" she asked.

"I don't know yet."

"Sounds good," Sara said. "See you for dinner."

*　　*　　*

Sara came home to fresh-cut flowers on the dining table, Yo-Yo Ma playing a Haydn cello concerto on the stereo, the smell of dinner cooking in the kitchen, and Patrick dressed for bed in his pajamas. She picked Patrick up from his playpen and found Kerney at the stove adding mushrooms and onions to a skillet of browned chicken.

She kissed him on the cheek. "How was your day?"

"Good," Kerney said. "And yours?"

"Fine." On the way home, Sara had decided not to tell Kerney about her planned end run around the brass at the Pentagon. She didn't want the evening to spiral into a discussion of why it would be best for her to resign her commission. "Did you get some playtime with your son?"

"He wore me out," Kerney said.

After dinner, Patrick got cranky. Sara examined his mouth, called Kerney over, and pointed out the tip of a small front tooth showing through his gums. She gave him a teething ring to chew on, which helped, but his discomfort kept him awake long past his bedtime.

Once he was finally asleep, they sat at the kitchen table, Sara sipping the last of her wine, Kerney reading the paperwork from George Spalding's 201 file.

"What about this CID investigation?" Kerney asked.

Sara put the wineglass down. "I talked by phone with the case investigator, a retired chief warrant officer named Noah Schmidt. He says the sergeant he busted, Vincent DeCosta, was involved in illicit gemstone trafficking. Mostly high quality rubies and sapphires smuggled into Vietnam from Thailand, transported stateside, and sold on the black market to dealers. But he couldn't prove it. He had enough on DeCosta to charge him with theft of personal property, which he did, while he continued to work the case. However, DeCosta escaped from the Long Binh Jail in Vietnam before he could be tried. He's never been seen since. He's still carried on the books as a deserter."

"Did Schmidt ever prove his smuggling case against DeCosta?"

Sara shook her head. "His informant in Bangkok went missing."

"How did DeCosta get away?" Kerney asked.

"During the pullout, the Army was shutting down the stockade at Long Binh and sending all the prisoners stateside. Schmidt thinks someone bribed one of the MP guards to look the other way."

"Schmidt is sure George Spalding wasn't involved in the gemstone smuggling?"

Sara shook her head. "Not at all. He thinks the smuggling ring consisted of a small group of enlisted personnel who worked with DeCosta. He just couldn't prove it. Spalding and the other cohorts were cleared solely on the basis of insufficient evidence. They alibied each other."

"Did Schmidt have a handle on the volume of smuggled gems?"

"Only one shipment was intercepted at the Oakland Navy base. According to the experts who examined the stash, countries of origin for the stones included Burma, India, Thailand, Pakistan, and Sri Lanka. All of the gems were cut, polished, and ready for sale. The estimated street value was a quarter of a million dollars for the shipment, at early 1970s prices."

"What kept Schmidt from following up on the case?" Kerney asked.

"He got promoted and reassigned. The investigator who took over the case was a short-timer who dropped the ball."

Kerney closed the file. "What do you know about Sergeant DeCosta?"

"Nothing more than you do, yet," Sara replied "We're waiting on his 201 file." She handed Kerney a slip of paper. "Schmidt is more than willing to speak with you. That's his home phone number."

"Thanks." Kerney put the paper on top of the Spalding documents. "How's your project coming along?"

"It's getting under way."

"Are you just too tired to talk about it, or trying to avoid the topic altogether?"

"Don't try to use your interrogation skills on me, Kerney. When are you taking me out to dinner?"

"Is tomorrow night soon enough?" he replied.

"That will work."

Later, as Sara slept beside him, Kerney tired to figure out what was bothering her. Was she in a bind at work because of her assignment to prepare a report on the sexual assault of servicewomen? Was she avoiding the issue for his sake while he was here? Or was it something he'd completely missed, something he had done?

It wasn't like Sara to hide her feelings or skirt an issue. He didn't know what to do other than wait it out.

ChapterFifteen

Kerney's time with Sara and Patrick passed quickly, but not without incident. By the end of his first week in Arlington, Sara seemed preoccupied and distant. She slept poorly at night but wouldn't talk about what was bothering her. As a result, their evening conversations kept to chitchat about Patrick, her plans to build a covered patio in the backyard, the events of Kerney's day at the academy, and similar mundane subjects.

Over the weekend, Kerney forced down every instinct he had to confront her uncharacteristic reserve. Sunday night, he could no longer contain himself.

"There's absolutely nothing wrong," Sara said in response to his question. She shifted her position on the couch to look at him and put her after-dinner liqueur on the coffee table.

"That covers a lot of ground," Kerney said from the other end of the couch.

"Meaning?"

Kerney sipped his cordial. "You're not one to leave things unsaid."

Rain began pattering on the side of the house and coming in through the old wooden window screens. Sara got up and closed the windows. "Don't get bullheaded on me, Kerney. Just give it a rest. Nothing's wrong."

"You're irritable, not sleeping well, and evasive every time I ask you what's wrong."

She returned to the couch. "If so, it's for good reason."

"I'd like to hear it."

She gave him a feisty look. "Okay, I'll make it short and sweet. I don't want to tell you what's going on because you'll harangue me about resigning my commission."

"I harangue you?"

"You have a tendency to lecture."

Kerney shook his head in rebuttal. "I don't mean it to sound that way."

"I believe that's true," Sara said. "But you knew what you were getting into when you married me. I'm career Army, and that fact alone makes family life hard. We live apart by your choice, and that makes it even more difficult. But never once have I asked you to quit your job, leave Santa Fe, and follow me from post to post until I retire. You could give me the same consideration."

Kerney was silent for a time. Finally he said, "I can see how you might think I've been pestering you to quit the Army. I won't do it anymore."

"Thank you."

"But I don't think you're telling me the whole story. Does it have something to do with that assignment on the rape of servicewomen?"

"Mostly," Sara replied.

"Want to talk about it?"

"Not yet." She slid closer to Kerney and ran her hand up his leg. "I know I've been a bit preoccupied with work, but I haven't been unapproachable, have I?"

"Are you trying to distract me with sex?" Kerney asked, breaking into a smile.

"Is it working?" Her hand moved to his crotch. "Oh my, what's this?"

*   *   *

Late in Kerney's second week at Quantico, Claudia Spalding was still on the loose despite intensive efforts to locate her, and Ramona Pino, who was back in Santa Fe, had been unable to find a money trail between Clifford Spalding and any past or present members of the Santa Barbara Police Department. However, fresh information about the George Spalding investigation had begun to come in. First, Jerry Grant, the forensic anthropologist, called.

"The narrowly angled pelvis, the rounded head of the femur, and the length of the femur, confirm it to be the skeleton of a male, slightly less than six feet in height," Grant said.

"You already told me this in Albuquerque," Kerney said.

"But I needed to verify my observations," Grant replied. "Now it's fact. The joints were completely fused with the bones and showed only slight wear, which is consistent with an age range of thirty to thirty-five years."

"Did you find anything that would help ID the remains?" Kerney inquired.

"Nothing," Grant said, "and lacking a skull, I couldn't even determine race. But there were no tool marks that would indicate the body had been dismembered."

"That's interesting."

"I thought so. What I did find was microscopic evidence that the body had decomposed badly before interment."

"I thought you said the bones had been cleaned."

"Yes, but not well enough. The evidence suggests the remains were exposed to the elements for a period of time. In Vietnam, a body could decompose down to cartilage, bone, and sinewy ligaments in a matter of a few weeks. That could explain why the skull, hands, and feet were missing. Predators could have easily scattered those bones."

"But you're sure the man was shot?"

"Absolutely. My best guess is by an automatic weapon, but I couldn't swear to it in court. I asked the Central Identification Laboratory in Hawaii to run all the information through their database. It yielded a list of seventy-six military and civilian Americans and thirty-nine foreign nationals who fall within the parameters. I'll fax it to you."

"Great."

"By the way, the Armed Forces DNA lab at Walter Reed has the results from the bone sample I took. They said they were expecting it when I called to tell them it was on the way. You must know people in high places."

"I do," Kerney said. "Has the lab in Albuquerque finished the mitrochondrial DNA comparison tests?"

"You should hear from them today," Grant replied. "I'll fax my report to you along with the list from Hawaii."

Sara called shortly afterward. "Vincent DeCosta, the sergeant George Spalding served with in Vietnam, has a cousin. He says De-Costa's younger brother, Thomas, emigrated to Canada during the Vietnam War to avoid the draft, and hasn't been seen or heard from since."

"Where in Canada?"

"I don't know," Sara replied. "We've asked the Canadian authorities to locate him if possible."

"Debbie Calderwood said she lives in Calgary, Canada."

"That's why I thought you'd like to know. I've got to run, I'm a busy girl."

Kerney called Ramona Pino. "Was there a Canadian connection in any of Clifford Spalding's personal or corporate financial records?"

"He owns several hotels in Canada, and a third of the proceeds from his estate will go to a foundation he established in Canada, the High Prairie Charitable Trust."

"What do you know about the foundation?" Kerney asked.

"Nothing, Chief."

"Look into it," Kerney said. "I want as much information as you can get. When it was incorporated, who directs it, what its purpose is, who the board members or trustees are, and any financial statements and annual reports."

"Didn't Debbie Calderwood tell her old college roommate that her husband ran a philanthropic organization in Calgary?" Ramona asked.

"She did," Kerney replied. "Query the Calgary police for information about her, her husband, a man named Vincent DeCosta, and his brother Thomas. They may have changed their names. Fax them the police sketch of Debbie."

"Who's this DeCosta?" Ramona asked.

"He's an Army deserter who served with George Spalding in Nam."

"I'll get on it, Chief."

Kerney put the phone down and went back over his notes on Ed Ramsey. During the past few days he'd used his free time at the academy checking into Ramsey's background.

Ramsey had started his law enforcement career in Missouri and worked briefly for a small department in Illinois, before moving to California and joining the Santa Barbara Police Department as a patrol officer and then moving up through the ranks. The police standards and certification boards in all three states had no disciplinary reports or formal complaints about him on file.

Ramsey's credit history proved to be more interesting. He had a sizable mortgage on his Stafford home, as well as personal loans for a boat, motorcycle, and two automobiles. Additionally, the report showed another real estate loan in the amount of two hundred thousand dollars for property in Maine. The bank that held the note reported it was for a summer home on the coast near the town of Camden and that Ramsey had purchased it two years ago. Ramsey's total loan payments added up to a six-figure annual nut.

He used his credit cards frequently, occasionally for big ticket items, but always paid the balances in full each month.

From the FBI Personnel Office, Kerney learned that Ramsey's civil service position was rated as a GS 12. From the California Public Employees' Retirement System, Kerney learned how much Ramsey received annually through the pension fund. Even if Ramsey was at the top end of his salary scale, his combined income from wages and retirement pay fell far short of the money needed to fuel his lifestyle. It pointed to an additional income stream that Kerney couldn't find until he knew where to look.

That afternoon, Kerney sat in on Ramsey's media relations class and did a Q&A about his efforts to improve coordination between his department and community agencies serving chronically mentally ill patients. Kerney explained how the deaths of two seriously mentally ill individuals had prompted him to appoint an ad hoc citizen task force to develop and implement a special training program for all sworn personnel.

After class, Ramsey shook Kerney's hand and thanked him for his participation.

"When do you head home to Santa Fe?" Ramsey asked as they walked down the hallway.

"I'm at work Monday morning, with a full plate waiting for me."

Ramsey flashed an understanding smile. "Isn't that always the case? From what I've been reading in the newspapers, you've still got the Spalding homicide hanging fire."

"She's still out there, but we don't know where. I understand you met her husband some time back."

Ramsey laughed and nodded. "When he was married to his first wife. We called her Crazy Alice. I spoke to him a few times."

"How did that come about?" Kerney asked as they descended the stairs to the ground floor.

"The woman had some hare-brained idea that her dead son was still alive. She was obsessed by it, and kept calling my department to report alleged sightings. Spalding found out what she was doing and came in to set the record straight. He brought full documentation with him of his son's death in Vietnam. He said he couldn't control her behavior, and asked for my understanding in the matter. From that point on, I had my detectives humor her whenever she called with a new lead."

Kerney nodded knowingly. "Cranks and crazies, they're everywhere."

"That's what makes a chief's job so much fun. But when they're rich and influential, you've got to placate them a bit more than the average civilian. Any ideas of why the current Mrs. Spalding killed her husband?"

Kerney stopped in front of his office. "A few."

"Probably for the money," Ramsey said. "He had a shitload of it."

"Interestingly, that hasn't popped up as a motive."

Ramsey shrugged. "I guess there are as many motives to kill as there are victims. We need to get you back here to teach again."

"I'd like that."

"Good. I'll make it happen."

After Ramsey waved good-bye and disappeared around a corner, Kerney smiled. From what he'd said about Alice Spalding, Ramsey clearly knew Kerney had been snooping into the case, and his most likely informant was Dick Chase. Ramsey had stopped short of probing the subject more deeply, but his curiosity about it had been real. It was also interesting that Ramsey had focused on money as a motive for Clifford Spalding's murder. Did he have a personal interest in Spalding's wealth that made him jump to that conclusion?

Kerney was now convinced, in spite of what Ramona Pino had told him to the contrary, that there had to be a money trail connecting Clifford Spalding, Ed Ramsey, and Dick Chase.

On his desk he found a note to call the lab in Albuquerque. He dialed the number and spoke to a senior tech, who gave him the results of the DNA comparison testing. The remains were not those of George Spalding.

*   *   *

Friday night, Sara came home at a reasonable time with news from the Armed Forces DNA Identification Laboratory at Walter Reed. As she fed Patrick his dinner in his high chair, she told Kerney what had been discovered.

"The remains in Spalding's casket belong to a chief petty officer. He was lost overboard when his strike assault boat came under fire during a mission to pick up a SEAL team operating near the Cambodian border in 1972. According to eyewitness reports, he took rounds in the chest. Several other sailors were wounded."

"At least he wasn't a murder victim," Kerney said, "which means we have one less crime to worry about. How was his body retrieved?"

Sara wiped Patrick's chin with a napkin. "There's no record that it was, at least by our personnel. The file does show that South Vietnamese naval commandos mounted several search and recovery missions for his body after the SEAL pullout. But there are no follow-up action assessment reports. They were probably burned before Saigon fell. Lots of official documents were destroyed to keep them out of the hands of the North Vietnamese."

"What about mortuary records?"

Sara held out the spoon to Patrick. He took it and banged it on the high chair. "According to the quartermaster corps, the sailor's remains were never received at either Da Nang or Tan Son Nhut. From what we now know, the likely scenario is that after Spalding faked his death, someone at the mortuary sent the body bag home under Spalding's name, and whoever processed it stateside made sure no questions were asked."

"I wonder how many gemstones were in the body bag, and how Spalding left Nam without getting caught."

"Given his job, it would have been easy for him to assume a dead soldier's identity. He probably came home on a chartered troop transport flight."

"He would have needed orders to do it."

"Which a processing clerk could have provided for a hefty bribe."

"That makes sense," Kerney said. "Has the sailor's family been notified?"

Sara shook her head as she tried to get Patrick to eat more dinner. He pushed the spoon away. "No, but when they are told, there will be no mention of the fact that his remains were unearthed in a casket buried over thirty years ago under another man's name."

"I think he's finished eating." Kerney took Patrick out of his high chair and plopped him on his lap. "That would be an embarrass-ment to the military."

Sara gave him a guarded look. "Do you think they should be told the truth?"

"I don't think that would be wise," Kerney said. "The family has had over thirty years to wonder, hope, and grieve. Let them bury him and move on. What are the Army's plans to find George Spalding?"

"JAG and CID have mounted a full-scale investigation into the en-tire gemstone smuggling operation. It's quite possible that a quarter-master officer, who has since retired at a fairly high rank, may have been involved."

"Why do you say that?"

"The officer in question authorized the release of the remains to Clifford and Alice Spalding *and* logged in the body bag containing the gemstone shipment that was intercepted."

Patrick smeared a sticky hand on Kerney's shirt and burped. "Are you still in the loop on the case?"

Sara shook her head. "Only peripherally, but I'll keep an eye on it. When will you tell Alice Spalding about her son?"

"Not right away," Kerney replied. "Although with her deteriorat-ing mental condition it might not matter when I did. Are you busy to-morrow night?"

"Of course not, it's Saturday."

"Good. I've booked dinner reservations at a Georgetown restau-rant. Afterward, we have tickets for a chamber music concert in the city. I've already arranged for a babysitter."

Sara smiled. "That sounds nice."

Kerney lifted a very smelly Patrick off his lap. "I think our young friend needs his diaper changed."

"Your turn," Sara said. "I'll do the dishes."

Kerney took Patrick away and cleaned him up. Through the open door he could hear Sara loading the dishwasher. She was still a bit preoccupied and overworked, and not her usual self. But the tension between them had diminished.

Kerney thought it best to let the situation ride. He didn't want anything to spoil his last two days in Arlington.

He put a clean diaper on Patrick and tickled his belly. "Let's have a great weekend, Champ, before I head back to Santa Fe."

Patrick giggled in agreement, burped, and kicked his little feet in the air.

*　　　*　　　*

A late afternoon summer sky greeted Kerney upon his return to New Mexico. The sun flooded golden light on the desert and made the distant peaks behind Santa Fe flutter miragelike against a hot blue horizon.

The thought of returning to the solitude of his empty ranch house depressed Kerney. After two weeks with Sara and Patrick, he didn't want to face the feeling of loneliness that would surely come as soon as he got home. Instead, he went to his office. On his desk was a memo from Ramona Pino and some material on the High Prairie Charitable Trust. According to the memo, the Calgary Police Department and Canadian federal authorities had not yet completed background checks on the staff and board members of the trust. Efforts to locate Debbie Calderwood, George Spalding, and the DeCosta brothers had just gotten under way.

Kerney turned to the charitable trust documents. Established twenty-eight years ago as a private foundation, its mission was to conserve, protect, and restore native prairies in Alberta and Saskatchewan, preserve historical sites in both provinces, and provide scholarships to agricultural students at Canadian colleges.

A small staff of four people ran the organization: a CEO, a director of development, a grants manager, and an administrative assistant. The board consisted of three individuals, including Clifford Spalding. It met twice annually to make grant awards and allocate funds. Except for Spalding, no familiar names were listed as staff or board members.

The permanent endowment came solely from gifts made by Spalding, and in the last two years, he'd tripled his annual contribution of cash and investments to the trust, which currently exceeded sixty million Canadian dollars.

The most recent annual report showed funding of program activities by category only. Over four million dollars had been disbursed in the reporting period, but there was no breakout of the organizations that had received funding or the amounts allocated.

Kerney eased back in his chair. The last light of evening had passed, along with his hope Pino would have found a money connection between Clifford Spalding, Ed Ramsey, and Dick Chase through the foundation. If one existed, it was hidden. He'd ask Pino to dig deeper.

Kerney had also hoped that the Canadian connection would lead him to George and Debbie, but nothing had surfaced. Still, it was conceivable that Clifford had been secretly bankrolling his son through the trust over the past twenty-eight years. Or perhaps, as Sara had suggested, George had bankrolled his father, and the trust was a blind used to launder and deliver George's cut of the corporate profits.

Kerney had strong evidence that Clifford Spalding had falsified his son's military records, probably with George's help. Did the two men do it to keep Alice Spalding in the dark about their ill-gotten gains? By making George out to be a good soldier who'd died in combat, did they hope she'd accept his death more readily? If so, it had backfired.

But what motivated Alice to keep searching for George? Did she have suspicions about Clifford's sudden financial windfall that got him started building his hotel chain? Or had Clifford tripped himself up in the lies he'd told to keep the truth from her? And why had she been kept from knowing the truth in the first place?

Kerney figured with Clifford dead and Alice mentally out of it, only George could answer those questions, if he could be found. Otherwise the reasons would stay buried in the past.

Kerney wondered why Spalding had tripled his contributions to the trust during the last two years. His will divided his estate in thirds, shared equally by Claudia, the trust, and Alice, who was entitled to her slice through the divorce settlement.

Had Spalding been moving cash and investments into the foundation to reduce the amounts Claudia and Alice stood to inherit? Did he want to penalize Alice for being a thorn in his side for so many years, and punish Claudia financially for violating the terms of their amended prenuptial agreement?

Kerney wrote out his questions, knowing he might never learn the truth. He attached them to a note to Ramona Pino asking her to look deeper into the trust, put it on her desk, and went home.

At the ranch, he heard the whinny of a horse through the open truck window. He drove toward the barn, and the two geldings he'd bought in California, a red roan and a gray, scampered to the far end of the corral away from the glare of the truck headlights. There was a note taped to the barn door from Riley Burke saying he had put Comeuppance in a stall across from the geldings to keep the animals separated, and the brood mare was stabled at his father's place.

Kerney walked to the corral on the opposite side of the barn and Comeuppance trotted over to check him out. He spoke to the horse in low, reassuring tones, but Comeuppance didn't buy it, and moved away, shaking his mane.

Kerney checked the stalls. They were clean, with a fresh mat of straw laid down, and the doors were latched open to give the animals access to shelter. The geldings were friendlier, and Kerney spent some time talking to them and feeding them a few horse biscuits.

He went to the house thinking that having the animals on the ranch made the place seem a whole lot less lonely. He'd call Riley in the morning and thank him for his good work.

There was only one phone message on the answering machine and it was from Sara, reminding him not to forget that she loved him. Although he still worried about her, it put a smile on his face.

*   *   *

In the morning, Kerney found it unnecessary to call Riley Burke and thank him. At first light through the kitchen window, he could see the young man inside the corral working with the gray gelding. The horse had a halter on, and attached to it was a lightweight, thirty-foot line.

Riley stood behind the horse outside of the kick zone and flicked the line against the gray's hindquarters. The startled horse took flight and Riley followed along, pitching the line gently against the gray's rear quarter until the animal broke into a canter.

After the gray made a half dozen turns around the corral, Riley reversed its direction and repeated the exercise. Finally, the gray slowed and lowered its head. Riley approached the horse at an angle, coiling the line as he moved in, and the gray retreated, refusing to join up. Riley backed off, flicked his line against the gray's hindquarters, and set the horse in motion again.

Kerney liked what he saw. Riley was starting from scratch with the gray, training it his way, gauging its agility, responsiveness, and temperament. He watched for a few more minutes, then showered, dressed in his uniform, and walked to the corral. Riley released the gray and met Kerney at the fence.

Tall and slim, Riley had his father's square jaw and deep chest, and the same widely spaced brown eyes and button nose as his mother. His sandy-colored hair was hidden under his cowboy hat.

They exchanged greetings and Kerney nodded in the direction of the gray. "What do you think?"

"Both geldings are well balanced," Riley said. "They got good, long muscles for stride and mobility, and their front legs match up nicely with their chests. All in all, I'd say they'll make fine cutting horses. But it will be a while before we know how good they are."

Kerney nodded, quietly pleased that Riley approved of his selections.

"You only bought one mare," Riley said as he climbed the fence and dropped down next to Kerney.

"I'm hoping your dad will sell me one of his."

Riley nodded. "I think he might consider it. Comeuppance is going to need a firm hand if you're planning to ride him."

"I already have," Kerney said.

Riley hitched a boot on the low railing. "I can't understand why he wasn't raced. He's got the bloodlines and the conformation for it."

"According to the trainer, he does fine on an empty track, but doesn't like running in a crowd. I appreciate the work you've done while I was gone."

"I wish I could have done more," Riley replied. "My dad's trail-riding business picked up last week, and he corralled me to take some tourists out on half-day trips."

Kerney knew that Riley's parents worked hard to keep their ranch afloat, and trail rides during the tourist season brought in some much-needed income. "That's okay."

Riley's comment about trail riding made Kerney think about Kim Dean's cabin in the Canadian River canyon lands. Last night at the office, he'd reviewed the status report on the hunt for Claudia Spalding and no one had thought to look for her there. According to Lucky Suazo, the Harding County sheriff, it would make a perfect hideout.

"I've got to go," Kerney said abruptly, turning on his heel. "We'll talk later. Thanks again."

Riley watched Kerney walk briskly to his house. In less than ten minutes, he came back out the front door, dressed in jeans, boots, and a work shirt, with his sidearm strapped to his belt. He got into his pickup truck and drove away, kicking up a trail of dust on the ranch road.

Riley wondered what had made Kerney switch getups so quickly and leave in such a big hurry. Behind him, the gray snorted quietly and he turned to find it had come closer, no more than three feet away. He moved slowly away from the animal, showing his back, and the gelding followed along.

Riley stopped as the gray closed the distance. He reached out, and rubbed the animal between the eyes. The gelding didn't flinch. Now the training could begin.

*   *   *

Only one highway traversed the Canadian Gorge, a state road that ran from the town of Wagon Mound to the village of Roy. A tangle of canyons and mesas, the gorge dropped off the high plains of northeastern New Mexico into breaks over a thousand feet deep in places.

Cut by rivers and streams, most of the Canadian was remote and wild, virtually empty of people, sprinkled with the remains of failed Hispanic and Anglo settlements.

Other than the locals, some hunters, and occasional tourists, few people visited the gorge, a forty-five mile swath of box canyons, slippery rock mesas, boulder-strewn streambeds, sandstone chutes, rock slides, and bottom land meadows. But there were signs that a more ancient civilization once used the gorge. Caves cut into the soft sandstone mesas were littered with pottery shards and flint. Rock art of birds, animals, feet, abstract symbols, and fantastic creatures were engraved in the perpendicular vermillion walls. Cliff overhangs were thick with the black smoke from a thousand years of campfires.

Kerney crossed the canyon and entered the most sparsely populated county in New Mexico. About eight-hundred people lived in Harding County, an area larger than the state of Delaware, and just about all of them resided and worked on the high plains grasslands.

He passed quickly through Roy, a village with a post office, school, one restaurant, a few small businesses, and a lot of shuttered, empty buildings. Not too many years ago, there had been a state park with a lake near the village, which had drawn tourist traffic and put some money into the local economy. But the lake dried up and the park was closed. To Kerney's eye, Roy looked about as dead as the lake.

North of the village, the Kiowa National Grasslands spread out over the prairie that rolled toward a flat, endless horizon. To the west, the Sangre de Cristo Mountains rose up into a sky peppered with enormous puffball cumulus clouds that crowded the peaks.

Kerney turned off at Mills, once a small hamlet that had served dryland farmers. A victim of drought, it was reduced to a few scattered buildings along the highway. Eight miles in on a dirt road, he dropped into the canyon. Juniper-studded mesas towered over the slow-moving, shallow river that snaked through the valley, parts of it hidden from view by stands of invasive salt cedar trees that lined the banks and sapped up precious water.

Instead of drought, a long-ago flash flood had wiped out the agri-cultural settlement of Mills Canyon. The torrent had left behind rock wall ruins of a few buildings, including an old hotel, and had inun-dated the bottom land crop fields, now reclaimed by junipers, yuccas, and cactus.

Kerney found Sheriff Lucky Suazo waiting for him near the hotel ruins. He'd brought along two saddled mounts in a horse trailer. Suazo ran a small cow-calf operation when he wasn't busy enforcing the law. Built close to the ground, he had a narrow face and a thick mustache that covered his upper lip.

Lucky's department consisted of himself and one chief deputy. To-gether, the two men policed over 2,100 square miles. Fortunately, crime wasn't rampant in Harding County.

"You made good time," Suazo said as he shook Kerney's hand. "How sure are you that this Spalding woman is at the cabin?"

"It's nothing more than a guess," Kerney said.

Suazo nodded and raised his chin at the mesa across the river. Flat-topped, with a wide band of sandstone that ran horizontally along the base, it was capped with rock.

"We'll skirt that mesa through a side canyon," he said. "The trail is good for a spell, but then it gets rough. Keep an eye out for rattlers. We've got plenty of them."

On the ride in, they followed a jeep trail that was much too rocky to accommodate a horse trailer. They saw signs of deer, bear, and mountain lion along the rocky trail cut.

Suazo briefed Kerney on Kim Dean's cabin. "It's on a little spit of high ground at the end of a small canyon near a clear spring," he said. "There's a cleft behind it where the trees thin out, but it would be a damn near impossible climb to the top. The cabin faces the canyon mouth, so we better go in on foot."

"Is there any cover and concealment?" Kerney asked.

Suazo reined in his horse where the jeep trail petered out. "Some mountain mahogany, a few cottonwoods and box elders, some piñons and junipers. We can leave the horses at a sandstone chute just outside the canyon, and get fairly close on foot without being seen. But the last quarter mile beyond a rock slide is all meadow, part of it fenced. If Spalding is there, she should see us coming."

Kerney swatted a mosquito. "Does she have a back door out?"

"If she can climb the cleft, she does," Suazo said. "But it would take her deep into the back country, miles from anywhere. Outsiders who go in there often get lost and some don't ever come out."

He pointed at the rimrock mesa six hundred feet above their heads. "We'll ride single file from here. The cabin was originally an old line camp on two sections surrounded by state trust land. Hadn't been used for years until Dean bought it and fixed it up. Got it dirt cheap, according to county records."

They moved slowly ahead, climbing the mesa, until the horses started lunging and stumbling on the trail, kicking up stones and puffs of gray dust. They dismounted and finished the ascent on foot, pulling the animals along.

At the top, they paused and sipped water from Suazo's canteen. Kerney could see Hermit's Peak, fifty miles distant, at the foot of the Sangre de Cristo Mountains. Beyond, the Colorado Rockies were dense and black against the horizon.

Suazo remounted and Kerney followed suit. They rode down an easy switchback trail off the mesa, cut across a dry streambed, and stopped at the sandstone chute at the mouth of the canyon.

"You don't sit a horse like a city cop," Suazo said as he swung out of the saddle.

Kerney dismounted and pulled his rifle out of the scabbard. "I've been riding some recently."

"You're thinking Spalding's armed and dangerous?" Suazo asked as he reached for his rifle.

Kerney studied recent boot prints in the sand. They were small, the right size for a woman. "Best to err on the side of caution. But my hunch that she'd be here looks like it was a pretty good guess."

"Let's go find out for sure," Lucky said as he started into the canyon.

*   *   *

From behind a piñon tree, Suazo covered Kerney's back, as he ran zigzag across the meadow toward the cabin. A redtail hawk screeched out of a pine tree, and Kerney looked up to see the figure of a woman climbing the cleft in the canyon wall.

He motioned Suazo forward, skirted the cabin, laid his rifle aside, and started up the cleft.

"There's no way out, Spalding," he yelled. "Climb down."

Spalding shook her head and kept moving. Kerney paused for a better look at her. She carried a backpack strapped to her shoulders and had a canteen on her hip. He didn't see a weapon. He glanced back at Suazo, who'd rounded the cabin and pointed at an outcropping twenty feet above Spalding's head.

"One round," he called out.

Suazo got the message and fired once. The round tore into an outcropping and showered rock fragments down on Spalding, who froze momentarily.

"Come down," Kerney ordered. "Do it now."

Spalding shook her head and started climbing again.

Kerney went up the split, using footholds where he could find them. Spalding cleared the outcropping before he could reach her and disappeared from sight. He looked down at Suazo, eighty feet below, with his rifle aimed and ready.

"Where is she?" he called.

"Standing on the ledge, staring at me," Suazo said. "She can't go any further. It's slick rock from there to the top."

"Any weapons?"

"Nothing in her hands," Suazo answered. "I think she wants to jump."

"If she moves toward the edge, blow her fucking head off," Kerney yelled.

"She's at the edge now." Suazo raised his sights a bit, but held his fire.

Kerney reached for the lip of the outcropping, and felt Spalding's boot come down hard on the fingers of his left hand. She looked down at him, red-faced and angry.

He pulled his hand free, found a crevice for his foot, swung up and over the ledge, kicked out a leg, and knocked Spalding back. He scrabbled to his feet, spun her around, and pushed her hard against the slick rock wall.

Spalding yelled in pain and slammed her boot down on Kerney's instep. She turned, and broke for the edge of the outcropping. Kerney grabbed for her with his injured hand but couldn't hold on. He lunged and caught her around the waist as she stood staring down at the barrel of Suazo's rifle. He pulled her back to safety.

He put her facedown on the outcropping, planted his knee on her neck, cuffed her using his uninjured hand, and raised her to a sitting position, holding on tight to the cuffs.

She turned and looked at him. Her nose and forehead were scraped raw and bleeding, and her eyes were riveted on Kerney's face.

"How are you going to get us off this ledge?" she asked matter-of-factly. "I'm handcuffed, and your hand looks broken."

Kerney's left hand ached badly. Except for the thumb, his fingers were swollen. He tried to move them, and pain shot up his arm. He wondered how many Spalding had broken. He tried to wiggle his wedding band off his finger with his thumb, but it wouldn't budge.

"We'll use rope and rig a sling."

"You're an interesting bastard," Spalding said. "Blow my fucking head off, indeed. How could you possibly know that would make me hesitate?"

"Call it a lucky guess," Kerney said.

"Seriously," Spalding said, "how did you know?"

"I read your diary," Kerney replied.

Above him, the redtail hawk swooped across the canyon, skimmed above the far rim, and veered out of sight.

ChapterSixteen

By the time Kerney and Suazo got back to Mills Canyon with Spalding in tow, Kerney's left hand was badly swollen. From the top of the mesa, Suazo had called ahead by cell phone and his chief deputy was waiting for them. He drove Kerney to the Las Vegas hospital while Suazo took Spalding to the Santa Fe County Jail.

The ring and little fingers of Kerney's left hand were broken and his wedding band was squashed. An ER doctor cut the ring off, took X-rays, which revealed that the breaks were clean, and immobilized the fingers with splints. He gave Kerney a prescription for codeine and told him to go home and rest, which in Kerney's mind wasn't an option.

The chief deputy drove Kerney to Santa Fe, where Suazo was waiting in Kerney's office at police headquarters. Together, the three men prepared the necessary reports, talked to the DA by phone, entered Spalding's arrest into the National Crime Information Center data bank, and notified the California authorities that Spalding had been taken into custody. After dealing with the outstanding homicide and fugitive warrants on Spalding, they did the paperwork charging her with the attempted murder of a police officer.

As soon as Suazo and his deputy left, Helen Muiz buzzed him on the intercom.

"Your wife is on the phone," she said.

"You called her?" Kerney asked.

"Darn tooting, I did," Helen replied.

Kerney punched the blinking button. "I'm all right," he said quickly.

"A smashed hand is not all right," Sara said emphatically.

"It's only two broken fingers. I'll be fine."

"You are not a twenty-something cop without a family, Kerney. Stop acting like one. Tell me exactly what the doctor said."

"I don't need surgery, and I'll be able to use the fingers when the bones heal. It's no big deal."

"It is to me. Are you going home now?"

"Yes, as soon as I send Sergeant Pino to the DA's office with all the paperwork."

"Good. I'll call you at home. Put Helen back on the line."

"What for?"

"Since I can't be there to take care of you, Helen has volunteered."

"To do what?"

"Whatever needs doing, but mostly to grocery shop, fix some meals to put in the fridge for you, and act as my spy."

"I suppose I have no choice in the matter."

"You do not," Sara said. "You could have been killed, Kerney."

Kerney looked at his mangled wedding ring. Without a crevice toe-hold he might well have fallen eighty feet to his death. "Don't be upset, Sara."

"I am upset. Put Helen on. I'll talk to you later."

*   *   *

Because of the swelling and pain, Kerney's hand was useless for the next several days. He got through the nuisance of it as best he could. Helen's home-cooked meals in the fridge made caring for himself easier, but getting dressed in the morning remained a bit of a challenge.

On Thursday morning, he called Penelope Parker and told her the remains in the coffin were not those of George Spalding. "That doesn't necessarily mean that he's alive," Kerney cautioned. "Will you let Alice know?"

"I will, although I can't promise that she'll understand," Parker said. "She's already forgotten that Claudia has been arrested for Clifford's murder, and she's taken to calling me Debbie, which she's never done before."

"I'm sorry to hear it," Kerney said.

"Perhaps if you came out and told her yourself," Parker said wistfully, "it would sink in more readily."

"I'll have to leave that in your good hands, Ms. Parker," Kerney said.

Ramona Pino stepped through the open door to his office with a pleased expression on her face. Kerney made his excuses to Parker and hung up.

"I've got news, Chief," Ramona said. "The Canadian Customs and Revenue Agency reports that Edward Ramsey and Richard Chase have both received annual consulting fees of a hundred thousand dollars U.S. each from the High Plains Charitable Trust over the past fifteen years. The deposits were made to a bank in Toronto."

"That's a nice sum of money to put in your pocket. Has it been reported as earned foreign income on their tax returns?"

"Not according to the IRS agent I spoke with."

Kerney smiled, "Good work, Sergeant. Any word on George or Debbie?"

"That's not going well, Chief. The Calgary PD has stopped talking to me. It seems that the U.S. Army has stepped in and wants to keep the investigation all to themselves."

"Let them have it," Kerney said.

"You want me to drop it?"

"It's a military matter that doesn't concern us now."

"Okay, Chief, but I hate to leave loose ends untied," Ramona said.

"That's one of the reasons you're good at what you do," Kerney replied with a laugh. "Give me a copy of your supplemental report on Ramsey and Chase as soon as it's done."

"It's on your computer, Chief," Ramona said as she waved from the office door.

Kerney pulled it up on his screen, read through it, and dialed the number of the resident FBI special agent.

"Would you be interested in a bribery case involving an FBI employee and a city police captain?" he asked.

"I always like a good bribery case," the agent said. "Is the officer from your department?"

"Nope, Santa Barbara, California."

"What kind of FBI employee?" the agent asked.

"A GS 12 who teaches at Quantico," Kerney answered, "who also happens to be the retired chief of the Santa Barbara PD."

"Intriguing. How big a bribe are we talking about here?"

"One point five million each, spread out over fifteen years."

The agent whistled. "You've got proof?"

"I do." Kerney printed Pino's supplemental report and stuck it in his case file.

"Can you bring it to me now?"

"I'm on my way."

He left the building thinking how absolutely grand it would be if the feds busted Ramsey and Chase at work.

*   *   *

Two months after the Army started looking for George Spalding and Debbie Calderwood, Sara called Kerney from her office with an update on the investigation.

"Debbie Calderwood is in custody," she said as she scanned the CID investigator's report.

"That's good news," Kerney replied. "Where was she found?"

"At the Toronto Airport about to board an international flight to Europe under the name of Caitlin Thomas," Sara replied. "It's her legal name. She changed it after gaining Canadian citizenship."

"What about George?" Kerney asked. "Did he change his name to Dylan Thomas?"

Sara laughed. "That's unknown, as are his whereabouts."

"Is Debbie cooperating?"

"Yes, indeed. She divorced George twenty years ago and hasn't seen him since. But she got a multiyear, multimillion-dollar settlement. The Canadian Customs and Revenue Agency is auditing her income tax records for a paper trail that should eventually lead us to him."

"You sound very confident about it," Kerney said.

"I am. No matter where George might be, he's about to discover that the world is a very small place. We'll get him."

"I've never understood why George colluded with his father to deceive his mother. Has Debbie shed any light on that?"

"According to Debbie, Alice sexually molested George until he got old enough and strong enough to resist her. He hated his mother."

"When I first spoke with Alice, she said that she never should have let George go. At the time, I thought she meant she should have talked him out of enlisting in the Army."

"Apparently, it was far more twisted than that," Sara said.

"Yeah," Kerney replied, thinking about Clifford Spalding. When it came to women, the man had picked two real humdingers to marry.

"I've got to go," Sara said.

"I'll call you at home tonight," Kerney said.

Sara hung up, put the report aside, and returned to the task of compiling all the data that had been gathered on the active rape cases her team had surveyed.

In six cases, vital evidence had been misplaced or lost. One CID investigator had been ordered by a post commander to destroy evidence, which the officer had refused to do. A victim with ten years' service had accepted an honorable discharge after being threatened with a letter of admonishment for a trumped-up minor rule infraction that had occurred after the rape.

In another case, an accused rapist, a master sergeant, had been allowed to retire before the paperwork could be forwarded to JAG for action. At JAG, several prosecutions had been dropped when victims had recanted their allegations after receiving spot-promotions and transfers.

Of all the cases surveyed by her team, only two investigations had been conducted without any evidence of interference or inappropriate meddling by higher-ups. The findings made Sara boil.

She entered the last of the information, saved the file to the computer hard drive, and made a backup copy. With the case sampling data now complete, Sara decided it was time to pass the results on to her Teflon-coated, chicken-shit boss. In all probability, she would pay a price for submitting hard, disturbing facts the general didn't want to hear. At the very least, a butt-chewing was likely.

But whatever the outcome, for the first time in weeks, Sara felt good about doing her job.

ABOUT THE AUTHOR

Michael McGarrity is the author of the Anthony Award–nominated *Tularosa*, as well as *Mexican Hat, Serpent Gate, Hermit's Peak, The Judas Judge, Under the Color of Law, The Big Gamble,* and *Everyone Dies*. A former deputy sheriff for Santa Fe County, he established the first Sex Crimes Unit there. He has also served as an instructor at the New Mexico Law Enforcement Academy and as an investigator for the New Mexico Public Defender's Office. He lives in Santa Fe.